RAVE REVIEWS FOR
ALTHEA & OLIVER

"Fans of Rainbow Rowell's *Eleanor & Park* will enjoy debut author Cristina Moracho's trip back to the 1990s in *Althea & Oliver*."

—CNN.com

"The bittersweet romance, Oliver's battle with his illness, and Althea's coming-of-age struggle should appeal to fans of John Green and Sarah Dessen who are looking for something new."

—*VOYA*

"Can boys and girls really be just friends? This endearing novel explores that, and a whole lot of other things." —TeenVogue.com

★ "Mesmerizing." —*Kirkus Reviews*, starred review

★ "It is the exquisitely created and painfully real, pitch-perfect characters who make it so memorable." —*SLJ*, starred review

★ "Moracho's coming-of-age story carries rare insight and a keen understanding of those verging on adulthood."

—*Booklist*, starred review

"A very grown-up story of redemption and self-discovery."

—*BCCB*

"Big-hearted and wiseassed and penetratingly smart."
—Jim Shepard, author of *Project X* and *You Think That's Bad*

"Marrying dazzling prose and sharp-eyed realism, *Althea & Oliver* is a gritty, sparkling triumph."
—Bennett Madison, author of *September Girls*

"Urgent and poetic." —HelloGiggles.com

"*Althea & Oliver* captures the painful state of longing that is adolescence perfectly."
—Corey Ann Haydu, author of *OCD Love Story*

"A gorgeous, glorious, unforgettable novel."
—Sarah McCarry, author of *About a Girl*

"It's mind-blowingly good." —Molly Templeton, WORD Books

"Even if the book weren't eloquent and hilarious, it'd be a must-read for all children of the '90s. But thankfully, it is, and if you're smart, you'll run out and grab a copy." —Bustle.com

A *Time* magazine Top 10 YA of the Year
An *SLJ* Best Book
A *Booklist* Editors' Choice
A *Kirkus Reviews* Best Book
A Junior Library Guild Selection
A YALSA Best Fiction for Young Adults Title

CAN THE RIGHT KIND OF BOY
GET AWAY WITH KILLING
THE WRONG KIND OF GIRL?

"I thought they'd say something," I said. The weed had me all confused; I struggled to find my words. "I don't know, sing a song for her, something."

"How could they?" Owen said. "With him sitting right there?"

"Still," I said finally, "it's not right."

Owen shook his head. "There's nothing we can do about it now." He tightened his fingers around the steering wheel. "Finley, I want you to listen to me. As far as this town is concerned, there's no proof she's even dead. You weren't here when it happened. I was. Everyone in Williston is on his side. They think his confession was some coerced bullshit and that she ran off with some dude. Leroy had Emily fired and now there's, literally, a new sheriff in town who does whatever Leroy says." Emily Shepard, one of Owen's many cousins, had been sheriff since I was in elementary school. Leroy Miller, Calder's father, was mayor of Williston. He owned the gravel mine just outside town, which had closed the year before so he could focus on opening a local factory that would make computer parts or something. Owen looked at me. "It's over, okay?"

But it wasn't over. Not for me. Not for Serena. For us, it was just beginning.

OTHER BOOKS YOU MAY ENJOY

All the Truth That's in Me	Julie Berry
Althea & Oliver	Cristina Moracho
Conversion	Katherine Howe
Daughter of Deep Silence	Carrie Ryan
Dreamland	Sarah Dessen
Exit, Pursued by a Bear	E. K. Johnston
The Fault in Our Stars	John Green
Looking for Alaska	John Green
The Morgue and Me	John C. Ford
Pasadena	Sherri L. Smith
Saint Anything	Sarah Dessen

A GOOD IDEA

CRISTINA MORACHO

speak

Moracho

SPEAK
An imprint of Penguin Random House LLC
375 Hudson Street
New York, New York 10014

First published in the United States of America by Viking,
an imprint of Penguin Random House LLC, 2017
Published by Speak,
an imprint of Penguin Random House LLC, 2018

THE LIBRARY OF CONGRESS HAS CATALOGED THE VIKING EDITION AS FOLLOWS:
Names: Moracho, Cristina, author.
Title: A good idea / Cristina Moracho.
Description: New York : Penguin Group, [2017] | Summary: "A girl returns to her small hometown in Maine seeking revenge for the death of her childhood best friend"—Provided by publisher.
Identifiers: LCCN 2016020075 | ISBN 9780451476241 (hardcover)
Subjects: | CYAC: Revenge—Fiction. | Mystery and detective stories.
Classification: LCC PZ7.M788192 Go 2017 | DDC [Fic]—dc23
LC record available at https://lccn.loc.gov/2016020075

Speak ISBN 9780147517036

Printed in the United States of America

10   9   8   7   6   5   4   3   2   1

$10.99
3/13/18
DC

i14287407

For Sarah

BEFORE YOU EMBARK ON A JOURNEY
OF REVENGE, DIG TWO GRAVES.

—*Confucius*

A
GOOD
IDEA

CHAPTER ONE.

I THINK IT started with the seizure. Serena and I talked about it later, and she agreed that if Ann Russo hadn't had an epileptic fit during the graduation ceremony, she would have been far less likely to contribute her own outburst to the proceedings. Something about the sight of Ann spasming on the ground, red hair gleaming against the aggressively green, meticulously manicured grass of the backfield, mouth opening and closing wordlessly like a fish, gave what had been until then an unnoteworthy ceremony—the valedictorian's relentless optimism about the future, the hungover graduates' heads dipping as they nodded off, their mortarboards shielding their eyes from the morning sun—a surreal quality that sent things firmly off the rails.

The students sitting around Ann called for help. The principal unwisely tried to continue with his speech until he was silenced by the crowd—"Shut up, man, we need a doctor"—and an uncomfortable, expectant hush fell over the entire field. In an instant, the pretense to which everyone had been clinging, that there was nothing unusual about this day, this ceremony, vanished, as if Betty herself had found a way to reach down from wherever she was. *Take that, motherfuckers.* Suddenly we were in a David Lynch movie. Suddenly anything could happen.

It was a crushingly bright morning, swimming-pool-blue sky and the sun an orange blaze steadily making its way to its zenith. The fog had burned off by nine A.M., and the breeze from the Atlantic carried with it a salty mist that reminded me of the ubiquitous lobster rolls of my childhood. Above the stage, a banner congratulating the class of 1998 snapped with the occasional gust.

I was sitting all the way in the back, behind the families of the graduates, barely able to see the podium where the principal stood, fiddling with his cuff links as he awkwardly waited for Ann to be removed so he could continue with his speech. If Betty had still been alive, I would have taken a seat right in front, next to her parents, ready to whoop my approval when she finally crossed the stage to accept her diploma. But Betty was dead, and instead I was waiting to see if there would be any mention of her at all. I was waiting to see what would happen when her murderer's name was finally called. So maybe the ceremony was already somewhat surreal before Ann Russo collapsed, even if Serena and I were the only ones who noticed. And I didn't even know Serena yet.

I was wired and anxious; I hadn't slept much the night before, then overcompensated with too much coffee on an empty stomach, and Ann's seizure did something to me, physically, the shock of it flooding my system with a large dose of adrenaline I definitely didn't need. Perspiration dampened the armpits of my T-shirt, and I had to press on my thigh with the heel of my hand to keep my leg from bouncing up and down. The other hand I held over my heart, like I was saying the Pledge of Allegiance, and I was alarmed by how rapidly it was firing inside my chest.

After the principal was finally able to finish his speech, it was time to start handing out the diplomas. I leaned forward, the hinges of my plastic chair protesting beneath me, thinking that surely when they got to Betty's name in the alphabet they would at least acknowledge her. I held my breath when they got to the Fs—"Brian Farmington, Melissa Ferris . . ."—thinking, *Here it comes, here's where they'll stop the ceremony and say something*, and when they got to George Flattery I half rose out of my chair, my whole body clenched and expectant—*say her name, say her name, say her name*—but there was no mention of Elizabeth Flynn, and then the principal moved on to the Gs and I was sinking back into my seat, eyes stinging, hands fisted at my sides.

I went to stand under a tree, where I could chain-smoke through the rest of the ceremony.

If I was outraged that they hadn't mentioned Betty, if Ann's seizure had given me a full panic attack, it was Calder's walk across the stage that truly brought on the complete out-of-body experience. He looked exactly the same as the boy I had known, back when he was Betty's boyfriend, not her murderer. Two years ago the three of us had spent an entire summer together, taking his two Labrador retrievers to run on the beach, picnicking in the woods on a scratchy flannel blanket, Betty's head on his stomach, my head on hers, while he read to us from *The Odyssey* and Roald Dahl.

I hadn't been jealous when they'd started dating, hadn't

resented sharing my closest friend in Williston; if anything, I was relieved there was someone else Betty could call when one of her black moods descended like an unexpected summer thunderstorm. *The unlights,* she called them, and while Calder did not have my years of practice at coaching her through their frequent visits, he seemed to have been gifted with a natural, boundless patience that made him an ideal match for someone who could be, frankly, exhausting. Still, I was suspicious of how much he seemed to relish her damage, his wide-eyed eagerness to swoop in when even the slightest hint of a shadow crossed her face—exactly the kind of behavior I knew would just encourage her—but if anything, I feared that Betty, master of self-sabotage, would get bored and break his heart. Which she did. And I guess his patience ran out after all.

He had drowned her in the shallows of a rocky beach, held her head under the frigid Maine waters while her blonde hair floated like seaweed or the tentacles of a jellyfish. Or that's how I pictured it. I had imagined it a million times that winter—her hands pulling at his wrists, heels kicking feebly, her muscles clenching and lungs aching, shuddering violently as the cold seeped into her bones. He had killed her at night; the scene I envisioned was lit only by the moon. I would lie in bed and hold my breath, timing myself, wondering how long she lasted until she gave up and let the water in. And afterward, the stillness.

Tall and rangy, fair-haired, he strode across the stage like he had never held someone underwater until her lungs filled with the ocean and her brain shut down and her heart stopped beating. The principal gave him his diploma as if he were any other student, resting a hand briefly on his shoulder as if Calder were in need of moral support. I ground my cigarette butt into the dirt.

I was about to turn away when I took one last look at the stage and saw a girl I didn't recognize—short blonde hair streaked with cotton-candy pink, skull and crossbones spray-painted on the back of her graduation gown—arguing with the principal. He must have already called her name, which I hadn't caught, because she was holding her diploma, but she wouldn't leave. I couldn't hear what they were saying; wisely, the principal had steered them away from the microphone, but she was gesturing furiously even as he crossed his arms over his chest, refusing whatever she was asking for. She was pleading with him, that much was clear, a request desperate and urgent, and while he showed no sign of relenting, there was something in the way he wouldn't meet her eyes—his gaze fixed at an indeterminate point over her shoulder—that gave him a guilty, shifty look. He never stopped shaking his head. A group of students in line to accept their diplomas were trapped onstage as the scene played out. One girl rolled her eyes; a couple of the boys looked genuinely nervous. Finally, the principal placed his hand on the blonde girl's back, steering her toward the steps that led offstage, a final dismissal, and that's when she started screaming.

I watched the girl's mouth, wild with the need to make out what she was shouting, but she was unintelligible. Then she said it: *Betty Flynn.* My whole body had been tensed with the ache of anticipation, and now that someone had said Betty's name I felt myself releasing, unfolding. The girl stormed down the stairs, striding up the aisle in a tearful rage, one hand held over her head, flipping off the faculty and students and attendees, still shouting, and I thought I heard Calder's name, too. She ripped her mortarboard from her head and threw it not to the ground like I expected, but into the rows of seats she was passing. Several people put their hands defensively in front of their faces; others ducked. She tore off her blue graduation gown and let the wind carry it away; it slid along the ground for several yards like something alive before coming to rest in the grass.

She passed only a few feet from me on her way to the parking lot. Her eyes were red from crying, but there were circles underneath that predated this morning's outburst; I pegged her as a fellow insomniac. She had a septum piercing that was oddly fetching, and chunky rings on almost every finger; her nails were rimmed with black, from the spray paint she'd used on her gown, I imagined, and though she was curvy in that way girls are when they never lose their baby fat, she still gave the impression of being fine-boned—slender wrists, well-defined cheekbones, long neck, and a pronounced clavicle. To my surprise, she wore a delicate gold crucifix, which lay right below the hollow of her pale, slender throat. As she went by, she wiped her eyes with the heel of her hand, a gesture that gave her a curiously childlike appearance, just for a moment, before the rage-filled look again took its place. She never even glanced in my direction. I wondered who she could be, how I could not know the only other person here who gave a fuck about Betty, but more than anything I felt oddly ashamed that this girl had had the temerity to make the scene that Betty deserved, had screamed her name onstage while I sat silently in the audience.

I ran off in pursuit, following the path she had taken into the parking lot. Scrambling onto the hood of the nearest pickup truck, I surveyed the area for a long time before I was willing to admit what I already knew: she was gone.

Behind me, the ceremony was concluding; Ann Russo had recovered in time to collect her diploma, and the graduates giddily threw their hats into the air, cheering.

"What the fuck are you doing up there?"

I looked down, shielding my eyes with my hand. "Owen?"

"You better get down before Principal Moore sees you."

"This is the principal's truck?"

"Yeah."

I climbed off the hood. "What are *you* doing over *here*? Shouldn't you be watching the ceremony?"

"I needed to get some air," he said, holding up a half-finished joint.

I took a hit, eyeing him through the smoke. To anyone else, he'd look dressed for a day of work on a construction site, but his fresh white T-shirt still smelled like fabric softener, and he wore clean brown Dickies and Doc Martens instead of his old Carhartt work boots. This was about as fancy as he ever got. His dark brown hair was brushed out of his face, but he still wore about three days' worth of stubble; apparently he had drawn the line at shaving.

Owen had been my neighbor growing up; he was three years older, and he came from one of Williston's largest families, the

Shepards, a prolific clan whose various lines ran through the town's history, beginning with its founding, occasionally converging in the marriage of distant relations, or so Owen had told me. I didn't even ask who he had come to see graduate; he claimed half the town as cousins once, twice, or even three times removed. Of all these relatives, Betty had been his favorite, although their familial connection was vague and tenuous; they'd been related by a marriage that had lasted less than a year.

He had played a role in my life not unlike an older brother, alternately mocking and tormenting me, only occasionally revealing a gentler side, like when I was eight and fell off his four-wheeler and cracked my head open, and he'd tended my wounds right there in the woods, using his wifebeater as a makeshift bandage, cleaning away the blood with creek water and singing a Johnny Cash song to keep me from passing out. A few years after I left town, our relationship had shifted with an inevitability I could feel in my blood long before anything actually happened; the mocking and tormenting never ceased, we just added sex to the mix. If I still lived in Williston year-round, I would probably have been in love with him; fortunately, I departed at the end of every August before the oxytocin could get the best of me.

"Did you see what happened?" I asked him, giving back the joint.

"Ann Russo? I had a feeling she wouldn't make it through the ceremony. She's been up for two days, I heard, getting drunk and snorting Ritalin. Not a good move for an epileptic. No wonder she had a seizure."

"Not Ann," I said, shaking my head, already feeling blurry from the weed. "After. That girl."

"What girl?"

"The one with the pink hair. She looked a little strung out. She was yelling about Betty."

Owen's eyebrows went up. "I don't know any girls with pink hair. What was she yelling?"

"I couldn't hear."

He pinched the tip of the joint until it was safely out and put the roach in his pocket. His face was inscrutable. "When did you get back?" he asked.

"Just yesterday."

"I wasn't sure you'd come home this summer." He took a step toward me, idly hooking a finger through one of my belt loops.

This always amazed me. We hadn't spoken once in the ten months I'd been away, but less than five minutes in Owen's presence and I was wondering how much longer I'd have to wait before he would take me somewhere and remove all of my clothes.

"I had to come. I had to see it for myself."

"See what?"

"That he's still walking around. Like it never happened. I didn't believe it. But I just watched him accept his fucking diploma."

"Yeah." Owen sighed. "Look, you want to go? I need to get out of here."

I nodded. He started to walk off toward his truck. I went to follow him, but hesitated; something about that girl had inspired me, compelled me to make a grand gesture of my own.

"Wait," I said. "Can I borrow your knife?"

He didn't ask any questions, just pulled the knife from his pocket and held it out to me, watching with amusement as I knelt down.

It's harder to slash someone's tires than you think; that rubber is thick as fuck. I pictured Principal Moore handing Calder his diploma, that sympathetic pat on the arm, as if commiserating with Calder over everything he had been through, and then I felt the rubber give. I smiled when I heard the hiss of escaping air. Owen waited patiently as I went around and did the other three. When I was done I stood, folded the locking knife, and held it out to him.

"Why don't you hang on to it? I've got plenty."

"Okay. Thanks." I slipped it into my pocket.

"You feel better now?" he asked.

"I think so," I said. "Let's go."

As Owen drove away from the high school, I watched the town where I'd grown up pass by the windows of his truck, and I felt the way I did every year when I came home, like New York City and my life there was just a dream I'd had, another dimension I'd managed to slip into sideways, but now it was back to reality, and reality was Williston.

Everything was the same, Main Street still cutting a broad swath through the town, woods on one side, the Atlantic on the other, an unwelcoming gray-green lined with jagged rocks instead of sandy beaches. The summer people didn't come here for the swimming; Williston was more of a pass-through town, where tourists stopped for a bathroom and a lobster roll on their way to Boothbay Harbor or Georgetown Island. Everything was still quiet—it was only the end of June, school had just ended, down the coast the summer people were just starting to pack for their summer vacations—but in another week, by July 4, Main Street would be an unmanageable shitshow of tourists the locals both relied upon and despised.

We passed the grim row of one-story buildings—general store, post office, ice cream shop and seafood shack, diner, dive bar—that made up the town's center. Manufactured homes on tiny lots, overgrown yards, a rusting tricycle upended in a driveway, a front porch sagging under the weight of hundreds of newspapers piled up in moldy stacks. That briny tang in the air, sinister now, at least to me. Cold green seawater slapping against rotting, wooden docks; the intermittent clanging of the buoys.

"So how was your year?" I asked, reclining my seat and propping my feet up on the dash.

"Go ahead, make yourself comfortable," Owen said. "How was my year? The same. Besides the whole fucking mess with Betty. The cabin's roof leaks. The diner needs a new Hobart. My tires are bald. You know the story, Fin. It's the same every year."

"Your parents doing okay?"

He just shook his head.

I looked out the window. We were right outside of town now, where the houses were larger and farther apart and set back on multiple acres, long driveways marked by mailboxes where they met the road, hidden under the canopy of trees. Owen was smart;

by all rights he should have been at school in Orono, reading Russian literature and studying abnormal psych and getting laid every weekend. But his older siblings had all moved away—he was the youngest of five by almost a decade—and by the time it was his turn to leave, his mother had developed arthritis and his father emphysema. They owned the local diner, and he had opted to stay and help them run it; it had been his choice, but still, I watched him grow more bitter every year.

"I heard you had some trouble in New York," he said.

"My father tell you that?"

"Frank didn't get specific. Just said you were having a hard time."

That was one way of putting it. My dad had called with the news about Betty the Sunday after Thanksgiving. It was late afternoon, but I was still in bed; my friends in college were home for the holiday, and I had been out all night, drinking forties on stoops in the West Village and listening to their stories about higher education, wondering if I seemed as suddenly young to them as they did old to me. My mother had come into my bedroom, her expression not unlike the one she'd worn when my parents told me they were splitting up—eyes narrowed, lips parted like she was about to speak but couldn't pick a place to begin. She turned on the light despite my protests, pulled back the curtains, and opened the window, letting in a gust of cold air that made me clutch my blankets around me. Then she held out the cordless, saying my father needed to talk to me, and I tried to take the phone under the covers, but Mom said, "No, Fin, you have to sit up for this," something in her voice thick and curdled,

and I stopped arguing, sat up, put the phone to my ear, and listened to Dad tell me that Betty was dead.

I walked into school Monday morning like someone doing
the Thorazine shuffle—empty-eyed, everything in slow motion,
asking anyone who talked to me if they could repeat themselves.
My friends were sympathetic in that hyper, almost giddy way,
eager to take care of me, constantly asking if I needed anything,
was there anything they could do. Most of them were like Betty
herself, melodramatic extroverts who appreciated the fact that
they would never have to fight me for the spotlight and enjoyed
my sarcastic running commentary. They really did want to comfort me, but they were also undeniably exhilarated by their proximity to a genuine tragedy. Soon I felt smothered and shaky and
on the verge of something I couldn't name. I made it to my lunch
period before I walked back out the school's front door.

Betty and I had sent our applications to NYU a few weeks
before. We'd both applied early decision to Tisch—her to the
Institute of Performing Arts, me to the Department of Cinema
Studies. It was a plan we had hatched together last year, during
one of her visits; finally, she would make her escape and join me
in New York. Freshman year, we'd live in the dorms together,
but after that we'd get a place.

I still remembered Betty's first visit to me in New York. The
way she bounded down our front stoop every morning, so eager
to see all the places I'd told her about—the dog run in Tomp-
kins Square Park, the theater marquees on Broadway, the old
dim sum parlor nestled into the curve of Doyers Street in Chi-
natown. I told her everything was closed at Coney Island, but

she wanted to go anyway; we took the F train to the end of the line just so she could take pictures of the Wonder Wheel and the Cyclone.

"Haven't I already sent you postcards from Coney Island?" I asked as I shivered on the boardwalk.

"Postcards aren't the same," she said. "The postcard means *you've* been here. The picture means *I've* been here."

She loved the city with a fearlessness surprising for someone from such a small town, and her frequent visits always included trips to places I never would have considered. When we talked about going to college at NYU, we skipped past freshman year as if it were an afterthought, arguing the merits of an apartment in the West Village (her preference) versus the East (mine). It was a constant battle made no less heated by the fact that the actual decision would not be made for two more years, although in the months before she died she'd been harder to bait during our conversations, as if her enthusiasm for our proposed future together were waning.

I mailed my application at ten thirty P.M. from the main branch of the post office, the one by Penn Station that never closed, so it would be postmarked November 1. And while our guidance counselors always warned us during those interminable assemblies that your admission could be revoked if your grades fell off too much, it seemed like one of those myths designed to keep the senior class from disintegrating into a complete state of anarchy by springtime. So when my acceptance letter and financial aid package came that first week in December, right after Betty was killed, I took it as permission to give up completely.

I stopped going to school; instead, I would take the train out to Coney Island and wade into the ocean, jeans rolled up, shoes in my hands, until my feet and ankles were numb; I'd use my fake ID to buy beer and drink it right there on the beach out of a paper bag, until the cops came along and wrote me a citation; later on, I'd tear it into pieces, scattering them over the subway tracks and leaving them to the rats.

Every morning that winter, I left the apartment with my messenger bag strapped around me and a thermos mug full of coffee, just as if I were going to school, and used my student MetroCard to travel all over the city in a numb haze. I took the tram to Roosevelt Island and wandered around the crumbled remains of the old smallpox hospital; I rode the Staten Island Ferry and hiked through Freshkills Park, trespassing through the abandoned monastery and Willowbrook State School; I walked across the Brooklyn Bridge and kept going until I got to Red Hook and the old sugar refinery. I skipped tests. I failed classes. I didn't care. I just had to keep moving.

Some days it didn't feel like it was about Betty at all. Some days I was just a misanthropic truant who would rather go up to Fort Washington Park and take pictures of the lighthouse than go to school. Some days I didn't think about her until I was in bed trying to sleep and her face would flash behind my eyelids and I remembered, and I'd realize it was the first time I'd thought about her since I'd woken up that morning, and I'd wonder what that meant, and if I could go eight hours without thinking about her, then maybe I could sit through a little bit of school. But something always stopped me—the next day would be a Saturday, or unseasonably warm, or I would have a dream where Betty called me on the phone to wish me a happy birthday and I could hear her voice so clearly, smooth and honeyed, perfect diction, slightly nasal on every *n*, and I would cry into the receiver about how much I missed her until I woke up, gutshot all over again.

And then NYU got word that I had practically dropped out of high school, and I was violently whisked out of my silent reveries along the various New York City waterfronts and into office after office, with my mother and the principal and the NYU assistant dean of admissions, and various guidance counselors and therapists, where I kept having to explain how depressed I had become after the murder of my closest childhood friend. It took more convincing than I thought it would. Grief they could understand; my way of grieving, not so much. If I had stopped eating or tried to kill myself, I probably would have seemed more sincere. It was my winter of sightseeing that confused them.

I had to start seeing a psychiatrist, who prescribed antidepressants I pretended to take and who eventually wrote a compelling letter about my progress to the NYU admissions board. My record was otherwise spotless, my grades and SAT scores impressive. I had never been particularly rebellious; unlike Betty, who'd constantly chafed against her family and church's repression, I lacked compelling reasons to act out. The shrink suspected I was "subconsciously harboring some serious resentment" toward my mother, whose unhappiness had defined most of my childhood and who then had forced me to choose between my parents and uproot my entire life, but even if he was right, I was perfectly happy to keep shoving those feelings deep down inside, in keeping with my New England heritage. The point is, I made a convincing case for being a good kid going through a hard time, and it worked. As long as I stayed in therapy and attended all my classes for the final quarter of the school year, NYU would still take me. I never found out if Betty had been accepted.

So that's what I did. I went to school, and I went to counseling. The charges against Calder were dismissed on a technicality. He would go off to Bates in the fall, and I would be back in New York, but for one final summer we'd overlap in Williston.

"Yeah," I said to Owen now. "Things got pretty dark for a while. It was a long winter."

He grunted, I assumed in agreement.

"Are you working today?"

He shook his head. "Got a family barbecue later. For the graduates, you know. To celebrate."

"You don't look like you feel much like celebrating."

"I don't."

"I thought they'd say something," I said. The weed had me all confused; I struggled to find my words. "I don't know, sing a song for her, something."

"How could they?" Owen said. "With him sitting right there?"

"Still," I said finally, "it's not right."

Owen shook his head. "There's nothing we can do about it now." He tightened his fingers around the steering wheel. "Finley, I want you to listen to me. As far as this town is concerned, there's no proof she's even dead. You weren't here when it happened. I was. Everyone in Williston is on his side. They think his confession was some coerced bullshit and that she ran off with some dude. Leroy had Emily fired and now there's, literally, a new sheriff in town who does whatever Leroy says." Emily Shepard, one of Owen's many cousins, had been sheriff since I was in elementary school. Leroy Miller, Calder's father, was mayor of Williston. He owned the gravel mine just outside town, which had closed the year before so he could focus on opening a local factory that would make computer parts or something. Owen looked at me. "It's over, okay?"

But it wasn't over. Not for me. Not for Serena. For us, it was just beginning.

After Owen dropped me off at home, I found the keys to my Subaru, a hand-me-down from my father that stayed in the garage ten months a year until I came back in the summers and reclaimed it. She was covered in a thick layer of dust, so I backed her out into the driveway, gathered Armor All, sponges, and a bucket, hosed her down, and gave her a thorough scrubbing. I even washed the tires and the license plates.

The sun was still out, the mosquitoes were mostly dormant, and the thrumming white noise of the cicadas was all around me, punctuated by the occasional call from a mourning dove. In the last few hours I'd added car keys and clasp knife to the list of items in my pockets, and that's how I knew I was home.

After I'd dried off the Subaru and changed into clean clothes, I was ready to go. The gas tank was half-full, courtesy, I imagined, of my dad. The radio was still tuned to the classic rock station. Being back behind the wheel gave me a small thrill of satisfaction; none of my friends in New York even knew how to drive. The Subaru was a manual and I was definitely rusty, stalling before I'd reached the end of our driveway, but I took a deep breath and remembered the advice Owen had given me when I was first learning. "Think of the stupidest person you know," he'd said. "That person can drive a car."

I don't know what I was expecting—that it would look haunted, I guess, the lawn overgrown and tangled with weeds, paint peeling off the front porch, the wooden steps rotted and sagging. But Betty's house was exactly the same as I remembered, the lawn groomed to perfection and the petunias blooming in the flower boxes. The front door was open, and I could see through the screen door into the house, where Montel Williams was on the television and someone was bustling around in the kitchen, turning the faucet off and on, cabinet doors being open and shut, everything so usual and familiar I expected to hear Betty come flying down the stairs—it was the parking brake on my car, she said, that always tipped her off to my arrival, so loud she could hear it from her bedroom on the second floor— and see her appear in the crosshatching of the screen, a darker, obscured version of her, and then, flinging the door open and rushing onto the porch to greet me, she would be revealed in full daylight as the bright, shining, ridiculous creature that she was.

I rang the doorbell and wondered if I should have brought something, flowers, a casserole, but then Mrs. Flynn was letting me into the house with a genuinely delighted look on her face—"Finley! Hello! What a welcome surprise!"—and I was being swept along into the living room.

Mrs. Flynn was blonde, like her daughter had been, although her hair was run through with coarse silver strands. She was soft without being matronly, and even though she was just doing housework she wore a smart pair of navy slacks and a white shell blouse. She turned off the television and sat down on the couch, gesturing for me to join her.

There were pictures of Betty everywhere. I guess I should have been prepared for that. Even the picture of Betty and Calder from the junior prom was still on the mantel above the fireplace. There was little physical evidence of their overzealous Catholicism—no crucifixes mounted on the walls, no pictures of a bleeding Jesus wearing a crown of thorns—but I knew how fervently she and Mr. Flynn believed.

Mrs. Flynn asked a flurry of questions—how was my mother, was I excited to be starting college in the fall—and I tried to answer all of them as honestly as possible without going into detail about just how fucked up my year had been.

"So," she said, after exhausting all the usual innocuous topics, "what brings you by?"

"I just came by to offer my condolences in person," I said.

Her face darkened, as if up until now this had just been a friendly visit and I'd spoiled it. "Thank you. And thank you for the card you sent, that was very thoughtful of you."

"I can't imagine how hard this has been for you. I just wanted to say if there's anything I can do, now that I'm back—"

"I appreciate that," she said, more polite and composed than she had any right to be, "but honestly, Finley, we're just trying to put all of that behind us now."

"I was wondering if—I don't want to impose, but—would it be okay if I went up to her room?"

Mrs. Flynn paused for a moment, took a sip of her iced tea like she was stalling for time. "Of course, honey."

As I followed her upstairs, I thought I detected a hint of sheepishness in the cast of her shoulders. When she led me into Betty's bedroom, I understood. While it was somewhat intact—the same furniture, her big sleigh bed still made up with its creamy lace duvet, mirror hanging over the vanity, the little stool tucked underneath it just so—what remained of Betty's belongings had been packed into a couple of cardboard boxes and shoved, unceremoniously, into a corner of the room. The walls and surfaces were all bare, a thin, grimy layer of dust covering all that mahogany furniture.

"Is this everything?" I said, unable to keep the judgment out of my voice.

"Everything from the house," Mrs. Flynn said quickly. "There's a box of her things at the school. Her notebooks, a few costumes. The guidance counselor has been holding on to them for me. I keep meaning to go pick them up, but, well, I guess I just haven't gotten around to it yet."

She retreated, leaving me alone. I sat on the plush carpet, unfolding the flaps of the first box and spilling its contents out beside me so I could sift through them.

There were old play scripts with her lines highlighted and notes about blocking in the margins, class photographs from elementary school—Betty's blonde hair in perfect curls, hands folded primly in her lap. Dried rose petals in a small plastic sleeve, the kind meant for preserving baseball cards. The sheer scarf, the color of lilacs, that matched her dress from the junior prom. Postcards I'd sent her from New York, *Playbills* from the Broadway shows we'd seen together.

I went through everything, repacking the first box when I was finished and opening the second. Here was a paper she'd written on *To Kill a Mockingbird*; the ruffled white dress she'd worn for her first communion; her Bible, the red satin ribbon marking a page. I opened it eagerly, reading a passage from the Book of Matthew before I decided the page had been saved at random. There was no hidden meaning, no secret message, no insight granted into Betty's heart. One thing was clear, though: no matter what the official story was, Betty's parents didn't think she was coming home.

Her copy of *Hamlet* was tattered, several cracks in the spine, a number of the pages flagged with small pink Post-it notes. She'd been cast as Ophelia in last fall's production. Her name was written on the first page, and that neat, feminine cursive brought me back to middle school, all those notes we passed in class and slipped into each other's lockers during the hours we were apart; all day, we would correspond, and still spend hours on the phone at night, receivers wedged between our ears and shoulders, sometimes watching the same movie, one eye trained on the television as we talked, sometimes absently doing our homework, comparing our answers and providing synonyms or correct spellings when needed. Usually my parents were fighting in the other room—their arguments, once begun, were like runaway trains, steadily gaining momentum until they were disaster-bound and unstoppable—and Betty, sensing that I needed a distraction, was unparalleled at keeping a conversation going indefinitely. Now, sitting in her bedroom, I tried to remember what we had talked about for all those hours, and I couldn't.

When I turned nine, I celebrated my birthday by hosting my first—and only—slumber party. I think I must have gotten the idea from a book or something; I had never been to one in my life. I was not the most popular kid, but I was not a social pariah, either. My mother insisted I invite every girl in my class, so no one would feel left out, and a decent number accepted, enough so I didn't feel the need to cover my face in shame, although I did, on the evening of the actual party, have a moment of deep conviction that no one would actually show up, and when the doorbell finally rang I was overwhelmed with relief. Though we barely knew each other then, Betty had been the first to arrive, and right away I loved her for that, just a little. I loved her even more, though, for what came later.

After my parents served us pizza and chips and soda, they graciously retreated upstairs so that our cabal of fourth graders could take over the living room. We spread out our sleeping bags, changed into our pajamas—I still remember Betty's, a creamy flannel with a lollipop print—and sprawled out to watch a movie.

Upstairs in their bedroom, my parents started to argue. First it was just a dull murmuring that we could only hear during the movie's quiet parts, but their voices grew slowly and steadily louder, as if someone had trained a remote control on them and was holding down the button that turned up the volume. I couldn't make out actual words, but when one of them—my mother, if I had to guess—slammed a door hard enough to rattle the pictures on the bookshelves, I knew I couldn't brush it off with some joke. Instead, I stared straight ahead at the television, trying to ignore the uncomfortable sidelong glances some of the other girls were exchanging. I buried my hands in my sleeping bag so no one would see my clenched fists.

Probably I was supposed to set my guests at ease somehow; I could shrug and tell the truth, that it was no big deal, that they fought like this all the time, that we should just keep eating our pizza and ignore them, that that was what I always did, but I suspected this tactic would fail to lighten the mood. I thought about setting the curtains on fire, to create a diversion. Upstairs, a door opened just long enough for one of Mom's piercing shrieks to escape, like a bat had gotten into the house, and when the door slammed again I knew it was too late. No one would want to stay here now, not with that thing on the loose. All around me I heard rustling as girls shifted uncomfortably in their sleeping bags, and I wondered who would be the first to say it.

Shelly opened her mouth. "I think maybe—"

And then Betty came down the hallway carrying my cake and singing "Happy Birthday," and the other girls were forced to join in, drowning out the noise from upstairs. While everybody else had been preparing their exit strategies, she had been searching my kitchen for candles and matches so that she could put an end to my humiliation. Just lifting the cake out of the freezer was practically an act of heroism; it was nearly as big as she was. She set it down precariously on the coffee table and told me to make a wish. I was going to wish for my parents to stop fighting—not forever, just for that night; even then I was a realist—but as the girls clustered around me, waiting for me to blow out the candles, I realized a hush had fallen over the second floor of the house, and that my parents had most likely heard the singing and called a truce, however temporary, when they understood that they were embarrassing me and ruining my party.

I glanced across the low table at Betty and gave her a shy smile of gratitude, but really I was in awe. Here was a girl who could grant your wish before you'd even made it. I took a deep breath, leaned over the cake, and blew out all the candles while the girls clapped and cheered. No one was thinking about leaving anymore.

"What did you wish for?" Rebecca asked.

"Come on," Betty said, pulling out the candles and licking frosting off their waxy ends. "You know she can't tell."

I never did tell—not even Betty, which is too bad, because I think she deserved to know. I think I always meant to tell her, eventually, and then we ran out of time.

I'd wished for her. For her to be my best friend, to be mine.

There was only one thing in the boxes that had come from Calder: a small stuffed lobster he had won for her at the county fair. She'd named it Jimmy, I wasn't sure why, and kept it on her vanity among her vintage gloves and tubes of red lipstick, stray buttons and ticket stubs, phone numbers scrawled on scraps of loose-leaf paper—her "bits," I had called them, all gone now, but this fucking lobster had somehow been worth saving. I squeezed it, feeling the stuffing give beneath my fingers; I turned it over in my hands, looking along the seams, as if, I don't know, as if she might have torn it open at some point, hidden something inside and sewed it back up. But of course there was nothing. There was nothing here for me to find.

I was looking for clues. Trying to turn something into a mystery when it wasn't. There was no puzzle to solve, no secret to uncover. No matter how many people tried to float the story that Betty was still alive, that she'd run away, that Calder's confession was nothing but a confused lie coerced out of a terrified boy, here in her house it was obvious that not even her parents believed that she was coming back. Betty was dead, and we all knew who had done it. Still, I tucked her copy of *Hamlet* under my shirt, and I took it with me when I left.

CHAPTER TWO.

THAT NIGHT OWEN picked me up and took me to a party in the woods. He'd heard about it at the diner and asked me, as a joke, if I wanted to go. I surprised us both when I said yes. He handed me a can of Narragansett as soon as I got into his truck; he drank wordlessly from his, steering with one hand, tucking the beer between his knees when he needed to shift gears.

"Thanks," I said. "For coming with me."

He grunted. "I can't believe I'm doing this. Going to a high school party."

"Technically, it's not a high school party if everyone graduated today."

We parked in a clearing and followed the sound of drunken chatter, Owen leading the way, holding my hand. We emerged into another clearing, filled with the graduates who had managed to escape their family celebrations; most of Williston High's remaining students were there as well. There were a couple of kegs set in plastic garbage cans filled with ice; everyone was drinking from red Solo cups. I was glad for the flask of whiskey

I had tucked protectively in my waistband. A dozen kids sat in a circle around a huge bonfire that threw out the occasional spark; someone was strumming on an acoustic guitar, and the sight of it made me cringe. It would just be a matter of time until everyone was drunk and maudlin and singing along to Green Day's "Good Riddance."

Owen must have seen the look on my face. "You wanted to come."

It occurred to me that I had graduated from high school, too. I hadn't gone to the ceremony, but I had passed all my classes; in theory, my diploma would arrive in the mail sometime in the next four to six weeks. In September I would start at NYU, live in a dorm, get a part-time job. In theory I had as much cause to celebrate as the rest of these people, but I did not share their jovial mood.

I kept looking around, past the throngs of recent graduates— faces I mostly recognized from my childhood in Williston and the summers since—trying to see into the shadows beyond the trees, the darkness untouched by the blazing campfire.

"Who are you looking for?" Owen asked.

"No one," I said, and he raised an eyebrow in a way that meant he didn't believe me.

"Whatever. You want a beer?"

"Yeah."

He walked off to find the keg. I lit a cigarette, leaned against a tree, and waited. Owen was right, I was looking for someone: the pink-haired girl from graduation. I didn't think she'd show up here, but I knew I needed to see her again.

"Finley! You're here!" A tall girl with red hair and freckles came barreling in my direction and gave me an enormous hug.

"Hey, Rebecca," I said. Rebecca had made a big show of being devastated when I moved away, which annoyed Betty no end, as she felt exclusively entitled to all the grief and concomitant sympathy related to my departure. During the summers Rebecca worked as a counselor at a sleep-away camp, so I hadn't seen her much. Betty had kept me up to date on Williston gossip, though, so I knew Rebecca had lost her virginity last spring at a party much like this one, to Danny, a friend of Calder's, and that afterward she had cried.

"How've you been?" she asked.

"I'm okay. It's always a little weird, you know, coming back. How are you doing?"

"I can't believe it. It's so surreal, you know?"

It took a second for it to register that she meant graduating from high school, not Betty's absence. "Who was that girl? The one who flipped out this morning at the ceremony? With the pink hair?"

"Oh, Serena?"

"Serena?"

She made a face. "Yeah. Serena Thomas. I don't know her that well. She just moved here a few years ago. Not that long after you left, actually."

"Can I see your yearbook?" I asked. Rebecca seemed like the only person who had brought one to the party.

"Sure," she said, handing it over.

I flipped to the page where Betty's picture would have

been, but there was nothing. After seeing how she'd been so completely omitted from the graduation ceremony, I wasn't all that surprised. I went back to the beginning and carefully paged through the whole book, the candid pictures of students sprawled on the lawn during lunchtime, the posed photos of the chess club and the swim team. Finally I found the drama club— Betty had been a member since freshman year—but she wasn't in the photo. They must have taken it after she died.

"You looking for a picture of Betty?" Rebecca asked.

I nodded.

"Here." She turned to a two-page spread in the back, a collection of pictures from *Hamlet*. I searched the faces of the actors onstage, caught mid-line, mid-gesture, but Betty wasn't there. I followed Rebecca's finger across the page, to where the crew had posed together, head-to-toe black outfits, headsets around their necks. Betty was standing on the end, her blonde hair a shapeless mess around her face, wearing a forced smile that wasn't fooling anybody.

"She was on the *crew*?" I asked, shocked.

"Assistant stage manager. I know. It was weird. She tried out for Ophelia and didn't get it. She didn't get *any* part. Not that there's a ton of parts for girls in *Hamlet*. A lot of students complained, actually, but Mr. McCartney"—the drama teacher; Betty had spoken of him often and fondly—"said he was sick of doing *Midsummer's* every other year and it was time for one of the tragedies. So Betty was stuck as ASM."

"She never played Ophelia?" I said. I was reeling. Betty had lied to me for months. *Months.* "She wasn't in the show at all?"

"No, but you wouldn't have known it. She would go around

reciting the monologues, weaving flowers into her hair. It was actually—" Rebecca stopped.

"What?"

"She would talk about drowning. About what it would feel like. It kind of spooked everybody, afterward. A few people said some pretty fucked-up things."

"Like what?"

"Like that she got to play Ophelia after all."

"Ophelia drowned *herself*," I snapped.

"It was just a stupid joke."

"Who?" I said, shoving the yearbook back into Rebecca's hands. "Who said that?"

"I don't know, just some of the guys," she backpedaled. "They were freaked out, okay? Everybody was. The kids working in the theater kept getting scared. It got so nobody wanted to be in there alone."

I gestured to the party. "Everyone seems just fine to me."

Rebecca looked at me, annoyed. "It's graduation night. Cut them a little slack."

Owen came back with the beers just as Rebecca was walking away, tightly hugging her yearbook, chin tucked to her chest.

"What did you do?" he asked, handing me a red cup.

"Nothing." I chugged the watery beer and refilled the cup with whiskey from my flask. "Want some?"

He shook his head. "I'm driving, remember?"

A group of guys were standing around the fire pit, throwing those little bang-snap firecrackers into the flames and then leaping back when they exploded, laughing like idiots. I drank my whiskey; Owen brought me another beer. A lot of people nodded at me from a distance, lifting a hand to wave across the clearing, but after Rebecca no one else approached. They didn't want to be reminded of Betty tonight, but she was all I could think about. If she were here, I would probably be doing the exact same thing— leaning hostilely against a tree, smoking cigarettes with Owen and getting lit—but I'd be watching her, too, gamely doing a keg stand or trying to rally a group into a game of spin the bottle, drunkenly doing cartwheels to prove how sober she was, getting dirty looks for flirting with somebody's boyfriend, pleading innocence with those big blue eyes.

Betty had told me she was playing Ophelia. I had even offered to make the trek up to Maine to see her perform, but she'd talked me out of it, told me to wait until I could visit for longer than a weekend. Now I understood why she hadn't wanted me to come. But why had she lied?

Across the clearing, I saw a boy—he looked too young to have graduated today, I pegged him for a rising junior or senior— catch Owen's eye, nodding at him and gesturing to a cluster of trees set apart from the rest of the party. Owen nodded back.

"I have to go talk to somebody," he said.

He threaded his way through the crowd until he reached the boy, following him until they both seemed to feel they had relative privacy. I didn't need a clear view of the proceedings to understand what was happening; the boy's face betrayed his urgency, though Owen remained expressionless. The actual shake-and-trade took less than a second, an impressive sleight of hand that would have fooled anybody who hadn't clocked quite so many hours in Washington Square Park. Owen put his hand on the boy's shoulder, leaned over and whispered something in his ear. The boy nodded; I could see how eager he was now, to get away from Owen and sample whatever it was he'd just purchased. Owen stopped at the keg to refill his cup, then joined me under the tree from where I had watched the whole thing.

"So," I asked him, "when did you become the town drug dealer?"

"It's not like that," he said. "Just a little something I'm doing on the side."

"Sure."

"Did you find whoever you were looking for?" he asked.

"I don't think she's coming."

"You'll run into her sooner or later. It's a small town."

"Tell me about it." I gestured to his pocket. "What have you got, anyway? Anything good?"

"Nothing for you, that's for sure."

"Come on. How about a little welcome home present?"

"Forget it."

The boys around the campfire had moved on from bang-snaps to bottle rockets; the girls shrieked, jumping up and leaping away. Owen put his hands on my waist, and I tipped my head forward so it rested on his chest. I breathed in his familiar scent, Old Spice and cigarettes and beer, his denim jacket rough against my cheek. He was right; Betty had been gone since November, and the town had moved on. What had I expected, to show up and find them all grieving? Stopped clocks, sheets over the mirrors? Why would they bother? They didn't even believe she was dead. I looked up at Owen, and I guess he saw the intentions in my eyes, how badly I needed a distraction, because he took my hand and led me away from the party, deeper into the woods until he was sure we were alone.

"I think I have a better way to welcome you home," he said, slowly unzipping my hoodie.

The temperature had dipped considerably since the sun had gone down, and I shivered as Owen slipped the sweatshirt off my shoulders, but not just from the cold. I reached inside his jacket, wrapping my arms around his waist and pulling him closer. His kiss was as rough and familiar as Owen himself. My winter of discontent, and the subsequent spring, had been incredibly solitary, and as Owen's fingers traced the skin around the waistband of my jeans, removing my flask and tossing it to the ground, something inside me stirred for the first time in many, many months. Sensing my urgency, he dispensed with the formalities and got down to the awkward business of trying to pull my jeans off over my sneakers.

"Shit," he whispered, and laughed for the first time since I'd seen him, a low, throaty chuckle that reminded me why I had been on the verge of falling in love with him for essentially my entire life.

He took off his jacket and laid it on the ground, gently easing me on top of it, and pulled a condom out of the same pocket that had earlier held the knife and the joint. We left my jeans as they were, and I opened my knees, ankles bound together, underneath him like a butterfly, pinned. His brief moment of mirth evaporated with an abruptness that unnerved me; suddenly his face was buried in my neck, teeth pressed against my skin as if he were grimacing in pain, his breath hot and jagged and loud in my ear. I stared up at the sky, at the stars wheeling overhead beyond the trees—twigs snapping beneath my hips, the distant roar of the party and the campfire smell and the hot lick of bourbon at the back of my throat—and tried to ignore the feeling that I was no closer to Owen now than I had been a week ago when I was still in New York. And then, almost like he was remembering I was there, he lifted his head and kissed me again and brought me back to him.

When we returned to the party, Calder was there. I didn't know when he'd arrived. Maybe he had been there the whole time. He was sitting around the fire, sipping from a red plastic cup and talking to Shelly, who had attended that ill-fated sleepover so many years ago. I searched her face for any sign of fear or fascination, some indication that she recognized Calder for what he was. There was none; he was just another classmate who had graduated that day.

"Did you know he was going to be here?" I asked Owen.

"I don't know. I guess I figured he might show up."

I stared at Calder, waiting, knowing if I kept my eyes locked on him long enough he would look up; it took longer than it should have, and I suspected he was actively avoiding my gaze, but finally he gave in. Our eyes met, and I felt my face slacken and go expressionless; he sighed, a pained exhalation of air that made his shoulders sag. He looked sad, sadder than I expected.

"I don't feel so good," I whispered.

The whiskey had snuck up on me, devious fucker. I took a step and stumbled. I was drunker than I realized. People were starting to stare, not at Calder, of course, but at me.

"Are you going to be sick?" Owen asked me.

I shook my head vigorously, as if by denying it I could make it so.

"Come on," he said. "I'll take you home."

I let him slip an arm around my waist and lead me back to his truck.

In the morning I stumbled into the kitchen, hungover. My father was sitting at the table, drinking a cup of coffee. The French press was still half-full, wrapped in a dishtowel to keep it warm. I poured the remainder of the coffee into a mug with a chipped handle and a picture of an orange kitten clinging to a tree branch wrapped around the side; the caption read, *Hang in there, baby!* It was the only mug I ever used; I had drunk hot chocolate from it as a child, sipped warm ginger ale from it when my stomach hurt and valerian root tea when I couldn't sleep. When my parents divorced and I moved to New York City with my mother, I had debated taking it with me, but in the end decided to leave it in Maine, more for my father's benefit than for mine; I imagined him seeing it in the cupboard every morning and being reminded that I still thought of this house as home. Every year when I returned, I was cheered to find it waiting for me, this one familiar object in a place that felt more foreign and alienating all the time. But there was little that orange kitten could do for me that morning—sour-stomached as I was, clammy with sweat that smelled like Old Crow, devastated by a headache that started at the base of my skull and radiated upward, culminating right between my eyes. I might have been "hanging in there, baby!" but it was only by a thread.

My parents split up when I was thirteen, the summer before I started high school. My mom was from Manhattan and my dad was from Williston; they'd met at college in Boston, a neat halfway point between their respective origins. Dad had apprenticed at the *Messenger*, Williston's local paper, since he was a teenager, learning the trade of putting out a local paper from Stan, his older, wizened predecessor. For Dad, there was no question that returning to Williston and eventually taking over the *Messenger* was his destiny. My mother's destiny, however, was back in New York City, where she planned to attend grad school and become a psychotherapist. By the time they graduated, this impasse proved impossible to overcome, and they broke up. Six months later, however, Dad made a completely unexpected romantic gesture, and visited Mom, telling her he was miserable without her, so miserable he would move to Manhattan if it meant they could be reunited. Thrilled, she accepted his offer, and they moved in together, Dad working as a freelance journalist while Mom got her master's degree.

What neither of them had anticipated was that there was one thing that would make my father more miserable than life without my mother, and that was life in New York City. Every rat that scurried across a subway platform, every trash-strewn, urine-soaked sidewalk that reeked of sour milk and human effluvia, every summer day when a thick filthy fog of humidity rose up and settled on his skin, leaving that grimy film with which all city dwellers are so intimately familiar, reminded Dad that this was not where he belonged.

It was the midseventies, and from what I've been told about the city then—the South Bronx in a constant state of smolder, Son of Sam rampaging freely across the boroughs—it's not hard to imagine why he felt that way. After Mom got her degree, Dad wasted no time impregnating her and then using their forthcoming offspring—me—as leverage for moving back to Maine. He insisted that Manhattan was no place to raise a child; Stan was ailing and wanted to turn over the *Messenger*'s reins; in Maine, my mother could start her own practice and not have to compete with the glut of therapists who had already set up shop in New York. She acquiesced, eventually, and so I was born in Williston.

Certain things, however, never materialized. Mom's practice never got off the ground; people in Maine don't particularly care to talk about their feelings. For a few years, she occupied herself with raising me, but then I was off to school and she was left every day with hours to fill, so many hours, and to be honest I don't know how she lasted as long as she did. She made no effort to hide her unhappiness—picking fights with Dad, sullenly preparing dinner and refusing to eat it herself, planting herself on the porch with the phone so she could call her friends in New York and cry about how miserable she was. She held out until I was finishing middle school, and then told Dad she was moving home with or without him.

Dad doesn't do well with ultimatums. When they sat me down to tell me they were getting divorced, I was so relieved—no longer would I have to endure their epic battles or my mother's almost tangible misery, which made every meal she prepared turn to a flavorless paste in my mouth—but I squeezed out a few tears, determined to produce the appropriate emotional response.

It was only when I realized that their divorce meant I would have to choose whether I went with my mother to New York or stayed in Maine with my dad that the tears came honestly. As difficult as she could be, my mom was my mom, but Williston was home.

Betty was dead set against my leaving. My father remained stoically neutral, Maine still in his blood, insisting again and again that it was my choice to make. My mother acted like it was a foregone conclusion that I would come with her, which was almost enough to make me stay in Williston out of spite.

In the end it was Owen, of course, who convinced me to give New York a chance. I'm not sure there was anybody else who could have. I think it horrified him that I would pass up the opportunity to trade a life in Williston for one in a big city—any city, really, let alone New York. And I think it horrified him even more because he knew if I stayed, he would be part of the reason; I'm sure he thought I was a ruthlessly calculating thirteen-year-old, biding my time, waiting for puberty to fully take hold so I could pounce and seduce him in the alley behind the diner. This scenario was not that far removed from my actual intentions.

He told me to go down there and give it a try. He told me if I hated it, I could always come back. So I followed my mother down there, certain I would be as miserable in Manhattan as my father had been. But I didn't hate it. I didn't hate it at all.

"How are you feeling?" my father asked, watching my tentative movements.

"Tremendous." I sat down across from him at the table and took a sip of my coffee. "This tastes fancy."

"I splurged on the good stuff."

"Thank you."

"You should call Owen later and thank him."

"Thank him?"

"For getting you home last night. You were in rare form. It took both of us to get you into bed."

I winced. "Sorry."

"Is this what it's going to be like all summer?"

I shook my head, a mistake. Sharp pain flashed inside my head like lightning and then dulled, settling in right behind my eyebrows. "I was upset. Seeing everyone at graduation, and then at the party, acting so normal. Talking to Calder like it never happened. It's so weird. It's like she never existed."

Dad shook his head. "That's not true."

"Yes, it is."

"You just got back. You'll see. She's on people's minds more than you think."

There was a time, right after Betty died, that I tried to convince myself she wasn't actually dead. It was easier than I thought it would be. Though Calder had confessed to drowning her in the ocean, her body had never been found; it had gone out with the tide, the initial theory went. Maybe it was some prank, some joke, and Betty had been in on it; she certainly had the requisite flair for the dramatic. Maybe she had wanted to pull a Tom Sawyer and watch her own funeral—but, of course, there had never been a funeral. If she had hoped to watch the town come together and grieve for her, surely she had been disappointed. And then Calder's confession became irrelevant, and the idea that she had run away—so much more palatable—took hold in Williston's collective imagination. Maybe she had taken off to start over someplace else, the thinking went, escape her bad reputation. Maybe she couldn't wait for NYU. Maybe she needed a quicker out, one with more panache.

But I knew she wasn't alive, because if she were, she would have come to me, found me in New York and let me in on her secret. She wouldn't have let me, her oldest, closest friend, who'd suffered so much in her absence, believe her body was drifting in the ocean, rotting, picked apart, if she were still alive and whole, still wearing Fire and Ice lipstick and listening to Billie Holiday on rainy days. If she had run off somewhere, she would have taken me with her.

And I think Williston knew it, too, knew that the story about Betty leaving on her own was nothing but a convenient fiction meant to soothe everyone's nerves, dispel the distasteful idea that the mayor's son might be a murderer by using Betty's reputation as a melodramatic slattern against her, the bow that neatly tied the whole narrative together. Because nobody from Williston— not Emily when she was still sheriff, not the toady with whom Leroy had replaced her, not an underling state trooper, not even Betty's parents—had ever called me in New York to ask if I had seen her. My mother's apartment, where Betty had her own goddamn toothbrush, would have been the most logical place to start looking, and nobody had ever bothered. I think they all knew there was no point. I think they all knew she was already dead.

"I just want to know why he did it."

My father raised his eyebrows. "Do you really think that would make a difference?"

"Yeah, I do," I said.

After he left for work, I dry-swallowed two aspirin, chased them with a glass of water, and lay down on the couch in the living room: hideous gold velour, overstuffed cushions splitting along the seams, the fabric rubbed bare in places. It always took me a few tries to remember how the remote control worked, and after several frantic minutes of pushing buttons, I began to despair that I might have to give up and read a book. Almost by accident, I managed to press the right combination, and with a comforting series of beeps the screen came to life. I flipped through the channels until I found the one that showed classic movies twenty-four hours a day. *Laura* was on, and though it seemed a little early in the morning for Otto Preminger, I let it play, closing my eyes and listening to the dialogue I knew by heart.

"I don't use a pen," Waldo Lydecker said. "I write with a goose quill dipped in venom."

In the movies, the murderer always dies at the end; the writers know the audience won't be satisfied if he's taken away in handcuffs. I wondered what would have happened to Lydecker if he'd been arrested instead; maybe he would have gotten a good lawyer, found a way to talk himself out of it, and Detective McPherson would have had to live with that, knowing that the guilty party had been allowed to walk.

I dozed but didn't sleep, vaguely aware when *Laura* ended and *Bunny Lake Is Missing* began. Even in my stupor, I felt a warm rush of sympathy for Ann Lake. I wished it were raining so I would feel justified staying inside all day; instead, the sunlight bled into the house around the edges of the curtains. I tried to summon the energy to get up and adjust them and failed.

Betty hadn't always been Betty. Growing up she was Liz or Lizzie, E-liz-a-beth when I was annoyed, and I needed every syllable for my outrage. Betty came later, when we were about to start high school and ripe for self-reinvention.

My last summer in Williston the weather fit my mood; it rained constantly, a steady drizzle punctuated by the occasional afternoon thunderstorm. The fog hung thick and low, and the ocean was just a vague, sleepy idea somewhere under the heavy blanket of mist. My parents were splitting up, my mother had already moved back to New York, and everyone was waiting on me to decide where I would live, whether I'd go to Williston High with the same people I'd known since kindergarten or join my mother in a place called the Upper West Side. Betty was both sympathetic and jealous of my misery; normally her dramas far outweighed mine.

We spent most of the time in her basement watching television. Eventually we tired of MTV's endless *Real World* reruns and discovered the classic movie channel. That week they were showing a Douglas Sirk marathon, and Betty fell for fifties melodrama. The histrionics and overwrought dialogue, those strange kisses—passionate yet close-mouthed—and, of course, the clothes. The fit-and-flare shirtdresses with the voluminous skirts, bolstered by tulle netting and petticoats; sleek wiggle dresses with scandalous necklines; silk dressing gowns and marabou mules.

TCM moved on from melodramas to film noir marathons, and Betty started wearing an anklet like Barbara Stanwyck in *Double Indemnity.* We watched *Vertigo* and *All About Eve, Out of the Past* and *The Third Man,* while Betty perfected finger-waving her hair. Finally, she started dragging me out of the basement for shopping expeditions, enlisting Owen as our begrudging chauffeur since we were both too young to drive, searching for the perfect shade of red lipstick. She adopted a signature scent, and with frugality in mind she chose the Body Shop's White Musk, but she kept it on her vanity in a vintage atomizer, so that even purchases she made at the mall were imbued with a bit of mystery and glamour. Seamed stockings are not easy to come by in coastal Maine, and these expeditions took us farther and farther afield, to thrift stores in Portland and beyond.

While our endless film marathons inspired her fashion sense

and love for acting, they instilled in me a passion for the movies themselves. I was never happier than I was sitting in the dark, watching the classics, trying to figure out how the story would end, why the camera moved the way it did, why some shots lasted for ages and other scenes were edited at a rapid-fire clip. I wasn't nearly as interested in whatever was at the local theater; I didn't think Kevin Smith was a genius. I was too busy watching Hitch-cock's *Rope* over and over, trying to spot the hidden cuts, or won-dering how *Sunset Boulevard* could still be so suspenseful even though it was narrated by a corpse and you knew from the open-ing scene where it was all headed. I didn't want to make movies or write movies or work on actual movies in any way at all; the col-laborative nature of the medium was not for me. I much preferred picking them apart to figure out how they worked.

During a phone conversation that August, my mother ob-served that I was the same way with people, more interested in their inner workings than anything else, and I told her she was one to talk, considering her profession, and I swear I heard her actually bite her tongue in an effort to avoid starting an argu-ment, and so in turn I refrained from making a snide remark about all the progress she was making with her own therapist, and we let the conversation stop there, both silently congratu-lating ourselves, I'm sure, on nipping that particular screaming match in the bud.

I made my decision after numerous lectures from Owen—surprisingly impassioned—and when it was time for me to leave, Liz, Lizzie, E-liz-a-beth announced she was calling herself Betty. I had to admit that "Betty" went with her new wardrobe, and possessed a certain vintage flair her other names did not, but still, I feared for her. This was small-town Maine in 1994; school shopping meant pilfering flannel shirts from your father and tearing holes in the knees of your Levi's. I'm sure when Betty showed up on the first day in heels and a pencil skirt, people must have reacted like she'd worn a wedding gown. If it bothered her, she never said a word to me, but then Betty thrived on feeling misunderstood.

She didn't want me to leave, but still, she swore that she'd be fine without me. It was a convincing performance.

I believed her.

She was not Williston's golden girl; she was not one of the popular crowd. She was too earnest, too flamboyant, stripped naked by her constant need for attention. The same boys who fucked her in the backseats of their cars, late at night after they'd dropped off their unwaveringly chaste girlfriends, always ignored her in the halls the next day.

She was nobody's favorite but mine.

Eventually I must have fallen asleep. I woke up, my mouth sour all over again, but my headache had receded and my thirst was less desperate. The sun had shifted lower in the sky, no longer leaking into the living room but backlighting the curtains with an orange glow. TCM had moved on from Preminger to Nicholas Ray. I shut off the television, suddenly restless in the empty, silent house.

I got dressed, grabbed my car keys. I left behind the gloomy little nest I had made in the living room—my body imprinted on the cushions, the chenille blanket lying on the arm where I had cast it aside, the curtains drawn, a pint glass of water on the end table next to the remote control—and drove to the high school. My car was the only one in the lot; the principal must have had his towed. The building was brick and sprawling; inside, it looked like all the lights were off. I took the flashlight from my glove compartment, testing its batteries and tucking it into my waistband, and slung my messenger bag over my shoulder.

I walked the perimeter of the building, testing all the doors, but they were locked. The first-floor windows were all covered with screens. Finally, I came to a small window just a few inches off the ground, which presumably opened into the basement. It was boarded over with cheap-looking plywood, which gave easily after a few kicks. I shimmied through, feet first, choking on dust.

I landed in what looked like the boiler room, surrounded by hulking, silent machinery. Turning on the flashlight, I swept it around until I found the door. I took the stairs up to the first floor.

Outside, the sun continued its slow slide toward the horizon. The beam of my flashlight gave everything an eerie shine—the glass in the trophy cases, the linoleum tiles, the rows of metal lockers lining the walls. I hadn't spent much time in Williston High, so I got lost easily, traveling in circles, covering the same territory. The only sound was my Chucks, rubber soles squeaking on the floor, until finally I found the guidance counselor's office.

Terrified the door would be locked, I used creative visualization before I turned the knob, imagining it turning smoothly in my hand and the soft click of the tumbler. To my amazement the door opened easily, and once inside I understood why. Where I had pictured cabinets full of private student files, there was only an old wooden desk and a small bookshelf filled with self-help nonsense like *Chicken Soup for the Teenage Soul*. By the look of it, the guidance counselor was only part-time and likely filled a lot of hours playing solitaire and Minesweeper on her aging desktop computer.

On the bookcase's bottom shelf was a small cardboard box labeled "Flynn." I used Owen's pocket knife—my knife now, I remembered—to slit open the brown packing tape that sealed it shut. Kneeling reverently on the cold linoleum floor, I tore back the flaps to reveal the last vestiges of Betty.

There was a picture of Betty and me, a cheap plastic mirror, an NYU bumper sticker I'd sent her last year, a collection of ticket stubs from movies, concerts, and plays—items that had all hung once, I was sure, inside her locker. Here, then, was the remainder of her bits, and I carefully removed them, collecting them in a neat stack before I placed them in the zippered pocket of my messenger bag.

The contents of the box were covered in a thin film of dust. It smelled like mold and pencil shavings, but beneath all that I thought I could detect that faintest whiff of White Musk. Notebooks, textbooks, her ASM binder for *Hamlet*. Betty's mom had been wrong; there were no costumes here, just a pair of black satin opera gloves, the kind that go all the way up past the elbow. To anyone else they might have seemed like part of a costume, but these were well worn, stretched out a bit in the fingers. Betty loved them like I might love a favorite T-shirt, and she found a way to wear them just as often.

I didn't bother sorting the rest of her things; I just grabbed the whole pile and shoved it into my bag. I would go through it later. I thought about at least throwing away the textbooks, but I was afraid to miss a single thing—a note scribbled in a margin, a doodle on the back cover.

I was debating whether to go down to the basement and exit the same way I'd come in or try my luck with the school's back door—would I fit through the window now that my bag was filled with Betty's possessions, or set off an alarm?—when I heard something. The sound was faint but familiar, the same kind of squeak my shoes had made as I crept through the hallways. Could it be a janitor, making a final sweep of the building? The total darkness made it unlikely. I remembered what Rebecca had said about the theater, the rumors about its haunting.

I got lost again before I found it. The auditorium looked like it hadn't been redone since the seventies—wooden folding seats in neat, slightly curved rows; the stage curtains parted, a worn black scrim hanging in front of the back wall. As I walked down the center aisle, I pointed my flashlight up and caught a glimpse of the catwalks above the stage, and the lighting grid, now bare.

I heard something, a shuffling of feet, and then a shadow

loomed large on the scrim, black on black, a person emerging from backstage, and my heart froze in my chest.

She stepped out from behind the scrim, and I exhaled sharply, all the oxygen rushing out of my body, rendering my hands and feet numb. It was the girl with the pink hair, the one from the graduation ceremony. Serena.

"Jesus," I said. "You scared the piss out of me."

She glanced at the crotch of my jeans. "Not literally, I hope."

"What are you doing here?"

"Same thing you're doing. Looking for a ghost. I guess you already heard the rumors?"

"Actually, I was picking up her stuff."

"You're Betty's friend, right? The one who lives in New York?"

"Finley." My voice echoed in the empty theater. I climbed up the stairs to meet her on the stage.

"I'm Serena." Stepping forward, she extended her hand. I shook it, smiling at her formality. The black paint under her fingernails had been scrubbed away. Her rings were cold against my palm, and her septum piercing sparkled faintly in the dim light.

"I've been looking for you," I said. "I was hoping you would be at the party last night."

She shrugged. "I don't really go to parties."

That I could easily believe.

I took her in. Now that I had her in front of me, instead of crying and screaming and fleeing the graduation ceremony, I could see the dark roots coming in under the bleached-blonde and pink hair, her gray eyes, the hard set of her jaw. She was wearing brown cargo pants, a white wifebeater, and Doc Martens; an outfit that wouldn't have looked out of place on Owen, except for the black bra straps that hugged her pale shoulders and the gold crucifix I recognized from yesterday. Had it just been yesterday I'd seen her for the first time? It felt like I'd been looking for her for much longer.

"I wish I had known that," I said. "I could have spared myself the hangover."

"I was wondering if you'd come back to town this summer." She said it like a challenge, like she wasn't sure I'd have the guts. Her voice was deep and raspy; instead of being amplified by the empty theater, it came out more like a hoarse whisper, and I had to lean in closer to make sure I was getting every word. Her eyes never strayed from mine.

"My therapist said I needed closure," I said. "Were you a friend of Betty's?"

"Not really."

"How did you know her?"

"We got sent away to church camp the same summer."

"Oh. I'm sorry." Betty's stories about church camp, the few of them that I had heard, had not been pleasant.

"It was rough. We sort of bonded while we were there, but we didn't really keep it up at school. How did you get in here anyway?"

"One of the windows to the basement was boarded up. You?"

"Master key."

"How did you get one of those?" I asked.

"There's a lot of them floating around. They get passed down from one senior class to the next."

"You haven't passed yours on yet?"

"I'm not done with it. Obviously. Usually I just use it to let myself into the office and make free copies on the Xerox machine. I was going to go backstage, look in the dressing room. You want to come?"

"Might as well. I'm already here."

I followed her offstage, down a hallway that led into the dressing room. Costumes from old shows were still hanging on the wardrobe racks. One whole wall was a vanity, white Formica counter beneath a long mirror framed by bulbs that came to life as Serena flicked the light switch. Another wall was covered in graffiti by the casts of various plays, going back almost a decade. I looked for Betty's name and couldn't find it. Her signature was nowhere on the wall.

"Her name should be here," I said, pointing to the long list of actors who had been in *Midsummer's*. "She was in this one, I saw the pictures."

Serena scanned the wall up and down. "You're right. Her name's not anywhere." She shook her head. "They probably found a way to erase it. Paint over it, or something. After all that shit started about people thinking the theater was haunted."

"How exactly did that start, anyway?"

Serena leaned against the wall, crossing her arms. "It was sometime in the spring, when rehearsals began for *The House of Yes*. One of the costume designers was here late, by herself, and she said she kept hearing things. And that the lights went out and came back on. Honestly, it was probably nothing, but she said she wouldn't be here alone after that. And then no one would be here alone, and that was all it took to make it into a thing, you know?"

"Did she come right out and say that she thought it was Betty?"

Serena shook her head. Her expression changed, and I got a glimpse of the rage I'd seen the day before. "Everyone knew that's what she meant, but she never said it. You'll see. No one ever says her name, but whenever something happens, she's on everybody's mind."

"I don't understand. I thought everyone thinks she ran away?"

"There's what everyone pretends to believe, and then there's what they all know is really true." She paused, fiddling nervously with her crucifix. "Was he there last night? At the party?"

"Yeah. He was."

We were silent for a while.

"What was it you said?" I asked her. "Onstage at graduation. To the principal?"

"I asked him if I could say a few words about Betty. I'm sure you can guess what his answer was."

"Why do you think Calder did it?"

She shrugged. "I don't have any idea."

"But you believe he did it."

"I do. I used to wonder why he did it, but now I don't think I care."

"Sometimes I think it's the only thing I care about."

"You must really miss her," Serena said.

"Yeah. Can I ask you something?"

"Sure."

"You said you guys weren't really friends, that you didn't hang out after camp. But you're the only person—" I thought of Owen and corrected myself. "You're one of the only people who seem to care that she's gone."

"I guess I was kind of in love with her," Serena said.

I found something about this admission oddly pleasing. Knowing that someone else had seen the same Betty as I had made me feel less lonely. "Then you must really miss her, too."

"Yeah."

Serena strolled over to the wardrobe rack, flipping through the costumes as if she were shopping in a department store.

"What if," she said, "there were something we could do to make them remember?"

We went to the diner to wait. It was full dark now, the night as clear as the day had been. I felt strangely energized as I drove us into town.

The Halyard smelled like hamburger grease and burnt coffee. The dinner rush was coming to a close, and people were filing out and into Charlie's, the bar across the street. We sat in a booth, the vinyl creaking beneath our weight, and looked over the laminated menus. There was a typo in the breakfast items, "two eggs and style," that normally would have made me laugh but barely registered now. My head was pounding; I shouldn't have waited so long to eat. Owen gave me a strange look from behind the counter; normally I sat on one of the stools near the register so I could bullshit with him while he worked. Even the waitress who took our order, Jenny, was surprised to see me at a table.

I heard the first fire truck then, the urgent wail of the siren, followed by another truck and then another. As they sped by in the direction of the high school, I avoided Serena's eyes, focusing instead on my iced tea and disco fries.

The Halyard emptied as the commotion outside grew, police cruisers following in the fire trucks' wake. Serena and I casually trailed outside along with the rest of the patrons; everyone was standing on the sidewalk with their hands in their pockets. Owen was there, too, dirty apron still tied around his waist.

The sky was hazy now, the stars blotted out by a thin scrim of gray smoke I might have mistaken for fog if it weren't for the acrid smell and the fact that I already knew its source.

"What's going on?" I asked.

"High school's on fire," he said. "Don't know much else yet."

But even as he said it, there was a rumor spreading like flame up and down the street, passing from one person to the next so quickly that its origin would soon be forgotten. Serena and I saw the worried faces and I knew she was filled with the same gladness that was fanning out inside my chest, and I recalled what she had said before, that no one would say Betty's name, but when something happened she was on everyone's mind. I felt her presence now, like I had at graduation when Ann Russo had her seizure, fighting back against Williston's tacit agreement to erase her from its memory. I saw the same ripple go through the crowd. Everyone was whispering the same thing—that the fire had started in the theater—and I knew that Serena was right, that we'd found a way, at least for tonight, to make them all remember.

CHAPTER THREE.

THE DAY AFTER the fire, I went to the *Messenger* office. Dad was out gathering information on the fire: interviewing witnesses, talking to the police and the firefighters, taking pictures down at the school.

The office was one cramped room above the creamery, with wood-paneled walls and shabby, threadbare carpet checkered with coffee stains. Most of Dad's desk was taken up by his keyboard and computer monitor, Post-it notes of various fluorescent colors stuck to both, phone numbers and reminders about upcoming dentist appointments and ideas for headlines; the rest was covered with back copies of the paper, legal pads filled with his illegible notes, and pink message slips. Buried beneath it all was one of those old desk telephones, the solid kind heavy enough to be used as a weapon in an emergency.

The rest of the office was equally disorganized, littered with stacks of cardboard boxes and empty takeout containers from the diner. The kitchenette against the back wall had a minifridge, a small sink, and a coffeemaker. There was a quarter inch of scorched black liquid in the bottom of the glass carafe. I dumped it out and started a fresh pot.

The Williston *Messenger* was a weekly paper and pretty much a one-man operation, with the occasional op-ed or advice column submitted by a mouthy local. Letters from concerned citizens took up most of the space. There was a calendar in the back that listed upcoming events like school board elections and PTA meetings and when the Traveling Heartbreakers, a Traveling Wilburys/Tom Petty and the Heartbreakers cover band, would be playing next at Charlie's. The police blotter was a perpetual source of amusement for me, chronicling what passed for crime in Williston—a taxidermied deer head stolen from above someone's fireplace, dogs barking too loudly, a teenager running off with the MS donation jar at the general store on a dare. The classified section was filled with ads from people trying to sell their old pickup trucks or give away kittens from their barn cat's latest litter; "will trade for guns" was a common refrain.

Today I was feeling less interested in Williston's many quirks than I was in reading the coverage of Betty's murder—or alleged disappearance. Dad had kept me updated, but I'd always suspected he wanted to shield me from the worst of it. I could have simply clicked through the articles on his computer until I found the ones I wanted, but instead I poured myself a cup of coffee from the pot I'd just made—it still tasted burnt—and started going through his archives, the cardboard boxes along the wall. I pulled every issue of the paper from November and December.

I began with the weeks before Betty died, more for context

than anything else, just to see what had been happening in Williston last fall. Dad had covered the high school's production of *Hamlet*; I was surprised to see that Calder had had the starring role, a detail I'd missed when I looked through Rebecca's yearbook. I checked the police blotter: someone had filed a noise complaint about a "rowdy gathering" that Saturday night, probably the cast party.

The following week's paper had a story about local election results; I was less surprised to read that Calder's father had been reelected as mayor. The police blotter reported two different incidents of "public fornication"; the first claimed that a couple had been spotted "in various states of undress" on one of the local beaches, the second that a car with "steamed windows" was parked in the alley behind Owen's diner. Had Owen himself been one of its occupants? I clenched my jaw. It was none of my business. There was no room for jealousy in our relationship, which technically only existed for two months out of the year, and even then hardly constituted a relationship.

Betty had been missing for two days before Calder confessed to killing her. Her parents reported it when they woke up on the Friday morning after Thanksgiving and found her empty bed. The *Messenger* had come out in the interval between then and Calder's confession, so the first articles were about her disappearance, not her death. It had made the front page, with the rather uninspired headline, "Local Girl Reported Missing." There was a picture of Betty alongside the article, a posed headshot that looked like her missing yearbook photo. Her head was tilted down slightly, turned just enough to the left to show off what I knew she thought of as her good side, one side of her hair pulled back with a vintage rhinestone barrette, lips in a suggestion of a smile.

Elizabeth Flynn, an 18-year-old senior at Williston High School, was reported missing yesterday morning by her parents, Thomas and Beverly Flynn, when they discovered her bed was empty and appeared not to have been slept in.

The girl was last seen on Thursday evening around 9 P.M., when she said goodnight to her parents and went upstairs to her bedroom. She is described as being 5 foot 3 and 115 pounds. She was last seen wearing a pale pink nightgown with matching silk robe. Mr. and Mrs. Flynn retired shortly after, leaving it open to speculation whether their daughter left the house of her own accord or was removed forcibly from the premises. The police reported there was no sign of forced entry or a struggle, strongly suggesting the former.

Several classmates, who all spoke on the condition of anonymity, said that Flynn had been acting strangely in the weeks before her disappearance. Disappointment over losing a part in a school play, coupled with a recent breakup with her long-term boyfriend, weighed heavily on the girl, who even her parents described as "troubled."

"We just want her to come home," said her mother.

Anyone with information regarding Elizabeth Flynn's whereabouts should contact the Williston Sheriff's Department.

So much had changed in the days after that story ran. The picture of Calder and Betty at the junior prom was splashed across the front page of the following week's paper. "Tragedy in Williston: Local Boy Confesses to Killing Ex-Girlfriend."

> Eighteen-year-old Elizabeth Flynn, who disappeared from her home last Thursday night, is now presumed dead in light of new information, according to the Williston police. Calder Miller, Flynn's ex-boyfriend, has apparently confessed to drowning Flynn in the ocean, on a small beach right outside the town's border.
>
> Police are not revealing any further information at this time, and the motive for the alleged crime remains unknown.
>
> It is now believed that Flynn's body, which remains missing, may have floated out to sea with the tide. Police have cordoned off the beach and are treating it like a crime scene as they search for evidence to corroborate Miller's story.

I read through the rest of the articles, detailing how the police had fumbled the investigation—Calder was still seventeen when he'd confessed, and without either his parents or an attorney present during the interrogation, everything he'd said was deemed inadmissible. Without his confession, the police couldn't even prove that Betty had been murdered; her body had never been found, and any physical evidence had been washed away. He'd had no motive, and if anything, the evidence pointed to her practically stalking him, playing the part of the spurned lover. Other members of the senior class said that she was always cornering him outside of rehearsal; phone records showed that she called him over and over. Finally, Shelly, who'd had a thing for Calder since kindergarten, went to the police and told them Betty had been talking about running away, that she'd been try-ing to get Calder to go with her, and when he refused she finally gave up and went off with another guy, one of the many she'd been sleeping with, and to where nobody knew. Conveniently, Betty had never mentioned a destination. It all sounded like bullshit to me, but it was enough for the county. The prosecutor had no choice but to let Calder go. Emily Shepard had been re-placed with one of Leroy's toadies.

By the beginning of December, the headlines had changed again. "Police Speculate Missing Girl May Have Run Away."

Dad came in as I was reading.

"Don't worry," I said, "I'll put them all back."

He walked over to where I was sitting and glanced down at the paper.

"So she's not even officially dead?" I asked.

He shook his head. "Officially, she's still a missing person."

"Did you ever see the transcript of Calder's confession?"

"It's sealed," he said.

"How sealed?"

"Forget it, Fin. I called in every favor I had with the cops, and they still wouldn't let me read it."

"Fuck."

He sat next to me on the floor and took a sip of my coffee. "God, this tastes horrible."

"It might be time to invest in a French press for the office."

He surveyed the stack of newspapers. "They really screwed this one up, didn't they? He was a high school senior—they just assumed he was eighteen. His birthday was only two weeks away, but it didn't matter. Without the confession, they had nothing." He sighed.

Dad had not liked Betty. He had been subtle about it, but I knew how to read him; inference was usually the only way to find out what he was thinking. He'd found her too brash, too brazen, too quick to give in to her impulses and emotions; Dad preferred steady people, thought moodiness was for the weather. Like most everyone in Williston, he'd been put off by her reputation with boys, although he seemed to feel sorry for her instead, a pity tainted with disgust. My mother told me that he held Betty's parents equally responsible for her behavior, that their self-righteousness and obsession with religion had sent her careening toward the opposite extreme.

He may not have liked her, but he didn't think she had it coming, and his sadness over her death was real; he was one of the few who saw it as a genuine tragedy.

"What's the story with the fire?" I asked.

"I'm not sure yet. The fire department didn't want to comment at all. But the cops are saying there's evidence of a break-in."

I looked at Dad directly, my facial muscles perfectly controlled. "A break-in?"

"Someone kicked in a boarded-up window to the basement. Went in through the boiler room."

I made a big production of reorganizing all the newspapers I'd pulled from the boxes. "I have to get going."

"I'll see you at the game later?"

Williston's softball team was serious business. Dad had to attend every Sandpipers game for the paper, and one of the few impositions he placed upon me every summer was that I accompany him, at least to the home games. Sports were the absolute last thing on my mind, but I wanted to keep him happy while I could. "Don't worry," I said. "I'll be there."

I drove straight from Dad's office to Serena's house after looking up her address in a dusty phone book I found under Dad's desk. She lived in an old Cape Cod a couple of miles outside of town, fallen into the sort of disrepair I'd expected at the Flynns'. The red paint was peeling, and the yard badly needed mowing. From the outside it looked empty—no cars in the driveway, all the curtains drawn—but I climbed up the porch steps and rang the bell anyway.

Serena answered after a couple of minutes. Her hair looked brighter than yesterday, as if she'd spent the morning freshening the color. It was still damp, and pink drops of water streamed down her neck, collecting in her collarbone and staining the white collar of her tank top.

"I need to talk to you," I said. "Can I come inside?"

"It's better if we go somewhere instead. Let me get my shoes."

She closed the door, leaving me waiting on the porch. When she reemerged, her jeans were tucked into her boots and she was carrying a sweatshirt, as if she thought we might be out late enough for the sun to go down and the temperature to drop.

I waited until we were back on the highway before I told her what Dad had said about the fire.

"It's not like I was wearing gloves. I could have left finger-prints all over the windowsill. And what about you? Who else knows you have that key?"

"Don't worry about it," Serena told me. "It's going to be fine."

"I never should have slashed the principal's tires. Anybody could have seen me do it."

"I had a feeling that was you," she said, apparently pleased to have this suspicion confirmed, and I found myself, ridiculously, hoping I had impressed her. She pulled out her key ring and wound the school's master free from the metal coil. "You take it. Just in case they start looking into other ways people could have gotten into the building. You were never a senior here, no one would think you'd have one."

"Okay." I wasn't sure that made much sense, but Serena's con-fidence swayed me.

"Where are we going, exactly?" she asked. "Did you have a specific destination in mind?"

"Would you think it's really morbid," I said, "if we drove to the beach?"

"You mean the place where he killed her?"

I flinched at her bluntness. "Yeah."

"I wouldn't think it was morbid if you wanted to visit her grave, but she doesn't have one, so I guess the spot where she died is the closest thing."

I looked out the window. "Thank you."

I knew the spot from the news reports; it had been a favorite of Betty's, a place where we'd had picnics and gotten drunk together countless times. It was just a small rocky cove, a narrow strip of sand with clutches of towering pine trees on either side. It was strange to think of him drowning her here—how had he gotten her out here? Had they gone into the water together? In November the ocean would have been freezing, too cold for swimming, even on a drunken dare. None of it made any sense.

Serena and I sat next to each other on a large, flat rock facing the water. I took my shoes off and buried my feet in the damp sand. She followed suit, unlacing her boots and easing them off her feet, then removing each sock, rolling them up into neat little balls, and tucking them inside her shoes, an economy and precision to her every movement that fascinated me. The waves were small and gentle, the foam rolling up just a few feet from our toes.

"You've been out here before," I said.

"I come out here all the time, but I've never been here with anyone else." She reached into her pocket and pulled out a tiny blue pill. She bit it in half and handed the rest to me. "Here."

"It's so small," I said.

"It doesn't feel small. Trust me. It helps if you chew it. Kicks in faster."

I obeyed without further objection, wondering briefly if Owen was her supplier. But Owen had said he didn't know any girl with pink hair.

"Tell me about meeting her. Tell me about church camp."

Serena snorted. "Oh God, that place. It was so awful. They sent me there for—well, I guess for the obvious reasons."

"How did they find out? Did they catch you with someone?"

"I wish. At least then I would have had a little fun first. No, I've never had a girlfriend. Slim pickings up here, you know? Not like in New York, I bet. I wrote a zine, and I traded with other people for theirs—mostly other girls our age. I had pen pals all over the country. We would write to one another and talk about how shitty it was to be trapped in these small towns." She paused and scratched at her septum ring. "There was one girl in particular, Monica. We wrote each other all the time, sent each other packages and mix tapes. Then we started talking on the phone. I guess it was as close to romance as either of us had ever gotten, which is pretty pathetic considering we'd never met. And then my mom found the letters. I think they'd always suspected, but once they had proof—that was it, off to church camp." She shrugged. "How much did Betty tell you about that place?"

"Not much. She didn't like to talk about it."

"I can't say I blame her. It was fucking awful. In the brochures, they make it sound like any other camp, just with Bible study. But it's not. There's all this emphasis on discipline. All the showers were cold, the food was just gruel. If you got in trouble, they made you stand in a corner facing a wall, not talking to anybody, nobody allowed to talk to you, for like ten hours a day. We called it the red shirt treatment. Once I was doing it and I got my period, and they wouldn't even let me go put in a tampon. I had to stand there with blood running down my legs until my ten hours was up for the day."

"Jesus."

"All in his name. A couple of kids tried to run away, and when they were caught they got the red shirt treatment for a week. Anyway, Betty was the only other person there from Williston. We were both on kitchen duty, cleaning dishes, scrubbing pots, so we got to talking. I almost didn't recognize her at first, it was so weird seeing her out of those fifties outfits, in a uniform just like everybody else. I liked her. She was funny. Even at that shithole, she still kept her sense of humor."

Betty had called me right before she was shipped off to camp, just a few days until I was supposed to arrive in Williston for the summer. She told me she had cheated on Calder, and that one night the cops found her parked in a car with some guy. She wouldn't tell me who it was. That kind of thing happened all the time in Williston, and usually they just let you off with a warning. But this guy was older, and she intimated it wasn't the first time she'd been discovered in the backseat of a car with her pencil skirt up around her hips. Anyway, the cops brought her home, told her parents. Word got around, Calder broke up with her, and her parents sent her off to Bible camp.

"For fuck's sake," I'd said to her on the phone that day. "Why did you do it?"

"I don't know, I don't know," she wailed, "it's not like I haven't done it before. But now he knows, the whole town knows."

"Who was it?"

"It doesn't matter."

"Come on, tell me."

"I mean it," she said sharply. "It doesn't matter."

"Why didn't you just break up with Calder if you didn't want to be with him anymore?"

"I never said I didn't want to be with him. I just did a stupid thing. It's so fucking textbook—I can hear your mom's voice in my head, telling me I don't think I deserve someone like Calder so I sabotaged it on purpose. I don't know, maybe I was just bored." There was a tinge of real hysteria in her voice, enough to make me feel shitty and powerless and so far away. "He broke up with me and now my parents are sending me away and by the time I get back he'll have a new girlfriend and it'll be like the last twenty-one months never happened."

I tried to find some words of comfort, but came up short. The truth was, she was probably right. For two months every year I swapped one home for another. I knew all too well how much could change in just one season.

The summer after my freshman year of high school had been a grim one; that spring, I had fallen in love with both New York City and a shy blond boy named Tad, who had delicate, almost pretty features and wore checkered Vans and black rubber bracelets. Our courtship consisted of him giving me skateboarding lessons in Washington Square Park, eating falafel, and combing the used-CD section of Generation Records. My face got hot every time his shoulder brushed mine or he clumsily reached for my hand. When I left for Maine, he gave me a mix tape (he'd used black and white paint markers to color it checkered, like his shoes) and one of his bracelets, which I didn't take off all summer. I spent the bus ride to Maine staring out the window, crying and listening to Tad's tape. By the time I came home, of course, he was eating falafel by the fountain with another girl and showing off his skateboarding tricks for her.

"She talked about you all the time, you know," said Serena, bringing me back to the present.

"She did?"

"She was pissed about being sent away for the summer because that was the only chance you guys ever really had to be together. She missed you."

"I missed her, too." We got by during the school year with our phone calls and visits and letters, but summer was when our friendship really flourished, and when she was at camp last summer we weren't even allowed to speak. It had been a long two months without her; I did some part-time work at the paper, archiving old issues and writing the occasional obituary, but there wasn't enough to keep me busy, and most days Dad cut me loose by lunchtime, leaving me with the rest of the day's endless hours to fill. I did my best—naps on the screened-in porch behind the house; trips to the beach, where I only sometimes found the courage to plunge into the icy Maine waters; long, aimless drives, a luxury for a New Yorker who normally lacked access to a car. Sometimes at night I went to the parties deep in the woods, where I hovered awkwardly around the fringes. I had grown up here, so I wasn't officially from away, but I lived in New York City, and I certainly didn't belong in Williston anymore; all the in-jokes and gossip were lost on me without Betty there to fill me in. I could only rely on Owen so much for entertainment; he was happy to provide me with frequent sex, but understandably reluctant to appear with me too much in public, since I was still in high school.

Betty and I had overlapped for just a week at the end of the summer, but she had been quiet and distant, beset by the un-lights, and I'd only seen her once, despite my frequent efforts to coax her out of her bedroom.

I'd shown up at her house uninvited and let myself in without ringing the bell. I found her curled up in a ball on the basement couch. She was wearing cutoffs and a plain black tank top, un-washed hair pulled back in a ponytail; no makeup, no lipstick. She smelled like stale sweat instead of White Musk. I was so used to seeing Betty in her vintage clothes, this simple outfit looked like a costume.

"Am I supposed to start calling you Lizzie again?" I'd asked.

"My mom made me donate all my clothes to Goodwill." I swallowed hard at the thought of her scrupulously curated col-lection of vintage dresses hanging from the racks surrounded by used polyester pantsuits and stained rayon blouses, the scent of her perfume overwhelmed by that ubiquitous thrift shop mil-dew. "She threw away all my makeup. Something about vanity and pride. I think there was a subtext about me being a whore."

"Come on, you're not a—"

"I don't know, I might be. By Catholic standards, I defi-nitely am. By small-town high school standards, it's still a little unclear."

"I'm not convinced monogamy is natural for seventeen-year-olds. You really shouldn't beat yourself up about this so much."

"Calder won't talk to me. He was going to break up with me anyway. I could tell. He was getting tired of me."

"So, what, it was like a 'fuck you'? Humiliate him before he could humiliate you?"

"If that was my intention, it seems to have backfired," she said ruefully.

"I can see that Jesus camp was a real morale booster."

"Everyone in town knows. At church people look at me like I'm the goddamn whore of Babylon."

"Fuck those miserable hypocrites. Maybe *you* were the one getting tired of *him*." I sat down on the couch and snuggled up next to her.

"You fall in love with Owen yet?" she mumbled into my shoulder.

"Not all the way."

"What percentage are you at?" We tracked my emotional attachment to Owen with various numbers and formulas.

"Coming up on eighty." This was a record high.

"Looks like you're leaving just in time."

"Yeah."

"If you guys did ever really get together, you'd never cheat on him. You'd never get tired of him."

"It's easy to think that when I only see him ten weeks out of the year."

"Will you get tired of me, too, when we're sharing our apartment in the West Village?" She put her head in my lap and looked up at me with those stormy blue eyes. "Am I going to wake up one morning and find you gone, having fled across town in the middle of the night?"

I sighed and stroked the stray hairs from her pasty forehead. "Hopefully when it is finally time for us to blissfully cohabitate in the *East* Village, you will have recovered from all this Catholic guilt bullshit. What the hell happened to you? Did they brain-wash you or something? Or is this just the unlights talking?"

"I don't know," she murmured, closing her eyes. "Sometimes it gets hard to tell the difference. You know what the worst thing was? That it worked, for a little while. They're good at what they do. For a few weeks, at least, I thought if I just prayed hard enough, believed hard enough, memorized enough Bible verses, that I could change. Or I would *be* changed. But it didn't happen. I'm still Betty. More and more every day."

So I left her there, in Williston, alone, without me or Calder to help her fight off the unlights. I tried to entice her down to the city for a visit, but she'd demurred, claiming she was too caught up in drama club and rehearsals for *Hamlet* and trying to make up with Calder. Now I wished I'd tried harder, or that I'd come back to Maine just once that fall. If I'd spent Thanksgiving with Dad instead of my mother—but that hurt too much to even think about.

"I miss her now," I said to Serena. "I miss her so much."

"Yeah."

"Did she know how you felt about her?"

She smiled faintly. "I flirted with her a lot. She liked it, liked the attention. She'd flirt back, just enough. I knew nothing would ever happen. It was just something to pass the time. When school started again, she kept her distance. She was so focused on getting Calder back, like if he were her boyfriend again, it would restore her reputation or something."

"Is that why she was so obsessed with being cast as Ophelia? Just so she could be close to him?"

Serena shook her head. "No, that was something else. She seemed—I don't know. She seemed really fucked up. I think she thought if she got to play Ophelia, everyone would see how much pain she was in. People were pissed—she'd already caused a lot of trouble. Slept with too many people's boyfriends, started too much drama. They just ignored her. I didn't know her as well as you did, but I knew her well enough to know she'd hate that more than anything."

Pulling her pant legs up above her knees, she stood and walked into the shallows, letting them wash around her ankles.

"It's cold," she said, wincing.

"How cold?"

"Like, heart attack cold."

I got up and followed her. I gasped when the ocean made contact with my calves. "Fuck."

My feet burned and went numb in the freezing water. I tried to imagine a world where Betty was still alive, where it was the three of us standing on the beach, summer stretched out in front of us as seemingly vast and endless as the ocean, but all I felt was her absence, the ragged, gaping wound of her loss, and under my grief a simmering rage that intensified every day.

The pill was kicking in; Serena had been right, it didn't feel small. A luxurious heaviness settled over my limbs, and something warm and good spread through my chest.

"If we knew why he killed her," I said, "maybe we could prove it somehow. Or at least get the police to start investigating again."

"Finley." She turned, fixing her wide gray eyes on me. It was the first time she had said my name. "Nobody cares. Nobody cares but us."

That night I went to the softball game in the park off Main Street. The park wasn't much, just a rickety playground in one corner, swings with rusty, squeaky chains and rubber seats, an aluminum slide made slick and shiny from years of use, and a merry-go-round that I had once, as a child, ridden until I threw up. The rest of the park was consumed by a baseball diamond lit by sodium lights and bleachers lined up against the chain-link fence. The Williston Sandpipers were in the dugout when I arrived, the ground at their feet littered with empty Narragansett tallboys and cigarette butts. The same firefighters and police officers who had rushed to the high school last night were now flexing their hands inside their mitts and taking practice swings. I spotted Owen by the number eight on the back of his shirt; his cap was pulled down low over his eyes, and if he saw me arrive, he gave no indication.

Dad was sitting on the bottom row of the bleachers, taking notes on a steno pad. The seats above him were filled with locals—Principal Moore was there, the bartenders from Charlie's (half of the team was composed of the regulars), most of the town council had shown up, including Calder's father. The field's scoreboard was lit, although several of the red LED bulbs needed replacing; the second *I* in VISITOR was dark, but there was no mistaking the fact that they were housing us, ten to two. It was only the fifth inning.

"This is demoralizing," I said, taking a seat next to my father. "Who are we playing anyway?"

"The Pullman Raptors."

"Raptors? Seriously? Like velociraptors? We've got sandpipers and they've got raptors? No wonder we're getting our asses handed to us."

"Their team captain is a big *Jurassic Park* fan. Anyway, it's just a game, Finley," he said. "All in good fun."

But it didn't seem like anyone was having fun. When the next player got up, he visibly wobbled for a moment as he settled over home plate, using his bat like a cane to steady himself. It seemed like a prodigious amount of alcohol was being consumed—even for Williston—both in the dugout and the stands. The batter swung wildly at anything that came his way; it took him barely a minute to strike out, and he threw his bat to the ground as he stormed back to the dugout, cursing while the crowd booed viciously.

Something felt off. Maybe it was the drugs. I wished Serena had come with me, so I could ask her if she felt it, too, but she hadn't wanted to come. I had dropped her off at her house around dusk. The sky was overcast, and I could hear the melancholy bleat of foghorns coming in off the ocean.

"What's going on?" I asked Dad.

"There was a big crowd of people at Charlie's before the game," he said, "talking about the fire. I'm afraid our team is at something of a disadvantage tonight."

"Come on, these guys play better drunk than sober."

"It's not just the alcohol. They're distracted."

Calder was the next at bat. I hadn't seen him in the dugout and the unexpected sight of him made my breath catch in my throat. Even Dad seemed to tense.

"You didn't tell me he was on the team now," I said, annoyed.

"I heard he wasn't playing tonight. I guess he changed his mind. I'm sorry."

At least Calder seemed sober, unlike the rest of his team-mates. He brushed the dirt off home plate with his cleat and raised the bat, settling into a flawless stance—hands up, front shoulder down, knees and ankles flexed—that brought me back, however briefly, to my childhood, to Owen teaching me how to hold a bat in his backyard, gently underhanding pitches in my direction while his beagle, Marty, ran circles around my feet and stole every ball I missed.

I looked in his direction again. His eyes were fixed on Calder, but then he blinked, shook his head, and turned away. When he saw me in the bleachers, he smiled weakly and gestured with his chin in the direction of the parking lot. I understood his wordless instructions perfectly; he wanted me to meet him by his truck after the game. I nodded my assent—not too eagerly, I hoped—and turned my attention back to Calder just in time to catch what happened next.

The other team's pitcher wound up, but instead of a typical

softball pitch, he threw an overhanded fastball that hit Calder directly in the solar plexus, dropping him to the ground as swiftly as if he'd been shot.

An uneasy quiet fell over the field and the stands, the same kind that had happened at graduation when Ann had the seizure. Calder's groans were audible; slowly, he came up to his hands and knees, and only when he lifted his head to glare at the pitcher did the crowd finally stir and make the requisite disapproving noises. Behind me, Leroy Miller was trying to climb down from the bleachers, swearing at people to get out of his way.

"I don't understand," I said to Dad softly. "Are both teams drunk?"

Calder staggered to his feet. With a strangely languid movement, he reached up and took the cap from his head, letting it fall to the ground. At the same time, Dad whispered, "Shit," and handed me his steno pad and pencil.

"What?" I said.

Before he could answer, Calder was lunging toward the pitcher's mound, his strides clumsy and uneven. The pitcher threw his mitt aside and held his ground, ready to fight. *Who the fuck is this guy anyway?* I wondered; the name *Emerson* was plastered across the back of his shirt but it didn't ring a bell. He looked around Owen's age, but I couldn't remember if I'd seen his face around town before. I turned to ask Dad if he recognized the guy, but Dad was already on his feet, racing to the mound.

Calder shoved the pitcher, planting one hand firmly on each shoulder and pushing with all his strength. Leroy had finally made it down from the bleachers, but Dad was still going to arrive there first. I was waiting for the pitcher to haul off and throw a decent punch—*Just one*, I thought, *I'll settle just for one*—but instead he raised his hands above his head in an "I surrender" gesture, and I was supremely disappointed. Calder pushed him again, and then Dad was there, inserting himself between the two players, forcing them apart, and Calder's voice called out a strident "What the fuck?" just as his father reached him and whispered something—what, I would have given anything to know—in his ear.

And, just as quickly, it was over. Calder came back to himself and looked into the stands, where everyone was staring at him. His father put an arm around his shoulders and steered him back toward home plate, stopping briefly so Calder could pick up his cap. I thought maybe they'd keep going, all the way out of the park, but instead Leroy just deposited Calder back in the dugout, where he sat on the other side of the bench from his teammates, hunching his shoulders and staring down into his hands. Even though no one had thrown a single punch I was still pleased, almost grateful, like Calder had done me a favor by reminding everybody himself what they were all trying so hard to forget—that he could be dangerous.

Dad took his seat next to me, and I returned his pad and pencil.

"So," I said, "are you going to put that in the paper this week?"

CHAPTER FOUR.

AFTER THAT WHATEVER remained of Williston's morale evaporated, the players phoning it in without much conviction and the crowd growing steadily more intoxicated. When the game was over—final score thirteen to four, Dad next to me with his head in his hands, everyone in both the stands and the dugout rushing to their cars and in turn, I imagined, to Charlie's—I met Owen by his truck.

"Come on," he said, opening the passenger door for me. "I could use some cheering up."

Enough of the crowd had dispersed that I felt comfortable giving him a kiss, which he returned with an eagerness that came perilously close to an actual display of emotion. "I didn't realize you were that invested in softball," I said.

"I'm just having a day. Let's go back to the cabin. I need a drink."

"You don't want to go to Charlie's with everyone else?"

"No," he said. "Fuck those people."

"You really are having a day."

"The Hobart finally died, and the guy can't come fix it

until next week. We had to do all the dishes by hand."

I climbed into the truck, settling comfortably into the thick layer of dust that covered the passenger seat, and lit a cigarette as I waited for him to come around the other side.

"Can I have one of those?" he asked as he started the engine.

"Take this one," I said, handing it to him and lighting another for myself. "If you need help in the kitchen, you know, it's not like I've got anything to do all day."

"Maybe," he said. "We'll see."

We drove silently out of town, Owen's hand on my thigh, removing it only when he needed to shift gears. For him this kind of behavior bordered on clingy, but I didn't complain, not even when he turned off a couple of miles before his cabin and pulled into an unfamiliar driveway, just far enough that his truck wouldn't be spotted by anyone on the road, but not so close that I could actually see the house. Like I said, Owen was smart. He killed the lights but left the engine idling; reaching over me, he took a battered brown envelope from the glove compartment.

"Stay here," he said. "I just have to run inside for a minute. I'll be right back."

He disappeared into the darkness almost immediately. I rolled down my window, listening to his footsteps shuffling toward the house I couldn't see. I thought I heard a voice, a door opening and closing, but that was all, and then there were just crickets and the trees shivering in the breeze and all the woodsy noises I'd grown up with that now scared the shit out of me. I closed the window and turned on the radio so I wouldn't have to hear them. I really had become a city girl.

Owen kept his radio tuned to the classic rock station, too. I listened to Cheap Trick while I rolled a joint from the eighth I knew Owen always had in the center console, hidden in a film canister, and wondered what he was selling. It probably wasn't weed—too conspicuous, too hard to carry around discreetly, too much weighing and measuring. Pills would be easiest, but still I worried. The Williston police had already proven to be pretty incompetent, but Owen never had any kind of luck but bad. I had no moral issue with him moonlighting as a small-time dealer to make a little extra money; I was more concerned about what it might cost him. By the time he returned, I had smoked half the joint myself and hotboxed his truck.

"Jesus," he said, coughing as he took his seat beside me.

"That's what you get for leaving me alone in your vehicle."

"Hand it over, at least."

I waited for him to take a hit before I spoke. "Seriously, O. Do you know what you're doing? I mean, with all this."

He exhaled thoughtfully. "Honestly? Probably not."

"Great. I feel much better now."

"Tough shit," he said, backing out of the driveway. "Tonight you're supposed to make *me* feel better, remember?"

Owen's cabin was set deep in the woods. It had been his grand-father's, a fisherman who died when we were young, someone I recalled vaguely—plaid shirt, weathered Carhartts, a long gray beard that reached his sternum. Owen told me once that he had never seen his grandfather's chin. After he died, the cabin had gone uninhabited for years, slowly falling apart, until Owen grudgingly decided to stay in Williston and run the diner. He'd also taken on the not-insignificant task of making the cabin livable again. It was that or stay at his parents' house, in his childhood bedroom.

The place had always reminded me of the inside of a small boat, with its paneled walls and uneven pine floor, the round window in the kitchen that looked out on the front porch like a porthole with a view of forest instead of water. A taxidermied sturgeon hung over the couch, which was a forlorn, faded blue badly camouflaged with flannel throw blankets. The table lamp had a scarred mermaid as a base, her hands stretched above her head to cradle the bulb. The place was tidy; it smelled like Murphy's Oil Soap, and the bed was neatly made.

I sat on the couch. Owen brought a bottle of Fighting Cock from the kitchen and placed it on the coffee table with two glasses.

"Say when," he said, and poured.

I waited three beats longer than was prudent. "When."

He didn't clink his glass to mine, just sort of leaned it in that direction before bringing it to his mouth and draining the contents. I did the same, even though it made my stomach lurch; for a brief, paralyzing moment my mouth filled with saliva and I thought I might be sick. In the end it stayed down, and Owen refilled my glass.

"You trying to get me drunk?" I asked.

"I'm trying to get us both drunk," he said.

It worked.

....

We were passed out in bed when the phone rang. I didn't know what time it was, but the sky outside was still dark; we were firmly in middle-of-the-night territory. Owen stirred but didn't get up. There was no answering machine to pick up so the phone just kept ringing.

I kicked Owen in the thigh. "Make it stop."

He staggered out of bed and into the kitchen. His side of the conversation was all I needed.

"What? No way. No, I can't now. I'm home, I'm lit, and I can't drive." He paused. "Do not come here. Don't show up at my fucking house. Come to the diner tomorrow. I don't want to see you before then." He hung up but lingered in the kitchen. As my eyes adjusted to the darkness, I could see him leaning against the refrigerator, his whole body sagging.

"You should get a pager," I mumbled when he rejoined me under the covers, rubbing his cold feet against my calves. "In New York all the drug dealers have pagers."

"I'm not a drug dealer," he said.

"Keep telling yourself that." I rolled over and went back to sleep.

Morning was miserable. It was raining and cold. I didn't want to get up but Owen had to open the diner, and his alarm went off at six. My car was still parked in town; I needed a ride from him or I'd be stranded. It didn't actually sound like a terrible prospect— sleep in as late as I wanted, spend the day reading books on his couch and listening to the rain—but I hadn't gone through the contents of Betty's locker yet. They were still in my messenger bag, shoved into the back of my closet at home. I roused myself and dressed wordlessly while Owen handed me a cup of coffee.

"Do you have any aspirin?" I asked him.

"Hangover?"

I nodded.

"We're going to have to build up your tolerance."

"That sounds like a long-term project. Right now I need a short-term solution."

He went into the bathroom and came back with a bottle of Advil.

I chased three with my coffee. "Why don't you feel this shitty?"

"What do you think we do here all winter? Not quite as much to entertain us as you've got down there in the city."

One of these days I was going to tell Owen to quit acting like a fucking martyr, but it wasn't going to be today. I sank onto the couch, facing the seemingly insurmountable task of putting on my shoes.

"What are you doing later?" he asked.

"I don't know, maybe I'll—" Something short-circuited in my brain. "Jesus."

"What?"

I looked up at him. "I was about to say 'maybe I'll see what Betty is up to.'"

He had no response to that, busying himself instead with washing out his mug in the kitchen sink.

"Did you see her around much, last fall?" I asked.

He sighed, loudly. "I haven't even been awake for an hour and you're bringing her up."

"Just tell me."

"I run one of the only restaurants in town. Yeah, I saw her. I see everyone, every fucking day."

"People are saying she seemed different. Did you notice?"

"Who told you that?" he snapped.

"It was in the fucking paper, Owen. Jesus."

"I don't know. I guess, maybe. A couple of times—" He stopped himself.

"A couple of times what?"

"She made me run lines with her. For *Hamlet*. She learned all of Ophelia's lines."

"For the audition?"

He looked at me like I was an imbecile. "After she lost the part. She learned it anyway. Like she thought somehow she'd get to be in the play."

I remembered the copy of *Hamlet* I'd rescued from the Flynns' basement, all those notes and dog-eared pages, and of course Betty's lie to me, that she'd be starring in the show. "Rebecca said some people made jokes after she died. About how she got to be Ophelia after all."

Owen didn't say anything, just took a fresh pack of cigarettes from a carton he kept in the fridge, slamming it violently against the heel of his hand, then carefully unwrapping it and throwing the cellophane and foil away under the sink. He lit two and handed me one, then sat next to me, staring straight ahead to where anyone else would have had their television. There were stacks of books reaching halfway to the ceiling. It occurred to me that Owen might slowly be losing his mind, trapped in Williston.

"Finley," he said finally. "This has been an incredibly shitty year. I'm glad you're back, I really am, but if you try to make me relive all the worst parts of it, we're going to have a problem."

"Right," I replied. "So I can't ask about Betty, but you can play softball on the same team as the guy who killed her."

"Put your fucking shoes on," he said. "You don't know what you're talking about."

"It's not weird to you? He's a goddamn murderer."

"You think I like it? You think I like serving him his fucking pancakes on the weekends and watching him play center field? But I'm the one who has to live here."

"You're not a fucking hostage, Owen. You can leave anytime you want."

"No, Fin, that's you."

"Fine," I said, angrily tying my shoes at last. "I'll leave right now."

I stormed out the door into the rain, up Owen's driveway toward the road. The screen door slammed behind him as he followed me.

"Get in the truck," he said wearily, standing by the door with his keys in hand. He looked exhausted, like I had worn him out before his day even started. "You're not walking back to town."

I knew what he meant. It wasn't the rain or the distance— about six miles—but the fact that someone might see me angry and soaked on the side of the road, coming from the direction of his cabin. Word would get around Williston by lunchtime. Owen didn't like people knowing his business. I stopped walking, trying to decide if it was worth ending up grist for the rumor mill just to make this particular point.

The ride into town was deeply uncomfortable, both of us seething silently, the only sound the *tsk*ing of the windshield wipers. I watched rivulets of water shimmy down my window and thought about drowning. Owen pulled over by my car, reached across me, and opened my door. I started to get out, and he grabbed my arm.

"You don't know how fucking lucky you are. You have no idea."

"Lucky?" I said.

"Because you weren't here. You get to remember her like she was. If I were you, that's what I'd be trying to hold on to. You can slash all the tires and set all the fires you want—yeah, I'm not a fucking idiot—and she'll still be dead and he'll still be going to college in September."

"Did people really hate her that much, O?" I said softly.

"Maybe she was easier to love from four hundred miles away. Did you ever think about that?"

I stared at him until he let go of my arm and looked away.

"I have to go to work," he said.

"Go to hell instead," I told him, and I got out of the truck and slammed the door, and stood there shivering like a wet dog, and I knew I wasn't done slashing tires and setting fires, not even close, not even a little. If it ever stopped raining, I might just burn the whole fucking town to the ground.

••

I went home to bed, where I slept restlessly until midafternoon, dreaming a series of heavily plotted, unsettling dreams I forgot immediately upon waking but that left me agitated anyway. It was still raining.

Downstairs, I put on water for the French press; my headache was mostly gone, but the fight with Owen lingered like a bad taste in my mouth. He was not turning out to be the ally I'd hoped for. The light on the answering machine was blinking; I waited a minute before pressing play, briefly entertaining the fantasy that it would be him, calling to apologize.

When I heard Serena's raspy voice, my disappointment vanished. She didn't say much, just asked me to call her back, which I did, immediately.

"Hey, it's Finley," I said when she answered.

"Hey."

There was a long pause.

"You called?" I said.

"Yeah. I just wanted to see what you were up to today."

"Actually, I was finally going to take a look at the stuff from Betty's locker."

"Really?" she said. "Have you started yet?"

"No, I just woke up," I said, looking at the clock and cringing. It was almost three.

"Don't worry, I don't judge."

"Why don't you come over? We can go through it together."

I gave her directions, and we hung up. I deleted her message, out of some vague sense of paranoia—we had, after all, set the high school on fire—but not before I listened to it a couple more times, just to hear her say my name. While the coffee steeped, I raced back upstairs, making my bed and throwing open the window. Finally, I dug my messenger bag out from the back of the closet and set it in the center of the floor.

While I waited for Serena, I watched television and drank too much coffee. An hour passed, and then another, and just as I was considering getting started without her—I was vibrating with nervous energy—I heard a car pull into the driveway. I ran over to the window and watched her run to the front porch, hood pulled over her head, trying to stay dry. I waited for her to ring the bell before I opened the door and ushered her inside.

We went upstairs and sat on the floor beside the messenger bag. I opened it up, gently removed the contents, and made several neat piles. Serena picked up a chemistry book, idly leafing through it while I sifted through a stack of papers, mostly old exams. Betty had never been a straight-A student, but this steady stream of Cs and Ds wasn't like her either.

"How was the game last night?" Serena finally asked.

"Weird." I told her about the pitcher nailing Calder in the gut.

"I'm sorry I missed that," she said.

"It was pretty great," I admitted.

"I can't wait to get the fuck out of this town."

"Are you starting college in September?"

"Just at Orono," she said. "But I'm hoping to transfer to Smith in another year. What about you?"

I told her about NYU, the whole story, how Betty and I had

planned to go there together and how I'd almost lost my spot after she died.

"Have you ever been to New York?" I asked her.

"Are you kidding? The East Coast capital of sin? Not exactly my parents' first choice when it comes to family vacations."

"You'd like it," I told her. "Come down sometime, after you start at Orono. Your parents will never have to know." Serena would prefer the East Village to the West, it was obvious.

"Careful, I might just take you up on that." She paused. "So, what's the deal with you and Owen?"

"Owen?" I said, surprised.

"I saw you guys looking at each other in the diner the other night. Is he your boyfriend or something?"

"It's not like that. I've known him since I was a kid. His family lives a few houses down."

"So you guys are just friends?"

"Right now I would say 'friends' is an overstatement."

She raised an eyebrow.

"We got into a fight. About Betty and Calder."

"Oh," she said, as if that explained everything, and it occurred to me that she'd probably had many similar arguments over the last few months.

"What about Calder?" I asked. "Everyone seems to agree that Betty was acting different before she died, but what about him?"

"I'm sure you knew him a lot better than I did, but I didn't notice anything, except that he went out of his way to avoid Betty. And the more he avoided her, the harder she tried to get his attention."

"Do you think—" I hesitated. I had imagined the most gruesome and minute details of Betty's murder many times, but rarely out loud. "Do you think he just snapped?"

"I don't know. If he lured her out to the beach to meet him, that seems pretty premeditated, doesn't it? Unless she got him to meet her there."

"The nightgown," I said suddenly.

"What?"

"In the paper, my dad wrote that she was last seen wearing her nightgown and a robe. I don't know if they ever found the nightgown. In the house, I mean. Wouldn't that have been sort of strange, if she'd gone to meet him in her pajamas? In November?"

"Can you ask your dad?"

"I will."

She stared at me.

"Like, now? Like, call him at work?"

"Can't you?"

I wasn't at all eager to speak with my father, considering I hadn't made it home the night before. "We kind of had a fight, too," I lied. "I might need to wait a day."

Serena smiled, a brilliant flash that called attention to its rarity. "You really have a way with people, don't you?"

I rolled my eyes. "I think they call it charisma."

"You and Betty must have made quite the pair. I wish I could have seen you together."

"Me too," I said.

We worked quietly after that, methodically making our way

through all of Betty's notebooks. Serena never asked what we were looking for; she knew, like I did, that we'd know it when we found it. I was hoping for something obvious—an angry note from Calder, a threat demanding he leave her alone, a link between them that started at his end, instead of the other way around—but there was nothing that helpful, just warnings from her teachers about poor grades, handouts from history class, pop quizzes on Virginia Woolf.

"What's this?" Serena said finally, pulling a thick, sealed priority mail envelope from a yellow spiral notebook whose metal coil had been partially undone.

I knew what it was before she even handed it to me, before I looked at the address printed on the front and saw "NYU Office of Admissions" in Betty's handwriting. I had mailed my college application in an identical envelope, handing it over to the postal clerk while my heart pumped like a fist inside my chest, as if I could will my admission into Tisch.

"It's her NYU application," I whispered. "She never mailed it."

"Because Calder killed her first?" Serena asked cautiously.

"Early admission. It was due November first."

Her eyes met mine across the books and papers strewn over my bedroom floor. "She never told you?"

I shook my head, bewildered. "No. She never told me."

Serena reached out and plucked the envelope from my hand, but as she was about to rip it open I snatched it back with a vehemence that surprised me.

"What?" she said, annoyed. "Don't you want to see what's in there? It might not even be her application at all."

I couldn't explain it. Here we were, shamelessly going through Betty's belongings, just as I had done in the Flynns' basement, but somehow this felt just too much like an invasion of her privacy. And I trusted Serena, I did, but a strange proprietary feeling had asserted itself. Betty was mine, I had thought to rescue her belongings from the school, and so by proxy the NYU application was mine now, too. I would decide if and when to open it, and I would do it alone.

"Sorry," I said. "I just don't think her transcripts and recommendation letters are what matter. It's that she never mailed it. Like lying to me about being cast as Ophelia. What was going on with her last fall? Did something else happen at that camp?"

"I don't know. I don't think so. Things didn't get really bad until after that, anyway, when we were back at school and she realized it hadn't blown over like she thought it would."

"What, cheating on Calder?"

"Yeah, and all of it, really. People were sort of sick of her shit, I guess, and since she wasn't with Calder anymore they could just ignore her, and they did."

I could imagine no worse fate for Betty than being relegated to near-invisibility, except, of course, for the one she'd been ultimately dealt.

After Serena left I got into my car and drove into town, Betty's NYU app on my passenger seat; I looked over at it occasionally, still in disbelief. I tucked it protectively into my sweatshirt to keep it dry and ran up the stairs. The police reports were off-limits to me, and Calder's confession was so inaccessible it was worthless, but my father had notes of his own somewhere, notes that might shed light on the identities of the unnamed sources in his articles, sources he would never reveal to anyone, not even me. Williston's *Messenger* may have been just a small-town paper, but Dad still took the rules of journalism seriously, and that meant keeping anonymous sources just that. Maybe not everything had made it into the paper.

I let myself into the office. The red light on the coffeemaker was still glowing; Dad had left it on, and now the place smelled even more like burnt coffee than usual. I turned it off, not wanting to be responsible for another fire.

Dad's system was incredibly basic. After he put out each week's paper, he gathered whatever legal pads and scraps of paper he'd used to research the stories, printed out the final versions of all the articles, and shoved everything into a manila folder along with a copy of the finished issue. These folders were arranged in the file cabinets more or less according to date, but the folders for the weeks surrounding Betty's death were missing. I went through each cabinet several times just to be sure.

I paced the office, looking again through the boxes of old newspapers, checking the cabinets above the tiny sink, pulling books off shelves at random, even rummaging through the closet where he kept the plunger and extra office supplies.

Frustrated, I sat down at the desk. I knew Dad wouldn't have thrown those notes away; they were too important. The slim top drawer of his desk was filled with stacks of unused Post-its, errant paper clips, and rubber bands, and in the bottom drawer were two thick phone directories for our county, one residential, one for businesses. I was disappointed that he didn't keep a bottle of whiskey hidden away in that drawer; in the movies, that was mandatory for all reporters.

I reached into the back, behind the phone books, and my fingers brushed against a stack of paper. I had to empty the drawer to pry it loose, but when I did, there it was. Dad's file on Betty's death.

The door at the bottom of the stairs opened and closed, and I recognized my father's tread as he made the ascent. Quickly shoving the folder into my bag along with Betty's application, I hurried to replace everything else in the drawer. By the time he was standing in the doorway with a confused look on his face, I had the phone receiver pressed casually to my ear as I swiveled back and forth in his chair. As soon as I looked up and saw him, I put it back in its cradle.

"There you are," I said. "I was just calling the house to see if I could find you."

"You looking for me?" he asked, dubious. "Everything okay?"

"Yeah. I just wanted to see what you were doing for dinner."

"I was going to cook," he said. "Spaghetti carbonara. I picked up groceries on my way home, but then I remembered I left the coffeemaker on. So I came all the way back." He headed toward the kitchenette.

"I did it already," I said. "Turned it off as soon as I walked in. Sorry you wasted the trip. Come on, let's go home. Spaghetti carbonara sounds perfect."

"You're just one step ahead of me, aren't you, Fin?" he said.

I just shrugged my shoulders and followed him out the door.

CHAPTER FIVE.

DAD'S NOTES WERE a mess. I spent the next morning on
the porch, drinking coffee and smoking, trying to make sense
of them. He'd interviewed the police after Calder's confession,
but all they did was confirm that he'd admitted to drowning her.
I couldn't bring myself to read anything about his conversation
with Betty's parents or the obituary he'd begun drafting; it was
the anonymous sources that interested me the most. Dad hadn't
used their names in the paper, but he'd taken down their information so he could follow up and fact-check later.

I compared the names with the contact list from *Hamlet* I'd
found in Betty's ASM binder; Shelly, the stage manager, had
been one of the sources. I thought about calling first, to make
sure she was home, but finally decided to just get in my car. If I
wasted a trip, so be it; it wasn't like I was so busy.

Shelly lived several miles out of town, at the end of one of
those long, shaded driveways, in a large two-story house made
of white bricks. The front door was painted bright blue. I rang
the bell and waited.

As soon as she answered, I knew I'd made a mistake. She flung open the door, shouting something back down the hallway at a group of people I couldn't see. Smash Mouth was playing on the stereo and Shelly was holding a beer; she was hosting some kind of party in the middle of the day while her parents were presumably at work. She finally turned to me, looking understandably puzzled. I hadn't been invited.

"Hey, Shelly," I said. "How's it going?"

Before she could respond, Rebecca came tearing out of the back room, shouting my name.

"Finley! What are you doing here?"

She was drunk enough to have forgotten my slight in the woods at the graduation party, but there was no way I could ask Shelly about Betty now. I could turn around and leave, or lie.

"Oh, you know. I got bored, heard there was a party." I shrugged, trying to seem casual.

"Come on in! It's so good to see you again!" As she embraced me, I realized we were having an exchange nearly identical to the other night, before I started acting like an asshole.

"It's good to see you, too," I said, and let Rebecca lead me inside.

I joined the dozen or so kids oscillating between the den and the back deck, grabbing a beer from a cooler and wishing I had one of Serena's blue pills to get me through this.

I drank instead, let myself be introduced to people whose faces were familiar but whose names I instantly forgot, smoked a cigarette on the deck, and took a hit off a joint being passed around. Rebecca did seem genuinely happy to see me, and this time I didn't ruin it; she talked about going off to Amherst in the fall and I asked all the right questions: did she know who her roommate would be, had she thought about a major, were the boys cute. And the whole time I tried to stay focused, thinking about Betty's NYU application collecting dust in the guidance counselor's office since November, and reminded myself I was here on a reconnaissance mission and not simply to get lit in the middle of the day.

Rebecca was rambling on about the pros and cons of an English major when I overheard some of the other kids talking about the fire in the theater.

"How could they not know how it started?" Shelly was saying. "I think it's really weird. I know that theater inside and out, and I've never seen anything that could just randomly combust like that."

"I saw plenty of weird shit this spring," another girl said. "Believe me, I wasn't surprised at all."

"What kind of weird shit?" I asked. Everyone looked at me. "I just got back to town, I'm not up to date."

"Just—things," the girl said. "Lights flickering. Strange noises. Once the fire alarm went off for no reason."

"Sounds like something with the electrics," I said. "A problem with the wiring could have caused the fire."

The rest of the group glanced around at one another uneasily.

"I don't think it was the electrics," she finally said.

"Then what?" I pressed.

She shrugged. "Whatever."

Someone changed the subject. I could feel them closing

ranks. Shelly went inside to get more beer, and I followed her into the kitchen.

"Need a hand?" I asked.

"Sure," she said. "There's a bag of ice in the freezer. You can grab that."

"So how was senior year?" I asked her. "Everything you hoped it would be?"

"Yes, it was," she said frostily. "This might all seem lame to you, keg parties and drama club and signing yearbooks. It's not like going clubbing in Manhattan, but we like it. Okay?"

"I don't actually go clubbing," I said.

"Whatever."

"You were stage manager on *Hamlet*, right?"

"Yeah. Why?"

"No reason. I just heard there was some weirdness between Betty and Calder while you guys were working on the show. And then, you know, what happened after."

"Oh? And what did you hear?"

"I heard he confessed to killing her," I said casually.

She snorted. "That was bullshit. The cops got him in a room alone, probably scared him to death, until he said whatever they wanted him to say. He's lucky he was able to get his dad to straighten everything out before he got into real trouble. Betty was practically stalking him the whole time we were working on the play. She wouldn't leave him alone."

"If Calder wanted to get away from Betty that badly, why'd he even audition? Didn't he realize she'd try out for Ophelia?"

She waved a hand dismissively. "His dad took care of that,

too. Once Calder decided he wanted to play Hamlet, his dad made a few calls, made sure Betty wouldn't get the part. Since she was in drama club, Mr. McCartney had to throw her a bone. No one thought she'd actually go through with being ASM. We thought she'd be so pissed that she'd just quit. That's how obsessed with Calder she was—she'd wear a headset and watch me call the cues, just to be at rehearsal with him every day. If you ask me, he's the one that was scared of her."

"No kidding," I said, adjusting the bag of ice under my arm.

"Look, I know she was a friend of yours. I had nothing against her. But something wasn't right."

"Last fall?"

She shook her head. "I think it started before that. In the spring."

"When Calder broke up with her?"

"It was the other way around. Calder broke up with her because something wasn't right. She got brought home by the cops for fooling around in some older guy's car, and everybody knew. Calder was humiliated, but I think, I don't know, he was almost—"

"Relieved?" I said.

"Maybe." She sighed. "He seemed really into her when they first got together. Anybody who saw them in the hallways together could tell. But at junior prom? I went outside to have a cigarette and they were screaming at each other in the parking lot. She'd pick fights with him, test him, and I think after a while he got tired of it."

"But he was still humiliated."

"Not humiliated enough to kill her, if that's what you're getting at."

"Then what do you think happened to her?"

"She wasn't herself, Finley. And she hadn't been for months. She was moody and depressed and a couple of times I even thought she might have been on drugs. She was miserable here. When she started talking about running away, I figured she was serious."

"Who was the older guy? The one the cops caught her with?"

"His name never got out."

"So Betty got publicly shamed and sent to church camp, and nothing happened to him?"

"You can't possibly be surprised."

"I'm not."

There was a silence. "You really don't think there's any chance she's still alive?" she finally asked.

I had tried so hard to convince myself of this and failed. "I really don't."

"I met her parents a few times, when they came to see her perform, and it can't be that shocking to you that she'd want to split. I've heard that camp they sent her to was no joke. Look, I'm sorry about Betty. But she had problems, okay? Problems that had nothing to do with Calder."

"So where is he, then?"

"What do you mean?"

"Why isn't Calder at your party?"

Shelly shrugged indifferently. "I don't know, he's probably coming later." She was a little too breezy about it, a little too eager to make like she didn't care if he showed up or not.

She carried the case of beer out to the deck, and we refilled the cooler. I meant to leave after that, I really did, but then she handed me a fresh beer. The deck was built into the side of a hill, overlooking a steep drop onto a cluster of mossy green boulders; I stood by the railing and imagined the whole thing collapsing—the splintering wooden planks and screaming, the floor disappearing beneath our feet, that falling sensation I felt so often in my dreams, the impact on the rocks below. Would we feel it? Would it hurt? And would everything end there, or would I wake up somewhere else, confused and groggy and dusting myself off? Would Betty be there? Was she still here somewhere, haunting the theater like everyone had implied, watching my half-assed, halting investigation with impatience? *Get it together, Fin*, I could hear her saying.

Give me a minute, I thought. *Let me just finish this beer, and then I'll get back to business.*

But it took more than one beer to drown the image of us all plummeting to our deaths on Shelly's back deck. The party wasn't winding down; it turned out Shelly's parents were out of town, not at work, and as it started to get dark more people were arriving. Practically pulling myself up the stairs by the banister, I went inside to find a bathroom.

There was one closed door on the second floor, which I knew had to be the master bedroom. Closed, but not locked; I let myself in.

I hadn't been able to stop thinking about Serena's tiny blue pills. I didn't know what they were called, but I knew I'd recognize them.

The medicine cabinet was a disappointment. I checked the drawers under the sink; among the tweezers and tubes of hand cream I found a consolation prize, an expired, half-full bottle of Vicodin that no one would miss. They weren't blues, but they'd do. I stuffed the bottle with toilet paper so the pills wouldn't rattle in my pocket as I walked, and then I went downstairs to say my good-byes.

"Finley, you're leaving?" Rebecca said. "Are you okay to drive?"

I wasn't. Quickly running through the list of people I could call—Owen, my dad—I realized I had alienated almost all of my potential rides. There was one person, though, who might still be glad to hear from me.

Serena showed up a half hour later. She didn't come inside, just pulled into the driveway and honked.

"Thanks for coming to get me," I said.

"What are you doing here, anyway?" she asked, annoyed, I assumed, that I'd been consorting with the enemy.

"Research. Here," I said, opening the bottle and shaking a few pills into the cup holder. "For your troubles."

"Where am I taking you?"

"What time is it?"

"Around eight."

Dad would be at the house. I couldn't let him see me like this again. "Anywhere but home," I told her.

She put a tape in the stereo and pressed play. It was a band I'd never heard before, a punk rock outfit helmed by a woman with a gorgeous, bluesy voice. I stared out the window and listened as darkness enveloped Williston. Serena drove around aimlessly for a while, avoiding the town's center and sticking to the back roads; still, I had the strong feeling that she was zeroing in on a target.

After about an hour she pulled onto a familiar street, killed her headlights and the stereo, and put the car in neutral.

"What the fuck are we doing here?" I whispered, sinking farther down in my seat.

She didn't answer, just stopped the car outside the Millers' house. Inside, all the lights were on; the whole family was there, on display, as if onstage, clearing plates from the dinner table and ferrying them into the kitchen.

"Don't worry," she said softly. "They can't see us."

"Do you do this a lot?"

Again, she didn't answer. Instead she reached into the cup holder and popped several Vicodin. "Doesn't it kill you," she said, "knowing that he's right there, and he has all the answers?"

I took a couple of pills myself, chewing my medicine thoughtfully, choking down the chalky paste as I watched Calder rinse a dinner plate and hand it to his younger sister to load into the dishwater.

"My dad tried to get the cops to show him the confession, but it's sealed," I said.

"I'd give my left tit to see that thing."

"Seriously."

"What were you doing at that party, anyway?"

I explained to her about Dad's notes and what Shelly said about Calder's confession being coerced.

"So you really *were* doing research."

"I told you. Getting drunk, that was, like, my cover."

She looked over at me and smiled. "Clever girl."

I shifted in my seat, closer to her so our shoulders were almost touching. Her crucifix glinted in the dim light. I reached out and held it between my fingertips; it was warm from lying against her skin. Suddenly I felt almost sober.

"Why do you wear this?" I asked. "If you don't believe."

"I never said I don't believe."

I waited for her to elaborate.

"I stopped wearing it after Bible camp, but after Betty died—not just after she died, but after they let Calder go— then I put it back on. I don't believe the same things my parents believe. I don't believe there's a bearded man in the sky, like, monitoring our thoughts and willing to send me to hell for masturbating or liking girls. I don't believe in fate, and I don't believe that everything happens for a reason. Betty's dead because Calder held her down in the ocean until she stopped breathing. And I don't believe that God will punish Calder if nobody else does."

"Then why—"

"Because otherwise I'll never see her again."

I didn't have a response to that. We sat silently while his parents finished clearing the table, his mother packing the leftovers neatly into Tupperware and stacking them in the fridge and his father pouring himself a drink, Calder and his sister laughing as they splashed each other with soapy water. It was strange to feel such an irrational surge of hatred toward Caroline, whom I had always liked; she'd worshipped Betty and tagged along with the three of us whenever we let her. Her company kept me from feeling like a third wheel and rounded us out to a more comfortable foursome, but her relentlessly cheerful demeanor and endless attempts to impress Betty made me feel invisible, like an outsider, even as they endeared her to me. Calder was unusually inclusive with Caroline, often encouraging her to join us instead of shooing her away, like I thought older brothers were supposed to do with their younger siblings.

One afternoon, during the summer between sophomore and junior year, we were all gathered in Betty's room. The Millers were having some kind of grown-ups-only luncheon at their house, so Calder and Caroline had escaped to Betty's, where until their arrival the two of us had been lying on her bed talking about sex. More specifically, I was pestering her for advice about sex. My relationship with Owen was close to crossing that threshold and I was determined not to let my inexperience show when it happened. When the Miller siblings showed up, I hid my consternation; Betty's exegesis on the finer points of blowjobs would have to wait for another day.

Calder kissed Betty hello and I instinctually moved from the bed to the rocking chair by the window.

"You don't have to get up," he said.

"I don't mind," I said, and I meant it.

Caroline sat down at Betty's vanity, where her makeup and vintage opera gloves and rhinestone jewelry were all scrupulously arranged. Caroline tried on a black fascinator and batted her eyelashes at us from behind the netting.

"What do you think? Is it me?"

She was wearing khaki shorts, tennis shoes, and a white V-neck T-shirt. In short, no, it wasn't her, but the rest of us were too polite to say so. Caroline lacked the drama necessary to pull off Betty's look.

"Here," Betty said, leaping off the bed. "This one might be a little more your style." She pulled back some of Caroline's blonde hair and pinned it with a hair clip made from peacock feathers.

"It's beautiful." Caroline gently stroked the feathers. "Where did you find it?"

Betty lowered her eyes. "That was a gift from my greatest admirer."

"Calder, since when do you know where to shop for stuff like this?"

"She meant me," I said. "They're a lot easier to find in New York."

Betty whisked over to her closet and threw open the doors. She dug out a powder blue silk housecoat. "Here," she said to Caroline. "Put this on. Just until I'm done."

"Done with what?" Caroline asked.

Betty didn't answer. She was already pawing through the piles of makeup, setting aside an eye shadow here, a lipstick there. I knew exactly where this was headed. Betty had tried numerous times to subject me to a makeover, but I patently refused to be tinkered with. Caroline, on the other hand, was more than willing, looking up at Betty with such gratitude I was forced to avert my eyes.

I sat next to Calder on the bed so we could keep each other company while Betty worked diligently on Caroline's transformation. Together, we watched as Betty made Caroline's eyes rounder, her lips fuller, her hair thicker, adding a gentle wave. Betty went back to the closet and found a green satin dress; Calder buried his face in a pillow so Caroline would have privacy while she changed. Opera gloves, a simple pendant, and, of course, the peacock feathers in her hair, and Caroline was hardly recognizable. Or, perhaps more accurately, she looked like Betty. I could tell Calder noticed the resemblance also, and it made him uncomfortable.

"You look beautiful," he told his sister, but it sounded tight and forced.

Caroline didn't notice. She was too busy staring at herself in the mirror while Betty smiled, satisfied with her handiwork.

"I'm hungry," I said. "Come on, let's go to the diner and get burgers."

"Oh, bullshit," Betty said. "You're not hungry, you just want to see Owen."

"Can't she want both?" Calder said.

"Owen Shepard?" Caroline said, glancing away from her reflection for the first time. "Are you guys, like, together?"

I didn't say anything. I knew the answer was no, we were not together, and we never would be, but I couldn't bring myself to admit it. If Caroline could play Cinderella for the afternoon, it seemed only fair I should be able to spend a few hours pretending that Owen was overwhelmed with joy every time I stepped inside the Halyard, that he lacked only the ability to articulate the depth of his feelings for me and not, in fact, the feelings themselves.

"It's complicated," said Calder. "With older guys, it always is."

"He's not that much older," Betty said, rushing to my defense, and the defense of my imaginary relationship.

Calder looked at Caroline. "Don't listen to them. You stay away from older guys, you understand me?"

Betty groaned. "God, don't you realize telling her that just makes them more appealing?"

"Fine," Calder said, with mock seriousness. "Just stay away from all boys, of all ages, forever. Okay?"

Caroline laughed. "Okay."

"Fin, if you want to go to the diner, we can go," Betty said.

I squirmed, suddenly restless and uncomfortable. The room seemed too small for all of us, and I needed to get out, but I didn't want to see Owen anymore. Calder got up and put his arms around Betty, kissing her cheek, whispering something in her ear that made her giggle.

"It's okay," I said. "I think I'm just going to head home."

"No, don't," Betty said. "Please?"

"I'm sorry," Calder told me. "You and Owen are none of my business."

"We don't have to go to the diner," Caroline said. "We could just go get ice cream."

It was three against one, so I relented, and we went into town together. Caroline had changed back into her regular clothes, but kept the makeup on, and the peacock clip in her hair. Calder held Betty's hand as we walked down Main Street, and jealousy spiked inside me. When we passed the Halyard, Owen saw me from behind the counter, smiled, and waved. I smiled back. Later that week I lost my virginity to him, but other than that, not much changed.

Now, in the car with Serena, I winced thinking about that day, how normal it all seemed. How normal Calder seemed. Affectionate toward Betty, protective of his little sister. "Sometimes I feel like it's my fault," I said suddenly, surprising myself. I had never revealed this to anyone—not Owen, not either of my parents, not my shrink in New York.

"Why?" Serena asked. "You weren't even here when it happened."

"I spent a whole summer with him, when he and Betty were together. It's like I must have missed something, a sign, a tell. He had me fooled as much as everybody else."

She didn't disagree, and I felt a rush of affection toward her. I was so tired of being bullshitted, it was a relief to be with someone who couldn't be bothered.

"I think we should go in there," she said, nodding toward the house.

"Now?" I said. "While they're doing the dishes?"

"Saturday night." July 4, I realized. "Everyone will be down by the water, watching the fireworks. We can let ourselves in and look around. Maybe there's something—I don't know."

Whether it yielded any answers or not, the desire to violate Calder in even the smallest way was too tempting to resist. I wanted to rifle through his belongings, wander through his house while he gathered with his family and the rest of the town, celebrating our nation's birth, oblivious to the fact that he wasn't as safe as he believed, that not everyone had forgotten what he really was.

He and his sister were finished with the dishes; Caroline went into the back of the house, leaving him alone in the kitchen. He took something out of a cabinet and put it in the microwave. I couldn't see but I imagined it was popcorn, that they were about to gather in the living room for a family movie night, and I was consumed with a fury that mingled with grief inside my chest, so powerful not even the Vicodin could stop the tears from filling my eyes until they overflowed. I wanted Serena to floor it, just punch the gas and drive into his house and kill him where he stood; I wanted to watch him take his last breaths pinned between her front fender and his refrigerator, the gleaming stainless steel covered in his blood.

"I know," Serena said, putting her arm around me and pulling me close. I buried my face in her shoulder; she smelled like baby powder and ChapStick and coconut shampoo. I was shaking.

When I stopped crying I sat up, wiping my face with my sleeve. "Saturday, then."

"Saturday."

The next afternoon, restless, I drove into town. Charlie's was doing a brisk business, the front door propped open to reveal a row of regulars slumped over the bar, their pints clutched tightly in their hands, cigarettes smoldering in their ashtrays. The rest of Main Street was still deserted, though, not a New York or Massachusetts license plate in sight. There were only a couple of days left until Fourth of July weekend, and I suspected it wouldn't be long until we were infested.

As I walked past the Halyard, I tried to resist glancing in to see if Owen was behind the counter, but I couldn't help myself. There he was at the register. He didn't look up as I went by. I wondered if he'd had the dishwasher fixed yet.

"Finley."

I turned around. My father was emerging from the side door of the creamery; to my surprise, Emily Shepard was trailing him. She was as I remembered—tall and blonde and solidly built, someone you'd put your money on in almost any situation, and though she still wore her jeans tucked into her boots and a loose button-down tucked into her jeans, without her badge and her gun there was no question that something was missing. The look on her face when she saw me was not pleasant.

"Hey, guys," I said.

"You want to join us for lunch, Fin?" my father asked. "We were just going to get a burger at the diner."

"No, thanks," I said. "I already ate."

Emily snorted, like she knew I was lying and just wanted to avoid Owen.

"Hi, Emily," I said.

She ignored me. "I'll go get us a table, Frank," she said, and disappeared inside the diner.

"What the fuck is her problem?" I asked.

"She's been a little cranky since she was fired."

"It must run in the family. You two on a date or something?"

This was meant as a joke; Emily's status as a lesbian was another of Williston's open secrets.

"I'm just picking her brain."

"About what?"

"A story. She may not be on the force anymore, but she's still got good connections."

I glanced inside the diner, where Emily was settling into a booth. Owen looked tense, like he wasn't any happier to see her than she had been to see me. "Do you have a girlfriend?" I asked my father, suddenly realizing I had no idea.

"A couple," he said with a wry grin, and I honestly couldn't tell if he was joking or not.

I got an ice cream cone at the creamery and took it down to the marina behind Main Street. Sitting at the end of one of the docks, I dangled my feet above the water and licked my coffee-flavored lunch while I considered everything Shelly had said. The false confession thing made sense, in a way—not that I believed it, but I understood how people could convince themselves of something like that.

Everyone I'd spoken to so far agreed that Betty had been unhappy in the months leading up to her death. Even if it predated the breakup with Calder, that didn't necessarily mean he'd had nothing to do with it. He could have cheated on her first, or, knowing Betty, he could have just stopped paying her the requisite amount of attention; that alone might have been enough to set her off. I remembered times I hadn't returned her phone calls quickly enough, and when we finally spoke she would have a chill in her voice, keeping her sentences short and clipped to communicate her displeasure.

But Calder had always been a vigilant boyfriend. In fact, he had pursued her, apparently charmed by the things so many before him had found alienating. He was a lacrosse player who liked to perform in school plays, someone popular who didn't look down on the artsy crowd.

When they first started dating, at the beginning of sophomore year, Betty had regaled me with tales of his affections: the flowers he taped to her locker door, the way he waited for her outside all her classes. The stuffed lobster he'd won for her at the county fair. His family embraced her; she had dinner at their house several nights a week, became friends with the worshipful Caroline, who was in her last year of middle school then, and joined the Millers regularly for their excursions out to the movies or the beach. It was a reprieve from her own parents, I knew, from the claustrophobia of being the only child to two of the most conservative Catholics in Maine. When Calder broke up with her, she didn't just lose him; she lost them all.

Caroline wouldn't even look at Betty in the hallways at school, but still I wondered how she felt when her brother was accused of her former heroine's murder. Did she believe his confession had been coerced as well? Or did she have her doubts?

I lit a cigarette and stared into the water. I missed New York. When I first moved down there I was so trepidatious about everything, from living with only my mother to navigating the subway system. With work to give her purpose again, Mom was no longer the shrieking harpy who had made our lives in Williston so unhappy. And every month in school, I was given a fresh subway pass and set loose on the island of Manhattan.

Soon I realized I had found my real home. To walk down the street and not be recognized, to not have every interaction with a cashier or a waitress include detailed questions about my family or myself, to not be expected to make eye contact and smile and say good morning to every fucking person I passed on my way to get a cup of coffee at the bodega on our corner—at last I could understand my mother's protracted misery in Williston, the claustrophobia she must have felt. I might not have forgiven her for infecting our entire family with it, but a newfound empathy gradually warmed me.

Our first apartment was a railroad. Mom slept on a pullout couch and had to walk through my bedroom to get to the bathroom. As her practice grew, picking up more and more momentum, we moved again, and then again, until we each had our own bathroom and there was a spare bedroom Betty eventually came to think of as hers.

In two months I would be moving into my dorm at NYU, with a roommate who wasn't Betty. Everyone—my mother, my father, my friends in the city, my therapist—had promised me that it wouldn't always hurt this much, that slowly, gradually, the pain would recede, like the tide going out, and that scared me shitless. Betty's death had hollowed me out, and I was sure if I ever stopped mourning for her, there'd be nothing left of me. I'd be as gone as she was.

CHAPTER SIX.

ON FOURTH OF July afternoon, I told Dad that I didn't feel up to going to the Sandpipers game, or the fireworks afterward. He tried to give me a hard time, but all I had to do was place my hand in the general area of my uterus and wince in feigned menstrual agony and he gave up, leaving me on the couch with the remote and my kitten mug full of steaming tea.

Serena arrived about an hour later. She had dyed her hair black.

"I thought the pink was a little bit conspicuous," she explained.

"Clever girl," I said, and smiled.

I filled my bag with the essentials—flashlights, knife, cigarettes. The plan was to hike several miles through the woods behind my house and eventually come around behind Calder's. We couldn't risk taking a car; there was nowhere to park where we could be sure we wouldn't be spotted. No one in Williston ever locked their doors, so once we knew the Millers were gone, we would just walk right in. And then—I wasn't sure what, exactly. We'd know when we got there.

It was still light out when we left, but the sky was the color of slate and it smelled like rain. There was a damp chill in the air, and I shoved my hands deep into the pockets of my sweatshirt.

At the edge of my backyard was a narrow deer trail that wound north. Serena led the way; I watched her march forward with confidence and told myself this was a good idea. There was no reason to be nervous yet; right now we were just two girls taking a walk in the woods.

"Whatever happened to Monica?" I asked her. "Do you two ever talk anymore?"

"No." Her shoulders tensed as she answered, and I thought it wise to let the subject drop.

We were quiet after that, although the forest around us was filled with sound—mourning doves calling from their perches in the trees and twigs snapping under our feet. A mosquito buzzed in my ear and I slapped ineffectually at the side of my head. There was no sun to dapple through the leaves, and the gloom increased as we slipped deeper into the woods.

"What about you?" Serena asked. "You seeing anyone back in New York?"

"I wasn't exactly ripe for romance this year."

"Fair enough."

We came to a shallow creek; a series of slick, glossy stones made for a potential path to the other side. Without looking at me, Serena held a hand out behind her back; I took it and followed her careful steps. After we crossed, she released my hand from her firm, solid grip, but not before giving it a slight squeeze.

It was a long time before we spoke again, but I didn't mind. I didn't exactly feel comfortable around her; something about Serena set me on edge, as if I'd never fully recovered from the shock of seeing her flip off the entire faculty at graduation, or the scare she'd given me in the theater the day we'd officially met. It was not an unpleasant sensation, though; it made me more aware of my body—my stomach clenched, my chest expanding and contracting with every breath, the place on my shoulder where the strap of my messenger bag bit into my flesh. Being with her felt like I was constantly bracing for impact, what I imagined it would be like in that split second before a car crash, when you can see what's about to happen but can't react fast enough to stop it.

It started to rain. We pulled up our hoods and trudged forward. Occasionally the path veered close enough to the road that I could hear cars passing by, water swishing under their tires as they drove toward town.

"Do you think they'll cancel the fireworks?" I asked.

"No way. Williston would celebrate Independence Day in the middle of a nuclear fucking holocaust if it had to."

"You're right."

She glanced at me slyly over her shoulder. "You're not looking for an out, are you, Finley?"

Was I? I pictured Calder accepting his diploma, and my resolve hardened. "No."

We finally came around the back of the Millers' house. The lights were off and the driveway was empty. I slid open the glass door, but Serena stopped me before I could step inside.

"Shoes," she said, pointing at mine. They were covered in mud from our rainy walk through the forest. I took them off and placed them neatly on the cement outside the door. She did the same.

"Okay," she said. "Now."

We slipped inside, just enough gray light still coming in through the windows that we avoided bumping into the furniture. I had forgotten about the fucking dogs, though. The two chocolate Labs rushed us as we came inside, barking wildly, and Serena shrank behind me; I crouched down and made a series of soothing noises, scratching behind their ears and whispering their names, Cassie and Gemini. I remembered them, and they, apparently, remembered me; Cassie licked my face while Gemini shoved his nose directly into my crotch, his signature move.

"It's okay," I told Serena. "They don't bite. Go into the kitchen, there should be a jar of treats on the counter. Grab a few."

Visibly shaken—the first time I'd seen her confidence falter— Serena obeyed, and soon the dogs were quiet, padding behind us as we headed for Calder's room, me leading the way through the formal dining room with its gleaming mahogany table and the den outfitted with a big-screen television and beige sectional. I could still remember the last time I sat on that couch, watching *12 Monkeys* on cable, Betty happily sandwiched between Calder and me, his arm around her—but chastely, so as not to make me uncomfortable. Dogs at our feet, Gemini occasionally eyeing the open bag of Doritos on the coffee table and whining, Cassie deep in REM sleep, her front paws racing to nowhere as she gamely chased squirrels in her dreams; Betty's head on my shoulder, its warm, solid weight an invitation for me to stroke her blonde curls back from her forehead, which I knew she loved. I complied with her silent request; she sighed contentedly as I did so. In four more days I would leave for New York and return to what I considered my real life, but that night—unlights nowhere to be found, thunder rumbling occasionally in the distance, Bruce Willis making his deranged attempt to save the world—I found myself wishing, for the first time I could recall, that my parents had never divorced, that I had never been forced to choose, and that both my time and my allegiance did not have to be split between Maine and New York City.

"Which way is his room?" Serena asked, bringing me back to the task at hand.

"This way," I said, and led her there.

Holiday fireworks or not, we took no foolish chances. Leaving the overhead light off, I took the flashlight from my bag—I was getting a lot of mileage out of it this summer, I thought—and made a sweep around the room while Serena booted up the computer. The bed was made, navy blue comforter tucked in neatly and the pillows propped up against the headboard. Calder's lacrosse sticks were leaned against a wall in the corner, his Beck and *Clerks* posters curling a little around the edges. I scanned the titles on his bookshelves, the typical fusion of assigned classics from English class—*Their Eyes Were Watching God, As I Lay Dying, The Sun Also Rises*—and the sorts of novels I knew were requisite reading for teenage boys: *Trainspotting, Fight Club, Fear and Loathing in Las Vegas*. I looked for the books he'd read to Betty and me, the Roald Dahl and Homer, but they weren't there.

His yearbook was, however. I pulled it off the shelf and handed it to Serena. "I can't," I said. "I just can't look at all those signatures, everyone wishing him good luck. Can you check it out, see if there's anything in there that might be important?"

She nodded and paged through it while I made my way around his room. There was nothing under the bed, not even dust or an errant sock. There were no papers on the desk, just the computer and a framed picture of him with Caroline; his dresser was equally disappointing, nothing incriminating tucked behind his boxers or beneath all those expensive wool sweaters that kept him warm during the long, dark winters.

"God, I hate these fucking people," Serena said, closing the yearbook. She spun around in Calder's desk chair so she was facing me, backlit by the blue glow of his monitor. "If you thought you could kill him and get away with it, would you?"

"Shit no," I said, the answer coming quick enough to make it obvious I'd asked myself that very question. I nodded toward the yearbook. "I'd rather kill my fucking self than watch all those people cry over him."

"Yeah," she said, somewhat sadly, then turned back to his computer.

I leaned over her shoulder and watched while she opened his documents and folders, finding nothing but schoolwork and his application to Bates.

"Wait," I said. "I want to see what he wrote his admissions essay about."

Serena double-clicked. "Why his father is the person he admires most."

"I'm going to fucking puke."

I wandered into his attached bathroom and checked the medicine cabinet, something that was quickly becoming habit for me. "Holy shit. Come look at this."

An entire shelf was lined with those translucent orange bottles I had recently come to covet so much, but the contents were unfamiliar, the names complicated and intimidating. Buspirone, sertraline, fluoxetine—I didn't recognize the generic names. Diazepam and alprazolam rang some bells. I wasn't even tempted to take anything; there was always, I supposed, the chance Calder could accidentally overdose on all this shit. Serena plucked one from the shelf—paroxetine—and examined the label.

"This is Paxil," she said. "These are all for depression and anxiety."

"How do you know?"

"My parents tried to put me on some of this shit. Medicate the gay away. I read about the side effects and told them to go fuck themselves."

"Yeah, they put me on drugs for a while back in New York, but it was nothing like this."

She put the Paxil back on the shelf and closed the medicine cabinet. We stood there for a second, looking at our reflection, and I was suddenly aware of the damp warmth radiating from her, the goose bumps on her forearms and the fine hairs all standing up at attention, behind the curve of her ear a streak of black dye that she'd failed to rinse away.

"There's nothing here," she said finally.

"I want to go upstairs," I said. "I want to look in Caroline's room."

"What the hell for?"

I remembered watching Caroline through the window, horsing around with her brother, and I wondered if she was as untroubled by Betty's death as she'd appeared. "I'm just curious."

I kept the beam of the flashlight covered with my palm as I led the way up the stairs, fingers cast in that eerie opaque red. Serena stayed close behind me, so close I could hear her tight, anxious breaths. We stood at the foot of that long dark hallway, lined with framed pictures of the Millers, and I tried to remind myself that what we had done at the high school was much, much worse, so really there was nothing to worry about.

Outside, there was a distant boom—the start of the fireworks—and the dogs resumed their hysterical barking. Startled, I dropped the flashlight, which landed on the hardwood floor with an impossibly loud clatter, and I felt Serena freeze.

We might have turned around and left right then—I was certainly tempted—but there was a beat between the thunder of the fireworks, when the dogs settled just long enough for us to hear something down the hall, a low murmur, a shifting, like someone mumbling and rolling over in their sleep. Serena tugged on my sleeve, eager to abort, but something drew me forward, the same reckless apathy that had governed me for months, and I took her hand firmly in mine and towed her toward the noise's source.

The door to Caroline's bedroom was open. Unlike Calder's,

it was filthy—clothes everywhere, a toppled pile of books on the desk, a haphazard collage on the wall above the bed, photographs and pages hastily torn out of magazines. It smelled stale, like cigarettes and dirty sheets, and I was wondering when Caroline had started smoking and how her parents felt about her doing it in her bedroom when I realized she was lying there, in bed, staring at us.

But she didn't seem to really see us. I stepped gingerly inside; a cigarette was smoldering in an ashtray on her nightstand, and even as she lifted it to her mouth I had a hard time believing she was actually conscious. Her eyes were glassy and she wasn't at all surprised or disturbed to find me there.

"Finley," she said lazily. The hand holding the cigarette drifted dangerously close to the bed. "It's good to see you. Don't turn on the light."

"Hi, Caroline," I said. "Why aren't you at the fireworks?"

"They can't take me out in public like this."

I came closer so I could get a better look at her. On the nightstand, next to the ashtray, were half a dozen lines of chalky blue powder, a hollowed-out Bic pen, and a neat row of pills, waiting to be crushed and snorted. Caroline took another drag of her cigarette. Outside the fireworks exploded again. The curtains were open, billowing in the salty breeze; the moon cast a frosty light over the room. Through the haze of smoke I could see Caroline's blue eyes, their pupils pinned as tight as fine, black needles, and her blonde hair greasy against her pillow. The fireworks kept roaring; downstairs, it sounded like the Labs were charging the front door.

"What the fuck are you doing?" Serena whispered from the doorway.

"She's high," I said. "Come look at this."

Caroline's head sank back into the pillows, and this time the cigarette did make contact with the bed sheet, which flared an angry orange until she slapped it with her palm a few times, sparks filling the air around her, then dying and drifting to the floor as ash. I was stunned to see her like this, Calder's adorable little sister who'd followed us around like a puppy, so eager to be included and yet horrified if I so much as lit a cigarette in front of her. When had she become another casualty of Betty's death? I felt sickened by, and inexplicably responsible for, her current state.

"Jesus," Serena said.

"Caroline, are you okay?" I asked.

"Never felt better."

"Where did you get these?" I picked up one of the pills. It looked identical to the one Serena had shared with me that day on the beach, the ones I had looked for at Shelly's party. Crushing up and snorting them was not something that ever would have occurred to me. Where the fuck had Caroline gotten the idea? "Who did you get this from?"

"From Owen," she said. "That's where everybody gets them."

I sighed and turned to Serena, to ask if that was where she got hers, too, but she was looking at the closet, its doors wide open. She snatched the flashlight from my hand and turned it on, shining it on the racks of dresses. Dresses we both recognized. I had zipped Betty into them myself, many times.

The bengaline leopard print, the blue wiggle dress with the matching bolero, the polka dot halter with the full circle skirt—it wasn't the whole collection, but it was more than I'd ever hoped to see again. I fingered the hem of a black tulle skirt with rosettes sewn into the fabric.

"I saw them at the Goodwill," Caroline said. "After Betty's mom made her give them all away. It seemed like such a waste."

Suddenly I had the grisly idea that if I flung back the covers I would find Caroline clad in the outfit Betty had last been seen wearing, the silk nightgown and the matching robe. For a minute, I considered actually doing it, but Caroline saved me the trouble, getting out of bed and revealing a plain black tank top and underwear. She stumbled down the hallway to the bathroom to vomit. It took a while; it sounded as though she retched long after she was empty. Then she returned as if our exchange had never been interrupted.

"I bought as many of her dresses as I could find," she said, climbing back into bed and lighting another cigarette. "Nobody knows I have them."

"We won't tell anyone. Are you sure you're okay?" I asked again.

"When I'm this high even the puking feels good."

"Do you ever get high with Calder?" Serena asked.

Caroline laughed. "He gets *his* drugs from the doctor. They're not nearly as much fun as mine."

"Why did he start going to the doctor?"

She sat up, barely, struggling to prop herself up on her pillows. "Hey, why aren't you guys at the fireworks?"

"I have phonophobia," Serena improvised. "It's a fear of loud noises."

"Bummer," said Caroline.

"I know. It's the worst."

"You know there are people who are afraid of tinfoil? I saw something about it on a talk show." She turned her murky gaze to me. "What are you afraid of, Finley?"

"Drowning," I said.

"He has nightmares about drowning."

"Calder?"

She nodded.

"Nightmares where he's drowning? Or nightmares about drowning Betty?"

"He didn't kill her."

"How do you know?"

"He's my brother, Finley," she said, something hot and nasty in her voice, just beneath the listless drawl of the opiates. She set her cigarette in the ashtray, leaned over the nightstand, and snorted another line. "I know he didn't kill her, because he's my brother."

"Okay," I said. "Okay."

"We won't tell anyone about the dresses," Serena said.

"I won't tell anyone you were here," Caroline replied. "But I think you'd better go now."

"Be careful, Caroline," I said, nodding at the nightstand as I backed toward the doorway.

"*You* be fucking careful," she said, petulant and childlike.

Serena and I were headed for the stairs when she called after us. "He didn't kill her, but sometimes I think he thinks he did."

"I don't even know what the fuck that means," Serena whispered.

"We can reflect on it later. Let's get the hell out of here."

In the distance, the fireworks were reaching their crescendo. Gemini was cowering under the dining room table, whimpering, while Cassie pawed at the front door, her claws scratching frantically at the wood, barking in pained, clipped yelps that hurt my ears. Serena and I ran for the back door, flung it open, and scrambled to find our shoes. My hands shook as I struggled to tie my laces.

In our haste we left the sliding door ajar, and like a bad dream I watched helplessly as Cassie flew past us, a brown streak that disappeared across the yard and into the woods even as I grabbed for her and came away with nothing but air. The fireworks had gone silent, and I could hear Cassie sprinting into the woods until she, too, was gone.

"Shit!" I whispered. "Shit shit shit!"

Serena shoved her feet into her Docs and grabbed my elbow. "Let's go, Finley, move your ass *now*!"

"We have to go get her!"

"She'll come back on her own, they always do."

"But they'll wonder how she got out."

"Caroline is nodding out upstairs, I'm pretty goddamn sure she'll be the prime suspect. Now *go*!"

We ran. At least the rain had stopped. We headed south, but it was impossible to tell if we were on the same path we had taken to get there, and I was afraid to use the flashlight, scared it would call attention to us in the darkness. I tried to keep our pace up—when we were running, all I could hear was my blood pumping thickly in my ears and my labored breath and the bass drum of my heart keeping a steady, frantic beat. When we slowed down, the sounds of the forest found their way in, and I wasn't having that.

It was Serena who brought us to a halt, bent over with a stitch in her side.

"Just give me a minute," she said, panting.

I leaned against a tree and closed my eyes. I kept seeing Caroline lying in her bed, the flare of the sheet igniting, the fleeting shower of sparks as she smothered the flame with her hand. I took a deep breath.

"Do you smell that?" I whispered to Serena.

"Smell what?"

I sucked in another lungful of air to be sure. "Eucalyptus."

"What?"

"Smell," I said.

She inhaled obediently and nodded. "Where is it coming from?"

"I'm not sure," I said, and then a gust of wind blew through the trees, carrying with it the bracing, soapy scent. "Wait. Over there."

I crept through the forest toward the source, Serena following me this time. In addition to the eucalyptus, I could smell a fire burning somewhere nearby, and hear the soft rush of a small creek. Soon we were following the flickering light until we were right outside a small clearing. Inside was a squat round structure that looked like it was covered in tarps, and a few feet away was a campfire in a pit circled with rocks. There were voices, or at least one voice, coming from inside the hut. I couldn't make out the words, but there was a weird rhythm to them, like someone was singing or chanting.

"What the fuck is that?" I whispered.

"I think it's a sweat lodge," Serena said.

"A sweat lodge?"

"It's a Native American ritual. You heat up rocks in the fire, bring them inside and pour water on them, breathe in the steam, sweat like crazy."

"So why is there one in the middle of the woods?"

"I don't know. I don't know where we are, I don't know whose property we're on."

"Let's get the fuck out of here."

I started to walk away, but Serena grabbed me, pulled me behind a tree with her, and put a hand over my mouth.

"Shh," she whispered. "Look."

Someone had thrown open the flap covering the entrance to the lodge. Three naked men emerged, glistening with sweat and shivering in the night air.

"Jesus," one of them said, gasping. "I thought I was going to fucking suffocate."

"Price of doing business," one of the others said.

A fourth man came out of the lodge, and unlike the others, he didn't seem to be in any distress. He was tall and sinewy; he stretched his arms over his head and I could see his muscles working beneath his skin. He, too, was naked, but wearing a beaded necklace and some kind of pouch around his neck; he had matted blond dreadlocks as thick as my wrist. Even from where I stood, they looked filthy.

I gently removed Serena's hand from my mouth. "That guy," I whispered, "does not look Native to me."

"How many more rounds to go?" one of the other men asked him.

"As many as I decide," he said.

"In that case, I better go take a piss."

The guy wandered to the edge of the clearing; Serena and I huddled together, silent, afraid even to breathe, as he unleashed his stream into the darkness. We exhaled simultaneously when he finished and turned back toward the fire. The dreadlocked blond was already ushering the others back inside the sweat lodge. Before he followed them in, he gave the woods a long, searching look, and that look terrified me. He seemed like just some dirty hippie poser playing at being Native, but somehow I knew he was more than that; something about him felt dangerous. He took a step away from the lodge, and another, past the fire and closer to the edge of the clearing. I felt Serena tense next to me, her whole body getting ready to bolt. I clutched her more tightly. I had no doubt that if we ran, he would catch us.

"Don't move," I breathed into her ear.

She nodded. Whatever this guy was, she sensed it, too.

Finally, one of the others stuck his head out the flap. "Silas, are you coming back in here or what?"

Silas turned in a slow circle, surveying the entirety of the darkness beyond the clearing, while Serena and I hid behind the trunk of a Douglas fir, pressed against its rough, sticky bark. After a long moment, he seemed satisfied at last.

"Yeah," he said. "I'm coming."

We waited until he was back in the lodge and the chanting had started again before we crept away, and only when we were certain we were out of earshot did we break into a run, Serena's hand in mine, fleeing through the woods, not stopping for cramps or stitches this time. Just running.

"Finley," Serena said finally. "Finley, it's okay. I think I know where we are. We can walk from here."

She was panting hard, and I relented, relieved to catch my breath. Above us, the clouds were breaking up to reveal a half moon, split neatly down the middle like a black-and-white cookie.

"Jesus Christ," I said, leaning against a tree for support. "What were we thinking?"

"It's okay," Serena repeated.

"Caroline saw us, we let the dog out, we were almost caught by some crazy hippie in the woods, it was a total debacle and for what? We don't know anything we didn't know before, except that Calder has bad dreams and his little sister could probably use a trip to rehab. And what the fuck is Owen doing selling that girl drugs?"

She put her hands on my shoulders. "Calm. Down."

"Is he your connection?"

"He's not. I swear."

"So where did you get it?"

"My uncle died of pancreatic cancer last year."

I paused awkwardly, not sure how to respond. "Oh. I'm sorry."

"Yeah, well, he's dead, but my suffering goes on and on. So. I stole all his painkillers after the wake."

She loosened her grip on my shoulders but let her hands linger there, her face only inches from mine. I shook my head sadly.

"We're never going to know," I said. "We're never going to find out what happened to her. You were right, Serena. Nobody cares. Nobody cares but us."

"They will care. We're just getting started. It's the Fourth of July and we've already set fire to the high school, broken into Calder's house, and interrogated his sister. Think of what we can accomplish by Labor Day. Just hold it together." She smiled.

I managed to force a weak smile back. She smoothed my damp, matted hair with one hand and slid the other from my shoulder to my cheek. The wet chill that had seeped into my bones suddenly vanished. I traced the gold chain encircling her neck with one finger, pale soft skin beneath the gleaming metal, and kept my eyes trained on the crucifix. I could see the pulse at her throat and I rested my thumb there, felt the blood racing through her arteries, propelled by a heart as dark and furious as mine. Finally I met her gaze, and she kissed me. *What the fuck*, I figured. I'd already done so many stupid things today, what was one more potential disaster? I kissed her back.

It shouldn't have surprised me that kissing Serena was as intense as any conversation with her, her mouth as forceful and unrelenting as her gaze, as if the whole world had been reduced to the space around our bodies and that world was shrinking fast, forcing us closer and closer together, until I was pressed up against a tree so hard the bark scratched me through the thick fabric of my sweatshirt. Owen was all I really had for comparison; his attention always seemed like it might wander away at any moment, and him along with it. Serena's intensity almost frightened me, like I was a thing she could devour, like she could consume me until there was nothing left, and I wouldn't even care.

I laid low. The break in the weather was brief, and before long the clouds had returned and cloaked Williston in a perpetual grim, salty mist. I used it as an excuse to stay home, where I established a comforting routine—coffee and a cigarette on the front porch when I woke up, usually long after Dad had left for work, then a couple of hours on the couch in the living room, flipping back and forth between MTV and TCM, until I felt restless enough to move to the screened-in back porch, where I'd listen to the rain *pock*ing on the roof and try to read until my thoughts inevitably drifted to Serena and I fell asleep. Eventually Dad would come home and rouse me so we could eat dinner together.

As the days passed, I watched him struggle between relief that I was spending my time contained safely in the house, and anxiety that I showed interest in absolutely nothing. At night, when I couldn't sleep, I'd look over Dad's notes in my room and feel the same hopelessness I'd felt right before Serena had kissed me.

The time finally came when I ran out of cigarettes and was forced to drive into town to the trader. I sat in the Subaru for a minute, trying to summon the requisite energy for brief, casual human interaction. Main Street, which should have been flooded with tourists by now, was empty; even the locals seemed to have been driven inside by the weather, except for a handful of people eating lunch at the Halyard and the Charlie's diehards lined up on their stools, hunched over their drinks and looking even more disconsolate than usual.

I went into the trader to conduct my business. There were no other customers. I recognized the guy behind the counter. It was Danny, the kid who had taken Rebecca's virginity in the woods the year before. I didn't know him well, but I had one vague memory of him from elementary school, poking at a dead raccoon on the playground, not to be creepy but out of a genuine fascination with the animal's corpse and the various flies and maggots that had come to inhabit it. He'd expressed concern to a teacher that the animal wouldn't decompose properly on cement, and asked if he could take it home and bury it in the woods behind his house. He was denied this request, and the raccoon was swiftly removed by a janitor. Danny had sulked for the rest of the day.

"Hey, Finley," he said.

"Hey, Danny. Can I get a carton of Marlboros, please? Reds."

"You got ID?"

I stared at him. "Are you serious? You know how old I am."

"Sorry. It's the rules. We got busted a few months back for not carding. Now we have to ask everybody. I get in big trouble if I don't."

I looked around the empty store. "There's no one else here."

He nodded toward the security cameras mounted on the wall behind him.

"Where is everyone, anyway?" I asked as I opened my wallet and flashed my New York license. "Has it been this quiet all week?"

He dutifully pulled the Marlboros out from below the counter and rang them up. "Must be the weather. Hope it picks up soon though. Everybody's hurting except Charlie's."

"The more everyone hurts," I said, handing over the cash, "the better Charlie's does."

"Yeah," he said, smiling vaguely.

I took my smokes. "Thanks."

"I'm sorry," he said. "About Betty. I know you guys were really close."

I stared at him, shocked yet grateful. "Thank you."

"I miss seeing her around in those dresses, trying to give this town a little class."

"She was wasting her fucking time," I said sharply.

He shrugged. "Maybe. But it was nice to watch her try."

"I thought everyone in Williston hated her?"

"I didn't," he said. "I didn't hate her at all."

"What do you think happened to her?"

"I think she's dead. Come on, you know it, I know it."

"I know that she's dead, Danny. What I mean is, how did she get that way?"

"You've already got your mind made up. I can tell just by looking at you."

"If I'm wrong, convince me."

He looked at me for a long minute, long enough for me to wonder if he actually did know something, but finally he just shook his head dismissively. "Christ, man, do you ask this many questions every time you go to buy cigarettes?"

"Maybe it's not the weather keeping all the tourists away," I said as I left. "Maybe it's the bad vibes."

On my way out I passed a flyer taped to the door. *Have you seen this dog?* it asked me. Below the text was a grainy picture of Cassie and the Millers' phone number. I tore it down and stuffed it angrily into my pocket.

Owen was standing in the alley beside the diner smoking as I walked back to my car. I kept going.

"Jesus, Finley," he shouted. "Are you gonna stay pissed at me forever?"

"Try apologizing, motherfucker, and then I guess we'll see."

I was strangely invigorated by all these encounters. Instead of driving home, I went straight to Serena's. She must have heard me in the driveway—maybe my parking brake gave me away, like it always had with Betty—because she came out before I had even left the car. I leaned over and opened the passenger door for her.

"Hey," she said.

"You think the master key to the high school will still work?" I asked her.

"Yeah, unless they've changed the locks. Why?"

"Because," I said, throwing the Subaru in reverse and tearing back down the driveway, "I have this really fucked-up idea, and I think you're going to love it. But we're going to need a copier."

CHAPTER SEVEN.

WE WERE UP all night working on our little project. When we finished, we went to the beach, the same rocky cove where Betty had died, to watch the sunrise.

"You want a blue?" she asked me.

"Why not?" I said. "I think we've earned it."

She took her wallet out of the back pocket of her jeans, unzipped the change purse, and fished out a couple of the tiny pills, giving me a whole one this time. We looked out at the water while the sky slowly lightened, the remainder of the clouds turning pink and the sun reluctantly creeping over the horizon, the orange flare reminding me how close Caroline had come to self-immolating in her bed.

"Think they'll know it was us?" I asked.

"Maybe. Do you care?"

"Not really."

"Still, we should probably stay out of town today," she said.

"Okay by me." My fingers crept toward hers in the sand, and then our hands were locked together. "I don't have anywhere to be."

"She did kiss me once," Serena said, looking me in the eye. "Betty did. Just once. To get a reaction, I think. Maybe she wanted to try it so she'd know what it felt like. Is that what that was, the other night?"

"No," I said. "It wasn't. I swear."

She grinned crookedly and pulled me closer. "Prove it, then."

Owen was waiting on the front porch when I got home. I could tell he was angry by the way he was sitting, perfectly still and tensed, eyes following me as I got out of the car and climbed the steps. A muscle in his forearm twitched as he took the final drag of his cigarette.

"So did you come to apologize?" I asked.

He pitched the butt over the railing onto the lawn, leaped out of his chair, and pushed me up against the side of the house in one fluid motion, so fast it was surreal. His fingers dug painfully into my shoulders, and I fought to keep my expression blank; I would never let him know he was hurting me.

"What the *fuck* were you thinking?" he snapped. "What in Christ's name is *wrong* with you?"

"What's wrong with *you*?" I said, trying to shove him away.

He gave me a rough shake for good measure and backed off. "Don't try that with me, Finley. You're a good liar, but you're not that good." He reached into his back pocket and pulled out a crumpled copy of the flyer Serena and I had posted all over town.

We'd both been pleased with how it came out. *Have you seen this girl?* it read, and then there was a picture of Betty, the headshot that never made it into the yearbook, a list of her stats, and the date she'd last been seen. At the very bottom, we'd added the phone number for the Williston Sheriff's Department. *Please call with any information.* In the middle of the night, long after even the most committed alcoholics had left Charlie's, we'd taken down all the posters of Cassie and replaced them with ours.

"You're lucky I open the diner as early as I do," he said. "I think I got them all before anybody saw them."

"You took them *down*?" I shouted, shoving him away. "The whole point was for people to see them."

"How much shit do you need to stir up, goddammit? The police are still investigating the fire at the school."

"Funny how they're still investigating that, but not somebody's murder."

"You've been asking questions all over town, and now this? You're not being subtle, Finley, and you're not being clever. Do you have any idea how much attention you're calling to yourself?"

"I don't care, as long as it draws the same attention back to him, and what he did to Betty."

"You're so certain he killed Betty."

"You know it as well as I do, don't act like you don't."

"Then what makes you think he wouldn't do it again?"

Owen reached into his cargo pants for his cigarettes; he took one out of the pack and his hand shook as he lit it.

"Oh my God," I said softly, finally understanding. "You're worried about me."

"You've seen how easy it is for a girl to go missing in this town.

You think it can't happen to you, too? You want me to say he's a murderer? Fine, you're right, I think he drowned Betty and got away with it. So maybe antagonizing him with shit like this isn't a great idea."

He sat back down, his anger replaced by the same weary expression he always seemed to get when I was around.

I sank into the chair beside his, took the cigarette from him, and inhaled. "I'm not scared of Calder."

"I wish you were scared of something," he said.

I decided to let Owen think he'd gotten all the flyers. I didn't tell him about the ones we'd put in the mailboxes all over town.

After Owen left, I went upstairs and passed out on my bed, on top of the covers, in all my clothes, falling into a sleep so deep and dreamless I woke up completely disoriented; the clock on the nightstand said it was four, and with my shades drawn I didn't know if that meant late afternoon or early morning. I didn't care. I buried my face in my pillow, hoping I could go back to sleep, but I was suddenly, hopelessly alert. I rolled over onto my back and stared at the ceiling, bewildered at how I was supposed to fill the endless hours between now and I didn't know when. Nighttime? College? The same empty ache that had propelled me around the five boroughs last winter forced me out of bed; I didn't know why I could spend nearly a week inside the house and never feel restless, and then suddenly be overwhelmed by the need to be in motion, but I felt that need now.

A quick peek out the kitchen curtains confirmed it was afternoon. I checked the mail, and among my father's bills and the catalogs addressed to "Resident" was a thick envelope with my name in my mother's familiar hand. It was my welcome package to NYU, all glossy pictures of Bobst Library and course descriptions that overused words like *pedagogy* and *ideology*. I'd received my room assignment, a one-room double in Brittany Hall; according to the paperwork, I'd be sharing it with a girl named Kate Shields, a student from the dance department whom I immediately hated. My mother had included a note imploring me to call her. I threw it all in the garbage.

I didn't bother changing, just went outside and got into my car. The skies were clearing, but the asphalt was still slick and glossy with rainwater. I drove without a destination at first, my only goal to get out of Williston for a while. Without realizing what I was doing at first, I found myself scanning the side of the road for Cassie's body. I did feel bad about letting her out. I hoped she was okay, that she'd find her way home, even if that home was the Millers'.

I drove south, following the water. There was nothing stopping me from driving all the way back to New York, to my mother's apartment and my friends, forties on stoops in the West Village and shows at punk clubs in the East. I was sick of the rain, sick of the Halyard's shitty coffee, sick of seeing the same faces, sick of all those faces being white. I missed the crowds of New York, the anonymity of the subway, the ability to walk down the street without having to stop and make small talk with nearly everyone I saw.

I could feel the city hundreds of miles away like a giant

pulsating heart, and the highway was a vein drawing me in. I could have kept going, it would have been so easy, but instead I got off the exit at Pullman, the town whose softball team had trounced ours.

Pullman was bigger than Williston, its downtown a square mile of wide, crooked streets that zigzagged toward the water; they were filled with brightly painted stores and buildings, art galleries and antique shops and clothing boutiques. Tourists strolled along, holding hands and window-shopping. Boats were pulling in and out of the marina; the whole town bustled with more activity than Williston had seen all summer.

The Emersons owned a roofing and remodeling business with an office in a strip mall a couple of miles past Pullman's center, sandwiched between a Rite Aid and a dry cleaner's. A bell jingled overhead as I walked through the door. Behind a beige Formica counter, a receptionist was on the phone. She was around my mom's age, her brown hair streaked with silver, and the lines around her mouth betrayed several decades of smoking. She eyed me warily as I waited for her to finish, standing awkwardly with my thumbs in my back pockets. I guess it was obvious I didn't need the siding on my house redone.

"Can I help you?" she finally asked, more politely than I'd expected.

"I'm looking for—" I realized I didn't know the pitcher's first name. "Mr. Emerson's son."

"Mr. Emerson's got three sons. You want to try again?"

"The one that pitches for the softball team."

"That's Jack. Can I ask what this is about?"

"It's kind of embarrassing."

She raised an eyebrow at me, as if to say, *Tough shit.* I was starting to get the feeling she was more than the receptionist. There were a number of framed photographs on her side of the counter, all facing away from me, but I was pretty sure if I reached over and took one I'd see it was of Jack or his brothers—her sons.

"I saw Jack pitch at a softball game a couple of weeks ago. I thought he was cute, but I didn't have the nerve to say anything afterward. Ever since, I've been kicking myself. One of my girl-friends finally talked me into driving down here, so I figured I'd just do it, before I changed my mind." I stared at my feet, trying to seem demure.

She chuckled. "That's sweet. So you drove all the way down from—where?"

"Williston."

The kindness drained from her face. "Williston?"

"That's right."

"Are you one of Caroline's friends? Did she send you down here to give a message to him or something?"

"Caroline? Caroline Miller?" I asked, confused.

"So you do know her."

"Everyone in Williston knows the Millers."

"Well, you can turn around and go back to Williston and tell the Millers to leave the Emersons alone. We don't want any more trouble with them. And my boys are done with girls from Williston, that's for damn sure."

"I'm sorry, I don't understand," I said, stepping back from the reception desk, confused. "I'm not friends with Caroline and she didn't send me down here. I just want to talk to Jack."

"Jack's working." The phone rang again, and as she held her hand over it, she gave me a pointed look. "And you'd better go."

She wasn't asking.

By the time I got back to Williston, I was too hungry to avoid the diner. I cringed as Owen looked up from the coffeemaker. Relief passed over his face just for a second before he reorganized his features into their normal mask of mild irritation. I kept my eyes down, went to a booth, and sat with my back to the counter and to Owen, paging through the Pullman newspaper to keep my hands busy until Jenny the waitress filled my coffee mug. Their town might be getting all the tourist money this summer, and their softball team was definitely superior, but their police blotter was a bore compared to ours. Someone sat opposite me in the booth and I sighed, assuming it was Owen. I took a sip of my coffee and made a point of not looking up.

"Hey, Finley."

It wasn't Owen. It was Calder.

I recoiled, my back pressed against the vinyl, as far away from him as I could get without running for the door. "What do you want?"

"I just wanted to say hi," he said softly. "You've been back for a couple of weeks now and I haven't had the chance. But I was walking by and saw you sitting here by yourself, so I thought I'd pop in and see how you were doing."

"You really shouldn't have worried about it," I said.

"How's your summer going so far?"

I wondered if he was high. I knew I wished I was. I forced myself to look at him.

He'd lost weight. His face and shoulders seemed more angular and he was pale. His eyes were set deeper in his skull. The pupils weren't pinned, so he wasn't on the same shit as his sister, but his irises were a muddier blue than I remembered. I'd never seen his hair so long; it reached his collar at the back, curling softly at the ends. He was clean-shaven, though, and his fingernails neatly trimmed; he wasn't unrecognizable, and nothing about him screamed "murderer" in quite the way I'd expected.

For all of my previous bravado, I was terrified, even though I was sitting in Owen's diner, and Owen's diner was my safe place even when we weren't speaking, and Owen was behind the counter, probably watching this exchange. My father was in his office down the street; I'd seen his car parked outside the creamery when I'd come in. It was the middle of the afternoon, and any minute I'd hear the cook hit the bell in the kitchen, and that would mean that my grilled cheese was ready. Maybe I'd get a to-go box and head down the street to Dad's office; maybe he had some filing he needed me to do, and after work we would go home together and I would lock all the doors and fall asleep later with the TV on. Just because Calder had killed Betty didn't mean he would kill me, too.

"It's okay, I guess." My mouth had gone dry but I was scared to take a sip of water, afraid my shaking hands would give me away. Somewhere in my head a chant was starting up: *Show no fear, show no fear, show no fear.*

"I wasn't sure you'd come back this summer."

"Yeah, I've been getting that a lot."

I had known that sooner or later this day would come, that somewhere I'd end up face-to-face with Calder. I'd imagined it many times, just like I'd imagined Betty's death, but not like this. There, I approached him, not the other way around, and I was clever and brave, and he was the one frightened of me. That I'd managed to convince myself of this—that I was some sort of threat to him—now seemed patently ridiculous and stupid, and suddenly I realized that maybe Owen had a point after all, the one about not antagonizing the person who had killed your friend, and I probably owed him an apology. And where the fuck was Owen anyway? I looked up but he wasn't behind the counter anymore.

"Do you remember that time we found the bathtub in the woods?" Calder asked, out of nowhere.

"Yes," I whispered.

It happened on a gray Saturday, the summer before our junior year, when Calder and Betty were still a normal, happy couple and I was the welcome trespasser hanging out with them nearly every day. It had rained all that week and we had exhausted our collection of movies and board games; even though there was still a damp, achy chill in the air, we were so relieved the rain had stopped that we'd made straight for the woods, trailing crumbs from our cherry Pop-Tarts and shivering. We had no plan or agenda beyond simply being outside and together, and we hiked farther in than we ordinarily would have had the patience to do.

I still remembered that walk with unusual clarity—Betty

leading the way, the occasional skip in her step, me following Calder, his red rain slicker in sharp relief against the lush, loamy green—and how abruptly it ended when we came upon a bathtub, a real claw-foot, cast-iron tub, just sitting under a tree in the middle of the woods. It was rusty and filled with several inches of dirty rainwater.

Betty was delighted—she immediately wanted to climb inside, and I had to convince her not to, remind her that she would be miserable hiking home in wet clothes, and I would be miserable listening to her complain the whole time—and Calder had a number of theories about the bathtub's origins, but something about the whole thing unsettled me deeply, the way I imagined seeing a UFO might. The tub had no business being there, there was no explanation for where it had come from, yet we were looking at it just the same.

I didn't know why Calder had brought up that day in particular, but it only disconcerted me further, that he'd chosen an incident that already made me inexplicably uneasy.

"Wasn't it weird," he went on, "how we were never ever able to find it again?"

The bell dinged in the kitchen, and a few moments later Jenny brought me my grilled cheese, for which I had lost all appetite. Still, I forced myself to pick it up and take a bite, the bread turning to a dry paste in my mouth, melted cheddar burning my tongue. *Show no fear, show no fear, show no fear. Now swallow.*

We never did find the tub again, as Calder said. We had looked, tromping through the woods again a few days later, this time with a small entourage in tow: friends of his from the lacrosse team, friends of his from the drama club who seemed to mostly tolerate Betty. Most of the guys carried forties or six-packs of beer, yet glared every time I lit a cigarette.

"You'd better not start a fire out here," one of them warned me, a particularly simian member of the group, thick-necked, brown hair shorn into a crew cut. All the lacrosse guys had nicknames, and his was Stupo.

We wandered around in circles all afternoon. The boys got buzzed and hit on the theater girls like they were doing them a favor; the theater girls stuck together in a tight clutch and only spoke to one another in stage whispers; Betty and I were far behind the others, her arm slung loosely around my waist as we tried to decide if she should visit New York for Halloween or Thanksgiving. Only Calder moved seamlessly among and between, talking team rivalries one minute and Shakespeare the next, falling back to plant a kiss on Betty's palm and then sprinting back to the helm of the whole party. We never came across the bathtub, despite his insistence that we had followed the same path, and I for one was silently grateful. I hadn't actually wanted to see it again.

"So what?" I said now.

"I was thinking about that tub the other day. How easy it is for things to get lost in the woods. Like Cassie. She's out there somewhere. Who knows if she'll ever find her way home. Poor Gemini's so upset he won't eat. "

"I know how he feels."

"You mean well, I get that, but you're making trouble for no reason, Finley," he said, to my bafflement. Then he leaned forward, and I stiffened. "Betty killed herself. Maybe nobody else will say it to you that bluntly, but that's what we all know happened."

"And how do you 'all know' that?"

"Because she was miserable. It was obvious to everyone. I bet it was even obvious to you."

"That doesn't mean anything."

"I miss her too, you know," Calder said. Then he got up and walked away.

As soon as the door closed behind him, Owen came over to the booth, leaned in, and put a hand on my shoulder. "Are you okay?"

I shrugged him off. "What the hell took you so long?" I tried to throw some money on the table—I think I had some idea about storming out—but Owen took my shaky hands in his and I, to my horror, dissolved completely into tears. He froze for a moment, not sure how to proceed, and then, like he had seen someone do it in a movie once, he put his arms around me and pulled me close so I could sob into his chest. "Where were you?" I managed.

"I'm so sorry, Fin, I was out in the alley having a cigarette. I'm sorry. He left as soon as he saw me come back in."

"I'm so stupid, O, I'm so fucking stupid."

He was, in his own way, too good to lie. "I know." He reached across me and pulled a fistful of napkins from the dispenser, then tried to use them to blot away my tears. I let him rub the scratchy paper against my cheeks a few times before I pulled away.

"You were right. Okay? I was wrong and you were right."

"Look," he said. "Why don't I close up early? Give me a few minutes and we'll get out of here."

"Can you do that?" I asked.

"It's my diner. I can do whatever I want. Besides, it's not like we're slammed at the moment."

I lifted my head from his chest and looked around. There was nobody there but us. For some reason, that got me crying all over again.

When I was done weeping, and Owen had sent Jenny and the cook home, and after he finished counting out his meager tips, we got ready to leave. I was still shaking and starving; that one bite of grilled cheese was all I'd managed to choke down. So when he offered to take me back to the cabin and make me something to eat, I agreed, not thinking past food or the comfort of being around someone I'd known my whole life, someone who seemed fairly invested in my continued well-being and physical safety.

The phone behind the counter rang as we were about to walk out the door.

"Shit," Owen said. "I have to get that. I forgot I was expecting a call."

"Seriously? Now?"

"I'm sorry," he said, squeezing my shoulders reassuringly as he sprinted toward the phone. "This'll just take a second."

I stood by the door hugging myself as he picked up the receiver; I looked up and down the street to make sure Calder was gone.

Owen's side of the conversation didn't give anything away; it was all "yes" and "no" and "okay, fine." I figured it was either his connection or another girl. I was still trying to decide which one was preferable when he hung up.

"Come on," he said, putting an arm around my waist and leading me out the door. "Let's go."

We got into his truck and I numbly fastened my seat belt. My stomach rumbled audibly, but I couldn't feel a thing.

"Are you okay?" Owen asked me.

"I don't think so."

He lit two cigarettes and passed me one. "Look, I have to run a quick errand on the way home."

I didn't answer, took a drag instead. I couldn't feel that either.

He drove farther out of town than I expected, passing the turnoff to his cabin. Wherever we were going, it wasn't on the way home. I didn't care. I searched the sky outside my window for a break in the clouds and came up empty.

"What did he say to you?" Owen asked. "Did he threaten you?"

"I'm not entirely sure."

"Fuck," he said.

"I'm not exactly in the mood for an 'I told you so,' in case that's where this is going."

"It's not, I swear."

He finally pulled into an unpaved driveway carpeted in wet, green leaves, so narrow that branches scraped against the side of the truck. Then he stopped, but didn't kill the engine.

"I need you to do something for me, okay?" he said softly.

"Get down."

"What?"

"Crouch down in your seat. This guy can be pretty paranoid and I don't want him to see you."

So it *had* been his connection on the phone. "Are you sure you don't want me to crawl into the truck bed? You can cover me with a tarp."

"I'm serious, Finley. I've got enough to worry about right now. Just do it."

"Fine," I said, slumping lower in my seat.

"That's not enough. I need you to curl up under the dash."

"Christ, Owen."

"And keep your goddamn voice down."

I unbuckled my seat belt and did as he said, folding myself up and wedging myself in the space underneath the glove compartment. The floor mat was filthy, my jeans immediately covered in dirt and ash; I tossed a crumpled beer can into the back of the cab. "Hurry up, okay?"

"Don't move, and don't make any noise. I mean it. This guy has, like, a sixth sense or something. If he knows I brought someone to his house, he'll lose his shit."

Satisfied that I was hidden from view, Owen finished pulling into the driveway. From my vantage point on the floor, I could see that the canopy of trees had opened up. Raindrops started falling on the truck's roof. I hugged my knees to my chest and thought about Owen's cabin, a whiskey for my nerves, falling asleep on the couch listening to the rain, his ratty old quilt wrapped around me.

"I'll be right back," Owen whispered, not looking down at me. "Hopefully before my legs start to cramp."

The truck shook when he closed his door. I massaged my calves, trying to keep the blood moving, and wiggled my toes so my feet wouldn't fall asleep. I needed to talk to Serena, make sure she was okay, see if Calder had tried to contact her, too, warn her that he might. Just the thought of Serena did something else to my blood altogether, and suddenly I could feel my stomach again, that warm flush low in my belly and between my legs. Could I convince her to let Betty's death go? Did I want to? What else could we do? There was no evidence that Calder had killed her, no way to prove he'd done it. And on top of everything, his father ran the town. Maybe I should hunker down, spend the rest of the summer picking berries and eating ice cream and letting Serena's mouth wander all over my body.

I pressed my face against my thighs and listened to the rain pummel the windshield and thought about Betty, how the summers were ours and he'd stolen this one from us, this one and all the others to come, and our late-night dorm room conversations and our fights over how to decorate our West-or-East Village apartment. I'd never have another new Betty story to tell, I'd only have the old ones to recycle over and over. Sometimes I had trouble remembering her voice. How much longer until I needed a photograph to remind me what she looked like? I thought about the crucifix that nestled in Serena's collarbone, and what Serena had said, that she believed in God because otherwise she'd never get to see Betty again. I wished I could do the same. As it was, I could only hope to see her in my dreams, dreams that left me feeling like the shit had been kicked out of my heart. I wanted her ghost to haunt me forever, as much as I wanted to put her to rest, as much as I wanted Calder to suffer.

The windows of the truck were rolled up, but I could hear muffled voices. Whoever Owen was talking to, he was incredibly long-winded; full minutes seemed to go by between Owen's familiar monosyllabic responses. Something about the first guy's voice was familiar, too; I couldn't place it, but I could feel the face that went with it trying to emerge from my subconscious. Despite all Owen's warnings, I slid out from under the dash, hands on the bottom of the passenger seat, pulling myself up just enough so I could peek out the windshield.

The truck was parked in a large circular clearing, alongside an enormous black Dodge Ram with a crew cab and a shiny canopy. The Ram looked brand-new, and trucks like that didn't come cheap, but it was the only ostentatious thing around. The house itself was nothing more than a shitty prefab not much bigger than a trailer, purple paint cracking around the windows, storm door sagging on its hinges and flapping angrily in the wind, slamming against the frame every few seconds with a gunshot sound that made me anxious. Beyond the house was a smaller wooden structure with a curved roof of logs that hadn't been stripped of their bark. The trees swayed in the rain and hundreds of feathers dangled from the branches—all sizes, some as big as eagle feathers and others small enough to have come from the tiniest sparrow I'd ever seen hop along a bench in Washington

Square Park, all of them glistening with rain and twisting on their tethers.

I knew where we were now, whose property we were on; a sick recognition filled me as I slowly turned my head and saw Owen talking to Silas.

Silas was shirtless and barefoot, wearing only patchwork corduroy pants and a fanny pack that would have looked ridiculous on anybody else. He seemed oblivious to the rain streaming down his chest, which was covered in tattoos; poor Owen was getting soaked, brown hair plastered to his head as he nodded his assent to whatever Silas was saying. I couldn't make out any words over the rain and my jagged breathing; slowly, I rolled my window down, just a crack.

"Seriously, man, the multiverse is a real thing. The quantum suicide machine proves it. Haven't you ever read Greg Egan? And think about it. The multiverse is the path to immortality. In an infinite number of universes, there always has to be one where you're still alive. We just have to figure out—"

I rolled the window back up. Perhaps Silas's minions had to suffer through his sweat lodges and insane ramblings—"the price of doing business," one of them had said in the woods— but I did not. I wanted Owen back in the truck, *now*, and when we got to his cabin I was going to drink all his whiskey, smoke all his cigarettes, and then beat the shit out of him for getting into business with a guy like this. I seethed. How could he lecture me about staying out of Calder's way when he was working for this crazy motherfucker? Owen was good with his hands, I had firsthand knowledge of that, and if he needed extra money he could start building furniture out of driftwood and selling it to the tourists. I slipped back into my hiding spot and waited impatiently for his return.

When he finally got back in the truck, he made a point of not looking down at me; I figured Silas was still standing there, watching him. Owen leaned over and put a brown envelope in the glove compartment, resting his hand briefly on my head before he strapped himself in. He executed a flawless three-point turn—there was a reason Owen had taught me how to drive—and took off back up the driveway.

"Stay down until I tell you to come out," he whispered.

I thought that would be when we were back on the main road. As soon as I felt asphalt beneath the tires I began to surface.

"Not yet," he whispered.

"How come? He can't see me now."

"Someone else might. And that somebody else might tell him. I don't want this fucking guy to know you exist, Finley. Got it?"

We were on the same page there. I shut up and stayed crouched under the dash until we were safely back at the cabin. He had to help me out; by then I had lost all feeling in the lower half of my body, and I hobbled inside on wobbly, gimped-out legs, promptly collapsing on the couch and reaching for the cigarettes. Owen did that thing that guys do when they get home, emptying his pockets onto the kitchen counter—Zippo lighter, wallet, keys—and taking off his watch and setting it neatly beside them.

"I'm sorry about that," he said, handing me an ashtray. "I had to stop by there, and I didn't want to leave you alone after—"

"It's okay," I said. "I understand. I respect your efforts to keep work and your personal life separate."

Owen rubbed my feet, trying to get the circulation going. "Thanks."

"When did you start?"

"You just said—"

"When?"

He got up, got the bottle—Powers this time, instead of Fighting Cock—and poured us each a glass, then he sank back into the couch, still rubbing my feet absently, eyes closed, a look of surrender on his face. "Last spring."

"So all last summer?"

"Yeah. But it was different then. That was just selling a little shit out in the alley behind the diner, or over at Charlie's. I didn't even meet this guy until a few months ago. I was getting it from some other guy, who was getting it from him. I guess I earned up enough goodwill to get the introduction, and now—now I'm stuck with him," he said ruefully.

"Is he, like, the hippie Mafia or something? Once you're in, you're in for life?"

Owen opened one eye. "You took a peek, huh? I fucking knew you would."

"What's with all the feathers?"

"He thinks he's Native American," Owen said, shaking his head. "Passamaquoddy, to be precise. He doesn't even live in the house, he lives in that fucking wigwam he built next to it. There was some kind of scabies outbreak in the house, no one goes in there anymore. I think he might actually be Canadian."

"Jesus Christ, Owen, are you listening to yourself? You've got to get another side gig."

"I need the money," he said simply. "If I stop now, the diner will go under. You've been here long enough to see what's happening. There's no tourists. No summer money. How the fuck am I going to make it through the winter?"

"That guy is bad medicine," I said. "Keep working for him, and I'm not sure you'll make it through the winter anyway. What happens if you get arrested?"

He sat up sharply, his moment of calm repose gone. "Don't even say that."

"You're selling drugs to kids all over town," I said. "You're selling to Caroline fucking Miller. What if her dad finds out?"

"How do you know that?"

"You've lived in Williston all your life, Owen. What makes you think you can keep a secret here?"

"I'm careful." He saw I wasn't convinced. "I promise."

"There's something about this conversation that's so familiar. Like we had one just like it, really recently," I said.

"Working for Silas is not the same thing as trying to get a rise out of Calder."

"It's not Calder I'm trying to get the rise out of."

"Then who is it?"

The blood had flooded back into my legs and feet, sensation returning on a painful wave of stabbing needles and sharp, rusty pins. I got up and circled the couch like a shark, trying to walk it off. "Everybody else in town."

"Good luck stirring up a lynch mob against Williston's favorite son."

"Good luck selling drugs for a psychotic hippie who thinks he's going to live forever in the multiverse."

I finished another lap and stood in front of Owen. He reached up and pulled me onto the couch, holding me so my head was buried in his chest. Sometimes I remembered that before Owen was anything else, he had been like my brother, and when we eventually stopped fucking he would be again. His fear was a strange reminder of that, because it was so deep and genuine that I knew it stemmed from that older, more familial connection, not the more recent developments of the last couple of years. I was surprised to find the same thing happening to me, that after years of balancing precariously on the edge of the cliff that was falling in love with Owen, being afraid for him pulled me back instead of pushing me over.

Still, I wondered if I should fuck him now. I knew Owen, stone cold. If I fucked him, he'd fall asleep. If he fell asleep, I could go out to his truck and get a look at the package he'd picked up from Silas. Then I'd know what he was selling and how much of it, precisely how deep he was in. And if there was enough of it, maybe I'd take a sample. Just so I'd know exactly what we were dealing with.

The phone rang before I could decide. I tried to stop Owen from getting up—"Let it ring," I said—but he shook his head.

"When I try that they just keep calling. Maybe you were right about the pager."

Suddenly I hated that idea. As though it meant admitting what he had become. I liked it better when he denied he was a dealer, like that meant it wasn't real, or only temporary.

"Hello?" he said, and raised his eyebrows at the response on the other end. I was startled when he held the receiver out to me. "It's for you."

"Hello?" I said tentatively.

"It's Serena. I've been trying to find you. Your dad said you might be at Owen's. You need to get down here."

"Hang on, hang on. Where's 'here'?"

"Charlie's."

"What's going on at Charlie's?"

"There's someone down here saying—" She took a long pause. "There's someone down here saying she saw Betty."

"What do you mean, 'saw' her? Like, the night she died?"

"No," Serena said impatiently. "She's saying she saw Betty last night."

"What?" I said, a little too loud. Owen stood over me, his face a furrowed question mark.

"Just get down here." She hung up.

I looked over at Owen, the receiver dangling limply from my hand like something I was afraid might contaminate me. "I'm on my way."

CHAPTER EIGHT.

MY CAR WAS still in town, so I had no choice but to ask Owen to drive me to Charlie's. When I told him what Serena had said, he balked, said he didn't want to go all the way back to Main Street to watch one of the local drunks spread a bullshit rumor, but I insisted, threatened to walk, pulled out all the usual stops until he acquiesced, strapping on his watch again, angrily shoving his wallet back in his pocket. Still, he held the front door open for me on the way out, and unlocked my side of the truck before going around and settling into the driver's seat with an aggravated sigh.

I don't know what I was expecting at Charlie's, maybe something more dramatic than the usual—people spilling out into the street, the place filled with that invisible electricity, that buzz characteristic of any noteworthy event in Williston. But it was just like any other evening.

The tiny NYC dive bars I'd weaseled into with my fake ID, Sophie's and Lucy's and Manitoba's and 9C, were all cramped and smelled vaguely like locker rooms, but Charlie's was different. Soft orange light spilled through the windows, washing over the long bar, illuminating every gouge and scorch mark in the wood. The regulars gathered here, all the faster to be served their next shot or beer. The large room had a stage and a dance floor, and a vast space around these filled with wobbly Formica tables, napkins wedged under their legs in a futile attempt to keep them stable. When there's only one bar in town, it better have enough room for everyone, and Charlie's had plenty.

Tonight, it was nowhere near full. A few tables were occupied by couples—almost nothing depressed me more about Williston than watching someone's date night unfold at Charlie's— and the barstools were mostly taken. Granted, the sun hadn't even gone down yet, but in July the place should have been lousy with tourists looking to use a bathroom or have one quick pint before they got back into their cars. Looking around, it might as well have been February.

Serena was sitting at the bar; when she saw me, she lifted one arm in greeting. When she saw Owen, she lowered it, annoyance flashing across her face.

"Hey," I said, sliding onto the stool next to her. "What's going on?"

"Shh," she said. "Listen."

Owen hovered behind us. I bowed my head as if that would allow me to hear better. First I had to tune out the jukebox, which was playing that Badfinger song "Come and Get It," and then I was able to pick up the voices drifting down from the other end of the bar.

"Don't you think you should tell the sheriff?" someone said.

"Tell him what? I know what I saw, but it's not like I got a picture of her."

"You're sure it was her?"

"I recognized her by the clothes. You remember how she used to dress? Like she thought she was in a movie? Long blonde hair, red lipstick, some fancy gown. Just walking down the road in the middle of the night."

I lifted my eyes to get a look at the raconteur. She looked familiar, but I couldn't think of her name. Her hair was a deep blue-black, pulled into a bun that sat primly on top of her head. She was wearing workout clothes, shiny nylon leggings and a purple top that looked like it was supposed to wick sweat or trap body heat or something equally fancy. Even though she was seated at the bar, I could tell she was unusually tall. She had perfect posture, unlike most Charlie's patrons, who tended to slump, the curve of their spines directly proportional to the amount of hours they had clocked at the bar that evening. At closing time, their noses were nearly touching the wood, except for those who fell asleep with their cheeks nestled cozily against the sticky varnish and needed to be roused by the bartender with harsh words and coffee so they could stumble outside to their trucks and drive home.

The woman was drinking a Bloody Mary; she paused to fish one of the olives out of the glass with her straw. She used it to emphasize the next part of her story, pointing the straw, olive still speared onto the end, at her companion, a woman who had her back to us.

"Can you imagine? Where on earth has she been this whole time? I know she was mixed up with a lot of different boys—she must have run off with some boy, that's what I think, and I bet now he's tired of her and she wants to come home—"

Serena half rose from her stool, eyes filled with hateful intentions at hearing Betty bad-mouthed. I gripped her tightly at the waist and whispered into her ear. "Don't." She glared at me, too, but settled down and took a big swig of her beer. I kept my hands on her, moved my stool a little closer. Her face didn't soften, but she didn't pull away, either.

"Or maybe," the woman continued, "she's just been playing a big joke this whole time. Some kind of prank." At last she ate her olive, chewing it more than seemed necessary. She plunged her straw back into the glass and sucked up the remainder of her drink. Her cigarettes and lighter were beside her; she slid them toward the bartender and stood up. "Can you keep an eye on these, Jed? Just put them behind the bar somewhere. I have to go teach an aerobics class. I'll be back in a couple of hours." Behind me, Owen snorted.

"Maybe it was her ghost," Serena said loudly. "Maybe you did see her. But that doesn't mean she isn't dead."

The aerobics instructor didn't respond, only smirked smugly in our direction and walked out the door without saying good-bye to the woman she'd been talking to. I figured they were just acquaintances, that the aerobics instructor had come down to Charlie's with the simple intention of telling her story to whoever happened to be sitting at the bar. But then the remaining woman turned her head, and suddenly I wasn't so sure.

"Jed, could I have another shot of Powers? And a Narragan-sett. Thanks," Emily Shepard said.

Before Owen or I could move, she was already coming our way. She had a good buzz going—something in her loose-limbed movements gave it away—but her eyes were still sharp, and when she settled them on Owen, he took a step back.

"Owen," she said.

"Emily," he answered.

"Come outside with me."

He followed her obediently onto the back deck, overlooking the water.

"Who is that?" Serena asked me.

"One of Owen's cousins. I forget how they're related, exactly."

"Why does she look so familiar?"

I waited until the bartender's back was turned, then I chugged the rest of Serena's beer. "She was sheriff for something like eight years. She was still sheriff when Betty died."

"You think she's seen Calder's confession?"

"I'm sure she has. She might have even been there when he gave it."

"Let's kidnap her," Serena said angrily. "Tie her up some-where, pull out her fingernails until she tells us what she knows."

"A lot of good it would do us. What could she tell us? Calder killed Betty? Yeah, news flash. Nobody cares." I sipped my drink. "She sure seems pissed at Owen, though."

"What were you doing at his place, anyway?" Serena asked.

"I'll tell you in a minute. Hang on."

I crossed the dance floor and stood just inside the door that led out onto the deck. I cracked the door open and leaned my ear toward the narrow opening. The deck faced the water; I could smell the ocean and hear the faint hiss of waves against the rocks. Over that were low voices, Owen's and Emily's.

"I mean it," Emily was saying sternly. "I can't protect you anymore. You need to get out. Now."

"It's not that easy," Owen said.

"You're a smart kid," she said. "Figure it out."

I'd heard enough, so I went back to Serena.

"So?" she said expectantly.

"So what?"

"You were about to tell me why you were at Owen's."

"I talked to Calder today."

"What?" Serena said, shocked.

I related everything that had happened—except for the part about seeing Silas again. After hearing what Emily said— knowing that even she knew about Owen's side business—I was suddenly thinking in terms of who could be called to testify. The fewer of us there were, the better. I was already regretting that clandestine look through the truck's windshield. Curiosity killed the cat, but satisfaction brought it back. Something like that.

"Jesus Christ," Serena said, whatever anger or jealousy she'd felt instantly evaporating. She put an arm around my shoulder, and I leaned into her as far as I could without knocking her off her stool.

"It's okay," I mumbled. "What do you think we should do?"

"Right now? I think we should wait. In a couple of hours, that prissy cunt will be back here and the bar will be full, and she'll be telling that story to anyone who will listen. I want to see what happens when she does. Let's find out who in Williston believes in ghosts."

"You know what she saw, right?"

Serena nodded. "Caroline."

"Dressed up in Betty's clothes, wandering around at night."

"Probably high out of her mind."

"Speaking of—"

Serena was reaching for her wallet before I even finished my thought. "Don't worry, Fin, I've got you covered," she said, and palmed me a blue.

"Thanks," I said. "I'm kind of having a day."

The back door opened and Owen and Emily came inside, both looking grim and unsatisfied. Emily returned to her seat at the far end of the bar, downed her shot of Powers, and started working on her beer.

"Everything okay?" I asked Owen.

He took in the two of us, heads angled together, the proprietary way Serena's arm was wrapped around my waist, and he shook his head. "I'm leaving. You're good here?"

"Yeah," I said. The heat of Serena's hand against the small of my back made it difficult to speak. "I'm good."

"You still want to help out at the diner?" he asked me.

I had offered to do that, hadn't I. "Sure."

"Come by in the morning, before the lunch rush. Don't wear anything fancy."

"Do I ever?"

"Who knows what the fuck you get up to, Finley," he said, and left.

"I take it you guys are fighting again," Serena said when he was gone.

"Not 'again.' More like 'still.' "

"You want a drink?"

"How are you getting served here?"

"Jed goes to my church. You want a drink or not?"

"Sure."

Serena signaled for the bartender. I lit a cigarette, and we were on our way.

True to her word, the aerobics instructor returned a couple of hours later. By then, Jed had told us more about her. Her name was Janet, and she was recently divorced. The aerobics class had been conceived as a way to help her—and other newly single women of Williston—work through their anger by bouncing medicine balls off the walls of the elementary school's gymnasium to a soundtrack composed mostly of Alanis Morissette and Meredith Brooks. Jed complained that the women usually arrived en masse afterward and ordered complicated blender drinks that took forever to make.

"You need a hand?" I offered. "I can blend the shit out of a margarita."

"You're a sweetheart," he said. "But it's bad enough you girls are sitting on that side of the bar. No way I'm letting you back here."

I reached for my wallet. "I've got a license right here that says I'm twenty-one."

"Don't bother. Finley, if your father walks in, you better hide in the ladies' until I send someone to get you."

"He won't," I said. "The paper goes to press tomorrow. He'll be at the office late."

"Better pray to fucking God you're right."

"Does my dad really spend that much time here?" I asked, suddenly very aware that for three-quarters of the year his life was more or less a mystery to me.

"Look around, kiddo. Where else is there to go?" The door opened and a dozen women in athletic wear poured in, Janet included. "Christ," Jed muttered. "Here they come."

"Good luck," Serena said, tilting her glass in his direction.

"All right," I said. "Let's watch the show."

They smelled like sweat and rubber, terry cloth headbands holding back their damp hair as they jostled around the bar and ordered margaritas and chardonnay and cosmopolitans. Emily hadn't moved from her stool in the last two hours, and she recoiled at the sudden commotion, then visibly sighed with relief as the group moved to a cluster of tables, away from the bar. Still, they were loud enough to drown out the jukebox, now playing Nazareth's "Hair of the Dog" and competing with the blender. Once the divorcees all had their drinks in front of them, Janet retrieved her cigarettes from Jed, took a long pull of her margarita, and asked if any of them could guess what she'd seen last night.

"Here we go," Serena said. "She's going to tell it again. I think I need another beer."

"Make it two."

"What?" one of the women asked, licking salt off the rim of her margarita glass. "What did you see?"

Abruptly Emily stood up, grabbing her beer and cigarettes and making for the deck again. She strode across the dance floor like she'd been drinking Sprite for the last few hours, and when she reached the back door she kicked it open with her booted foot, a move she'd clearly perfected on the job.

"Wow," Serena said. "And why exactly isn't she still sheriff?"

"You tell me. I don't even live here anymore."

I got down from the stool, the floor undulating briefly beneath my feet. Janet was about to launch into her story, but right now the woman who had been sheriff when Betty had died was drunk and alone on the back deck, clearly upset about something. If I was ever going to get any information out of her, this would be the time.

"Where are you going?" asked Serena.

I nodded toward the deck. "Fresh air. You stay here and listen to this. I want to talk to her."

"I thought you said there was no point."

That had been two hours, four beers, and an unknown number of milligrams ago. Now I saw things a different way. Why not talk to Emily? So what if she couldn't give me any information? Who cared if she told me to go fuck myself? When the summer was over, I'd never have to come back to Williston again.

Outside the rain had stopped and the fog had rolled in across the sea. The clouds were either dispersing or simply gathering their strength, I couldn't tell, although a few snatches of inky black sky showed around the seams. Emily didn't turn around when she heard the door close behind me.

"Hey, Finley," she said.

"How'd you know it was me?"

"I used to be a cop, remember? Besides, I figured if there was anyone else who couldn't bear to hear that twat tell her story again, it would be you. And now she's going to tell all her little friends, and by tomorrow it'll be all over town."

"You don't believe her?"

Now Emily turned to me. "I know you and Betty were close. Don't let that dumb bitch get your hopes up. I don't know what she saw, but it wasn't Betty."

"But they never found her body. How can you be so sure?"

Emily's eyes were, unbelievably, as sharp as they had been two hours ago. "Don't insult me by playing stupid. You're not stupid, I know that much."

I dropped all pretense. "Nobody ever called me. In New York. If she had run away, she would have come to me, and I never even got a call from any of you people, asking if I'd seen or heard from her. Yeah, I guess I did the math."

"If you know so much, why are you bothering me?" she said wearily.

"That's just what I know. You know a hell of a lot more."

"I can't tell you any of that."

"So what *can* you tell me?"

She cleared her throat. "I was already on my way out when it happened. I'd been fired as sheriff, given notice at the department. I'd gone up against Leroy Miller too many times. He wanted someone more, I don't know, agreeable. And then Betty disappeared, and his son was the prime suspect, and I knew if I didn't clear the case while I was still sheriff it would never happen. I had my chance, and I blew it."

"The confession?"

She looked away, over the balcony. "I can't answer that."

"Was there ever anything to go on, besides the confession?"

"There was nothing. Nothing washes away evidence like the ocean. We never found the witness."

I lit a cigarette, trying to stay composed. "The witness?"

Emily shook her head. "I meant *a* witness, any witness. Someone who could put them together that night. Someone who might have been on the beach, or saw what happened from a distance." She took a deep drag of her cigarette. "If there was someone like that, we never found them."

"Right."

"There's three ways Betty's killer could still be caught and punished. One, her body turns up, and somehow there's enough physical evidence left to lead us back to who did it. Not us"—she corrected herself—"them. It's not my job anymore. Anyway, I don't think that's very likely. Second, a witness comes forward, says he or she saw what happened that night. After all this time? Seems pretty unlikely, too."

"And the third?" I prompted.

"If whoever did it confesses."

"Which you also think is unlikely."

She looked me straight in the eye, and I held on to my composure. "What was your plan, huh? Rattle him hard enough and let his conscience do the rest? Do you know who you're dealing with?" She lowered her voice. "Leroy Miller would never let it happen. If you mess with his family, he won't come after you. He'll go after your father. He'll go after Owen. He'll go after your new girlfriend in there. You're here for what, another month? Think about the people who'll stay behind. You want my advice? Leave it alone."

"Can't you just tell me why he did it?" I pleaded.

"You know, if I thought it would help, I actually might." She took a swallow of her beer. "Now it's my turn to ask the questions. Is Owen working for Silas?"

"I can't answer that."

She rested her elbows on the railing and hung her head. "Christ Jesus. I thought I was helping him. He's family, he was in a bind. Who cared if he sold a little shit behind the diner once in a while? So I looked the other way. But this, Finley—he's in over his head. I've seen that guy's record, it's not pretty. God, I have never felt so fucking helpless in my life."

"Tell me what to do," I said. "Tell me how to help him and I'll do it."

"Convince him to stop doing business with Silas."

"I never said he was. But let's say, hypothetically, I had tried that already and it didn't work. What then?"

"Tell him to sell the diner and go to college. There's enough Shepards in this town to look after his parents."

"Why don't you tell him that?"

"I did. I don't think it took."

I finished my cigarette and threw it over the side, where it disappeared into the spray on the rocks below. "I better get back inside."

"You be careful with that girl," Emily said.

"Careful? Careful how?"

"A little discretion never hurt anyone."

As I started for the door, my mouth filled with saliva, and bile backed up into my esophagus. I swallowed hard.

"I'm sorry, Finley," Emily said. "I really am. I let her down."

"Yeah," I said hoarsely. "I'm sorry, too."

Inside, I headed straight for the ladies' room. I locked the door and dropped to my knees, barely managing to get the seat up in time. I threw up the beers and that single bite of grilled cheese from the afternoon, heaving so violently into the toilet my eyes filled with tears. Even when my stomach was empty, the convulsions kept coming—hands gripping the porcelain, my whole body shuddering, body slumped over the bowl, until finally I was beyond empty and I sat there on the floor wiping my face and laughing. There was something cathartic about it, like this was exactly where I should be, what I deserved. I knew it was just the pills that made me feel that way, but I remembered what Caroline had said, and I knew what she meant now: even the puking felt good.

"So what's the verdict?" I asked Serena as I took my seat again on the stool beside her. "Does Williston believe in ghosts?"

"Are you okay?"

"Better now. Did Janet finish telling her story?"

"Yeah."

"Do they really think it was Betty?"

"They seem a bit divided on the subject," Serena said, looking over her shoulder. The divorcees were still in a huddle at their table. "It's going to be all over town by tomorrow. I don't like this. If word gets around that someone saw Betty alive, Calder might start to relax."

"Or he could just look in his sister's closet, and he'd know what Janet really saw."

"We could just tell people, you know. That it was Caroline."

"No." I couldn't explain it, but I still felt strangely protective of her. If Caroline was becoming addicted to painkillers or slowly losing her mind, I wasn't going to be the one to out her. "Maybe it won't be a bad thing if Calder lets his guard down a little."

"What did Emily say?"

I sketched out the conversation, and Serena listened, thoughtfully sipping her beer.

"She said 'the witness' the first time? You're sure."

"She's pretty lit. She probably just misspoke."

"Or maybe she was trying to tell you something."

"Why would she do that one minute, and then turn around the next and tell me to quit fucking with the Millers?"

Serena shook her head. "You know, it doesn't matter if it's true. All we have to do is make people *think* that it's true. Make Calder think that it's true. If we could get him to believe someone saw him do it—"

"And how are we supposed to do that?"

"We do what Janet's doing. We start a rumor."

....

I made it to the diner by eleven A.M. Owen gave me a once-over, a disapproving glance, and an apron, then pointed me toward the kitchen, where the breakfast dishes were waiting.

"Jesus H.," I said when I saw the mess.

"No complaining. You volunteered for this."

"Yeah," I said, pulling the apron over my head, "but I never thought you'd actually take me up on it."

"I want you where I can keep an eye on you."

"And who's going to keep an eye on *you*, Owen?"

"Just get to fucking work. Here," he said, handing me a pair of yellow rubber gloves. "You should probably wear these."

I snapped them on like I was getting ready to perform surgery. "Thanks," I grunted.

"I don't know what you're so cranky about. At least back here you don't have to talk to anyone."

"Oh, yeah?" I said. "You want to trade places? You can do dishes and I'll pour people coffee and make chitchat."

"No dice."

"That's what I thought," I called after him as he went back out front.

I washed the dishes. All the dishes. I hosed them down with the sprayer and scrubbed them with Brillo pads, racked them and set them aside to dry. I washed every fucking coffee mug from breakfast, and used steel wool to scrape bacon grease off spatulas until my forearms ached. Just as I was finishing, fantasizing about going out the back door and smoking a cigarette in the alley, the lunch rush started and suddenly the sink was full all over again.

A couple of hours later, when the Halyard had quieted down again, I followed Jenny out the back door when she took a smoke break.

Jenny had been a few years ahead of us, quiet, the middle child of a large brood whose most memorable feature was her ability to stay out of everyone's way. She wore her straight brown hair pulled back in a ponytail, an apron over her jeans and black V-neck T-shirt. This was her first summer at the diner, but she seemed okay. She moved with efficiency and economy, and since Owen didn't complain about her I assumed she was a decent waitress.

"Hey," she said as I stepped outside.

"Hey."

The sun was making a rare appearance, but in the shade of the alley I still felt chilled; it didn't help that my clothes were soaked beneath the apron. My cigarettes were tucked safely in my back pocket, and I lit one with relief, leaning against the wall next to the Dumpster and sighing.

"Rough night?" Jenny asked.

"Is it that obvious?"

"You're not the only one. There were a couple of ladies in here before, looked like they overdid it at Charlie's."

"Oh, yeah?" I said, trying to be casual.

She looked into the distance, smoke curling up around her face. Then she turned to me. "Hey, you knew that girl, right? Owen's cousin Betty? The one who disappeared?"

"We were friends, yeah."

"These ladies, they were saying someone saw her. Just a couple days ago. Walking down the side of the highway at night. You think it could be true?"

I took a drag of my cigarette and shook my head. "Not unless it was a ghost."

"Really? You think she's dead? I'm sorry, that's awful."

We start a rumor, Serena had said. *Sure, why not.* "You know how they arrested Calder Miller but never charged him?"

"Yeah?" Jenny said, moving a little closer to me.

"I heard there was a witness. Someone who saw him do it."

"Where did you hear that?" Her voice was skeptical.

I shrugged. "My dad runs the *Messenger.* He has a lot of contacts." After a meaningful pause, I added, "I can't really say anything else."

"If there was a witness, why wouldn't they go to the police?"

"Maybe whoever it was, they were too scared to say anything when it happened, but now, I don't know, maybe their conscience is getting to them." Another meaningful pause. "I probably shouldn't have said anything."

"Jesus. Then who was wearing Betty's clothes on the side of the highway?"

"What?" I said. "You don't believe in ghosts?"

"You don't really think—"

"I don't know what else to think. But something about Williston feels different this summer. Off. There was that fire at the high school. There's no tourists. As far as I'm concerned, this whole fucking town is haunted." I crushed my cigarette under my heel, picked up the butt, and threw it in the Dumpster. I didn't know if it would be enough, but telling

Jenny was a start. At least the last things I'd said were true.

Inside, I went behind the counter and poured myself a cup of coffee. I took off my sodden apron and handed it to Owen. "It's been a pleasure." I took a sip of coffee, but it had been sitting on the burner too long. "This tastes like shit."

"Leaving already?" he said dryly. "I was so enjoying your company today."

"How was your chat with Emily last night?" I asked, unable to help myself.

"Be here again tomorrow. Same time. Try to stay out of trouble between now and then."

"You should really do something about that coffee," I said, and left.

I drove to the beach, to the place where Betty had died. I watched the last light drain from the sky, and when it was dark, I stripped down to my underwear and walked into the ocean.

The water was so cold it hurt, but I forced myself to keep going, diving in and swimming out toward the horizon. I rolled over onto my back and stared up at the stars, this patch of sky that had been the last thing she'd ever seen, and I thought about how cold the water must have been in November, and I kept swimming, like if I went far enough out I might be able to find her again.

But there was nothing there. Just cold, wet darkness, just my own guilt and grief, and the shore so far away. This was what Betty had meant when she talked about the unlights. *Finley,* I thought, when I saw how far I was from the shore, *you dumb bitch*.

I started back, slow and steady, but when I tired I didn't stop and think, *Why bother?* I thought, *Fight, bitch, fight.* I forced my numb legs to keep kicking, I forced my weak arms to keep moving through the water until I could feel sand beneath my feet again, and I walked out of the Atlantic and collapsed in a shivering, exhausted heap next to my clothes, too spent to get dressed, and I still didn't feel any better, and I wondered if I ever would.

CHAPTER NINE.

WE GAVE IT about a week. Serena told a few of her fellow churchgoers about the potential eyewitness, and we waited for word to spread. I kept working at the diner to keep Owen and Dad happy, and even though I was mostly exiled to the kitchen I made it a point to emerge periodically, to clear a table or grab a cup of coffee, so I could hear the chatter among the patrons and see if the rumor had stuck. On the nights Jed bartended at Charlie's, Serena and I posted up there, drinking beer and feeding the jukebox, listening.

It took a few days, but finally one evening as Serena and I were programming the jukebox with every track from *Appetite for Destruction*, more for our own sanity than anything else—"If 'Brown Eyed Girl' comes on one more time," she said, "I will fucking stab someone"—we overheard a conversation at one of the tables. It was a middle-aged couple. The man was eating peanuts and throwing the shells onto the floor. Serena and I stilled when we heard Calder's name.

"I think it's ridiculous," the man was saying. "Calder Miller didn't kill anybody. They don't even know if that girl is dead. Didn't someone just see her near town the other day?"

"I'm just telling you what I heard."

"Well, it sounds like bullshit to me."

"Fuck," I whispered to Serena.

She angrily punched the code for "Rocket Queen" into the machine, and we went back to our seats.

"At least they're talking about it," I said.

"What good does it do if they don't believe it?"

"We can't make them believe it."

"Maybe we can," she said.

"Oh, yeah? How?"

She looked at me, narrowing her gray eyes. "They'll believe it if they read about it in the paper."

I snorted. "You think my dad will put something like that in the paper just because I ask him to? Are you kidding?"

"I wasn't really thinking about asking his permission."

My smile faded. "No way. No fucking way."

"Come on. You've got keys to the office, right? How hard would it be to go in there one night after he's put the paper to bed and just make a few changes?"

"Do you have any idea how much trouble he could get into?" I lowered my voice, not that anyone could hear me over "Welcome to the Jungle." "You and I telling a few lies is one thing. Putting something like that in the paper? That's libel. Leroy could sue my father, bankrupt him, shut down the paper—"

"Okay, calm down. It was just an idea."

I grabbed my cigarettes and headed for the deck, welcoming

the fresh air after sitting inside for so long. The clouds had returned, bringing with them a prickling drizzle. Leaning over the
railing, I watched the waves far below.

Serena approached me softly, putting her arms around my
waist. "I'm sorry, okay? It was a stupid idea." She stroked my hair
back from my forehead and kissed me, hard. "Please don't be
mad at me."

I pushed her away. "I'm not mad. I don't know what I am. I'm
just sick of feeling—" What had Emily said? "So fucking helpless."

"I know, Finley. I know how you feel."

I stared out at the water for a long time, thinking. "Maybe
there is a way. To slip it into the paper. Without mentioning any
names, so my dad can't get in trouble. He still wouldn't be happy
about it, but I don't know. It might work."

"What might work?"

"The police blotter."

We spent the rest of the night crafting the perfect two-line item
(*Caller reported witnessing a crime last November, claiming he
wanted to come forward but was afraid he would be prosecuted for
not doing so sooner*) and the next night, after Dad put the *Messenger* to bed around nine, it was easy enough to sneak into the
office and make the tiniest addition to the files on his computer.

The day the paper came out, our softball team was playing
Pullman again. This time, we were the visitors, and everyone
drove to the game like they were going to a funeral. I dragged

Serena along; if Jack Emerson nailed Calder in the head this time, I didn't want her to miss it.

We sat at the top of the bleachers, where we could better survey the entire scene—Leroy in the bottom row with Mrs. Miller, Caroline nowhere to be seen; Calder in the dugout, staring straight ahead and not talking to any of his teammates; my father, notebook in hand, mini-cooler of beer at his feet; Owen flexing his hand inside his glove and chewing gum like he was hoping he might choke on it and be put out of his misery. From the pitcher's mound, Jack scanned the Williston bleachers, and I had a feeling I knew who he was looking for.

I pressed my thigh against Serena's; finally, perhaps, we were making some progress. A hush had fallen over Williston, a tense expectancy heightened by the fact that it was clear now that the tourists weren't coming, the weather wasn't getting any better, and come winter the town would be fucked. The Williston side of the bleachers was filled with tight, worried faces, and my heart swelled with an evil gladness when I looked at them. The more miserable they seemed, the better I felt. Let them all get what they deserved.

The game itself was uneventful. They scored, then we scored, whatever. It wasn't a blowout like the last one, but in the end we still lost in a sort of bored, desultory fashion that implied we had other things on our minds. When the crowd began to disperse—the Pullman side to its local bar to celebrate, the Williston side back to Charlie's, but with far less cheer—I grabbed Serena's hand and we followed Jack, at a distance, as he made his way back to his car.

He was parked on a side street. I started to speed up—I wanted to catch him before he drove away—but Serena yanked my arm suddenly, pulling me behind someone's minivan.

"What is it?" I whispered.

Look, she mouthed.

Caroline was waiting for Jack, sitting on his hood with her back against the windshield and her arms spread out crucifixion-style. She wore one of Betty's least flamboyant outfits, a plain black shirtdress and espadrilles that tied around her ankles; no one else would have recognized its origin, no one besides me and Serena. Even as Jack approached, she didn't move. Then he called her name, and finally she stirred.

"What took you so long?" she said.

"What are you doing here?" he said.

"I wanted to talk to you."

"Caroline, I don't think that's a very good idea. Where's the rest of your family?"

"I don't know. I came alone."

He cupped her chin in his hand and pulled her face close to his, squinting; he shook his head in disgust. I guessed he was trying to get a good look at whatever was left of her pupils. "Goddammit, Caroline, not again with that stuff."

"Oh, please, what the fuck do you care?"

"Don't say that."

"Then why—"

"Let's not do this again. You know why."

"I can only say 'I'm sorry' so many times."

"It's not your fault. You're just a kid, and I should have known better. But you shouldn't be here. If your dad sees us, or your brother—"

"Then let's go somewhere." She slid off the hood of the car, her skirt riding up and briefly revealing a plain, good-girl pair of white cotton panties before it fell back down to her knees. The espadrilles had a good four-inch wedge heel, and she wobbled unsteadily, listing to one side like a sinking ship until Jack grabbed her shoulders and righted her.

"No way," he said.

"Please?"

She sounded so desperate and entreating, I don't think I could've said no to her, but Jack held fast. He must have been legitimately frightened of Calder and Leroy, and I didn't blame him.

"Why are you so scared of them?" Caroline asked.

"Because when Calder told your father about us, he almost shut down our business. He sent in inspectors, held up our building permits. My dad had to pay thousands of dollars in fines. We're still recovering," he said, irritated, like he had explained the situation to her a dozen times before. "Come on, Caroline, you know all of this."

Serena and I glanced at each other. Was it possible that Jack's animosity toward Calder had nothing to do with Betty? Were we crouched behind this vehicle for no reason?

"Are you sure that's it?" Caroline asked. "And it's not because you think my brother killed Betty?"

Jack said nothing for a long time. "You were sure he didn't do it."

"What if I'm not so sure now?"

"Why would you change your mind?"

"I didn't say I had."

"You're not making any sense. You should go home and sleep it off. And flush the rest of those pills down the toilet. And you tell Owen Shepard if he sells you any more, he's going to get a lot worse than a softball to the gut when I see him next." Christ, was there anyone in Maine who didn't know Owen was a drug dealer?

Jack got into his car and slammed the door. Caroline stood on the sidewalk hugging herself, crying softly. I felt sorry for her; it sounded like Calder had destroyed whatever she and Jack had, and then Leroy set out to punish Jack for having it with her in the first place. I thought about what Emily had told me, that Leroy wouldn't come for me but for the people I loved, the people who would be trapped in Williston long after I'd moved into my dorm room at NYU. And the Emersons didn't even live in Williston. Just how vast was Leroy's reach?

Jack drove away, leaving Caroline behind.

"Should we say something to her?" I whispered to Serena.

She shook her head. "Let's get out of here."

I kept one hand on Serena's thigh as I drove, silently replaying Caroline and Jack's conversation. Were we the reason she was having doubts about Calder's innocence? Had our campaign, the posters and the rumors and our little item in the paper, been that successful?

But Caroline wasn't the one who was supposed to be tortured by it.

"Charlie's?" Serena asked, like she was reading my mind.

"Let's get a closer look at Calder," I said. "I want to know why Caroline's having doubts."

I parked off Main Street. "Wait," Serena said before I could open my door.

"What?" I said, turning to her.

She sprang at me from the passenger seat, kissing me, hands in my hair, pulling at my shirt, frantically unbuttoning my jeans. She pushed her seat back and reclined it, then guided me over the gearshift so I was half-sitting, half-lying on top of her, both of us facing the windshield, her hands prowling under my shirt, exploring farther and farther. I craned my neck so I could keep kissing her, but when her fingers reached their destination I threw my head back, gasping quick and sharp. I came in less than a minute, my thighs shuddering, whole body convulsing in a way not unlike when I had gotten sick in the bathroom at Charlie's. Serena stroked my stomach gently while I tried to catch my breath, but when I moved to reverse our positions, she stopped me.

"No?" I asked.

"Later," she said, grinning mischievously behind the curtain of black hair that had fallen over her face.

"Okay," I said, and kissed her.

My knees were still trembling when we got out of the car.

"Wait," she said, trying to smooth my mussed hair. She shook her head. "It's no use."

"What?" I asked. "How do I look?"

"Freshly fucked."

"Oh, well," I said, taking her hand and leading the way to the bar.

We separated before we walked in, unconsciously putting negative space between our bodies. I could still feel her hands on me, her breath on my cheek, hear my own muffled cries echoing in my ears even as we were swallowed up by the din and chaos of the bar. People looked at us as we made our way inside, and I could see the knowing in those looks, and I realized my relationship with Serena was as much an open secret as Owen's dealing, and what I had been trying to tell him all summer—that there were no secrets in this town—applied just as much to me.

I felt as exposed as if I'd opened my eyes while Serena had her hand in my pants and seen them all there, watching us through the windshield.

Sweat bloomed under my arms. Serena must have sensed my anxiety. "Just ignore them," she said.

"I'm trying," I replied.

Everyone was there. Or at least that's how it seemed. Logically, I understood there was no way a town of 1,300 could fit inside a bar even as spacious as Charlie's, but I recognized every single person. The softball team still in their uniforms. Calder sat at a table with Rebecca and Shelly and a bunch of kids I recognized from Shelly's party. Charlie's was pretty relaxed about serving older teenagers if their parents were there. I looked around until I spotted the elder Millers, Leroy drinking a Budweiser like it made him a man of the fucking people, his wife sipping tentatively at a glass of white wine I was sure had come out of a jug. I didn't see Caroline anywhere. Janet and her divorcees had commandeered two tables, and the usual regulars were lined up on their barstools. I figured Owen was underneath the deck, selling somebody something, and that eventually he would surface.

"I'll get us a couple of beers," Serena said. "See if you can get close enough to Calder to hear what they're all talking about."

I was heading in that direction, reaching for my cigarettes, when a hand clamped down on my arm, hard. I looked up, annoyed, expecting Owen—I blamed him for anything that irritated me—and instead found myself face-to-face with my father, whom I had scrupulously avoided all week.

"Come with me," he said.

For once, I didn't argue. I let him steer me out the door, to the farthest corner of the back deck. It was chilly, and I'd left my hoodie in the car, so I tried to chafe the goose bumps from my forearms and avoid eye contact with Dad.

"I warned you, Finley," he said. "I really did."

"What are you—"

"You thought you could slip something into the police blotter and I wouldn't notice? Or you knew I would figure it out eventually, and you just didn't care?"

"It's all anonymous. There's no names, no way for you to get in trouble—"

"You snuck into my office, you altered my newspaper before it went to press, you printed something false in my fucking paper. Great, so the Millers can't sue me. That doesn't make me feel any better. That doesn't solve my problem."

"Which is?"

"You're unrecognizable to me," he said. "I don't know who you are, I can't trust you, and I don't want you living in my house anymore."

"Dad, I'm sorry—"

"I don't believe you. I don't believe anything that comes out of that mouth. Tomorrow you can call your mother and tell her you're coming home. And I want to be there when you do it. I want to make sure you tell her why."

I was ashamed, because I knew he was right. I was a liar, and I wasn't sorry about what I had done, and even as I stood in front of him trying to arrange my facial expression into some approximation of contrition, I was already scheming—he could make me leave his house, but he couldn't make me leave Williston; I could sleep in my car; I could stay at Owen's; I had Serena and we had unfinished business, Betty's and our own. I would do it again, and I would do worse, until Calder had gotten what I decided he deserved.

"Give me your keys to the office," he said.

"Seriously?"

"Seriously."

My cheeks flushed with shame as I unclipped the carabiner from my belt loop. That's another thing about small towns; you end up with keys to everything. I had my car keys, the keys to the house, the master key to the high school, a set to Owen's cabin and the diner, even a set to his parents' house in case of an emergency; I still had my spare keys to Betty's, too, and I flipped past them sadly until I got to the pair that unlocked my dad's office.

"Here," I said, handing them over. "Do you feel better now?"

"I know you think you're doing all this for Betty, but you're not. You're doing this for you. And that other girl. Serena."

"That's bullshit."

"Whose idea was it? Yours or hers?"

Even my dad knew about me and Serena. "It was my idea," I said, meeting his eyes defiantly, making a point of not moving mine to the left, the classic liar's tell you learn if you watch enough movies.

"Let me tell you something," he said, leaning down so he could whisper in my ear. "And if you've got a brain in that fucking head, you'll take this to heart. You're not half the liar you think you are. When you get home tonight, you better start packing."

He left me there, shivering. I lit up with shaking hands and smoked, listening to the muted sound of Charlie's at full bore. No one else was on the deck. As I was about to finish my cigarette, Serena showed up with my beer.

"Your dad?" she asked.

I nodded, taking a long pull. It only made me colder; I wished it were whiskey instead. I would have even settled for Fighting Cock.

"I just saw him leave," she said. "He looked pissed."

"He found out. About what we did to the police blotter. He wants me out of the house. He told me to go back to New York."

She put her arm around me. "It'll blow over. We'll figure something out until it does."

"Yeah. I know," I said, leaning into her.

"Come on, you're freezing. Let's get you back inside." I followed her numbly as she took my hand and led me through the back door. No point being discreet anymore.

Something was happening. We both felt it before we saw it. A hush had fallen over the room; every conversation had died, every patron was frozen in place, some with their drinks en route to their lips. REO Speedwagon was playing on the jukebox, "Can't Fight This Feeling," and beneath it all was that hum of anticipation that only comes in the instant before something terrible happens—before someone throws the first punch, before the storm takes out the power, before the flames catch and start climbing the walls like vines.

For one second, I thought the crowd was going to unpause and turn toward me; I don't know why I thought that, aside from my own self-absorption, but it did occur to me that the jig was up, so to speak, and that I was about to pay, in spades, for every shady thing I thought I'd gotten away with so far that summer. It had already started, with my father. I'd targeted Williston's golden boy, and now the lynch mob I'd tried to send in his direction was going to come after me.

It was Serena who brought me back from this brief, dark reverie, elbowing me and pointing toward the door. "Look," she said, grabbing my beer and setting it down on a nearby table.

I was about to protest the loss of my drink at the moment I might need it most when I saw them—the two police officers standing just inside the door, scanning the crowd.

We drew closer together as they came farther inside. One spotted the Millers and made the smallest indication to his partner, but still, we all saw it, I *felt* us all seeing it.

Calder was standing with his parents, and as the cops began walking toward them, he shrank back. Leroy put a reassuring hand on his son's shoulder, but a grim expression spread across his features, as if he knew he was finally facing the inevitable. Calder's face remained impassive, but I actually saw his eyes flicker toward the back door, possibly contemplating an escape attempt.

This was *it*, it was finally *happening*, and in front of the whole fucking town, no less. They were going to slap the cuffs on Calder in the middle of Charlie's, and his life would be ruined and at last I could get on with mine. Mission fucking accomplished. Serena and I were going to watch Calder get arrested and then find someplace to have epic, victorious sex.

The cops spoke to the Millers quietly, so no one else could hear, although not a single person in that bar bothered to pretend they weren't straining to catch the conversation. When Mrs. Miller let out a desperate wail I had to force myself to hold back a triumphant cry of my own. I could feel it forming in my throat, and I grabbed Serena's wrist in an effort to control myself. An unfamiliar madness took hold of me, and I was terrified I might start laughing or clapping with childlike delight.

But something was wrong. The police weren't handcuffing Calder or leading him away. They were not eyeing him with suspicion or contempt; they did not look satisfied to be, finally, apprehending a murderer who had managed to elude them for the better part of a year. No, they looked sympathetic and grave, as if they were delivering bad news, and now tears were streaming down Calder's face and my fleeting giddiness was replaced with a horrible understanding. The police led the Millers out of Charlie's, and as soon as the door closed behind them it was like someone had turned the volume back up. I looked at Serena; I was leaning on her for support now. The news swirled around us but her name was already on my lips.

"Caroline."

She'd been in an accident driving home from Pullman. No one knew if she was alive or dead, but Charlie's was on fire with speculation. We'd seen her with Jack, we'd known what shape she was in, we hadn't given a single thought to how she was getting home—but I had to put my guilt aside if I wanted to prevent the next inevitable, terrible thing from happening.

I dragged Serena out the door and found a pay phone on the corner. The Halyard was closed; the cabin phone was busy. "Fuck!" I dropped the receiver and sprinted to my car.

"Where are we going?" Serena asked as I floored it.

I didn't answer. I drove as fast as I dared on the dark, slick highway, certain that at any minute I would hear sirens behind me, that I wouldn't get there in time, that the universe had somehow misinterpreted my fervent desires and tonight Owen would be the one I'd see handcuffed and taken away.

The driveway was empty; the cabin was dark. I kicked the side of the house in frustration and sank into a defeated crouch, my head in my hands.

"Finley," Serena said gently, guiding me to sit next to her on the steps, "tell me what's going on, and we'll figure it out. Let me help."

"When they find the drugs in Caroline's system, they'll come for him. There're enough people in this town who know what he does. And if he gets arrested—" Between Leroy and Silas, Owen would pay.

"Okay," Serena said calmly. "He's not at home, or at Charlie's, or at the diner. So where could he be?"

I knew Owen. Stone cold. And I knew where to find him. But none of us were going to like it.

I passed the narrow driveway by accident the first time, missing it in the dark; I drove past on purpose the second time, pulling a quick U-turn farther down the road and killing the headlights. As soon as I pulled in I put the Subaru in neutral and turned off the engine, coasting just far enough that my car would be hidden from the road.

"You stay here," I said to Serena as she started to unbuckle her seat belt.

"No fucking way," she said.

"Do you know whose place this is?"

"I think I'm starting to put the pieces together, yeah."

"Then please, I'm begging you, stay in the car."

"Not a chance." She got out, holding the latch inside the door so the dome light stayed dark.

We crept up the narrow drive. The rain had started again in earnest, and this time I was glad, hoping the sound would mask our weak attempt at stealth. I tried not to think about what Emily had said about Silas's criminal record, or whether or not Caroline was dead; instead, I tried to calculate the over/under of Owen ever speaking to me again after tonight, if he would weigh the fact that I was trying to save his ass against the absolute, inarguable stupidity of what I was doing. I put the odds at an even fifty-fifty.

His truck was parked in the clearing, and I sighed with relief. At least I had successfully located him. Sort of. There were no lights on in the house, but I remembered Owen telling me it was essentially abandoned.

"Is that a wigwam?" Serena whispered.

"I'm afraid so."

The wigwam, Silas's actual dwelling, looked dark as well, but for all I knew it had no electricity. We got closer, sticking to the edge of the clearing where there was some coverage from the trees and brush. I was glad Serena couldn't see the feathers; I suspected they would have freaked her out even more. I strained my senses—could I hear voices? Smell a fire?—but all I could tell was it was fucking pouring.

"Maybe we should just go back to the car," I whispered. "Wait for him to leave, catch him on the way out."

"So if the cops show up we'll be the first thing they see. Great."

"What do you suggest then?"

She shrugged. "In for a penny, in for a pound." Leaving the relative shelter of the clearing, she strode toward the wigwam.

Silas appeared out of the darkness like he'd been there all along, watching us with amusement. I honestly couldn't tell where he had come from. Shirtless and barefoot, wearing the same patchwork corduroy pants, his enormous blond dread-locks glistening with rain, his hemp necklace lying among the few sparse hairs of his tattooed chest.

"Good evening, sisters," he said. "Can I help you?"

Serena was back at my side in an instant. It was up to me, apparently, to do the talking, which made sense. Owen was my friend, after all. My family.

"I need to talk to Owen," I said, loathing myself for being so terrified of this hippie. "It's an emergency."

"And how did you know to find him here?" Silas asked.

"Please, there's not much time. It's his dad," I said with urgency. "His dad's just been rushed to the hospital, he needs to go now."

Silas came closer, and I tried not to step back. He looked me up and down in a way that made me very aware of how my wet shirt was clinging to my skin. "What's your name, sister?"

"Finley."

He glanced at Serena. "And your girlfriend?"

"Never mind about her. Where's Owen?" I said, raising my voice in the hope that he would hear me over the rain if he were nearby.

As if I had willed it, Owen emerged from the wigwam. "Silas? Everything okay?" He saw me and Serena, and I recognized both the murder he had for me in his heart right then, and the fear brought on by my proximity to Silas. "What the fuck—"

I cut him off. "Owen, we have to go. It's your dad. It's an emergency."

He raced toward me, and even in the rain I could smell the

weed on him. "Jesus Christ, what happened? Is he okay?"

"I'll explain everything, you just have to come with me right now." I tossed Serena my car keys. "Take my car, I'll go with him."

Serena didn't have to be told twice. She turned around and sprinted through the clearing and back up the driveway. Owen was already headed for his truck and I hurried to keep up with him.

"I'm sorry, dude, I have to go," he called to Silas over his shoulder. "Where am I going?" he asked me when we were back in the truck. "To the hospital?"

"Just drive. I'll explain when we're back on the highway." I waited until Silas's place was behind us before I said, "Your dad's fine. Where's your stash?"

Owen almost swerved off the road. "Wait, what?"

"Caroline Miller wrecked her car driving home from Pullman. She could be alive or dead, I don't know. What I *do* know is that it's pretty common fucking knowledge that you're her dealer, and when they find that shit in her system Leroy is going to come for you, so tell me, Owen, where's your fucking stash? Is it in your house? Your truck? The diner? Are they going to find it when they show up? What about the cash? You need to get rid of everything, *right now.*"

"It doesn't work that way. I can't just flush ten thousand dollars' worth of—"

"Ten thousand dollars?" I cried.

"—OxyContin down the fucking toilet. Then I'm in to Silas for ten grand."

"So hide it."

"Hide it? Hide it where?"

"I can keep it at my house."

Owen laughed. "So when they finally come to arrest you for the fire, they can find my stash in your mattress? I don't think so."

I fingered the master key on my carabiner. "Okay. Neutral ground, then."

CHAPTER TEN.

THE NEXT DAY, the story was the talk of the diner. Caroline had flipped her car on the highway somewhere between Pullman and Williston; luckily, someone driving behind her had seen it happen. They said she just swerved off the road; maybe she'd been trying to avoid a deer, someone theorized, but I was nine out of ten she'd nodded off behind the wheel.

She wasn't dead, but it had been close, and it still wasn't a sure thing that she'd make it. No one was allowed to see her but family.

Owen closed early, right after lunch, and went home to wait, rather than be confronted in public at the diner. The police, as I'd predicted, came for him that afternoon. I was surprised it had taken Leroy that long to get the warrants through, but he had been tied up at the hospital, after all. The cops searched Owen's cabin and truck and came up empty; after they were gone, I went over and found him sitting on the porch smoking a cigarette, his hand shaking as he brought it to his lips. He was clammy and pale.

"Are you okay?" I asked.

"I threw up. As soon as they were gone. I was afraid if I puked when they were here, it would make me look guilty. So I managed to hold it. And then as soon as they left, I got sick. Then I called you." He looked at me pathetically. I thought he might start crying. "Do you think my parents know? Do you think they've heard yet?"

"I don't know," I whispered.

"What the fuck was I thinking, Fin? What am I going to do?"

I put my arms around him. "It's going to be okay."

"If she dies, it's on me."

"Not entirely," I said, and I told him about seeing Caroline in Pullman after the game.

"I didn't know she was that bad, I swear. I thought she was buying it for her and her friends, I never thought she was doing it all herself. Oh my God Finley, what if she dies?"

"She's not going to die."

"I don't know what to do. Silas is going to want his money. I can't sell anything if the cops are watching me. What do I do?"

"You do nothing, O. You keep opening the diner every morning. You keep checking in on your parents. You stay away from Silas for now. You're just a local who runs the Halyard and serves coffee to everyone in town. And Caroline will get better, Leroy will leave you alone, things will calm down, and we'll figure it out."

"How did shit get so bad so fast?" he asked me.

"I hate to tell you this," I said, as he buried his face in my shoulder, "but shit has been going south for a long time."

"Just please don't say, 'I told you so.'"

I stroked his hair. "I wouldn't dream of it."

The best thing I could do for Owen, I figured, was get him drunk to the point of unconsciousness and put him to bed, even though it was barely five in the afternoon. So I went inside and found a bottle of bourbon, and I sipped one drink while I refilled his glass again and again. Just as I had when Dad had confronted me, I was already scheming, working out a way to get Owen off the hook, out from under Silas, and a vague plan was starting to form in my mind, a nuclear option I wouldn't even consider deploying unless the situation got considerably more dire.

In the meantime, I focused on filling him with liquor until his eyes were red and glassy, the lids tinted purple and starting to droop.

"I know what you're doing," he said.

"And what's that?" I raised an eyebrow, blatantly imitating one of his go-to facial expressions.

"Thank you," he said. "I know I can be a real asshole sometimes, but—"

"Don't get sentimental on me, okay?"

"Just listen to me. I know I'm a hypocrite. I know I have no business saying this after I've been selling that shit all over town. But promise me you'll stay away from it. If anything happened to you—"

"Nothing's going to happen to me. I swear. Come on." I put an arm around him and helped him up. "Let's get you inside. You can sleep it off. Tomorrow is another day."

"Will it be better than this one?"

"It will. You'll see."

But I was wrong about that, too.

Serena wanted to go to Charlie's that night, a reconnaissance mission to gather more information about Caroline and whatever other rumors might be flying around, but I told her she was on her own.

Seeing Owen so shaken had undone something in me—driven home, I supposed, the real-life consequences of what up until now I had essentially treated like a game of Risk or Monopoly. Yes, Owen had sold Caroline the drugs that had gotten her fucked up enough to flip her car; yes, Serena and I had seen her in that condition and not thought twice about whether she'd be driving. But I couldn't stop thinking about her conversation with Jack, the sudden wavering in her belief that her brother was innocent. That was why she had been so upset; that was why she had made the trip to Pullman in the first place. We had done that, Serena and I, and while I should have been glad—wasn't that our intention? To make people realize he was guilty?—it seemed safe to say our plan had backfired, at the very least. Caroline was in the hospital, Owen was closer to being arrested than Calder, and Betty's death—or disappearance, as some in Williston still insisted—was more an afterthought than ever.

Somewhere along the line, I had fucked up.

What if I could choose? Would I have Caroline die, if that would be Calder's punishment? Could I live with my part in it if he knew it had all started with him? If she died, there'd be a body to bury, and a proper funeral, and the whole town would mourn her. No one would pretend she'd never existed, no one would say she had been asking for it. They'd plant a tree for her in the middle of town, they'd name the library after her. Next year, they'd dedicate the yearbook to her and sing a song for her at graduation. And Leroy would make sure that someone paid for it, whether that person deserved it or not.

I wanted her to live. The last thing I wanted was to watch the whole town console Calder and Leroy. I had to believe there was still a way for Calder to get what he deserved.

These were not feelings I particularly wanted to feel. Luckily, I had a couple of blues Serena had given me for a rainy day. It rained every day in Williston now, but I decided this was the day I'd been saving them for. Dad wasn't home yet—I thought about the conversation we'd had on the deck at Charlie's; Christ, wasn't I supposed to be packing and calling Mom?—so I went up to my room, leaving my door ajar so I could hear if he came in, and cleared a space on my desk. I laid a crisp twenty-dollar bill over the pills and pounded them with my lighter until they were fine enough to be carved into lines with my driver's license. Then I rolled up the bill and bent over the desk, resolutely snorting everything in sight.

I took my cigarettes to the screened-in porch at the back of the house and lay there, waiting. A few minutes later, I felt the familiar warmth starting at the base of my spine, spreading over me like a soft blanket. It worked. I stopped picturing Caroline in her hospital bed; I stopped imagining Owen in a prison jumpsuit; I stopped seeing Betty's dead body floating toward the open sea. I stopped thinking much of anything coherent and lost my-self in a blank, pleasant numbness.

Dad must have just followed the smell of cigarette smoke to the back porch; by then I was lying in complete darkness. He sat down beside me. I could sense him weighing his options, trying to decide how to begin.

"You know I wish you wouldn't smoke in the house," he said.

"Technically, this isn't the house."

"You know I wish you wouldn't smoke at all."

"You smoked for twenty years. It's in the blood."

He sighed. "Are you okay?"

"You've been to the hospital? Talked to the cops?"

"Yeah."

"Is she going to die?"

"They still don't know."

"It's my fault." I could say it out loud now without feeling anything.

"No, it isn't, Fin. Don't say that."

"Do you still want me to leave?"

My father surprised me then. He shook one of my cigarettes loose from the pack and lit it with the deftness that comes from muscle memory. It amazed me sometimes, the way the body re-membered things. He stretched out on the chaise lounge next to mine.

"Do you think you can handle being here?" he asked after a moment. "Because so far it doesn't seem like it."

"I don't know," I said. "I really don't know."

He took a deep drag and exhaled. "That is the first thing you've said, since you've come back, that sounds like the truth to me."

The doorbell rang. Dad looked up, startled. I didn't move.

"You expecting someone?" he asked.

"Nope."

He sighed, handed me his cigarette, and went inside the house. I heard him open the front door, the faint murmur of voices. My eyes kept closing without my permission, but I was vaguely aware of footsteps coming in my direction. I sat up and tried to quell the nausea that rippled through me. Looking down at the cigarette in my hand, I somehow knew that even one more drag would push me over the edge and make me sick. I stubbed it out reluctantly and smoothed my hair, hoping I could pass for sober.

Dad flicked on the porch light, and I winced.

"Your friend's here," he said.

Behind him was Danny, who I hadn't seen since he'd sold me cigarettes at the trader. He looked pale and sallow, damp T-shirt sticking to his skin. I stared at him blankly, not sure what he was doing at my house.

"Hey, Finley," he said.

"Hey, Danny," I replied, trying to pull myself out of my stupor.

Dad excused himself as gracefully as he could. "I'm going to make some dinner."

"I'm not hungry," I said.

"Suit yourself," he called over his shoulder.

Danny didn't move. He just stood dripping on the floor and staring at me nervously.

"Have a seat," I told him, and he obediently sat on the edge of the chaise Dad had vacated. "What's up?"

"I need to talk to you. Can I have one of those?" He gestured to my Marlboros.

"Sure." I handed him the pack and lighter, waited for him to take a couple of drags. He coughed the way I had when I'd first learned how to smoke; this was a new habit for him, it was obvious.

"Sorry," he said, covering his mouth with his fist.

"It's okay. It takes practice."

"You always make it look so easy."

"You don't have any news about Caroline, do you?"

He shook his head. "This isn't about Caroline. Well, maybe it sort of is. Mostly, it's about Betty."

I sat up straighter on my chaise. "What's going on?"

"You know how Janet Payne says she saw Betty, on the side of the highway? I don't know when it was exactly, a few nights ago."

"Yeah, I heard about that."

"When she first started telling people, I thought she was full of it. Making it up, I don't know, so she'd have an excuse to sit around Charlie's and collect free drinks. I liked Betty, you know I did. I even asked her out a couple of times but she always said no because she was so hung up on Calder. But I don't think she's out there wandering around Williston at night. I don't think she's out there at all." The ash on his cigarette had grown perilously long; I handed him the empty Diet Coke can I'd been using as an ashtray. Oblivious, he started to raise it to his lips.

I managed to stop him in time. "Christ, Danny, that's an ash-tray. Are you okay?"

"No, I'm not okay," he said. "And I'm trying to explain why."

I fought off another wave of nausea. "I'm listening."

"I was working at the trader last night. It was dead, everyone was in Pullman for the game, but I had to stay open until ten, because I knew everyone would stop in when they got back, buy smokes or chips or whatever before they went over to Charlie's. I was alone in there for hours. You know how the counter faces away from the windows?"

"Yeah," I said, wishing he'd get to the point.

"Well, I was at the counter, doing a crossword puzzle, listening to the radio, just trying to kill time. And I started getting this weird feeling, like someone was watching me. But I knew there was nobody in the store. So I looked outside, and Main Street was totally deserted, but I swear, across the street, under one of the lampposts, I saw her." He tried taking another drag from his cigarette but it only turned him green. Defeated, he dropped the rest of it in the can, where the remains of my soda extinguished it with a soft, final hiss.

"Saw who, Danny?"

He looked up at me for the first time since he'd started talking and wiped his matted hair out of his eyes. "Betty. I swear to God, I saw Betty standing there. She waved at me. I just froze. And then she turned away. I came tearing out from behind the counter, ran out the front door, but by the time I got outside, she was gone."

"Look, Danny," I said. "I don't know who you saw, but it wasn't Betty. Betty's dead."

"I know that!" he cried. "Don't you think I know that? Why the fuck do you think I'm so freaked out? She's dead and I saw her standing around on Main Street. I saw Betty, I swear, and then I heard about Caroline, and I thought maybe, I don't know, Betty had something to do with it. Maybe Betty scared her off the road somehow, caused the accident—"

"Betty would never do something like that."

"Maybe not when she was alive, but now—"

"Are you being serious? You think my dead best friend is going around Williston terrorizing people?"

"I don't know what to think, okay? But I haven't slept since it happened, and I'm scared."

"Why would you have any reason to be scared of Betty?" Something that had nagged at me ever since my visit to the trader was beginning to surface in my mind. I leaned in, so close our knees were almost touching. "Why are you so sure she's dead?"

Danny was nearly in tears now. "I just am."

Nobody can read a liar like another liar. I grabbed him by the shoulders and gave him a good shake. "What aren't you telling me?"

"Nothing, I swear," he said, cowering.

"Bullshit. Whatever it is, I'm going to find out one way or another, and when I do, you really will have something to be afraid of. Do you think I came back here this summer for the fucking lobster rolls?"

"I know why you're here," he said, taking a deep, quivering breath and wiping his eyes. He sniffled and collected himself until he could look me in the face again. "You're here for revenge.

I get it. But I think that's why she's here, too."

"What does that have to do with you? Why would Betty be angry at you?"

"Because," he said, standing up, "she asked me to do something and I wouldn't do it."

"What?" I asked impatiently. "What was it?"

"If you want to know the rest, talk to Owen."

"Owen? Why Owen?"

"Because she asked him first." He turned to go.

"Danny, wait."

He paused in the doorway. "Yeah?"

"Do you still think she killed herself?"

"I wish it were that simple," he said, and left.

When he was gone, I tried calling Serena and then Owen, but there was no answer. I guessed Serena was still at Charlie's gathering intelligence, and Owen was undoubtedly still sleeping off the booze. I did not for one second believe that Danny had seen Betty's ghost, and the timing meant that he hadn't seen Caroline dressed in Betty's clothing either—Caroline had been on her way back from Pullman then, but of course she'd never made it.

There were myriad explanations for Danny's story—he'd fallen asleep at work and dreamt the whole thing, he was a blossoming schizophrenic experiencing his first psychotic break, or it had just been some girl with a passing resemblance to Betty who'd skipped the game and was waving hello to the only other soul on Main Street. But what I couldn't dismiss was the obvious admission that Danny knew more about Betty's death, and his intimation that Owen did, too, left me deeply, deeply shaken. I would have driven to the cabin to confront Owen, but I was in no shape to drive, and Owen was in no shape to answer. I had no choice but to wait until morning.

Unsurprisingly, I couldn't sleep. I thought about my short-lived moment of near triumph at Charlie's, when I thought the police had come to arrest Calder. I imagined them handcuffing him and reading him his rights and taking him away, but even then the dark thoughts crept in and ruined my fantasy. Leroy would get him a sharp, cunning lawyer, a shark in a five-thousand-dollar suit, and Calder would get off by pleading temporary insanity; even if Calder were convicted, he could be out in just a few years. Was there any outcome that might actually satisfy me?

And when I had worn myself out thinking about Calder and justice and revenge, and whether I could even distinguish between those last two anymore, my weary, addled brain settled on the one subject I had painstakingly avoided as much as possible—Betty herself. Not dead Betty, not ghost Betty, not Betty the murder victim, but the girl she had been.

I remembered her with all her flaws intact; her huge-heartedness had always made up for her insecurities and her exhausting, mercurial nature, but there had still been times I wanted to fling myself out of whatever car we were trapped in together rather than endure another recursive conversation about why a certain boy might or might not like her. The endless analyses of looks exchanged across the hallway at school, the mind-numbing decodings of notes slipped into her locker. And all this when we were still in middle school.

Part of me knew that if I'd stayed in Williston, if we'd gone to high school together, we would have drifted apart in a particularly painful way, Betty clinging ever tighter while I desperately tried to shake her off. But my moving to New York had somehow cemented us together: joining me there became her hope for the future, while she was the main thing that kept me tethered to Williston, besides Dad. Our separation meant that I got all the good parts of Betty without having to weather the daily storms of her moods and heartbreaks, without having to constantly face that abyss of need I knew she'd never fill.

But I *had* loved her, whether it was a love left over from our childhood together, or a blind love based on my own uncharacteristically optimistic idea of the person she might someday become. Or maybe it was all of her—that honeyed voice on the other end of the phone, the return address written on her letters in that all-too-familiar cursive, having one person who knew me best and having that person be her. Never in all our years as friends, no matter how long we were apart or how frustrating she became, had that proprietary feeling left me, that she was *mine*, and that meant I was the only one who could roll my eyes at her when she gave in to the histrionics, or comfort her when she was battling the unlights. Me, and nobody else. She'd been mine, and she'd been stolen from me. Taken.

I seized on that word—*taken*—as I lay in bed watching my room slowly brighten as the sun rose, and, like a CD set on repeat, my mind went back to the beginning and started playing track one again, and track one was Calder.

I fell asleep around eight A.M. and woke up at ten. Every part of me that had been so deliciously hollowed out by the pills the night before was now filled with dread as hard and sharp as a diamond in my chest. I was pretty sure Serena's blues had depleted my brain of some essential neurotransmitters; perhaps it was time to take a break. The sleep deprivation didn't help either.

The Halyard was locked, the Closed sign hanging on the inside of the door. All the lights were off. I went into the alley, expecting to find Owen smoking a cigarette, ready with some explanation about how he was too hungover to deal with people today so he was going to do inventory in the basement and the customers could go fuck themselves. But there was nobody there, either, and the back door was locked, too.

"What the shit?" I muttered. Maybe Owen had rallied last night after all, gone on a tear at Charlie's and was too sick to come to work. But Owen was never too sick to come to work. I tried to remember if I'd laid him on his stomach when I put him to bed, or if there was a chance he'd choked to death on his own vomit.

"Finley."

I snapped to attention at the sound of my name. It was Serena, standing at the far end of the alley, by the sidewalk. She was nervously worrying her crucifix on its chain, and her pale face, glowing brightly beneath her shaggy black bob, was tight and anxious.

"What is it?" I said, hurrying to meet her. "What happened?"

"I called your house and nobody answered, and then I remembered you were supposed to be working at the diner, so I got here as soon as I could. I wanted to make sure you heard it from me."

"*Heard what?* What the fuck is it now?"

"It's Owen," she said calmly, raising her hand when I tried to interrupt. "He's okay. But he was arrested this morning."

"For what? They couldn't find anything, they had nothing. What could they arrest him for?"

"Come with me. I can't tell you the rest here."

"Why not?"

"Because you're screaming."

I followed her to her car. I didn't protest or demand more information; I just stared out the window and wondered when it would start raining and if Owen's parents knew yet and who would bail him out. I waited until we were on the beach, the same beach as always, the place where Betty and I used to picnic with Calder, the place where he'd killed her, and where Serena and I had gone on what I sort of considered our first date, the place where my morbid curiosity had almost bested my will to live. Serena led me to the same log where we'd sat that first night and put her arm around me.

"Now will you tell me what happened?" I said.

"I don't know all the details. My mom was at the Halyard when it happened."

"They arrested him at the diner?" I said, horrified, picturing Owen led away in front of all his patrons. I started to cry.

"It's going to be okay."

"How do you know that?"

"They're not going to be able to make it stick."

"He's a fucking drug dealer. Everybody knows. And what about Silas?"

"They didn't arrest him for drugs, Finley."

"Then what?"

"They arrested him for arson. For the fire at the high school."

I cried harder.

"I guess when Leroy found out Owen had covered his tracks with the pills," Serena went on, "he decided to pin something else on him. But look, we know he didn't do it, we know there's not a single shred of proof. This is just a stunt Leroy is pulling. Owen'll be okay. Please stop crying."

I did, abruptly, like a faucet turning off. I stood up.

"Where are you going?"

"All I have done since I got back here is make things worse. At least this I know how to fix."

"What are you talking about?"

"I'll go in there and tell the police I did it, and they'll let Owen out. So I go to prison. Who fucking cares? Maybe NYU will let me defer for the length of my sentence."

"Are you joking?"

"I don't know, am I?"

"You can't do that."

"Don't worry, I'll leave your name out of it. I'll say I acted alone."

"Finley, look, just think for a minute." She came after me, grabbing my arm.

I whirled around in a rage, and for one hideous second I thought I might hit her. She had the same thought; I could see it in the way she flinched, dropping my arm and taking a step back. It occurred to me that Serena had never seen me like this; she'd seen me angry, because I was angry all the time now, but she'd never seen me lose my temper.

"Owen is in jail because of something that we did. That *I* did. Caroline is in the hospital, and when she gets out she'll probably get shipped off straight to rehab. Danny—you know Danny? From the trader?—came to my house last night to tell me he thinks he saw Betty's ghost waving at him from across Main Street. He nearly had a breakdown on my back porch. My father threatened to kick me out and send me home. I don't know what the fuck we thought we were going to accomplish, but we failed, okay? Even that goddamn dog that ran away—that was us. There's been nothing but collateral damage. Betty's still dead and Calder's still free, and the world has one more lacrosse-playing sociopath on the loose, despite all our best efforts. But if I can help Owen, then I will." I started walking away.

"And what about me?" Serena called after me. "You think they'll believe you did it alone? You think you and I are some big secret?"

"I told you, I'll leave your name out of it."

"Goddammit, Finley! You were at graduation. You saw what I did. That makes *me* the girl most likely to set fire to the school.

Nobody really thinks Owen did it, it's just Calder's dad trying to scare him, trying to scare us. If you tell them you did it, they'll know I was there, too, no matter what you say, and then they'll come after me next."

I stopped.

"If you wait a week," she went on, "they'll drop the charges and we can get back to business. What happened to Caroline is not our fault. Her brother's a murderer and she knows it and it's fucked up her head big-time. You're telling me that Danny thinks he saw Betty the other night? Come on, we've got these people seeing fucking ghosts. We can't blink now."

I didn't say anything.

"Let's at least go talk to Emily, okay? See what she says. If she really believes they can make a case against Owen, then fine, go confess, martyr yourself, whatever. But for Christ's sake, he's only been in jail for like an hour. They're probably still taking his fingerprints. Just breathe and think about what you're doing."

"Fine," I said after a long pause. "We'll go see Emily."

Emily lived right outside of town, in a small one-story house you could actually see from the road. Her place looked shabby and cozy, the porch crowded with a precarious-seeming swing and old rocking chairs; hummingbird feeders and long vines of night-blooming jasmine hung from the railing. She hadn't always lived alone; when I was a kid she'd had a willowy "room-mate" with auburn hair and a kind smile. One summer I'd come back to Williston and she was gone.

Emily herself emerged as we were pulling into the unpaved driveway; she watched us from the front door, drinking a PBR longneck inside a Red Sox beer koozie.

"Can you do me a favor?" I asked Serena.

"What?"

"Will you wait in the car this time? Please?"

The pleading tone in my voice must have softened her. "Fine," she said. I leaned over and kissed her, hard, before I got out.

"I was wondering when you would show up," Emily said, taking a seat in one of the rocking chairs. "Come on."

I took the sagging steps up to the porch and joined her. There was a moment of silence.

"So you heard," she said.

"Yeah."

"Poor kid." Emily shook her head and took a long pull from her beer. "Poor kid."

"What's going to happen to him?" I asked.

"He'll spend the night at the station. Tomorrow they'll set his bail, and I'll post it. He'll come home, and then we'll see. Maybe they'll drop the charges, maybe they'll try to indict him. From what I understand, there's no evidence, but Leroy's got it out for him pretty bad. He knows Owen was selling to Caroline, even if he can't prove it. And even if the police drop the charges, they'll be watching him. I'm afraid Owen's little side business is over."

I thought of Silas, and the ten thousand dollars' worth of pills I'd helped Owen hide, and my heart constricted inside my chest. It seemed possible Owen would actually be better off in jail.

"How are his parents?" I asked.

Emily just shook her head again.

"What do we do?"

She looked at me like I was an imbecile. "I'm pretty sure, Finley, that the best thing for you to do is nothing. Do you understand now what I was talking about that night?"

"You said that Leroy would go after the people I love. Is that why he's doing this to Owen? Is it because of the drugs, or is it because of me?"

Emily rocked in her chair and stared out over her front lawn, the grass lush and almost psychedelic green from all the rain. "He's not an evil man. I don't like him, and I never have, but I don't think he's evil. I think he's just trying to protect his family. You should be able to understand that. You two share the same brand of blind loyalty."

"But—"

"Have you ever asked yourself what you would do? If it were Owen? Or your dad? Or even her?" She nodded toward the car, where Serena was still waiting patiently in the driver's seat. "Or Betty. If Betty killed somebody, would you turn her in? Would you call the cops? Or would you help her hide the body? Would you do everything in your power to protect her? The difference between Leroy and the rest of us is he's got more power than most. Owen's guilty, Fin. Maybe he's been accused of the wrong crime, but he's guilty, and if you could just make that go away, you would. So would I. You think about that the next time you want to have a go at Calder. That's Leroy's son. His *son*." She sighed. "Maybe this'll be the best thing for Owen. Scare him straight. I don't know."

"It's not that easy. It's not like he can give two weeks' notice and just quit," I said.

"Owen's smart—"

"I know how smart Owen is," I snapped.

"Then you know he's smart enough to figure something out. Once this stunt with the arson charge blows over—and I'm pretty sure it will—he'll be motivated to get his shit together. He's young enough, he can still leave Williston, go to college and do whatever he wants, and someday he can look back at this as the dark times, and he'll just be grateful that he made it through."

"Do you think that'll happen to Calder?" I asked quietly. "That he'll grow up and once in a while think about that time he killed a girl, until maybe it starts to seem like a dream he had? Maybe he'll actually convince himself he didn't do it. Or he'll remember when he confessed to murder and got away with it anyway, and he'll be so grateful, too."

"What exactly is it that you think you want?"

"To see him punished."

"Look around you," Emily said. "This town is hanging on by a thread. All it needs is one more good yank and it'll come straight apart at the seams. We're *all* being punished. And that's exactly what I think you want. You'd see all of Williston burn to ashes if you thought for one second it might make you feel better."

"I'm not fucking delusional, Emily. I don't think anything's going to make me feel better. Not even watching Williston self-destruct, although I'll stick around to watch it happen, and if anyone wants to blame me I'll be flattered they think I have that kind of influence around here. If Williston's unraveling, it's not because of me—it's because of Calder. He killed her, and everyone's trying to pretend he didn't, and that's what's poisoning this town. It's like you've all been having the same dream. And you know what? It's time for everybody to wake up." I stood. "Thank you for helping Owen. Tell him to call me when he gets out."

"Be careful, Finley. That's all I'm saying," Emily said as I went down the steps.

I turned to her from the lawn, where the grass, still damp from the last rain, came up well past my ankles and soaked through my Chucks. "I think I'm done being careful. But thanks anyway."

Serena drove me back to my car, still parked in front of the Halyard. We made plans to meet later that night, but in the meantime all I wanted to do was go back to sleep. She kissed me good-bye standing by my Subaru—I'd meant it when I told Emily I was done being careful—and a few minutes later I was shambling inside my front door, shucking off my tennis shoes with my toes, leaving my sweatshirt and messenger bag in a pile on the floor. I headed to the back porch to smoke one last cigarette before I went upstairs and passed out.

I smelled him before I saw him—weed, patchouli, body odor. He was sitting in the shadows, waiting for me. His feet were bare, as usual, but this time he was wearing a shirt, a striped Baja pullover hoodie. A damp, briny breeze swept in through the window screens to let me know more rain was on the way. I froze in the doorway and Silas smiled.

"Finley," he said. "Hello, sister."

I didn't ask him what he was doing there. I didn't ask him how he got in. I didn't ask him what he wanted, because I knew if I stood there long enough he would tell me. My sense of self-preservation might have been wildly underdeveloped, but I knew the less I said, the better. I just tried to concentrate on staying perfectly still so he wouldn't see me shaking.

"I heard a rumor about our mutual friend. Heard he went and got himself arrested. You know anything about that?"

"It's got nothing to do with you," I said, my voice coming out in a whisper. "He got in trouble for something else, something he didn't do."

"It doesn't work like that. Everything that has to do with Owen now also has to do with me."

I didn't answer.

Silas stood up and came toward me, his calloused, filthy feet soundless on the floor. His toenails were long and yellow, like an old man's. "Sometimes when people are in jail, they'll say anything they think might get them out. Start telling tales out of school, so to speak. I like to think Owen's better than that, that he'll keep his head down and his mouth shut, but really, you never know what someone will do until they're tested, and Owen, he's being tested now."

I resisted the urge to take a step back; I didn't want him to know how scared of him I truly was. "I told you," I said, "he's in there on a bullshit, made-up charge that has nothing to do with whatever it is he's got going on with you. It'll get cleared up in a day or two, and then everything will be back to normal."

"Maybe so. Nevertheless, in the meantime, he has something

of mine. I know Owen's too smart to keep the shit at his place. I checked there anyway. And then I thought, why not come ask Owen's little friend? She knows where I live, so maybe she knows some other things, too. So tell me, sister, where did he put it?"

"I don't know." Even as I was saying it, I remembered what Owen had told me, about Silas's sixth sense, but I kept my eyes focused and my voice even, and I swear even I would have believed me.

"You sure about that?"

"Look, dude," I said, "I don't want to be a part of your drug operation. I don't want to know anything about what Owen does for you, and he certainly wouldn't have told me where he put his stash."

Lying to Silas was risky, but if he had his drugs back he wouldn't need Owen anymore; someone else could sell the pills, and Owen would just be a loose end. As long as Silas needed something from Owen, I reasoned, Owen would be safe—as safe as he could be from Silas.

"You tell Owen he has four days to get me what he owes me."

"Is that, like, four days from right now? Or four days starting tomorrow?"

Silas only grinned. His teeth were perfectly straight and a vivid white; further proof, to me, that he'd grown up in a Canadian suburb somewhere with a great orthodontist. "I like you, Finley. Tell Owen I said that, too. I like you, and I wouldn't want anything bad to happen to you. Not like what happened to Betty."

You've seen how easy it is for a girl to go missing in this town, Owen had said.

"What do you know about Betty?"

"She was a friend of mine," Silas said. "When Owen wouldn't sell to her anymore, she started coming straight to me. She had a bold, troubled soul. Lonely, I think. I wasn't surprised at all when I heard about what happened. You get what you ask for in this life, sister. A lot more than people realize."

"She wasn't asking for it," I said. "She didn't want to die."

"Are you sure about that? When the darkness comes—what did she call it? The unlights?—you make a choice to let it in. And Betty let the unlights in. You should be careful you don't make the same mistake. You're so angry, so full of negative energy." His voice dropped to a whisper. "Don't you know how vulnerable that makes you? What happened to Betty could happen to you, too. But there are worse things, I guess. Wherever she is now, she's happier than when she was alive. Her suffering is over."

"Don't talk about her like that, like she was an old dog that needed to be put down." I didn't know what enraged me more, the way he spoke about Betty or that she'd told him about the unlights, a word that was part of our secret language.

"I'm sorry," he said. "I wasn't trying to be disrespectful. I just want you to understand that she's free now. I had a vision of her in the sweat lodge, a few months after she disappeared. She was a sparrow, watching over Williston, flitting from house to house, looking in on all the people she loved. And later, when I came out of the sweat, there were sparrows everywhere, hundreds of them, all around me in the forest. I felt her spirit then. Sometimes I think I feel it still. I miss her laugh. Don't you?"

I nodded mutely.

"Not everyone is meant to live a long and happy life, Finley. We're born with a certain number of breaths, and when we've used them all up, we die. Every year we celebrate our birthdays, but as those months go by, we pass our death days as well. We just don't know when they are yet."

I had the horrible notion that this kind of faux profundity scored Silas an unbelievable amount of pussy. To me, it was clearer than ever that he was just a little bit insane, but his particular brand of crazy, combined with how seriously he took himself, was what made him truly dangerous. He seemed like he might kill someone, not necessarily out of malice but out of the conviction he was doing them a favor. *Please, God,* I thought, *I hope Betty never fucked this guy.*

"I never slept with her," he said, and I struggled not to show how unnerved I was. "It wasn't about that. I just liked her energy."

"You just said she was all about the darkness."

"Everyone needs a little darkness sometimes, to balance out the light. But I can tell that right now, your whole world is darkness. You might think it can't get any blacker, but believe me, it can. So I'll ask you one more time. Where is my shit?"

I forced myself to meet his glacial blue eyes. *Show no fear.* "I don't know."

He nodded thoughtfully. "Not bad. I almost believe you. Almost, but not quite."

Then he punched me in the face, a sharp hook to my cheekbone that knocked me back a couple of steps and rang and rang inside my head. He took me by the shoulders and straightened me up, propping me against the wall; I was sure he was about to hit me again, but instead he took my chin in his hand and surveyed his work.

"I think that should do it," he said almost thoughtfully. "You show that to Owen, and you tell him four days, and that's four days starting from right fucking now."

My face throbbed where he had hit me, but something about it felt almost good at the same time, bracing, exhilarating, like a plunge into an icy lake. I surprised myself by laughing, maybe a little hysterically, but also with something like relief.

"My God," I said, wiping away the tears that streamed from my swelling eye. "You have no idea how long I've been waiting for someone to do that."

Through my good eye I saw it—a momentary crack in his cool, mellow facade, a flash of discomfort across his face, proof that I'd succeeded in unsettling him, even if it was just for a second. He hit me in the stomach and the laughing stopped; I deflated like a balloon, sliding down the wall until I was on the floor.

"Four days," he repeated, and then he slipped out the back door and vanished into the woods behind the house.

When I could finally get up I went inside, put my shoes and sweatshirt and bag on again, and got back in my car. I glanced into my visor mirror and winced; a perfectly cinematic shiner was already forming around my eye, blooming like a flower in vivid purples and blues. I had no doubt Silas had done it that way on purpose; this was part of his message to Owen.

I drove to Owen's cabin; no one would look for me there, with him in jail. The place had been trashed, I assumed by Silas, searching fruitlessly for the pills. The mermaid lamp was on the ground, bulb shattered; the corny thrift-store oil paintings I'd always teased Owen about had been torn from the walls and slashed open; the stacks of books painstakingly arranged in the living room had all been toppled over. I sighed as I looked around at the damage. It would take the whole night to clean it up.

The cans of beer in the fridge were still intact, so I cracked one open and took a few hearty swallows. I wrapped some ice cubes in a dishrag and pressed it to the side of my face, wincing. The ashtray I found under the couch. I righted the coffee table and sat smoking, drinking, trying to keep the swelling down, trying to think of a plan. Maybe Owen could come up with Silas's money in time; maybe he could simply give Silas back his product. But that didn't solve the problem of Silas in general. Emily was right; Owen was guilty, and I didn't care about anything besides how to protect him. And myself. Between Silas and Calder, Williston was starting to feel crowded with sociopaths who had it out for me.

So I cleaned the cabin, sweeping up the broken glass and cigarette butts, putting the furniture back where it belonged, rebuilding the towers of books in the living room. Even the small bathroom had been ransacked—the toilet tank's porcelain cover lay in two pieces, the medicine cabinet was open, its contents spilled everywhere, and the tiny cabinet beneath the sink had been emptied onto the floor. I tidied it all, neatly placing the unused rolls of toilet paper back into their basket, sifting through the debris to determine what was still worth keeping, lining up the boxes of Q-tips and bottles of Advil in the meticulous rows I knew Owen liked.

Kneeling down, I reached behind the toilet for an errant tube of Crest, and a small plastic cylinder rolled across the floor, coming to rest by my foot. It was a tube of lipstick, and that old jealousy began to rise inside my chest, even as I reminded myself I was with Serena now, even as I told myself all the usual bullshit, that Owen had never been my boyfriend, that of course he fucked other girls and, who knew, maybe even dated once in a while, and if I was willing to come up with some sort of scheme to keep Owen safe from Silas, it shouldn't be that hard to wish Owen all the best when it came to finding a nice girlfriend.

Then I looked closer at the lipstick in my hand, pulling off the cap and twisting the bottom, and I saw that unmistakable red, that signature shade I would have known anywhere. Fire and Ice. Betty's.

I slept until the next afternoon, curled up in a ball on the couch underneath flannel blankets that smelled like Owen. Whenever I started to wake up, I remembered everything that had happened in the past few days and willed myself back into unconsciousness. I didn't want to think about why Owen had one of Betty's lipsticks in his bathroom, or how much time was left until Silas's deadline was up, whether Owen would get out of jail today or if the police would come for Serena and me next. The constant effort I'd exerted, ever since I came back to Williston, trying to be brave or clever or convincingly deceitful, had left me spent.

It wasn't until the front door opened and Owen walked in that I finally allowed myself to surface. He looked terrible and I forced myself to stem a tide of sympathy for him, reminding myself he wasn't the only one who'd been through an ordeal in the last day or two.

"What are you doing here?" he asked, but I could tell he was glad to see me.

"It's a long story," I said, slowly sitting up, the blankets still wrapped around me.

"Jesus Christ, what happened to your face?"

"That's part of it."

He sat beside me on the couch. "You should probably start at the beginning."

"Before we get into that, maybe we should talk about this first." I pulled the lipstick from my pocket and tossed it to him. He caught it with one hand and looked down at it with grim recognition.

"Finley—"

"Did you fuck her?"

"What difference does it make now?" he asked.

"All the difference," I yelled. I was awake now for sure. "I've been waging a goddamn war of attrition with this entire piece-of-shit town for her. Yesterday I got beaten up by your connection and I still came here to clean up the house that he trashed so that you wouldn't have to do it when you got home from jail.

So, yeah, Owen, it makes a difference to me whether you were fucking my best friend."

"Wait, *Silas* did that to you?"

"That's not what we're talking about right now. How could you do it? How could you sleep with her? She was my best friend. And your cousin, for Christ's sake."

"Only by marriage."

"Owen! Was it you they found in the car with her? Are you the reason she got shipped off to Jesus camp?"

"It wasn't me, I swear."

"I don't believe you."

"Okay, fine. You want to talk about loyalty? I'm out on bail for a crime I know you committed, something I've conveniently neglected to mention to the police, because who fucking cares if I go to jail, you're the one with the bright future."

"God, are you ever going to stop acting like such a martyr? Stop pretending that these things just keep happening to you. Everybody makes choices."

Owen stood up and began to pace. "What did Silas say? Did he threaten you?"

I thought about the deadline Silas had given me, considered passing the message on to Owen as instructed, but I didn't trust Silas, didn't believe that obeying his order would keep Owen or me from getting hurt. Or hurt worse, I guess. I didn't want Owen to work out some kind of deal with him. I wanted Silas out of the picture, period.

"It doesn't matter. I think I know a way to get rid of him."

"Stop," he said, holding up his hand. "Not another word. Get up. Put your shoes on. We're leaving."

"Where are we going?"

"I'm taking you to your dad's, we're going to pack up all your shit, and then you're getting your ass back to New York."

"No way."

"Don't argue with me."

"I'm not leaving!"

Owen crouched down by the couch and put his hands on my knees. "Listen to me. I am sorry about sleeping with Betty. It's complicated, okay? And I know you had some well-intentioned, ludicrous idea that you'd come home this summer and—I don't know, exactly, what your plan was. But it's not working. Going after Calder, that was stupid, and futile, and I tried to tell you a hundred times. But this thing with Silas—this is my doing, it's my fault, and now you need to go somewhere he can't get to you."

"And what about you? We need to do something about Silas so that he can't get to *you*."

"Finley, I am begging you. Literally, on my knees, begging you. Please. Let me put you on a bus today."

"No."

"What about a train? I'll even spring for a train ticket."

"No."

He leaned forward, resting one hand on my bruised cheek. "Does it hurt?"

"It's a little tender."

"If you stay, it's only going to get worse."

"I don't care."

"I know you don't care," he said, "but I really need you to start."

The phone rang. "Answer it," I said. "Maybe it's good news."

He laughed mirthlessly and went into the kitchen. "Hello? . . . Oh, hi, Mr. Blake. . . . Yeah, she's here. She didn't tell you? I'm sorry. . . . Yeah, I'm okay, thanks. . . . No, but thank you, I appreciate that. Here, why don't you talk to her?" He put his hand over the mouthpiece as he stretched the receiver into the living room. "You didn't tell him you were sleeping here?"

"I didn't know I was going to sleep here until I passed out."

He shook his head and handed me the phone.

"Hi, Dad," I said, reaching for my cigarettes.

"Hey, Fin," he said. He didn't sound angry at all.

"I'm sorry about last night. It's a long story."

"It's okay, I'm not mad. I'm just glad you're all right."

"Are you all right? You sound a little, I don't know, a little weird." I looked up at Owen. *I think he might be crying*, I mouthed.

"Tears of frustration," Owen muttered. "From dealing with you."

"Dad, are you there?" I said.

"Yeah, I'm sorry," he said. "It's just been a tough morning."

"What's going on?"

"Maybe you should come here, and I can tell you in person."

"Whatever it is, just tell me now."

He cleared his throat. "I'm so sorry. They found her. They found Betty."

"What?" I said.

"Her body. They found Betty's body."

CHAPTER ELEVEN.

MY FATHER WASN'T at the office. Instead, he was at home—the better for him to comfort me, I supposed—and he didn't seem surprised when I showed up with Owen, both of us shaky and pale.

Dad told us what he knew. Her body—*what was left of her*; I could hardly bear to think of it—had been found in the woods, in a shallow grave, nowhere near the beach where Calder had once claimed to have killed her. The police would need to use dental records to make a positive identification, but they were reasonably sure it was her, because of the scraps of peach silk found with her, and because of the long, blonde hair. Owen and I sat at the kitchen table while Dad talked, drinking his French-press coffee, Owen's arm around me as I sank lower and lower in my chair.

"Will they even be able to tell how she died?" I finally asked.

"I don't know," Dad said. "I really don't know what will happen now. I'm so sorry, Fin."

"It doesn't make any sense. He said he drowned her. Why would he take her all the way out to the woods and bury her?"

"At least the police will have to reopen the investigation now, right?" Owen said. "Maybe they'll be able to find something— something that will prove that it was him?"

"I don't know," Dad repeated. "The cops finally have proof that she's dead, so in theory, Owen, you're right; they'll have to investigate. That doesn't mean they'll focus on Calder. And if it turns out she didn't drown—if they can even figure out how she died—they may stop looking at him altogether."

"What about her parents?" I asked. "Have they heard yet?"

"The sheriff told them this morning. Once the medical examiner releases the body, there'll finally be a funeral."

"Oh my God," I said, the finality of it sinking in. I'd had no hope, none, and still this news tore me open all over again. For eight months my imagination had led me astray. I'd been picturing Betty drifting in the Atlantic, when she'd been here in Williston all along. "Where did they find her?"

Dad hesitated.

"Where?" I asked again.

"Off the hiking trail that starts out by the highway. The one across from the scenic overlook."

I wondered if Serena knew yet, if there was still time for her to hear it from me. I stood up so quickly that my chair almost tipped over. "I have to go," I said.

"What happened to your face?" asked Dad.

"I was drunk," I said, gingerly touching the tender bruises

around my still-sore eye. I wondered if I had any of Serena's blues around to take the edge off. "I think I fell. I don't really remember."

He met my gaze. "I don't really believe you."

"I don't really care."

Dad glanced at Owen.

"Don't look at me," Owen said. "I was in jail."

"I don't know about you guys," I said, "but I can't wait to see this week's police blotter."

When Serena answered the door, I could tell she didn't know yet. Her gray eyes were narrowed in anger—and at that moment I remembered we'd had plans the night before, plans I'd totally forgotten, and that she was legitimately angry with me—but as soon as she got a good look at my face her mouth formed a horrified O, and she grabbed my wrist and pulled me inside, into the foyer.

"Jesus Christ, Finley, what the fuck happened to you? Are you all right?"

"It's not important. Really," I said.

"What do you mean, 'it's not important'? Who *did* this to you?"

"I'll tell you everything later, okay? First, I need to talk to you about something else."

She must have read my grim expression. "What's wrong?"

"Something—" I faltered on my first try. "Something's happened."

She led me toward the stairs. "Okay. Okay. Come on."

Serena's house smelled of flowers and whatever it is they put in Earl Grey tea—bergamot oil, I think. It was bigger than it seemed from the outside, with dark hardwood floors and lots of little mahogany tables covered in delicate vases and Tiffany lamps. She led me upstairs and down a long hallway lit by sconces, and finally into her room—unmade bed, an armchair by the window, dusty gray curtains open, showing the clouds outside threatening to burst. Her belongings were a series of nests: a pile of laundry by the bed, cassette tapes spilling out of their cases on the floor in front of the stereo, a stack of books resting against the chair.

"Where are your parents?" I asked.

"Doing something at church." She sat on the floor and patted the spot next to her.

I joined her, hugging my legs and resting my chin on my knees.

"Is it Caroline?" she asked gently.

I swallowed. "It's Betty. They found her body."

"What?" Serena said sharply, one hand anxiously reaching for the crucifix around her neck.

"In the woods. I don't know much yet."

"In the woods? What was she doing in the woods?" she said, her voice rising.

"I don't know."

"How did they find her?" Her eyes bore into mine, accusatory.

"I don't know," I said defensively.

"So are they going to arrest him? They found her body, they

know she was murdered, doesn't that mean they arrest him now?"

"Serena," I said softly, "that isn't what this means. Unless there's something that can link her body to Calder, this doesn't change anything."

"This changes *everything*!" she screamed, and then she surprised me—both of us, I think—by bursting into violent, hysterical sobs.

I put my arms around her, stroked her hair, her back, made every soothing noise I could. She was as inconsolable as any small child I'd ever seen melt down over a stolen toy on a playground, those same bewildered tears. *Why is this happening to me? It isn't fair. It isn't fair!*

"I know," I whispered. "I know."

"I don't want her to be dead anymore. They say it gets better, but it doesn't. She keeps getting more dead and I keep feeling worse and I don't think it's ever going to get better."

A wave of irrational helplessness swept over me as Serena convulsed in my arms. For some reason, I remembered those childhood assemblies in the auditorium of Williston Elementary, the principal onstage explaining that the solution to any problem was to tell a grown-up. But he never told us what to do when the grown-ups were incompetent or had their own problems or just didn't fucking care. Serena's sobs were tapering off, more from exhaustion than anything else, and I was filled with a fresh, raw grief—not just for Betty, but for the way the world was supposed to work, and my sinking suspicion that Serena was right, and we would feel this way forever.

I wiped away her tears. I kissed her forehead and her mouth, and she kissed me back with the same vehemence and desperation that had just powered her furious outburst. I took off her shirt and laid her down on the floor, unfastening her jeans, pulling them down, my hand between her legs. She whimpered as I touched her, turning her face away from mine, grimacing and arching her back, fingers splayed out and flexing against the rug as her breathing came faster and faster until she cried out, wordless, guttural, and I watched her as she came and went to that secret, inward place; until slowly she returned, panting, opening her eyes and smiling at me and pulling me closer so she could kiss me.

"Thank you," she whispered.

"My pleasure," I whispered back.

"Do you know where it is?" she asked, abruptly ending the moment as she shimmied her pants back up around her hips.

"Where what is?" I asked her.

"The spot they found her body."

"I think so, yeah."

She stood up, looking for her shoes. "I want to go there."

"Are you sure?" I asked.

She answered me only with a look.

"Okay," I said. "If that's what you want."

We drove out to the highway. I parked by the scenic overlook, which was already crowded with cars. Across the road, I could see the trailhead; it wasn't blocked off, as I had been secretly hoping. I guessed the cops hadn't wanted to hang crime scene tape along the side of the highway where drivers could see it; bad publicity for Williston's already withered tourist trade.

But the news was out. Even as we climbed the trail, I could hear the buzz and hum of voices in the woods above us. The crime scene tape started about halfway up the hill, wrapped around the trees on the side of the path, flapping in the salty wind.

The crowd was made up of people I recognized from town, from Charlie's, from the Halyard—vaguely familiar faces whose names I couldn't place, and a few who I could, like Jenny the waitress and Janet the aerobics instructor. A TV reporter stood in a small clearing filming a segment, and I wanted to knock her cameraman's equipment from his shoulder and ask the two of them where the fuck they had been last November. Betty disappearing hadn't been news worthy of the TV reporters from Portland; now her body turned up in the forest and suddenly they had a story on their hands. I was sorry we'd come, knowing that to anybody else we'd appear to be just another pair of rubberneckers.

"Look," Serena said, nodding at a huddle of kids farther up the trail. Rebecca was among them, and Shelly, and some others that I remembered from Shelly's party. Rebecca was crying, her face red and crumpled. She had one hand pressed firmly over her mouth, as if she could hold the tears back that way. Her shoulders heaved with the effort. Then, as if she felt me staring, she looked over. She came down the path slowly, dragging her feet through the dirt.

"Finley," Rebecca said. I hugged her, not knowing what else

to do. "I can't believe this is happening. I can't believe she's really dead."

Serena and I looked at each other coolly while Rebecca wept into my sweatshirt. There were a lot of appropriate reactions to Betty's body turning up eight months after she'd disappeared, and I was reasonably certain disbelief wasn't one of them.

"I know," I said, rubbing Rebecca's back. Serena rolled her eyes.

"I just don't understand. Who would do something like that?"

Serena's irritated expression began transforming into something much more dangerous. *Don't*, I mouthed.

"Maybe now the police will finally be able to figure out what happened," I said to Rebecca, unsure how I'd been so abruptly tasked with the job of comforting her.

"I never thought she was *serious*," she wailed. "If I thought she really *meant* it, I would have told somebody."

"Meant what?" I said. I stopped rubbing her back and my hands fell to my sides. "What are you talking about?"

Sniffling, she wiped her eyes with the hem of her shirt, briefly revealing her soft, white belly. Everyone in Williston was so goddamn pale this summer, like they'd all been living in their basements. The sun never came out anymore; the puddles in the driveways never went away; everything smelled damp and rotten and sometimes worse—that fetid stench of decay, as if there were shallow graves like Betty's all across town, and hers was just the first we had discovered.

Maybe I'm exaggerating. Maybe that's just how it felt. But I looked around and saw how tired everyone seemed—stooped shoulders, puffy, unfocused eyes. To an insomniac, the world always has a slightly surreal quality, and a lot of people had that dazed expression I knew I wore when I couldn't sleep. They had plenty to worry about, from the lack of tourists to the mold growing in their houses, brought on by the relentless moisture in the air, to the ever-growing popularity of Silas's pills. Caroline's accident, Owen's arrest, and now a dead body in the woods. Or maybe they hoped this would be the end. That if we laid Betty to rest, everything would be just like it had been before.

"Rebecca," Serena said, "what do you mean, you never thought she was serious?"

Rebecca stared at her blankly. "You changed your hair."

Before Serena or I could push for an answer again, Shelly and the rest of them arrived.

"Come on," Shelly said to Rebecca. "Let's go to the hospital. Maybe they'll let us see Caroline."

"How is she?" I asked.

Shelly looked at me suspiciously. "She's not dead yet."

A soft drizzle began then, a mist that seemed to rise up from the ground as much as fall toward it.

"I can't believe it's raining again," Rebecca said. "I swear it's like this place is cursed."

"Maybe Betty cursed it," said Serena. "Could you blame her if she had?"

Shelly snorted. "You're so fucking clueless. Believe me, Betty got exactly what she wanted."

"Really?" I countered, pointing toward the police and the crime scene. "You think this is what she wanted?"

"I feel so sorry for you two. I really do. She's been gone all this time and you're still making her the center of your universe." Shelly put her hands on her hips and looked at us with sheer disdain. "Do you think she would do the same for you, Finley? What about you, Serena? From what I recall, she barely said hello to you in the hallways—"

Serena lunged forward and gave her a hard, vicious shove. Shelly stumbled backward and her friends caught her before she went down. I grabbed Serena in a bear hug, ignoring her struggles as I restrained her.

"Get it together," I whispered in her ear. "There are cops here, there's a fucking TV reporter. I don't want to end up in jail or on the news."

And yet, Shelly wasn't done. "It's funny how the people who spent the least amount of time with her before she died are the same people who think they knew her best. You two didn't know shit. You're a couple of dumb cunts who deserve each other," Shelly said. She shook her head and started down toward the highway, the rest of her friends following, Rebecca bringing up the rear, giving me a last, sorrowful look over her shoulder before the trail led her around a curve and she disappeared. I kept Serena in my embrace long after they were gone.

I took her back to my house to watch the news. Dad was staying late at the office, trying to get the paper out a couple of days early. If nothing else, I hoped that the day's grisly discovery would keep Owen's arrest from ending up in the *Messenger*. It was hard to imagine anyone giving a shit about that now. As we settled onto the couch, a million random details flitted through my mind— what I would wear to the funeral; whether the medical examiner would find any evidence, something that could miraculously incriminate Calder; would it be raining in the cemetery when we buried her, as it always seemed to be in the movies. Still, I couldn't stop thinking about Silas's deadline, one day already gone, three to go.

There was only one thing we learned from watching the news that we hadn't already known. All the rain that summer had disturbed Betty's grave, the topsoil slowly washing away while the water level rose underground, until finally some part of her surfaced, and then it was just a matter of time until some poor hiker stumbled across her bones piercing the moist, raw earth. The reporter didn't identify whoever it was; she just said the sheriff's department had received an anonymous phone call with the location of the grave. By the time the news aired, the medical examiner had gotten hold of Betty's dental records and confirmed that it was her. The reporter finished the segment by saying there were no suspects in the murder, but the investigation was ongoing.

I turned off the television with an angry flick of the remote and slumped against Serena.

She played with a lock of my hair. "What was she doing in the woods? It doesn't make any sense."

"I just can't figure out—" I paused.

"What?"

"I've been here for a month. Talking to people, snooping

around, eavesdropping at Charlie's and the diner, going through my dad's old notes and files. And I still have no idea why Calder would kill her. She broke his heart, sure, she slept around, but that was all months before it happened. Everyone says he was avoiding her, and that she was the one who was acting strange. All that shit about Ophelia, not mailing in her NYU application. Whatever."

"Are you wondering if he did it at all?" Serena asked.

"No," I said quickly. "I'm not. But he must have done it for a reason. If they had a fight and he lost his temper, what were they arguing about? What were they doing together that night in the first place? If they were hanging out again, someone would have known. There's no secrets in a small town, remember? So what are we missing?"

"Rebecca knows something. She was about to tell us when Shelly started in."

"I need to talk to her again. Get her alone, sometime before the funeral." I thought about this for a moment, how to catch Rebecca at her most vulnerable, with nobody else around.

"So," Serena said, "are you going to tell me what happened to your face?"

"Silas," I said.

"Why?"

"To get to Owen."

"Fuck."

"Owen thinks I should leave town. Go back to New York."

Serena stiffened. "Is that what *you* think you should do?"

"Of course not," I said, putting my hands on her hips and

pulling her close to reassure her I wasn't going anywhere. "I told him no way. Even before we got the call about Betty."

"So what do we do now?" she said, pressing her lips to my collarbone.

"About Calder?"

She kissed my neck. "About Silas."

"Don't worry about it," I said. "I've got something in the works."

"Great," she said, pulling away and rolling her eyes. "Now I'm fucking terrified."

"It's cool," I said, playing with the crucifix around her neck. "We've got God on our side."

Dad came home late that night, long after Serena had left, and found me lying on the couch in front of the classic movie channel again. This time it was musicals. I was watching *The Band Wagon*. Fred Astaire was getting his shoes shined in the middle of some weird arcade, and I was leafing through Dad's notes again, searching for some clue I had overlooked, someone I hadn't spoken to yet, an unlikely source of information who could tie it all together for me so it would finally make sense. Instead I kept coming back to the unsettling thought that there were still bits and pieces of the story I knew about yet had failed to learn, from Rebecca and Danny and Owen, and I didn't know how to ask again and get a different response. Maybe the funeral would shake something loose, but in the meantime I was stuck on the couch, riffling through the same legal pad over and over.

"Hello?" Dad called as he came in the front door. "Finley?"

"I'm in here," I yelled back.

"I've been looking for those," he said, gesturing to the notes in my hand.

"Shit, I'm sorry," I said. "I borrowed them and I was going to put them back, but then I couldn't get back into the office."

"You could have just told me you had them. If you'd asked in the first place, I might have even let you see the file."

"I'm sorry," I repeated, handing over the pad. "Most of it was illegible anyway. Why do you need them now?" I moved my feet so he could sit next to me.

He sank into the couch and sighed. "There's a draft in there, that I started—I never ran, you know . . ."

"The obituary," I finished for him.

"Are you okay?" he asked.

"Not really. Any news about the funeral?" I asked.

"Day after tomorrow," he said. "There'll be a service at the Flynns' church."

"So the medical examiner released her body?"

"First thing tomorrow morning."

"Did he find anything?"

Dad shook his head. "She didn't have much to work with."

"Cause of death? Did she drown?"

"They can't be sure, Fin. I'm sorry."

"Did they rule it a homicide?"

"A possible homicide."

"Possible?" I said. "She didn't bury herself in the fucking woods."

"Obviously the circumstances around her death all point to homicide. But—" He paused. "Do you really want to hear this?"

"Yes," I said impatiently.

"There was no head trauma. No broken bones anywhere."

"If Calder drowned her, there wouldn't be."

"If she did drown, there would be no way to tell."

"She didn't drown," I corrected him. "She didn't swim out too far and get tired. He drowned her. That's different."

"Look," Dad said, resting his hands on his knees and staring at the television. "The police have a theory about what might have happened. You're not going to like it, but I'm going to tell you anyway, because I'd rather you hear it from me. I just ask you do your best to not let this send you into some kind of emotional tailspin."

"I will make no such promise."

He sighed. "The police think it's possible she may have overdosed on drugs. And that whoever she was with at the time panicked, and hid her, buried her in the woods, because they were too scared to tell anyone. So they tried to make it look like she disappeared."

"That is bullshit!" I shouted.

"Finley—"

"Please tell me you're not printing that in the paper."

"I don't have a choice. It's in the sheriff's statement. I can't just leave it out."

They'll believe it if they read about it in the paper, Serena had said.

"You can't print that. If you print it, people will think that it's true."

"I'm sorry, I really am." He tried to rest a sympathetic hand on my ankle.

I jerked my foot away. "Who do you really think came up with that story? The sheriff, or Leroy Miller?"

"I know this is not what you wanted to hear. Okay? I understand that. But you're going to have to accept that we may never know what happened to her. It's a miracle her body turned up at all, that we even get to know for sure."

"What is with this delusional uncertainty?" I yelled. "Calder sat in the fucking police station and told Emily Shepard that he killed Betty. Just because he was only seventeen when he said it doesn't make it any less true. How is there still room for doubt after something like that?"

"Because that's how it works. That's how the law works. And it's not for you to decide whether he's guilty."

"Of course he's guilty!"

"How do you know, Finley?" he asked me. "How do you know? Because of a confession you never heard? Because of all the evidence they never found? Tell me, what gives you the right to be so certain?"

It took me a few moments to gather my voice. I realized now that my father had never outright asserted that he was as convinced of Calder's guilt as I was, but it had never occurred to me that he wasn't on my side, that he actually thought there was a chance that—"Wait a second," I said. "Are you saying you think he didn't do it?"

"I'm saying I don't know. That nobody knows. And that it seems more likely than ever that we'll never know. The funeral might actually be a chance for you to find some closure, and say good-bye, and maybe move on, and stop dwelling on what happened to Betty."

"Stop dwelling on it?" I said. "Are you kidding? By tomorrow everyone is going to be saying that Betty died of a drug overdose, because that's the most convenient story. If the police could prove she'd been killed, Leroy would have come up with a story about a drifter passing through town. What's next? Maybe he'll get some witnesses to come forward, and get the whole thing put to bed, and that'll be the end of it. And next year, when some girl at Bates disappears, what then?"

"She's not coming back, Finley. No matter what you do. No matter how angry you get. She's never coming back."

"Somebody buried her," I said, choking on a sob. "Somebody dug her a grave in the woods and left her there to rot forever. You're supposed to be a fucking reporter. Aren't you at least a little bit curious about who it was? Why aren't you the one out there looking for answers?"

"Don't you think I tried that?" he said, gesturing toward the notes I was still clutching in my hand. "If I couldn't find out what happened to her, what makes you think you're going to?"

"I know what happened to her," I said. "I just don't know why."

The phone rang, the cordless blinking at us furiously from the side table next to the couch. Dad leaned over and picked it up with a sigh of resignation, like he was expecting more bad news.

"Hello?" he said. "Sure, hang on a second." He held it out to me. I eyed it suspiciously. I wasn't expecting bad news, per se, but I certainly wasn't anticipating anything good.

"Finley?" said the weepy voice on the other end.

"Hey, Rebecca," I said.

"Are you busy right now?"

"Not exactly, no."

"Can you come meet me? I need to talk to you."

"That's funny, I need to talk to you, too."

Rebecca was waiting for me in the playground next to the soft-ball field, sitting silently on one of the swings. I sat down on the swing next to her, the worn rubber curving around my ass, and ran my hands along the rusty chains. The rain had stopped, for the moment, but the clouds hadn't cleared.

"Where's Shelly?" I asked.

"They were all going back tonight," Rebecca said. "They wanted to hike back up. Like they might get to see her ghost, like it might be fun or something."

"Why didn't you go with them?"

"I don't want to see her ghost," she whispered, looking down at her feet.

"Why not?" I spun around in my seat, twisting the rusty chains as tightly as I could.

"Have you talked to Danny?"

"Yeah."

"So he told you." She met my eyes with what seemed like a great effort.

"That he thinks he saw her? Yeah."

"You don't believe him?"

"Not really." I shrugged, picking up my feet so the chains unwound and the park whizzed around me in a blur.

"I do."

"Since when do you believe in ghosts?" I asked her, digging my Chucks into the ground to stop myself, kicking up a damp clump of dirt.

"Did Danny tell you anything else?"

"No, but I think he knows more than he's telling."

"He does."

"What is it, Rebecca? Just tell me already." I was starting to lose my patience.

"Nobody can know I told you. I'm scared I'll get in trouble for not saying anything before."

"Fine."

"I didn't think she was serious. If I thought she was serious, I would have tried to help her, I swear. You know how she was. It just seemed like typical Betty, trying to get attention. And even if she did mean it, I never thought anyone would actually do it."

"Do what?"

"Kill her," Rebecca said flatly. "I think that she asked Calder to kill her."

CHAPTER TWELVE.

I LISTENED TO Rebecca's story, such as it was—disjointed, incoherent, completely unbelievable. She couldn't say where she had first heard it, or who had told her, or when; perhaps most importantly, she didn't know why.

"Let me see if I understand this right," I said. "Someone was going around saying that Betty had asked Calder to kill her, but not why she wanted him to do it?"

"I *told* you, I didn't think she was serious."

"Did you ever ask her about it?"

"No."

"So you never talked to her about it at all."

She hung her head. "No. When she went missing, I thought, there's no way, she must have been pulling some kind of prank. And then Calder confessed, and I thought it must have been some kind of mistake. Even if she had asked him, he would never have done it. For a long time I didn't believe that he had done it. But now—" She started crying again.

"Did it ever occur to you that maybe Calder was the one

who started that rumor? Maybe he was planning to kill her so he wanted to make her sound suicidal. How many people know about this? Did anyone ever mention it to the police?"

"I don't know, I don't think so. Please don't be mad at me, Finley."

"I'm not mad," I tried to assure her. "I don't know what I am."

What I was, primarily, was skeptical. The idea that Calder had killed Betty at her request was patently ludicrous, and I knew better than anyone how easy it was to spread a rumor around Williston. Was this better or worse than people thinking she had OD'd? I wasn't sure. Either scenario made Betty the architect of her own death—the very idea I'd been trying to disprove since I'd arrived back in town—although there was something particularly galling about Calder murdering her under circumstances that might still make Betty seem like she had brought it on herself.

Serena and I had prayed for a valid motive to present itself; this was not the one I'd had in mind.

The lights around the softball field were off tonight, and only streetlamps lit the park. Rebecca's tears glistened on her cheeks.

"Shelly believes it, doesn't she?" I asked. "That's why she went to the police and told them Betty was planning to run away. She knew Calder was guilty and she was trying to protect him."

"She wasn't a hundred percent sure. I think she wanted to believe he said no, and that Betty went around asking people until somebody said yes."

I went cold inside.

She asked me to do something and I wouldn't do it, Danny had said. *If you want to know the rest, talk to Owen.*

She asked him first.

I'm not particularly proud of this, but I was high at the funeral. I woke up that morning to Talking Heads' "Take Me to the River" playing on the radio and I didn't think I could do it, any of it. Get up, put on a black dress, face Betty's parents, watch them put her body in the ground. So I took a handful of the Vicodin I'd stolen from Shelly's parents. As I swallowed a few, I looked at myself in the mirror above my dresser. The bruise on my face was fading to yellow around the edges; I would have tried to cover it with makeup, but I didn't own any. I pressed my fingers against my cheekbone and winced. It still hurt. But not for long.

The funeral service wasn't about Betty. It was about Jesus. I sat next to my father and stared at the casket, and honestly that's pretty much all I remember until everyone filed outside and saw that the sun had come out for the first time in ten days. I was relieved to have a reason to put on my sunglasses, hide my black eye and missing pupils. People squinted up at the sky like they didn't recognize it.

Everyone was there with their families: Owen helping his parents into the car, situating his dad in the backseat with his oxygen tank; Serena standing miserable and silent as her mother spoke to the priest; Rebecca crying into her older sister's armpit.

We're all just kids, I thought. *How did we end up here?*

Dad put a hand on my arm to steady me, and I realized I was wobbling in my heels.

"Are you okay?" he asked, looking down at me with concern.

I tried to articulate what I was feeling, the all-consuming sense of dread spreading through me like a fast-moving infection, the sudden, helpless understanding that I—we, all of us in that parking lot, the town of Williston itself—had been irrevocably damaged by what had happened to Betty, that her death had set in motion a series of events that had not yet fully played out, and that things would get markedly worse before it was over, if in fact it ever would be. It didn't matter that the sun was finally shining; from here on out it would be all unlights, all the time.

What I managed to say was, "This is a mistake," and I knew Dad didn't understand what I meant, and that it was probably better that way.

Over time I have managed, with a moderate degree of success, to eradicate my memory of the burial. The pills helped for sure, so that whatever recollections I might have had were certainly murky to begin with, but a large part of it was willful. For years afterward I would be doing something completely innocuous—writing a paper in my dorm room, waiting for the subway, putting on my shoes and jacket in preparation to leave my apartment—and that morning would come back to me, unbidden, that image of us all standing around her grave as they lowered the coffin, and I would be leveled. Sometimes I gasped out loud, clutching my stomach like I had been punched; sometimes I would cry. But every time I would push the memory away until all that was left were a few hazy impressions: my heels sinking into the grass and my arms prickling in the sudden summer heat, Betty's mother crying and crying. It's funny to me now, in light of everything that came after, that the moment we put her in the ground, when she was finally laid to rest, so to speak, is the one that I can't bear to think of.

Afterward, we all went back to the Flynns' for the reception. Claustrophobia immediately set in; it smelled like too-sweet lavender air freshener, although when I looked around I realized that was just all the flowers. The photographs of Betty were still all over the place, even the one of her and Calder on the mantel. The dining room table was flush with casseroles and bowls of potato salad. The fog around me was lifting, unfortunately, but at last the tight family units were loosening, and I was able to corner Serena and lead her outside to the patio. I wanted to tell her about Rebecca, what she'd said, but then I saw Serena's face, and I knew it wasn't the right time.

"You're scratching your nose," she said.

"Am I?"

"Yeah. Are you high?"

"Maybe. A little, I guess."

The corner of her mouth lifted slightly, stopping just short of a smile. Her cheeks weren't as round as they'd been a month ago;

her collarbone stood out farther from her neck. Her eyes had a haunted look I recognized all too well. I pulled her in for a hug, squeezing her tight, inhaling her baby-powder deodorant and coconut shampoo. Her hands rested on my waist, and suddenly all I wanted was to leave with her, take her someplace deep into the woods where nobody could find us, or get her into my car and just start driving. We'd never even gone on a normal date; no picnics on the beach, no hand-holding at the movies. And now here we were, awkwardly milling around the Flynns' living room after watching Betty's casket lowered into the ground.

"What are you doing later?" I asked her.

"Nothing. Why?"

"Let's go into Pullman. Go out to dinner or something."

"Like a date?" she asked, raising an eyebrow at me.

"Like a date."

"Okay." She nodded at something over my shoulder. "Check this out."

I turned around. Jack Emerson was there with two other boys I could only imagine were his brothers; one was a little taller, the other a little thinner, but all three had the same black Irish looks—dark hair, fair skin, blue eyes. All three were wearing suits with white shirts and striped ties. Add aviator sunglasses, and they could have passed for young FBI agents.

"What do you think he's doing here?" I asked.

"I have no idea. Maybe one of his brothers knew Betty?"

"Maybe. Seems like a weird coincidence, though."

"There are no coincidences," Serena said. "I want to talk to him."

"What are you going to say?"

She began walking toward the Emerson brothers. "I have no idea."

I went back inside to find Owen. I waded through a river of unfamiliar adults, members of the Flynns' church, I figured, or relatives from other parts of Maine. The Shepards were out in force. I only sort of recognized Owen's distant relatives, but I didn't see him anywhere. Finally I spotted Emily, unwrapping a cobbler at the table.

"Do you know where Owen is?" I asked her.

"Hello, Finley. Nice to see you, too. Wish it were under different circumstances. The service was lovely, wasn't it? Et cetera."

"Please, Emily, I need to talk to him. It's important."

When she was done making room for the cobbler, she balled up the cling wrap in her hand and looked down at me. Her nostrils flared when she saw my face. "I told you to be careful, didn't I?"

"Congratulations, that makes you the winner of a brand-new 'I told you so.'"

She shook her head. "Fucking idiot."

"I won't argue with you there."

"I wish I could say I never understood what he saw in you, but unfortunately, it makes perfect sense."

"What about Betty? Do you get what he saw in her?"

"Misery loves company. You should know that better than anybody." She grabbed a bottle of wine and a glass from the center of the table. "He dropped his parents off at home after the burial. He'll be here soon, don't worry." Instead of pouring herself a generous helping of chardonnay, she tucked the whole bottle under her arm and headed for the patio door. I vacillated between absolutely despising her and holding her up as some kind of role model. For the moment, I decided to follow her example and filled a coffee mug with red wine from a box.

"Finley."

I set the mug back on the table and wheeled around. "Mrs. Flynn."

She had clearly composed herself for her guests. There was a glassy sheen to her eyes that could have been tears or Valium, I wasn't sure. I wondered if I could slip upstairs long enough to search the medicine cabinets without anybody noticing. Betty's mom was wearing a tea-length black dress with simple jewelry, a single strand of pearls and a stud in each ear, and her silver-blonde hair was swept up in an elegant, mystifying knot. She was gracious enough not to mention my black eye.

"Thank you for coming," she said. "I'm sorry I couldn't find a moment to visit with you sooner."

"It's okay, really," I said. "I'm so sorry. About Betty."

"I'm just relieved we were finally able to have a proper service for her."

"If there's anything I can do—"

"It's good to see you. Here in the house. It brings back a lot of happy memories of Betty as a little girl. All those sleepovers you two had. She would get so excited when you were coming over. She loved you so much."

"I loved her, too."

"I know. She knows it, too." Mrs. Flynn glanced around the

room at the other mourners. "I didn't want to do any of this. I wanted a small private service, not all this fuss. These casseroles. But Mr. Flynn reminded me that you do things like this for the living, the people left behind. Death really is easiest on the departed. It's everyone else who does the suffering, gets angry, looks for someone to blame."

"But someone *is* to—"

"Do you know the parable of the unmerciful servant?"

"Sorry?"

"It's from the Bible; Matthew. Bear with me, I know you're not much of a believer."

I swallowed hard. "I'm listening."

"A king was collecting debts from his servants. There was one servant who owed the king a large sum of money, but the servant couldn't pay, and his master ordered him to be sold. The servant fell to his knees, begging his lord for patience, and the king was moved by compassion, released the servant, and forgave his debt. Later, that same servant found a fellow servant who owed him a much smaller sum of money, and instead of showing him the same forgiveness, even when the man was on his knees asking for mercy, the first servant insisted on being paid, and had him thrown in jail. When the king found out, he was furious that the servant hadn't been able to show another person the same kindness that had been shown him, so the king gave the servant to the tormentors until he could pay the king his debt, which was no longer forgiven. And Jesus said to Peter, 'So my heavenly Father will do to you, if you don't each forgive your brother truly from all his misdeeds.' Do you understand?"

I looked into her glassy eyes, watched as she tucked a gray-blonde lock of hair behind her ear. "Have you really forgiven—whoever did this?" I asked her.

She nodded. "I have. And you will, too."

"When?"

"When you're ready for your suffering to be over." She hugged me, a surprisingly strong embrace. She smelled like lilacs and coffee. "It's good to see you again. Stop by anytime and see us."

Then she was gone, whisking off into the kitchen in a graceful black blur. I reclaimed my mug of wine and took a few generous swallows. Suddenly Owen appeared, beelining toward me with great purpose. There was a sheen of sweat on his forehead; he put a damp, sticky hand on my elbow.

"Are you all right?" I asked him.

"I need you to do me a favor. Go outside to the patio, right now. Please."

"Why? What's going on?"

"Goddammit, Finley, why can't you ever do what I ask you? Can't you just trust me?"

"Apparently, I can't," I said.

"What, you're still upset about that?"

"Still? I just found out a few days ago."

"Fine, be mad, whatever. Go be mad in the backyard."

He tried to ease me toward the patio with a firm nudge, but I planted my feet in the carpet. I actually enjoyed playing games like this with Owen; I'd been doing it since I could talk, and battling with him over something inconsequential was as pleasant a diversion as I was likely to get at a funeral. But when I stopped to look at his face, I saw sheer panic and realized he was serious. Something terrible was about to happen, and he was trying to protect me from it. I understood a second too late, right when the air in the room changed.

The house didn't go silent, not exactly, but there was a pause in all the chatter, and when it started up again it was a little too loud—that uncomfortable, feigned nonchalance, people talking without moving their eyes, trying to avoid whatever was in their peripheral vision. It didn't take me long to see it, the tall blond figure in the black suit, moving through the crowd without stopping to talk to anyone.

"Oh my God," I said. "What is Calder doing here?"

"Please go outside."

"Not until I know what he wants."

Calder was carrying some kind of bundle in his arms.

"The fuck?" Owen said. "Did he bring his laundry?"

"Oh, no," I said. "Oh, no."

Mrs. Flynn emerged from the kitchen, and this time the conversation did die.

"Where did you get those?" she asked.

"I found them in my sister's closet. She says she bought them at the Goodwill. I don't want them in our house anymore. I think they brought us bad luck. I was going to burn them, but I thought you might want them back."

He held out the armful of Betty's clothes. Mrs. Flynn froze. I looked around for Mr. Flynn, but didn't see him. Even Owen was rooted to the spot. Serena and Emily were still outside. There was no one else.

I stepped forward. "I'll take them." I glanced at Mrs. Flynn. "Is that okay? I can bring them home, and you can decide if you want them or not."

"That's fine," she said, her voice thin and quiet.

I held my arms out toward Calder, took a deep breath, and raised my eyes. His were bloodshot, and he smelled like seriously cheap whiskey, but his suit was neatly pressed and his shoes were perfectly shined. He was listing to one side, slanted like a Dutch angle from an Orson Welles movie. Drunk as fuck. I wondered how well all his medications went with alcohol.

"Why don't you just give them to me?" I told him calmly. "And then you should probably go."

He carefully handed me the pile of clothes, making sure none slipped and fell to the floor. His hand grazed mine as we made the transfer. It was trembling. It was so hard to imagine this slip of a boy hurting anybody, but at the same time I was more certain that he had done it than I'd ever been. I closed my arms around the heap of fabric, hugging it to my chest.

"I've got it," I said. "I'm good." I took a step backward.

"Caroline's awake," he said conversationally. "She's been asking about you."

"Asking what?"

"When you're coming to visit her."

"How's she doing?"

"Sixty-forty. That's what the doctors say."

It took me a second to realize he meant Caroline's odds of surviving.

"Tell her I'll come tomorrow."

He nodded and looked back toward Mrs. Flynn. "I'm sorry about Betty."

"Thank you. I'll keep your sister in my prayers."

He turned to leave, but something captured his attention on the other side of the room. I followed his gaze to the junior prom picture above the mantel. He started toward it, and people shrank from him as he went by, as if a skinny, drunk, emotionally disturbed lion were suddenly roaming the Flynns' home. Halfway across the living room, Owen stepped in—fucking finally—halting Calder by planting a hand on his chest.

"Seriously," Owen told him. "You better get back to the hospital."

"Don't touch me," Calder said.

Owen lowered his voice and tried to say something soothing, but Calder cut him off.

"Why are you acting like you're scared of me?"

"I'm not scared of you," Owen said.

"What about the rest of them? I see how they're looking at me. Like I'm some kind of monster."

"They're looking at you like that because you're loaded, in the middle of the day, at a funeral. Come on, it's time to go."

Calder laughed. "Owen Shepard. Williston's favorite son. Why do you get to be here, and I have to leave? I know all about you. I know what you do. Everybody knows. You see how they're looking at me now? Soon they'll be looking at you like that."

I laid Betty's clothes on the arm of the couch and hurried to Owen's side. "Last time I checked," I said to Calder, "you were hardly an outcast."

"God, Finley, what a hypocrite you are. So self-righteous, now that you're here. Where were you last fall when she needed you?"

I slapped him across the face, so hard my palm stung and the sound echoed through the living room. "Don't you *ever* imply that I had something to do with Betty dying. It isn't my fault that she's dead."

"If you'd been here, you'd understand. It's nobody's fault that she's dead. It was an act of mercy."

I don't know how long Serena and Jack had been watching, but suddenly they were both there, flanking Owen and me, so it was the four of us facing down Calder in the Flynns' living room, Jack's brothers hovering just in range.

"Get out of here," said Serena, "before an act of mercy happens to you."

Slowly, Calder backed toward the front door. Everyone watched with trepidation, like they were afraid he might burst into flames. As soon as he stepped outside, I heard an engine turn over; his ride, I figured, and I was relieved he wouldn't be driving himself home in that condition. With Calder's luck he would sideswipe a Saturn carrying a family of four and walk away without a scratch while the kids were being scraped off the pavement.

Out of curiosity, I sidled up to the window, wondering who it was, what asshole would drop off someone that drunk at a funeral. Who set Calder loose on us like that?

And then I saw the Dodge Ram pull away from the curb, and I stepped away from the window and hoped the driver hadn't seen me. Owen was already on his way to the patio, cigarettes in hand, so I followed him out.

"Owen," I said. "Owen."

"Jesus, Finley, now what?"

"Please. Tell me. What the *fuck* is Calder doing with Silas?"

CHAPTER THIRTEEN.

THERE WAS ONE person who had been noticeably absent at the service, the burial, and the reception, but I knew where to find him. Danny was working, of course, behind the counter at the trader, and it was about time for me to buy a new carton of smokes anyway.

"Oh, no," he said when I came in. "Please. Seriously, Finley, just go away." He buried his head in his hands.

"I know how you feel, Danny, believe me." I threw down my license and some cash. "Another carton of Marlboros, please."

"Take them and go," he said. "I'm begging you."

"Hey, you came looking for me last time, remember?"

He sighed. "How was the funeral?"

"Worse than I expected."

"Jesus."

"Yeah."

"What happened?"

"You'll hear about it soon enough. Let me ask you something."

He glared at me. "I knew you weren't just here for cigarettes."

"I'm multitasking."

"What do you want to know?"

I glanced at the security camera over his shoulder. "That doesn't record any sound, right? Just video."

"Yeah."

I leaned in anyway, and lowered my voice. "You said Betty asked you to do something. That she asked Owen and then you."

"I can't believe you remember that. You were so fucking high when I told you."

Surprised, I flinched before I could stop myself.

"Christ, Finley, half this town is hooked on that shit. What, you think I can't recognize the signs by now?"

"You told me you'd seen a ghost. What can I say, the conversation stuck. Whatever, yes, I remember." I took a deep breath. "Danny, did she ask you to kill her?"

He looked so tiny, hunched over the counter, greasy hair falling into his eyes, a pale sliver of skin showing through the place in his T-shirt where the collar was coming unstitched. I felt sorry for him, this boy who truly thought he was haunted.

"Fuck you," he said, with a vehemence that actually made me take a step back. "Everything was fine until you came back to town."

"No, it wasn't," I snapped. "If someone goes around asking people to kill her and eventually finds a taker—then no, Danny, everything is *not* fine, no matter how much everybody wants to pretend it is. Now tell me, *what did she say to you?*"

"If I do, will you leave me alone? Find another place to buy your cigarettes until it's time for you to go back to New York?"

"Fine."

He turned around and looked out the front window, across the street at the spot where he'd sworn Betty had appeared to him. He spun back toward me, his face tortured. "Yes, okay? Last fall. I didn't think she was serious. She brought me up into the catwalks one afternoon at school, in the theater, after rehearsal. I was excited—like an idiot, I thought maybe she'd finally come around and wanted to make out or something. But instead she said she'd been trying to screw up the nerve to throw herself off the catwalk, but she couldn't do it. She asked me if I would push her. And I laughed and she didn't, and I realized that she meant it."

"What did you say?"

"I asked her what was going on. She got all pissy—you know what I mean—and told me to forget it, that she'd find somebody else. I wanted to know if she'd asked anyone besides me yet, and she said yeah, Owen, but he was a real jerk about it."

"Because he wouldn't do it?"

"Right. And I asked her if this was about Calder, and I tried to give her some shitty pep talk, you know, there'll be other guys and all that, but she just laughed and said I wouldn't understand. I said, 'Try me'—I wanted her to talk to me, you know—but she just went back down the ladder and never mentioned it again."

"When was this? How long before she disappeared?"

"I don't know, like a month? They were already in rehearsals for *Hamlet*, but the show hadn't gone up."

"Did you ever talk to Owen about it?"

"And say what? I barely know the guy."

"So who *did* you tell?"

"I might've mentioned it to Rebecca, but not until after Betty disappeared."

"And that's it?" I tried to remember if Rebecca had told me when she'd heard about it. And hadn't she specifically said that Betty had asked Calder?

"I know this sounds weird," Danny continued, "but I didn't really think about it much afterward. It was just this brief, strange moment, and then it was over. I mean, what about you, Finley? Didn't you talk to her last fall? Did she ever say anything to you?"

I was about to snap at him—what kind of stupid question was that?—but then I caught myself. Maybe it wasn't such a stupid question, after all. No one else had listened to Betty, why should anyone assume I was different? I had spoken to her during the months before she vanished, and it did sound like something was bothering her, but other than a few clumsy attempts to learn what it was, I had let it go. We'd talked a week before *Hamlet* went up, when I'd offered to come to Williston.

"You know I love watching you perform," I'd said.

"Seriously, don't worry about it. Don't bother," she said, trying to sound cavalier.

"Are you angry at me? Did I do something?" The physical distance between us didn't make it any less likely that I could have offended Betty without realizing it.

"No, you didn't do anything."

"Then what is the problem?"

"Nothing. It's not you."

"I take it Calder hasn't come around."

Silence.

"Does he have another girlfriend?" I asked gently.

"No. Shelly's been sniffing around him in a pretty big way, but he doesn't seem interested. I don't think he's fooling around with anybody." If anything, she sounded even more despondent.

"Isn't that good news? Doesn't that mean there's hope?" I asked, knowing I shouldn't. Rather than offering encouragement, I should have been telling her to move on. Fuck Calder—in less than a year, she'd be living in New York, where there would be more cute boys in one acting class alone than there were in all of Williston. Once she left, she'd realize that he was a provincial hick not worth another second of her time, someone who was unimportant outside of hometown and high school. I knew she would thrive just as soon as she had the bigger stage she needed.

"I think it's almost worse this way," she said. "If he were with somebody else, at least I could take a good look at her and know what I'm up against. But he'd rather be alone than be with me." She sighed. "Being with me was really that bad?"

"Being alone isn't all that awful," I said. I was a bit touchy about this subject. I hadn't had a boyfriend since Tad, and other than the occasional make-out and groping session—at a party in someone's apartment while their parents were at the country house for the weekend, in the crowd at a show—Owen was the sum total of my sexual conquests.

"I know you think it's, like, pathetic that I'm not over Calder yet, but don't act like you're any better when I know you're down there pining away for Owen. Believe me, Owen isn't sitting around Williston missing you."

I swallowed hard and forced myself to ignore that last shot. "I never said I thought you were pathetic."

"It is though, it *is* pathetic. God, I'm so sick of myself," she went on. "No wonder he won't even talk to me. I can't believe you haven't hung up on me yet."

"Would you like me to?"

"No."

"Then why don't we just pull the self-pity bus over to the side of the highway, turn off the engine, and get out and stretch our legs, okay?"

She gave her throaty chuckle, and I slumped against the wall of my bedroom with relief. "You're right," she said. "I know, I know you're right."

It seemed I had successfully dispatched the unlights, at least for now. "Okay, I'll ask you one more time. Are you *sure* you don't want me to come up this weekend and see you in *Hamlet*?"

"Yes, I'm sure. I'll come down over winter break, how about that? We can go see the windows on Fifth Avenue and do something for New Year's. A weekend wouldn't be enough. I need a longer visit."

"Okay," I said. "Sounds good."

"It's not just about Calder, you know."

"Is it the unlights?"

"Kind of. I don't know, not really. I just feel invisible lately, like this specter that nobody can see."

I could tell she was gearing up again, and I knew I needed to get off the phone before my patience wore out altogether. "Betty, in a week you're going to get onstage and perform in front of the whole goddamn town. How much more visible do you need to be?"

"Yeah," she admitted. "You're right. I know. Thanks for listening to me. I'm sorry."

"Don't be sorry," I said. "You've got nothing to be sorry for. Break a leg next weekend. Let me know how it goes."

What an asshole I felt like now, thinking of that conversation. Betty feeling invisible—I should have known how dangerous that was, what it might lead to.

"I'm just trying to understand," I said to Danny now. "Why would she want to die? She was so close to getting out of here."

He shrugged. "Maybe she wasn't as close as you think. Just because she was supposed to go to NYU with you doesn't mean she would have gotten in—or if she had, that her parents would have let her go. They sent her to that crazy Jesus camp last summer. Do you honestly think they would have let her go live on her own in the city?"

"She didn't need their permission. If they didn't want to pay for it, she could've taken out loans or something. Maybe she would have gotten a scholarship. We talked about it. She had options."

Danny looked at me sharply. "Maybe she didn't have as many options as you thought."

"It's a pretty big leap from not being able to go to NYU to wanting someone to shove you off the catwalk to your death."

"I'm not saying it makes sense. I'm just telling you what I

know, like you wanted." He handed me my smokes and pointed to the door. "Now. It's your turn. To do what I asked."

I didn't have to go far to find Owen. He was in the alley next to the Halyard, pacing and smoking. He rolled his eyes when he saw me stalking toward him.

"Not now, Finley, whatever it is."

I shoved him, hard. He dropped his cigarette.

"What the fuck?" he said.

"Why didn't you tell me about Betty? About what she asked you to do?"

"Oh, Christ—"

"I've been making myself crazy trying to figure out what happened to her, and it didn't occur to you to mention that she asked you to—" I went to push him again, and he grabbed my wrists.

"Not here," he said. "Not outside."

He dragged me into the diner through the kitchen door, brought me around the counter, and sat me firmly on one of the stools. Then he circled back so he was on the other side, filled two mugs with coffee and a third with water. Only when he lit another cigarette did I glance around and realize that there was nobody else in the restaurant. The booths were empty, and the sign hanging in the front door had the Open side facing toward us.

"What's going on?" I asked, confused. "Why are you closed in the middle of the day?"

"We got shut down by the health department," Owen said.

"What? Why?"

He ashed into the mug of water. "Leroy."

"I don't understand."

"The police dropped the arson charges. They had to. I was here the whole time, I was able to give them a dozen names of people who saw me working when the fire started."

"What does that have to do with—"

"Don't you get it? Leroy couldn't catch me dealing, he couldn't frame me for the fire, so he switched gears and shut the place down. He probably figures without the diner, I'll have no choice but to start selling again, and this time the cops will be paying attention."

"So don't start selling again," I said.

"Then what the fuck am I supposed to do?" he snapped.

"I don't know, we'll think of something."

"There's no 'we,' okay, Finley? You're leaving in a month, re-member? There's just me, doing it all by myself, as usual. I'm the one who'll think of something. 'Owen Shepard, Williston's fa-vorite son.'" He snorted. "But you didn't come here to talk about my problems, right? You came here to talk about Betty."

I crossed my arms over my chest; I wasn't going to budge. "I just want to know the truth."

"Fine." He dropped the butt into the water. "I started sleeping with her last fall, after you left. That was my first mistake. Then I started selling to her. That was mistake number two. I didn't want to, okay? She was getting it from somewhere else, and then her supply got cut off and she went into withdrawal." It was torture for me to hear this, picturing Betty dope-sick and desperate, and

279 A GOOD IDEA

me, oblivious, hundreds of miles away. "She was sick, really sick, so I gave her a bunch of pills. She was supposed to use them to taper off. Instead, she took them all at once. I woke up and found her facedown on my bathroom floor, and I couldn't wake her up. I didn't know what else to do, so I called Silas. He brought over this medicine they give people when they overdose on opiates, and he helped me give it to her. And you know what she said when she finally came to?"

"What?"

"She was pissed. She said she didn't want to wake up, that she wanted to die, and that she'd finally found a way to do it that wouldn't hurt. I said if that was the case, why do it in my house where I could stop her, and she said because she didn't want her parents to find her. Silas helped me talk her down. After that, I wouldn't sleep with her or sell to her, but it was too late. She'd already met Silas, and he'd taken a shine to her, and she didn't need me anymore."

"Why would Silas keep selling to some girl with a death wish?"

"Because he's fucking insane, don't you get that?"

"Of course," I said, my voice rising. "Believe me, that shit is abundantly clear."

"She came to me once, maybe a week after that night, and asked me if I would do it." He did not have to explain what "it" was. "She said she could find somebody else if she had to, but she wanted it to be me—someone she knew, someone she trusted. Of course I said no, and then a month went by and she didn't mention it again, so I figured she was okay."

Owen's story was missing a key element that had featured in both Danny's and Rebecca's—the part where they didn't believe her, didn't think she was serious. Owen had known how much she meant business, and still, he'd done nothing to stop her.

"You're lying," I said. "You didn't think she was okay."

"I wanted to believe it, all right? And I thought she was wrong about finding someone who would do it."

"How did you know Silas wouldn't?"

Owen shook his head. "He liked her too much. He wouldn't have done anything to hurt her."

"Not even if he thought he was doing her a favor?"

"What, you think Silas did it now?"

"We just agreed that he's insane. How do you know what he would or wouldn't do?"

"Silas may be crazy, but he wouldn't take that kind of risk unless he had to. He's been to jail already, I don't think he's too keen on going back."

"I just—"

"What?"

"All summer long, I've been trying to figure out why Calder would do it. A fight, a jealous rage, something. I just can't picture him killing her because she asked him to." Maybe I just didn't want to imagine that Betty had been so desperate and unhappy without my knowing. That she'd ask Calder for such a twisted, morbid favor before she'd unburden herself to me.

"'An act of mercy.' That's what he said after the funeral."

My hands were shaking so badly I needed both to pick up my mug. "Why didn't you tell me?"

Owen looked down at the table, scratching a nick in the Formica with a thumbnail. "I knew you wouldn't be satisfied until you had the whole story. About the overdose, about me and Betty sleeping together. I didn't want to hurt you any worse than you were already hurt." He stared down at the counter. "I'm sorry, Fin, I really am. For everything. God, every time I look at your face I feel like shit."

"Thanks."

"You know what I mean."

"Bruises fade, O. I'll be fine. You will be, too."

"Oh, yeah?" he said, unconvinced. "How?"

Owen didn't want any part of saving his own ass, because he didn't think he deserved to be saved; he was waiting for whatever punishment was coming his way, in the form of Silas or financial ruin or felony charges that would actually stick. He was taking his usual martyrdom to new levels.

I was still angry and I would be for a long, long time, but I couldn't bring myself to leave his fate in the hands of Leroy or Silas.

"Like you said," I told him as I got up to leave, "you'll think of something."

I had promised Serena an actual date, and while a trip to see Caroline in the hospital was likely not what she'd had in mind, she was easily swayed by the promise of dinner and more to follow. As we rode up in the elevator, I told Serena about Leroy shutting down the Halyard.

"That fits," she said. "He did the same thing to Jack, you know, because he thought Jack was too old for Caroline. Leroy sicced inspectors on the Emersons' business, had their permits held up, everything he could think of."

"Is that why they broke up?"

She shook her head, lips pursed with frustration. "He wouldn't say exactly why it ended, or who ended it. But I got the impression all that stuff with Leroy came later. After they were already broken up. That's all he could tell me at the reception."

When we got off at Caroline's floor, Serena agreed to stay outside the room and keep an eye out for any of the Millers.

I wasn't prepared for the girl in the hospital bed. Caroline's nose was a broken, swollen mess, and the bruises around her eyes were black and purple. Her hair was so greasy it didn't even look blonde anymore. There were a couple of bouquets of flowers around her room, although not as many as I thought there'd be. Her right leg was in a cast that I stared at a little too long.

"It was crushed," she said matter-of-factly, "underneath the steering column."

"I'm sorry," I told her. "How are you feeling?"

She held up her morphine button. "Very little." Her voice was hoarse and scratchy.

"I'm surprised they let you have one of those things."

"I think they figure if I die, it won't matter. If I live, it's off to rehab. I haven't decided which way I want it to go yet."

"Don't say that. You're going to be fine."

"Can you imagine a Miller in group therapy?" She snorted. "We're WASPs from Maine. We don't talk about our feelings."

She had a point. "I saw your brother. He said you were asking for me."

"I'm sorry I missed the funeral."

"It's okay. You would have been there if you could. Just worry about getting better." I sat in the chair next to her bed. "Jack came."

She pushed the morphine button.

"He says hi, and get well soon. And that he's sorry."

Caroline took a deep breath and looked away. "Have you seen her yet?"

"Seen who?"

"Betty."

"Seen her?" I asked, confused. "How would I have seen her?"

"Shelly was here before. She said they hiked up to the grave after dark and saw Betty's ghost."

"Shelly is a lying piece of shit." I got up and paced over to the window. There was a vase full of lilies on the sill, and I fingered the creamy white edge of a petal that was just beginning to wilt.

"I know." Caroline adjusted herself in her bed. "I was kind of hoping, I guess. For a little piece of Betty to still be around. I figured if she'd show herself to anyone, it would be you."

"Well, she hasn't yet. If she is here somewhere, I don't know what she's waiting for."

"What happened to your face?" she asked bluntly.

"I got beat up by a drug dealer," I replied. I couldn't help but enjoy the irony a little bit. My father had refused to raise me in unsavory New York City, and yet it was small-town Maine where I'd gotten wrapped up with an unstable criminal.

"Owen did that?"

"Not Owen. His dealer."

Her eyes widened. "Silas?"

"You know Silas?"

"It's a small town. What'd you do to piss him off?"

"Nothing really. He just did it to get at Owen."

"Poor Owen." Caroline shook her head. "Seems like every-one's got it in for him these days."

"It's definitely starting to feel that way."

"You have to be careful, Finley," Caroline said, her tone abruptly serious. "My dad and Calder, they're starting to come apart. How much longer are you supposed to be here?"

"About three weeks."

"Why wait? Why not just leave now?"

It was a valid question. Betty's body had been found; I knew who had killed her, and I knew why he'd done it, and after his display at the funeral I knew other people were finally start-ing to wonder about Calder. Maybe the drug overdose story wouldn't take; maybe the police would investigate for real; maybe Calder would have a nervous breakdown and confess, again. I wasn't sure what else I could hope to accomplish in Williston, but suddenly the idea of leaving Serena and Owen and even Caroline seemed impossible. I hadn't been around when Betty had unraveled but I was here now, and the least I could do was stick it out until the shit storm I'd helped create had passed.

"I don't know," I said. "I'm just not ready to go yet."

"If I were you I wouldn't hang around too long. God, you're so loyal. You're like a character on television. What are you trying to do, defend her honor? Even she didn't care. She couldn't be bothered. You're taking punches for Owen. Bringing me messages from Jack. Maybe you're just getting in the way. Did you ever think of that?" She clicked her button for emphasis.

"Is your brother friends with Silas?"

"Silas doesn't have friends. He has minions, and people who listen to his bullshit so they can score."

"And which of those categories does Calder fall into?"

Caroline sat up in her bed, leaning toward me, her eyes bright and glassy but suddenly very lucid. "Let's make a deal. I want you to promise me something."

"What?"

"If I die," she said, "you'll leave my brother alone. Actually, no. If I die, you leave, period. I don't even want you sticking around for the funeral. You catch the next bus back to New York after they call time of death."

"Jesus, Caroline."

"Promise me."

"Okay, okay. I promise. And if you live?"

She pushed the morphine button again and sank back into her pillows. "I'll tell you everything I know about what happened that night."

Serena was waiting in the hallway. She linked her arm through mine and steered me toward the elevators.

"How did that go?" she asked. "How's she doing?"

"I don't know. Okay, I guess. Something about that girl really freaks me out."

"Are you too freaked out for dinner now?"

Honestly, the last thing I felt like doing was sitting in a restaurant, but I had promised. "No, let's do this," I said, hitting the down button with what I hoped was a sufficient amount of enthusiasm.

We waited, Serena's arm snaking around my hips, and I tried to keep my body from stiffening at her touch, which normally thrilled me no end. Something was off today, even more than usual. I wasn't thinking about dinner, or what Serena might do to me in her car or on the beach afterward. I was already five moves ahead, my mind on Silas and Calder and how long it would be until Caroline was ready to tell me whatever she knew.

"Whoa," Serena said, pulling away. "Where did you go, just then?"

I opened my mouth, prepared to satisfy her with another one of my lies, when the elevator dinged its arrival and the doors slid open to reveal, of all people, Leroy Miller.

He wasn't as tall as Calder, but where his son was lanky and slender, Leroy was broad-shouldered and solid; his brown eyes missed nothing, lasering in on me. I met his gaze and instinctually moved closer to Serena, putting myself between the two of them, as if I were trying to protect her. His eyes did not waver, and my dread magnified. It was like he knew everything—every move I'd made since the graduation ceremony, from the moment I'd asked Owen for his knife so I could slash the principal's tires until now, making some sick deal with Caroline for information about Betty's death. My father had tried to warn me that I wasn't as good a liar as I thought, and now, finally, I understood what he meant. My intentions had been transparent from the beginning, and compared to Leroy I was a rank amateur.

Oh my God, I thought. *What the fuck have I done?*

"Hello, Finley," Leroy said. He held the elevator doors open, not once taking his eyes off me. "Were you here to visit Caroline?"

"Yes, sir," I said.

"That's very kind of you. She seems a little better today. We're cautiously optimistic."

"That's good. It was good to see her."

"I won't keep you. Maybe I'll see you at the softball game later?"

"Yeah, maybe."

"Have a nice night. Drive safely," he said, and smoothly stepped out of our way.

Serena and I got into the elevator. He turned to look at me, smiling as the doors closed. I slumped against the wall.

"Jesus," Serena said.

I couldn't speak. I felt sick.

"Okay," I finally said when we got down to the lobby. "*Now* I might be too freaked out for dinner."

I dropped Serena off at her house with a promise that I'd call her later, and made a quick stop to use a pay phone to call Emily.

"I need to ask you something," I said when she answered.

"What?"

"Is there anybody in the police department you still trust? Maybe someone who worked for you when you were still sheriff?"

She paused warily. "What's this about, Finley?"

"I just want to know. If I had information about something, who could I tell?"

"Whatever you're thinking about doing, don't do it. Talk to me, and I'll try to help."

"If you could help, you would have done it already. Just give me a name."

Emily sighed angrily into the phone. "Fine. Here." She rattled off a number that I scribbled on my hand with a Sharpie. "Make sure you talk to Officer Hanlon. He's clean."

"Thank you."

While the rest of the town was at the softball game, I went back to Williston High, letting myself in with Serena's master key. I padded through the hallways silently in my Chucks, afraid to turn on my flashlight.

We had hidden Owen's stash in a locker tucked in a corner on the first floor, wrapped in a pile of old clothes. I stuffed the whole thing into my messenger bag. My knees popped as I stood up again, rearranging the bag across my body and taking a deep breath. It had been well over a month since the fire, but I still thought I could smell it, that acrid scent burning the back of my throat. I followed it toward the theater.

The repairs hadn't started yet, and the damage was still evident. I stood at the back of the house and looked at the stage where Betty had so loved performing.

If she were anywhere, I reasoned, she would be here. Not at the beach where she had probably died, not lingering on Main Street in front of the trader, not up on the hillside where someone had buried her. She would be here, in the theater, the place she loved most.

Her love affair with the stage hadn't actually begun with acting; her parents had signed her up for ballet lessons in grade school, which she'd dutifully attended despite her middling aptitude. Her outsized personality was a lousy fit for a potential ballerina; she lacked the precision, the economy of movement, that would have made her great.

But the same outsized personality that made her a lousy fit for a corps de ballet made her a star attraction. You couldn't take your eyes off her. I was biased, of course, but I remembered every recital, watching her clumsy pirouettes, her loose and sweeping jetés, the way she covered the stage as if she was struggling to contain a wild magic she'd been born with, something bigger than her that she hadn't yet learned to tame. After those performances, I would rush backstage to help her remove her bobby pins until she could free her long, blonde hair from the bun that had been threatening to come undone all night. Covered in sweat, she'd take off her ballet slippers with trembling fingers while I detailed all the highlights of her performance and she countered with a litany of her mistakes.

Then, the summer before I left for New York—the summer

we discovered the classic movie channel—Betty found her true calling, like a terrier laying eyes on its first rodent and understanding all at once not only that it has a special purpose on this earth, but what that special purpose is.

She quit dance immediately and practiced monologues and facial expressions. We played a game where she would cover her face up to the bridge of her nose—she used a marabou hand fan—and I would have to guess what emotion she was trying to communicate through her eyes alone. I don't know if it was her talent or our connection, but I was almost never wrong. We reversed roles a few times, but Betty never guessed correctly, and always gave up after one or two tries.

"Pissed," she would say. "You just look pissed."

I'd never made it up to Williston to see her in one of the school plays, something else I could add to the list of things I felt endlessly shitty about, but I could picture her up there perfectly, even with the curtains gone and that big black scorch mark spread out across the stage. Costumed, made up, pretending to be somebody else. Who had Betty wanted to be? Had she really been ready to die that day, when she asked Danny to push her from the catwalk to the unforgiving floor thirty feet below?

What about that night with Calder? How had she convinced him to do it? Had she gone along with it right until the end? Had she changed her mind during those last moments, decided when it was too late that she wanted to live after all, when she was pinned under the water and Calder could have misconstrued any struggle as the grim, final reflex of her body crying out for oxygen, instead of a capricious girl having a desperate change of heart?

Is this really what she wanted?

I needed so badly to feel her there. But as per my usual, I felt nothing.

CHAPTER FOURTEEN.

ONLY AS I was creeping through the woods toward Silas's house did I start to wonder if I should have waited until morning. While it had seemed prudent to attempt this mission under cover of darkness, in the moment I realized that Silas was likely a nocturnal creature who would probably have slept through my visit if I'd had the good sense to make it in the daytime.

I could have aborted, turned around and gone home, or to the softball game, or to Charlie's, but instead I pressed on, over a carpet of damp leaves that had been beaten into the mud by all the rain. Under my hoodie and T-shirt I was wearing, ridiculously, Betty's elbow-length opera gloves, the same pair I had taken from the school with the rest of her belongings—they were the only gloves I'd been able to find.

The weather had cleared again, so beyond the canopy of trees the moon was out, guiding my way. I tried to keep my breathing slow and even and quiet, eyes on the ground so I wouldn't stumble and make too much noise. I was approaching the property from the opposite side of the sweat lodge, so if Silas were holding one of his bizarre, culture-appropriating rituals tonight he would be at a safe distance from the house and the wigwam. My hope was that the brief respite from the summer's endless rain meant he would be off by his fire pit, heating rocks and calling the four corners with his cronies.

When I got to the clearing by the driveway I stayed back, deep in the tree cover, trying to assess the situation. Silas's Dodge Ram was there, and two other cars I didn't recognize. There were no lights, no voices, no smell of weed wafting toward me on the cool night breeze. I waited as patiently as I've ever waited for anything, motionless, watching the house and the wigwam and the cars, until I was certain they were all deserted. Still in the shadows, I circled around the clearing to get a better look at the house, which I had only ever seen from the front. There was a back door, and after one more thorough glance around—no motion sensor lights mounted in the trees, no vicious guard dog snoozing with the proverbial eye open, still no sign of Silas—I left the safety of the woods and stepped into the moonlight.

To my surprise, even Silas kept his door unlocked. I didn't understand why Silas didn't have more security, why he would leave his house so vulnerable, but then I thought, why would he? He didn't live in it, surely didn't keep any valuables or money or drugs inside, so why bother? I doubted it would have been as simple to get inside the wigwam, but for my purposes it didn't matter. All of the land belonged to Silas, so it didn't matter where the police found the pills. It would be on him.

Silas's house felt all wrong. This was definitely a place where terrible things had happened. The walls breathed mold and mildew, and the stale air had a faint, sharp odor of bleach. There was no door between the kitchen and whatever was in the next room; I couldn't see much in the darkness, just the vague, hulking outlines of what I hoped was furniture. I waited for my eyes to adjust before I dared try to navigate my way around.

I eased out the Ziploc bag that Owen had thoughtfully hidden inside an empty box of Lucky Charms. In the shadowy kitchen light, the overly enthused leprechaun on the front had never looked so sinister. I flipped the box around so he was facing away from me as I contemplated the best place to hide it. It had to be believable, somewhere covert enough that the police would be convinced Silas had put it there himself, but not so imaginative that they would miss it altogether. Slowly the objects around me came into focus, and I gingerly moved into the living room.

It was not the hovel I'd expected, a well-used drug den filled with empty pizza boxes, dirty needles, and used condoms, but I suspected the benign look of the place belied its unsavory history. Maybe Silas had cleaned house after the scabies incident Owen had mentioned. The living room was sparsely decorated, with a couch that was in better shape than Owen's and a nonspecifically Native-looking throw rug that could have come from Pier 1 Imports. On the wall across from the couch was an enormous painting of either a wolf or a coyote—in the dim light, it was impossible to be sure which—howling at a red moon hanging low in the sky like a piece of bloated, overripe fruit. I didn't need to check the signature to be reasonably confident that Silas had painted this clichéd atrocity himself, perhaps in the midst of one of his peyote-guided vision quests.

The bathroom was off the hallway between the living room and bedroom. Here, things were more in keeping with my expectations. The walls were covered in pornography, page after page cut out of magazines, lined up neatly and stapled to the plaster. The toilet seat and lid were a scorched gray-black, as if someone had gotten so frustrated with a plumbing problem that they had simply torched the shitter. The tub was filled with used, reeking cat litter, and the mirror above the sink had a single, fine crack running across it diagonally, like something you'd see on a delicate porcelain teacup. Something about that crack made my stomach go cold—I couldn't pinpoint why, but it would have bothered me less if the glass had been shattered altogether.

I reached out—some habits die hard—and gently opened the medicine cabinet. It was empty save a single, gigantic roach, which swiftly made a desperate leap from shelf to sink. I leaped back myself, into the hallway.

The door to the bedroom was ajar, and as I pushed it open, my satiny glove gleaming slightly, I thought about what I would do if I were wrong, and Silas was inside, waiting for me. In my pocket I held tight to Owen's knife, but that was just for false courage. I had no doubt I would be at Silas's mercy.

I should have been more scared than I was. I should have been terrified, but I wasn't, and I wondered if Betty's death, her desire to die, hadn't been motivated by the deep depression I'd imagined but by apathy. Maybe the unlights deserted her but left nothing in their wake, no joy, no anger, nothing. Maybe she'd just gotten curious. Maybe Calder had been curious, too. Maybe it was fate being its most devastatingly efficient, pairing up two teenagers with complementary, morbid curiosities, one who wanted to die and one who wanted to see what it felt like to kill someone.

In any case, Silas wasn't inside the bedroom. There was just a bare, stained mattress on the floor and a dusty dream catcher nailed to the wall above it. The closet was empty except for a few wire hangers. This left me with something of a dilemma. There was so little actual stuff in the house that there were no decent hiding spots for the pills. I supposed I could leave them in the cereal box, put it in one of the kitchen cabinets, and go the "hidden in plain sight" route.

There was one more thing. According to Owen, I was holding about ten grand worth of Oxy, more than sufficient to get Silas slapped with a trafficking charge. So in the end, a few pills more or less wouldn't make any difference. After all, no one actually ever notices if anyone picks out a few of their favorite marshmallows in an actual box of Lucky Charms.

Even if Silas was in jail by the end of the night, there were surely more stressful days ahead. My best-case scenario had me back in the kitchen at the Halyard by week's end, washing dishes for Owen for the rest of the summer, my inevitable punishment for saving his ass by doing this unbelievably stupid thing.

Whatever happened, it was best to be prepared. I unfolded the cardboard flap on the top of the box, reached in and grabbed a handful of pills, and tucked them away safely in the pocket of my bag where I kept my keys, cigarettes, and MetroCard. A beat later, I decided to slip a couple in the pocket of my jeans, next to Owen's knife. Just to have them handy.

I braced myself as I opened the cupboard above the kitchen sink, expecting more antennaed creatures to break for freedom. I had a different kind of surprise. There was actually a small but tidy collection of canned goods lined up on the shelves—tuna fish, chicken soup, garbanzo beans—and some packets of instant oatmeal. The cereal wouldn't look quite so out of place, after all. I slid the box between an old Cup O'Noodles and a bag of brown rice, wiped the dust from my—Betty's—gloves on my thighs, and headed for the door.

I'd been in Silas's house for less than ten minutes, and that was plenty of time for me to get cocky and careless. I should've looked out the window before I opened the back door. Instead, I made it halfway down the steps before I realized Calder was waiting at the bottom.

I turned and ran back inside, heading straight for the front door. I flung it open, raced down the stairs and toward the driveway as Calder came around after me. My Chucks pounded the wet dirt as I sprinted up the overgrown path—maybe I would reach the road and a car would be driving by and I could flag it down—but he was right behind me, those long legs giving him all the advantage he needed. He'd spent the last four years playing lacrosse; I only ran to catch the subway. Still, I gave it everything I had, even when tears started to blur my vision and my atrophied muscles were screaming in protest, and I made it farther than I ever thought I would, and I even had time to think, *So, this is what running for your life feels like,* right before he reached out and grabbed my messenger bag and tackled me to the ground.

I landed facedown in the dirt, hands splayed in front of me, Calder on top. I threw a wild elbow and caught him in the throat—not enough to do any real damage, but enough to startle him for a second. I tried to wriggle out from underneath, but he caught me by the legs, dragging me back toward him while I kicked violently, hoping for another stroke of luck, but mine was all used up.

I'd pushed it far enough, and now the universe was pushing back.

Calder flipped me over and held me down by the shoulders. I slammed the heel of my hand into his temple and his grip loosened—too briefly. Grabbing my hands, he pinned them beneath his knees, straddling me, panting, and I was trapped.

"Get the fuck off me," I said weakly.

"Goddammit, stop fighting me, Finley," he said. "I don't want to hurt you."

"Bullshit." I tried to wrest one hand free and he dug his knee in harder, until the sensation in my fingers dimmed.

"Listen to me," he said, leaning forward so his face was only inches from mine. His breath was sour, and the rest of him smelled like sage and fabric softener.

I rallied what abdominal muscles I had, raised myself off the ground like I was doing a stomach crunch, and snapped my head forward on my neck, my forehead hitting him square in the face, so hard his nose started bleeding and my vision went momentarily gray. When it cleared, nothing had changed. I was still pinned beneath Calder, but now he was seething. I looked at him, really looked at him, and for the first time that night I had the good sense to be truly afraid.

"Are you finished?" he said.

I nodded mutely.

"I'm going to get up now, and then you're going to get up, and then we're going to take a walk in the woods to go see Silas. Okay?"

"No fucking way," I whispered.

"He doesn't mean you any harm. He just wants to talk to you."

"Then tell him let's meet for a beer at Charlie's tomorrow."

"He's got Serena."

"I don't believe you."

He let go of my hands long enough to fish something out of his pocket and dangle it above me. It was Serena's crucifix.

"Oh my God," I said. "Is she—"

"She's fine. For now. But we'd better get going. Okay?" He stood up, reached down, and extended one hand. I was winded and sore, but I still wouldn't take it. I rose on my knees, slowly, and then came up the rest of the way.

"What does Silas want?" I asked.

"To help you find the answers to your questions."

"I don't need him for that. All I need is you to finally tell the truth."

"I killed her," Calder said. "She asked me to, and I did it. Are you satisfied? Was that everything you wanted to know? Is that all you needed, this whole summer?"

I hated him for killing her, but I hated him almost as much for being right. He hadn't told me anything I didn't already know, and I was still far from satisfied. "Fine. Where are Silas and Serena?"

"I'll take you to them. Right now."

I took one last glance over my shoulder toward the road. I thought I saw the fleeting glow of headlights, heard the rumble of a diesel engine. I'd made it closer than I thought, but not close enough.

"Okay," I said. "Let's go."

Calder followed me through the forest, keeping me in front so as not to let me out of his sight. He held on to the strap of my messenger bag like I was a dog on a leash. The path was narrow, barely wide enough for one person, and the woods surrounding us were dense and thick. Out here, the moonlight didn't penetrate, and we hiked silently in the dark, the only sound our feet shuffling along the ground. I stumbled on a rock hidden under a pile of leaves, and Calder yanked me up by the strap of my bag before I could face-plant in the dirt.

"Are you all right?" he asked.

"What the fuck do you care? Aren't you marching me to my death?"

"I told you, Silas doesn't want to hurt you."

"What are you doing hanging out with that asshole, anyway? What happened to you, Calder? You used to be such a nice guy."

"I'm not so bad. You've met worse."

"Like your father?"

"He can be a real dick, it's true. He's got a few surprises up his sleeve, though." He laughed. "You know he gets high?"

I stopped short and Calder bumped into me. "On blues?"

"He smokes weed, you idiot." He nudged the small of my back and I got moving again. "He even used to grow it himself. Not a whole lot, just a few plants in a patch out in the woods behind our house. I knew where he hid his stash in the garage, and I used to help myself now and then. When he decided to run for mayor, he got a little paranoid and burned it all. I went looking for a bud one day and found a fifty-dollar bill instead. I know how to take a hint."

"So that's how you met Silas? Buying drugs for your father the mayor?"

"It's not like I was getting it by the pound. Just the occasional eighth."

I hoped I lived to see this piece of intelligence revealed in the police blotter. "And that's it? That's all you ever bought from Silas? You were never, say, the middleman between him and Owen?"

"I wouldn't know anything about that."

"I'm sure you wouldn't."

We trudged on through the night quietly after that. I could hear the creek somewhere to our right; I knew we must be getting close. I guessed at the odds that Silas just wanted to "talk" to me, and they came up less than favorable. The righteous cloak of anger I'd worn all summer was threadbare by now, and I was as weary as I was terrified, but I refused to linger in the woods or drag out this forced march so I could feel the fresh air on my face a little longer. I actually found myself walking faster, eager to get to our destination, Calder quickening his stride behind me to keep up. Whatever Silas had planned, I just wanted to get it over with. And then I figured, what the hell, I was probably going to die anyway, it might as well be painless. I fished the pills from my pocket and slipped them discreetly in my mouth. I had no spit—*Scared spitless*, I thought, and almost laughed. I chewed the blues into a fine powder and swallowed it down.

I smelled the sweat lodge before I could see it. Sage, and campfire, and a hint of weed; wood smoke drifted through the trees in a gray fog that stung my eyes. The fire pit illuminated the clearing in the distance, and just beyond the flames was the squat outline of the sweat lodge.

Silas emerged, pushing the flap aside. He was alone, as if he sensed us coming, which I figured he had. Why not? I wouldn't put anything past him at this point; for all I knew, the birds were his familiars and had been tracking me since the second I stepped onto his property, reporting back to him at regular intervals.

He was completely naked except for his hemp necklace and a thin sheen of sweat that covered his entire body. He was at least a foot taller than me.

"Hello, sister. You made it," he said, as if I had just arrived at a dinner party.

"Here I am," I said, spreading my arms wide and gesturing to my person. "Where's Serena?"

He nodded behind him. "She's inside."

"Bring her out. I want to see her."

"She's fine, Finley, you'll see. You can come join her."

"I'm claustrophobic. I don't do well in small spaces."

Silas turned the bullshit fountain back on. "There's infinite space inside your mind, and that's where the real ritual takes place. It's not about the physical."

"What am I doing here, Silas?"

"You tell me. You're the one who was trespassing on my land tonight. Do you have any tobacco?"

"I have cigarettes," I said, confused.

"That's fine. You have to make an offering to the fire before you can go inside the sweat lodge."

I reached into my bag and took out a cigarette. With shaking hands, I tore off the filter; following Silas's instructions, I walked all the way around the fire, stopping at each of the four directions to toss in a pinch of tobacco.

"You know the difference between a white man's fire and a native man's fire?"

I shook my head.

"The white man takes a few huge logs and uses them to start a fire. But they burn down quickly, and he spends the rest of the night running back and forth into the forest, looking for even bigger logs to keep the fire going. What's the point of building a fire if you nearly freeze to death keeping it alive? The natives, we know better. We collect a great big pile of sticks, build ourselves a nice modest fire, and spend the night feeding it without having to leave its warmth. Are you ready?"

"I guess."

"Take off your clothes."

"What?"

"It's about a hundred thirty degrees in there. At the very least you'll want to strip down to your underwear."

"He's right," Calder added. "You don't want to go in wearing jeans."

I lifted my bag over my shoulder and let it fall to the ground with an exaggerated thump. I kicked off my shoes, peeled off my socks, and rolled down my jeans, hoping the outline of the knife didn't show through the pocket. My sweatshirt and tank top I draped on top of the pile. Finally the opera gloves came off. I wondered if by morning my things would be tossed into a Dumpster somewhere in a different county.

I tried not to think about my parents, or a hiker stumbling across my body someday, when there was nothing left of it but hair and teeth and my naked bones, maybe a few threads of my black cotton panties and the plastic underwire of the Victoria's Secret bra I'd bought on sale in New York.

I shivered in my underwear, arms crossed over my chest, and looked up at Silas. "Okay?" I said.

"You too, Calder," Silas told him.

Calder obediently stripped down to his boxers, and we followed Silas into the sweat lodge. Once he shut the flap behind him, the darkness was nearly absolute, except for the tender orange glow of the rocks piled together in the center. The air was thick and wet with steam, like the inside of a sauna, but hotter than that—hotter than anything I'd ever felt.

"I can't do this," I said, panicky. "I'm suffocating."

Calder gently took my elbow and guided me around the

rocks. "Lie down," he whispered. "It makes it easier to breathe."

I felt my way down to the floor, immediately recognizing the raw, prickly hair of some animal hide, and lay supine, trying to control my breathing.

"Finley? Is that you?"

My eyes hadn't adjusted to the darkness yet, but I'd recognize that voice, that tone anywhere: irritation laced with the slightest bit of affection. "Owen?"

"You stupid motherfucker, what did you do now?"

"You're supposed to be at the softball game. Where's Serena?"

"Over here." She was also lying on her back, but she lifted one arm, and even in the almost darkness her pale skin gleamed like a beacon.

I crawled over to her, running my hands up and down her arms, legs, torso, checking for injuries. She was soaked in sweat, as if she'd just climbed out of a swimming pool. "Are you okay?"

"I've seen better days."

"What are you doing here, anyway?"

"I was worried, so I followed you. Silas found me hiding in the woods and dragged me in here."

"Don't listen to her," Owen said weakly. "Don't believe a fucking word she says."

"What are you talking about?" I asked.

"Be quiet," Silas told us.

He ladled water over the rocks, and a fresh cloud of steam filled the sweat lodge, which seemed to contract around me. My breaths came fast and shallow; I couldn't get enough air. I sat up too quickly, and the world turned to white. I managed to get up and start stumbling blindly toward the door. Silas grabbed me around the waist.

"I'm going to be sick," I said.

He took me by the hand and led me outside, where I promptly dropped to my knees and vomited heartily into the grass until my eyes and nose were streaming. My stomach was wrenching itself inside out; I couldn't stop dry-heaving. A breeze came through the woods and licked at the sweat on my bare skin, and I shuddered.

When the puking finally stopped, I was left sobbing and shaking, hugging myself, grass tickling my knees and Silas standing over me, his voice oddly distant, telling me to get the fuck up, but I couldn't move or speak. Finally he reached down, grabbed me by the armpits, and pulled me to my feet. I wrested free of his grasp and made a desperate dive for the pile of my clothes, frantically trying to locate the pockets of my jeans, but my hands were shaking too badly. Silas grabbed me by the armpits again. My knees buckled, but he held me upright.

"Are you looking for this, Finley?" he said, and I saw he was already holding the knife. He opened it, laying the blade across his palm. "What exactly did you think you were going to do with it?"

Suddenly my tears dried up. A weird calm swept over me and I went numb. Maybe it was the drugs kicking in or an almost comforting sense of inevitability, as if I had been courting this moment for weeks, months. Since Betty's death.

"Fuck you," I said. "I'm not going back in there."

"Yes, you are."

I saw the punch coming but I didn't have the reflexes to

dodge it. His fist caught me square in the temple and this time the world went mercifully black.

When I came to, I was back in the sweat lodge, curled up in the fetal position. I guessed Silas had laid me on my side so I wouldn't choke to death if I started vomiting again. So considerate of him.

My head was throbbing, my mouth was dry and tasted like bile. I rolled over onto my back and cried out in pain, a small, agonized mewl, all I could muster. I closed my eyes; maybe I could go back to sleep and wake up when this was all over.

"Fin," Owen whispered, stroking my damp hair off my forehead. "Finley. You have to stay awake. You probably have a concussion."

"Leave me alone."

"I'm not going to let you slip into a coma."

"You would probably be doing me a favor."

"Just sit up."

With a great deal of effort, I managed to obey Owen's instructions. Silas was pouring more water on the rocks; the temperature had risen significantly.

"Just breathe," Owen said. "Breathe through your mouth, it helps."

"What are you doing here?" I whispered at him.

"He tricked me into coming. He told me you were here."

"And now she is," Silas said. "The order in which you all arrived is irrelevant. We're here because of Betty. Her death has poisoned all of us in some way. We need to purify ourselves of what happened to her, and of whatever role we played in it."

"I call bullshit," Serena said weakly. She was lying on the ground to my left. I reached for her damp hand and took it in mine. She looked over at Calder. "You killed her. Nobody else but you."

"Nothing is that simple," Silas said.

I closed my eyes and let my head fall to my chest. I'd lost all sense of time. Was it last call at Charlie's yet? Was my father there, having a beer and scanning the crowd for me, wondering where I'd gone off to? My mind drifted, and I thought about the fountain in Washington Square Park and my first boyfriend, Tad, sitting next to me, awkwardly kicking my foot while the sun spangled the water and I ate my falafel sandwich and a warm rush of happiness flooded my belly. I squeezed Serena's hand and wished we'd had even one day together like that, sly sideways glances and the slowly dawning realization that the person you want actually wants you back; that first kiss, when you're stupefied by your unbelievable good luck. Serena and I were rage and drugs and desperation, and maybe I loved her anyway; I wasn't sure, but I did know for certain I didn't want to die with her in this sweltering cauldron.

"She came to me," Calder said. "She asked me, over and over again. I said no so many times. She wouldn't let it go. But she meant it. I knew her well enough to know that she was serious. I told her I wouldn't do it, that I couldn't. I'd never hurt anybody. But she kept after me, until finally I said yes. I still never thought it would happen. I thought I'd take her out to the beach and she'd change her mind. I thought maybe she needed to feel like she was actually going to die to realize she wanted to live.

But then we got out there and she just waded into the water like it was nothing, and I started to wonder—" He suddenly stopped.

"You wondered what, Calder?" Serena asked impatiently.

"I wondered if I could do it after all. What it would feel like."

"Jesus Christ, you sick fuck," I said. "You sound like you're talking about going skydiving. She was a person, a living, breathing person."

"Don't act like you've never thought about it."

"Of *course* I've thought about it! I'm thinking about it right now! That doesn't mean I'd ever actually *do* it!"

"Why not?" Calder said. "What's stopping you? What's stopping any of us? You show up here, Finley, so self-righteous and out for justice, and everything's so black and white for you. There's right and wrong, except when it doesn't suit you. Owen gave Betty the pills that almost killed her the first time, he sold my sister the drugs that got her in the hospital, but you'll bend the rules for him, and why? Because in your heart you just know he's such a good guy?"

"That's different," I said.

"Different how? Look, at least I finally told the police where she was buried. It's not like I don't have a conscience at all."

"You made the anonymous phone call?" I said, confused. "I thought it was some random hiker."

"I thought maybe it would help, if she finally got a proper funeral." He looked at me dolefully. "I saw the flyers you had made, the 'Have you seen this girl?' poster with that picture of Betty, and I thought, I knew where she was, maybe that was all you wanted, to know where she was. I thought finding her might be enough for you. I just—I thought it would help."

"Help what?"

He looked at me across the darkness of the sweat lodge, but I couldn't read his features. "Everything."

"Why?" Serena asked.

"Why what?" Calder said.

"Why were you able to do it? So she asked you? So what, she asked a lot of people. You got curious, you wondered if you could. And then you did. How?"

"I just did it," he said softly. "Like sneaking out of your house or shoplifting or doing anything you're not supposed to do, anything you think you can't do, and then you do it, and you realize this is all just made up. There's nothing holding any of this together. You have no idea, Finley. You have no idea how easy it all falls apart."

It was falling apart for me right now. The darkness had become a living thing with a pulse and hot, wet breath. At some point Serena's hand had slid out of mine, and though I knew the others were still there, only a few feet away—shadowy outlines on the floor, Silas's skin lit a faint, sinister red by the coals—I felt them recede until I was alone, or might as well have been, and I thought about the night I swam out into the ocean, how easy it would have been for me to give up, slip under, disappear; how hard I had fought to make it back to shore. I wasn't sure I had another victory like that in me. I was so tired.

But I wasn't Betty. I could see the appeal of the thing, the potential relief, but that was different than seeking it out and embracing it. And I wasn't Calder either, somehow managing to paint himself as both a victim of circumstance and its architect. What scared me the most, though, was that I could see his point. That heady, liberating feeling the first time you defy your parents and walk out the front door even though they've forbidden you to go to the party, and you realize their authority is based on an agreement you made as a child and are now free to break at any time, that the rules are all made up. And how quickly that exhilaration can turn on you, spin into a terrifying vertigo when you discover that if your parents are not in charge, then no one is, and therefore nothing is standing between you and every conceivable impulse—to storm out the door to the party, to set the high school on fire, to sleep with your best friend's un-boyfriend, to drown your ex-girlfriend in the ocean on Thanksgiving night.

I struggled to prop myself up on my elbows. "Betty didn't start asking people to kill her until after she OD'd at Owen's. After he stopped selling to her." I looked at Silas. "After she started coming straight to the source. You."

"What difference does it make?" Silas said. "She wanted to be at peace, and she lacked the courage to do it herself. All I did was tell her there might be another way."

"Then why didn't you do it yourself?" Serena said.

Silas shrugged casually. "I have to keep a low profile, if I'm going to protect my business."

"Holding us hostage in a sweat lodge, does this count as low profile, too?" I asked.

"I'm not holding you hostage, Finley, I'm hosting a ceremony."

Silas scared me the most when he talked like this, like a perfectly reasonable psychopath. "I'm trying to help all of you move on. Isn't that what you want?"

"The only thing that's going to help me move on," I said, "is seeing Calder punished for what he did."

"Don't you understand? He's not the only one responsible. If Calder's punished, doesn't that mean we all should be? What if it could be the opposite? What if we could all be forgiven? What if I could make all of Owen's problems go away? Reopen the diner, forgive his debt to me, let him start over? What if I could fix it all for him, and in return all you had to do was live with the fact that Calder would never be punished? She's already dead, she'll never know. Could you do it?"

"What about Serena?" I said. "She had nothing to do with Betty's death."

"Now I call bullshit," Owen said, his voice steadier than it had been since I came into the sweat lodge. "Who do you think started getting Betty high in the first place?" He glared at Serena. "She flirted with you like she flirted with everyone, and when you realized you would never have her, you cut her off from the pills, from everything. She thought you were one of the only real friends she had here and you stopped speaking to her."

"You're lying," Serena said.

"For months after she disappeared, you said nothing, did nothing, and then suddenly Finley shows up in town and you're raring to go, losing your shit at graduation, ready to go after Calder. What were you doing in the meantime, huh?"

"Owen, what are you saying?" I asked, not sure if I understood what he meant—not wanting to understand.

"I'm saying she was waiting for you, Betty's best friend, to come back to town. She bided her time until you were here so if anything went wrong there'd be someone else to blame."

"It wasn't like that," I said.

"You don't sound so sure," Silas said.

"I don't feel so good." I lay back down on the floor, ignoring Owen's protests, Serena leaning over me, her worried face peering into mine. I closed my eyes and saw Betty, the Betty of my childhood, nine years old and plump-cheeked, wearing a green velvet dress she'd been given special for Christmas that year. It was Christmas Eve, and I was over at Betty's for dinner, wearing a red-and-black-checked dress with a starched white collar that itched my neck, and my belly was full of lobster and cod, and in another couple of hours I would tag along to midnight mass with the Flynns. But first we were going to play Snapdragon. Betty's mom cleared the table, and her dad turned down the lights in the dining room.

"You girls ready?" he asked.

Betty squealed with excitement while I pulled anxiously at my dress. It was our first Christmas together, and Snapdragon was a Flynn family tradition Betty was eager to share with me; she'd spoken of it frequently in the weeks leading up to the holiday. Betty's dad filled a wide, shallow bowl with rum and raisins; with a flourish, he set the liquor alight so that blue flames danced across the surface and gave his face an eerie glow that only tightened the knot in my stomach.

"So now what happens?" I asked.

"It's easy," said Betty. "I'll show you." She jumped out of her chair, rolled up her velvet sleeves, and reached without hesitating into the bowl, retrieving as her prize a rum-soaked raisin, still aflame. She blew it out and popped it in her mouth.

"It doesn't hurt?"

"Sometimes it stings a little," she said after she swallowed. "You've just got to be quick about it."

I watched as Betty and her parents played, laughing as they snatched their hands from the bowl filled with blue tongues of flame; sometimes they came up empty, but that didn't seem to be the point.

"Come on, try it!" Betty urged.

"Finley, you don't have to play if you don't want to," Mrs. Flynn reassured me. "I know it's a peculiar game."

"No," I said abruptly, standing up and pushing back my chair. "I want to play."

I held my hand over the bowl, hypnotized by the flames—really, they weren't very big, and they moved back and forth across the rum, and all the Flynns had done it and remained unscathed, so there was nothing to be scared of, and if I was scared anyway, I wouldn't let it show.

Show no fear. Okay, then.

So I plunged my hand in and plucked out a raisin, and it stung but just a little; it didn't really hurt. The Flynns all clapped, so I did it again, and again, and then let Betty have another turn, until we were raking the bottom of the bowl with our hands to find the last few raisins and the flames had nearly gone out. In the fading light all I could see was her smile and her bright blue eyes.

"Finley," Owen said, shaking me by the shoulders. "Wake up."

"Leave her alone," Silas told him. "She's not asleep, she's having a vision. It happens all the time during a sweat."

"She's not having a vision, for Christ's sake, she's nodding out," Serena said. "Seriously, you two goddamn drug dealers can't tell the difference?"

"I'm fine," I said, brushing Owen away and sitting up slowly on my own. "I'm just dehydrated. We all are."

"What did you see?" Calder asked softly. "Did you see Betty?"

I was about to tell him to go fuck himself when Silas, surprisingly, leaped to my aid.

"Not cool, man. You never ask another person about their visions. That shit is private."

"I'd rather see us all punished," I said. "You asked me if I could live with it, if Calder got away, if you made all of Owen's problems disappear? The answer is no. If we're all responsible for Betty's death, then we should all pay for it somehow. But first I want to know one thing. How did you get her body into the woods, Calder? If you drowned her in the ocean, how did her body turn up miles away, off the highway? There's no way you carried her up that hill alone. Emily said something that made me think there was a witness, that somebody saw you do it, but now I think I had it all wrong. It wasn't a witness. It was an accomplice. Who was it?"

Calder didn't answer. I crawled over to where he lay. My arms were tingling and my vision blurred around the edges. I didn't know how long a normal sweat ceremony was supposed to last, but Silas had kept us trapped inside the lodge for what felt like hours at this point. I took Calder's wrist weakly and shook it, but he didn't move. He was limp, blond hair plastered to his forehead with sweat, but his skin was surprisingly dry, like he'd run out of perspiration.

"Calder, wake up," I said, but he didn't stir.

"Jesus Christ, is he dead?" Owen said.

On the other side of the sweat lodge Serena started to retch.

I checked Calder's pulse with trembling fingers—it was fast, erratic, but still there. "He's unconscious, but I can't wake him up." I was dangerously close to passing out myself. My eyes closed and I shook myself awake. "I don't know what to do."

"Let him die," Serena said, wiping her mouth with her wrist.

"You said we should all be punished," Silas said to me. "Maybe this is how it happens."

"No fucking way," I said.

Owen tried to stand up but his legs collapsed beneath him. I looked at him across the shadows, his sorrowful face slack, softened, once again the boy I'd grown up with. I knew what he was thinking about—who would take care of his parents, what would happen to the diner, all the books he'd never read. I implored him with my eyes—*Just try again.* He nodded, knowing what I needed him to do, smarter than I'd ever be, and crawled toward the door. Silas turned, startled and distracted.

"Sit the fuck down, man." The knife gleamed in his hand, outstretched in Owen's direction.

Hunched over, I hobbled to the pit of rocks in slow motion. Silas had his back to me just long enough; his focus was on Owen, and as Silas started to close the gap between them I thought of

Snapdragon, how afraid I had been, and I realized I'd never actually been afraid before, never known fear in my life until now. I knew it was going to hurt; I could only hope the blues I'd taken earlier would mask the worst of it, and if I was lucky I wouldn't have permanent nerve damage.

I grabbed a rock the size of a softball from the top of the pit. It seared the skin on my palms and filled the lodge with the scent of scorched flesh. I cried out, a guttural, inhuman sound, and for once my utter lack of self-preservation worked in my favor—every part of my body was telling me to let go, but I didn't. And when Silas turned my way I swung my arms like a baseball bat, just like Owen had taught me, and caught him in the temple with a deeply satisfying crack that I still hear sometimes in my dreams. He slumped over backward, a bemused look of surprise on his face, the knife slipping from his hand and skidding across the floor, and I dropped the stone, falling to my knees and bending over my ruined hands, the pain worsening with every passing second.

"Owen?" I cried out in the darkness. "Serena?"

"I think Serena passed out, too," Owen said. On hands and knees, he made his way to the door and opened the flap, letting in a rush of cool air that I inhaled greedily. I was horrified to see the sky was lightening; we'd been in the sweat lodge all night.

"It hurts so bad, O," I managed.

"We're going to be okay, Fin. I'll go get help."

"You can't even stand up."

"I can do it. I'll be fine."

"I'm so tired," I said, sobbing.

He put my head on his lap and stroked my hair. "You have to stay awake."

"I really don't think I can."

Owen slapped my face. "Goddammit," he said, "I'm not going to let you die, too."

Maybe this was how Betty felt. Maybe this was what Calder had been talking about—standing on the edge of the precipice and realizing there truly is nothing to stop you from allowing yourself to fall. You could just let go.

Somewhere outside the lodge there was a rustling in the trees, faint enough at first that I thought it was the wind. But it grew stronger, and louder, and then there were footsteps and voices, and suddenly Emily was there, crouched in the doorway, blocking the light and gloriously backlit by the rising sun.

"*In here!*" she shouted over her shoulder to whoever was on the path behind her.

Inside, she surveyed the damage—Silas unconscious and bleeding, Calder and Serena passed out around the rock pit, Owen cradling me in his lap as the skin blistered on my blackened hands. To her credit, she didn't ask us if we were okay. "Just hang on, guys."

"One of these days," I said to her, "you'll have to tell me how it feels to be right all the time."

She crouched down to get a better look at my palms, and ruefully shook her head. "Not nearly as good as you'd think."

CHAPTER FIFTEEN.

I WOKE UP in the hospital with my hands wrapped in bandages and my very own morphine drip. Dad was there, slumped in a hard plastic chair, his feet crossed at the ankles and his hands folded across his belly. For a second I thought he was asleep, but when he saw me open my eyes he scooted his chair closer, leaning over and kissing me on the forehead.

"Hey, girl," he said. "How are you feeling?"

"Is he dead?" I asked. I wasn't even sure who I meant.

"Nobody's dead."

I didn't know if I was relieved or not. "Serena?"

"She's down the hall. Owen and Calder, too. You're all being treated for dehydration. Severe dehydration. The doctor said if you'd been in there for much longer, you could have gone into organ failure." Dad paused. "Silas is in surgery."

"I need to talk to Emily."

"Look, whatever happened up there, you can tell me. You're not in any trouble yet, as far as I know."

"Please," I said. "Just find Emily."

....

He returned with her a few minutes later, brought her into my room, and excused himself.

"Close the door," I said. My throat was still dry, my voice raspy. I felt like I'd never not be thirsty again.

"I shouldn't even be talking to you," she said. "Your father's been lying to the police, telling them you're still unconscious, and then he snuck me back here."

"I needed to talk to you first. How did you find us?"

"It wasn't that hard, Finley. Your father called me when you didn't come home, and he couldn't get hold of Owen or Serena, and after you and I talked, I had a feeling you would try to do something stupid. So I got in touch with Officer Hanlon, told him to meet me at Silas's property."

"And?"

"We found the drugs, if that's what you're asking. I don't know if you were the one who planted them in his house or not, but if you did, you did a decent job keeping your prints off the bag. That was clever, too, with the cereal box."

"I don't know what you're talking about."

"Practice that line, Finley. You're going to be saying it a lot in the next couple of weeks. Do me a favor. Don't say a word to the police until you've got a lawyer."

"What about Calder? He admitted everything. He told us all he killed Betty."

"While you were being held hostage in a sweat lodge? Hallu-cinating, dehydrated, going in and out of consciousness? It won't hold up, Finley. Not for a second."

"So that's it?" I shouted. "He just goes free? Again?"

She sat down in the chair Dad had vacated, hands in her pockets, weary and resigned, the Shepard family's signature look. "That's it. For now."

I swept my arm across the bedside tray table, knocking the remains of my last meal and a plastic pitcher of water to the floor. If my hands hadn't been bandaged I would have started throwing things. I was filled with an outsized rage and there was no place for it to go. Instead of hurling the vase of flowers Rebecca had sent me at the wall so I could savor the cathartic sound of glass breaking, I broke down into guttural, violent sobs.

It had all been for nothing. All of it. Back in June, Owen had been right. *You can slash all the tires and set all the fires you want and she'll still be dead and he'll still be going to college in September.* They had all been right, Owen and Emily and my father, and still I had stormed into Williston arrogant enough to believe I could give Betty justice. But all of it—the arson, the libel, the breaking and entering, all that sneaking around in the middle of the night and the amateur detective bullshit and hijacking the police blotter, nearly suffocating to death and permanently scarring my own body—it had all been for nothing.

Emily, bless her heart, made no move to comfort me. She simply waited until I had worn myself out. I swiped at my cheeks clumsily with my gauze-mittened hands.

"How's Owen?" I finally asked.

"He'll be okay, I think. Silas is in some pretty serious trouble, once he makes it out of surgery. His brain was hemorrhaging. You really nailed him good, Finley."

I looked down at the bandages covering my ruined hands and tried to remember reaching into the pit of smoldering rocks. "Yeah, but I'll never play the piano again."

Emily erupted in an unexpected laugh. "Always the smartass."

"But Owen—"

"Owen doesn't have to worry about Silas anymore. And neither do you."

Owen would be okay. Silas would go to jail. And Calder— they'd pump him full of fluids, keep him overnight for observation, and send him on his way. Was I satisfied yet? Had we all been punished enough?

I took a shaky breath. "Can I ask you something?"

"Sure."

"Who do you think buried Betty in the woods?"

Emily shook her head. "You know I can't talk about that."

"But it wasn't in the confession. If he'd told you where she was buried, you'd have dug her up, inadmissible or not. You wouldn't have let her rot there all winter long. I know he couldn't have buried her alone."

"I'm not going to just speculate wildly—"

I held up my bandaged hands and cocked my head so she could see the bruise on my temple where Silas had hit me. "I almost died last night trying to find out what happened to her. I think I've earned the right to a little speculation."

Emily was quiet for a moment, choosing her words carefully. "Let me put it this way. Who would you have asked? Think about it, think about it hard. You loved Betty, you trusted her, right? But would you have trusted her with something like that? How about Owen? With everything he has to lose—the diner, his parents—when his back is against the wall, could you count on him to keep your secret? You and Serena made a hell of a mess together this summer, but you've barely known her for two months." She narrowed her eyes. "So say it happened to you. It's the middle of the night, you've got a dead body on your hands. What would you do, if you weren't you? If you were Calder?"

I closed my eyes and once more conjured the scene I'd played out so many times—the moonlit beach, Betty's red lips a chilly blue—but now I tried to imagine it from Calder's point of view. What happened next.

Maybe he panicked for a moment before he realized he could make up any story he wanted—it was an accident, she swam out too far, he tried to stop her, whatever. He didn't have to tell the truth; we never *have* to tell the truth. But maybe Calder wasn't confident in his ability to sell the lie, which he shouldn't have been, considering he broke down in Emily's interrogation room days later. So he needed to try it out on someone, someone he could trust to help him either way, someone who cared more about him—cared more about protecting him—than anything else. And lucky for Calder, that same person had the power to do it.

"Oh my God," I whispered. "You think Leroy buried her."

"I never said that," Emily replied, giving me a stony, level stare. "I never said that at all." She stood up and came closer to the bed, idly glancing over the IV bag steadily dripping fluids into my arm. "But look at what you were willing to do for Betty, even after she was gone. It's not hard to imagine what a father might do for his son, is it?"

"No," I said. "I guess not."

Emily leaned over me, her face softening for the first time I could recall that summer. "You've done enough, Finley. No one could have tried harder. But no more, you understand?"

To my utter humiliation, my eyes filled with tears and my chin quivered. "But I failed."

"We all fail. We all suffer. You've done enough damage, and I don't mean to Williston, or Silas, or the Millers. Go back to New York. Go to college. Hang her picture in your dorm room, and when your new friends ask about her, tell them who she was." She got up and strode toward the doorway.

"And Finley?" She stopped and turned back to look at me, all the compassion erased from her features. "Don't come back next summer."

I pressed the button on my morphine drip and closed my eyes.

Later, there was a knock on the door and I looked up expecting to see Serena or Owen or the sheriff, but it was just one of the nurses, telling me I had a visitor. Before I could answer, she wheeled in Caroline.

"I'll leave you girls alone for a few minutes," the nurse said.

"You look a lot better," I told Caroline.

"Thanks," she said. "You look like shit."

"So it seems like you're going to live," I said.

"I guess so," she said, not sounding thrilled by the prospect. "When I get out of here, they're sending me straight to rehab.

Some place in Arizona, with horses and shit."

"That doesn't sound so bad to me."

"How are your hands?"

"Pretty fucked up."

"Sorry."

"I'll be okay."

"So it sort of sounds like you saved my brother's life."

"Ironic, isn't it," I said.

"I guess a promise is a promise, then?"

"Wait," I said, struggling to sit up a little straighter in bed. "Let's do this the other way. Why don't I tell you everything I know about what happened that night?"

A wary look crossed her face, and Caroline narrowed her eyes. "Okay . . . we can try it that way."

I steeled myself, and looked straight at her. "Betty had asked Calder to kill her weeks before. He said no, and she kept asking, and when he realized she wasn't going to drop it, he finally agreed. Maybe he never thought he'd go through with it, maybe he thought she'd change her mind at the last minute, decide she wanted to live after all. Sometimes I picture it like this fucked-up game of chicken, with neither one of them wanting to back out. So he did it"—I saw a fleeting expression cross her face—"and then he panicked. He put her body in the trunk of his car, drove home, and asked your dad what to do. I think Calder probably lied at first, said it was an accident or something, but your dad's smart, and I doubt he ever thought it was that simple. So they buried Betty in the woods. But when she went missing, Emily came after Calder, got him alone in that interrogation room somehow, and he cracked. It didn't take much. I wonder if your dad knew that would happen—knew Calder would confess, knew it would be inadmissible. Maybe he just wanted to get that part over with. How am I doing so far?"

Caroline said nothing.

"And then it all just seemed to go away, except it didn't. Calder coming apart, that I can understand. He's the one who did it, after all. But you? You went way down some dark rabbit hole. Maybe it's knowing that your brother killed someone and your father helped him get away with it." I coolly leveled my gaze at her. "But then I saw Jack Emerson hurl a fastball into Calder's gut."

Her face tightened at the mention of his name. "What does any of this have to do with Jack?"

"At the end of last spring, Betty got in trouble with the cops. They found her parked in a car with some older guy, and no one ever said who it was."

"So? It was probably Owen."

I shook my head. "They didn't start fucking until after the summer. I think she was in that car with your old boyfriend Jack. No one ever knew who it was, but Calder knew, because he's Leroy Miller's son, so he knows everything. And Calder found out, and broke up with Betty, but he didn't know Jack was your boyfriend, did he? Because Jack was too old for you, and you were trying to keep it a secret. But there are no secrets in a small town, are there?"

Caroline sat up straighter in her wheelchair. "You're close, Finley, but you're not quite there. I found out about Jack and Betty first. Jack told me himself. He said he didn't want me to hear about it through the rumor mill. He said he was sorry, he wanted me to forgive him.

"But I wanted everyone to be just as miserable as I was.

"I turned around and told my father everything, and I told Calder, too. I knew Dad would go after the Emersons' business, and that Calder would break up with Betty. She got sent off to church camp, and when she came back she wasn't the same. I turned everyone against her. I made sure she didn't get to play Ophelia. I watched her fall apart. And I was glad. At least at first. But then she disappeared, and I knew exactly who was to blame. And I did it all out of spite."

"But, Caroline, you're not the one who killed her."

"Maybe not. But maybe if I'd forgiven her, she'd still be alive."

"It sounds like you'll have plenty to talk about in therapy," I said.

"Watch it with that thing," she said, nodding to the morphine button in my hand. "You don't want to end up my roommate in Arizona."

"Probably not," I said. "I can't stand horses."

Caroline scratched at her leg, trying to get at the skin under the cast. "You're lucky you didn't kill Silas, you know."

"How do you figure?"

"I just think it's better, for you, I mean. I think there's certain things about ourselves we're better off not knowing. What if you'd done it, and you'd liked it? What would you do then?"

"If I'd done it, it would have been in self-defense."

"Why didn't you try to kill Calder in there? You could have done it, made up any story you wanted."

I didn't know how to explain it to her, that I didn't want to learn whatever Calder had learned because he had drowned Betty. That getting away with murder might be as terrifying as going to prison for it—seeing the world as a place where that could happen, learning the exact delicacy of the framework that holds all of it together.

When Calder had passed out next to me in the sweat lodge, it would have been as simple as pressing my hand over his nose and mouth; in the darkness, maybe no one would have even seen it happen. But I would have known.

"I never wanted to see him dead," I answered.

"What did you want, then?"

"I don't even know anymore. But I'm pretty sure it wasn't this."

Serena didn't come see me while we were in the hospital, and I didn't go see her. She and Calder were discharged before I was. Silas was recovering on another floor, but he'd already been placed under arrest. When he left, he would be going directly to jail.

Dad stayed with me the whole time, installed in my bedside chair, reading Mary Roach's *Stiff* while I stared at the ceiling and clicked my morphine button ruthlessly anytime the fog around me started to lift. For the first time in years, the newspaper didn't go to press on time. I didn't ask Dad how he planned to cover the story, and I didn't make any jokes about the police blotter. I never really slept, and I was never really awake. When the nurses changed the bandages on my hands, I couldn't stop myself from looking at the raw, peeling skin. They all liked to tell me how lucky I was, that I could have lost a finger. At least there'd be no permanent damage, they'd say, and I'd just laugh and laugh.

I didn't know where Owen was, either. Dad said he'd been the first one released, but the diner was still closed, and no one was answering the phone at the cabin. I hoped maybe he'd taken the hint, finally packed up his truck with his books and left town, but I had a feeling he was around somewhere, lying low, maybe hiding out at Emily's or camping in the woods.

When I finally got to go home, I started packing. Not just the clothes and books I'd brought with me for the summer, but things I'd kept at Dad's house for years, even the chipped kitten mug I used for my coffee every morning. He said nothing, but we both understood my intentions. At last I had taken some of Emily's advice to heart. When I left Williston this time, I wouldn't be coming back.

I was taking a break from filling boxes, sitting on the screened-in porch and struggling to light a cigarette with my damaged hands, when I heard the front door open. It was the middle of the afternoon and Dad was still at work, but I didn't get up. Owen's knife was in my back pocket—never out of reach now—but I didn't bother going for it. I recognized the quiet footsteps as they made their way through the house to where I was staring out at the woods and fumbling with my Bic.

"Hey," Serena said.

"Hey."

She took the lighter from me and sparked the flame. I leaned forward, Marlboro in mouth, inhaling gratefully.

"Thanks," I said.

She sat next to me on the chaise. She'd changed her hair again, shearing most of it off into a pixie cut that made her neck seem even longer and more graceful. Her brown roots were growing in, and only the very tips were still black. The crucifix had been returned to its rightful place, nestled in the hollow of her throat. I let my gaze linger there for a moment, recalling the many kisses I'd planted in that exact spot, and then I had to look away.

"When are you leaving?" she asked.

"As soon as I can."

"Weren't you even going to say good-bye?"

I took another drag of my cigarette. "No."

"I guess I can't blame you. I just wanted to say I'm sorry."

"You loved her," I said. "I get it. I was just a proxy, the next closest thing. She was all we ever had in common. Betty and the blues."

"It wasn't just that. I wanted someone else who cared as much that she was gone."

"And you knew I'd be it. That first night," I said. "Did you follow me to the high school?"

She nodded. "I watched you break in. I needed a partner in crime. You didn't take much prompting."

"And that whole scene at graduation? Was that all for my benefit?"

"I wanted to get your attention, sure. But I meant every word of it. I wasn't pretending."

"And the rest of it? Which parts were pretend?"

She put her hand on my thigh. "Come on, Finley. Some things you can't fake."

Even now her touch had the power to alter my blood flow; I felt like my veins were dilating. I moved away, putting some distance between us on the chaise. "So what was your plan? Wait for me to get back and start making noise about Calder and Betty, then kill him and make it look like I had done it?" I felt sick. "The sweat lodge was your idea. Silas didn't find you wandering around his property—you went to him. Then you used yourself as bait to get me in there, too."

"I thought you wanted revenge, just like I did."

"I guess you're an even better liar than I am, because I thought you wanted me."

"I did. I still do."

"Well, all I want is to get the fuck out of this town. No offense or anything, but I can't wait to never see any of you people again."

She wasn't about to let me get away that easily. "Finley—"

"Don't—"

Then she was kissing me.

Afterward, I gave her the chance to zip up her jeans; then I stood. "I think you need to go."

I didn't walk her out. We didn't say good-bye. I waited until I heard her car drive away before I sank back down to the floor, the taste of her on my lips for what I knew would be the last time.

I haven't seen her since.

CHAPTER SIXTEEN.

THE DAY BEFORE I planned on going back to New York, I went to the beach where Betty died one last time. I thought about going to the cemetery, but there was no marker or headstone on her grave yet, and I felt oddly unsentimental about the box of bones beneath it. The spot where she drowned had kept its hold on me all summer long, so it was there I went to say whatever half-assed good-bye I could muster.

I took off my shoes, rolled up my jeans, and waded into the water, letting it wash around my ankles, sand sucking at my toes. The ocean was as cold as it had been when I'd arrived two months before; there'd been no sun to warm it, all summer long. Tomorrow I'd go home, and soon after that I'd start orientation at NYU. I'd move into my dorm room, meet my roommate, Kate the dancer, and register for classes. Life would, ostensibly, return to normal. No more mission of vengeance, no more wandering around the woods in the dark, lying and scheming and fixating on how to make Calder pay for what he'd done. I had tried, and failed, and nearly been killed in the process. I was already thinking up what lie I would tell when people asked me about the scars on my hands. I was leaning toward inventing a baking accident.

"Finley."

I turned around and there was Owen, walking toward me across the beach, also barefoot, shoes in his hands and Dickies rolled up to his knees.

"Hey," I said.

"I called your house and Frank said you're leaving tomorrow. I thought maybe I'd find you here."

"I was going to say good-bye, but I didn't know where you were."

"It's okay," he said. "I wanted it that way. I needed some time to think."

"And?"

"And I was pissed at you. Really fucking pissed. All I've done since you got back is try to protect you, and all you've done is get yourself into more trouble."

I fumed. "That's funny, Owen, because I could say the same thing about you."

"I tried to tell you, Finley. I told you to leave it alone, I told you to go back to New York, but you wouldn't listen. What you said to Calder in the sweat lodge? About how you thought there might be a witness, but then again it might be an accomplice? You were right, and you were wrong. There were both."

"What are you talking about, Owen?"

"I never wanted to tell you this. Because I knew you'd never forgive me. But you're leaving now, and I have a feeling you won't be back, so I guess it doesn't matter."

"Whatever it is, you don't have to tell me."

"Yes, I do," he said. "Because soon everyone will know, and I don't want you to hear about it from your father, or read it in the paper." He looked away from me, out at the water. "I was here that night, Finley. I saw everything."

I didn't say anything, just stared ahead at the water.

"She came by the diner that day. I blew her off at first. I thought maybe she was just trying to score. But she sat at the counter, had a cup of coffee, and it turned out all she wanted was to talk. There was something strange about it. She was cheerful like she hadn't been in ages, and when she said good-bye she came around the counter and gave me a hug, and a kiss on the cheek, and I got this feeling, like something wasn't right. I don't know, I can't explain it. But when she said good-bye, I didn't like the way it sounded. And she quoted *Hamlet* to me, one of Ophelia's lines. I recognized it from when she'd made me fake-rehearse with her. 'Lord, we know what we are, but know not what we may be. God be at your table!' And then she left.

"So that night, after I closed the diner, I drove by her house. Her light was on, I could see her upstairs, so I thought, *Okay, she's fine, I was overreacting*. And then Calder pulled up, and she snuck out and got into his car.

"I followed them, feeling like a creep—for all I knew they were getting back together, coming out here just to fuck. But it was cold, that made no sense, so I sat in my truck and watched them go down to the water. She was in her pajamas, I didn't understand what was happening. She took him by the hand and led him out until they were about waist deep." He shivered. "God, she must have been so cold."

I found my voice. "And then what happened?"

"She kissed him, and then she lay back in the water. She looked like one of those born-again Christians, being baptized in a river. And he held her under by the shoulders—"

"Stop," I said. "Stop talking." I couldn't bear to hear any more.

"You don't understand, Fin. She didn't seem to mind. She didn't fight it at all. I barely realized what was happening until it was over."

"*You watched her die?*" I said. "You watched Calder kill her? *And all this time you've said nothing?*"

"He came back with Leroy. *Leroy.* I watched them move her body together, watched them—"

"Don't tell me!" I shouted. "Why are you telling me this now?"

He shoved his hands deep into the pockets of his Dickies. "I didn't know what to do! When he confessed a few days later I thought, *Okay, fine, he'll go to jail, I don't need to get involved.*"

"And when the charges were dropped, you still said nothing?"

"It was my word against theirs. Yeah, I run the local diner, most people in town have a little soft spot for me, but we're talking about Mayor Leroy Miller and his kid versus the local drug dealer. Calder knew Silas, he knew I was selling—if I said anything, he could have pinned it on me. I decided to stay out of it and hope that the cops would eventually do their job. Instead, Emily got pushed out of the force and everyone pretended that Betty had just run away or something. I honestly didn't think it would make a difference if I spoke up. But then you came back."

He tried to brush the hair out of his face, fighting a losing battle against the wind.

"And?"

"You rolled into town like you weren't afraid of Calder or Leroy or Silas, like butter wouldn't melt in your goddamn mouth, and I just felt so ashamed."

"Of course I was afraid of them, I was terrified."

"And you reached into the rock pit anyway. And that's the reason we're all still here. So this is the least I can do. Better late than never."

I didn't know what he wanted from me. Forgiveness? Reassurance? For me to do what I had done all summer, promise that everything was going to be okay? "But it'll still be your word against his. Your word against Leroy's."

"I don't care anymore. You almost died trying to do what I could have done all along. Besides, something's changed now, you can feel it. The cracks have been starting to show for a while. People won't be so able to dismiss it this time."

"I hope you're right, Owen. I really do."

"Leroy shut down the diner. With Silas in jail, I'm straight, out of business. Nothing to lose."

"Why didn't you try to stop Calder?"

He stared out over the water, and when I followed his gaze I knew I was looking at the exact spot where it had happened. "I almost envied her. On some level it seemed like such a good idea, to have it taken out of your hands, to let someone else put you out of your misery. Take away all that pain, all that unhappiness. The way they looked at each other in the moonlight right before—there was no malice in it, no anger. It wasn't like he was hurting her. It was like he was giving her this gift. For a second, I almost wished I'd had the courage—to be the one to do it for her."

"That is," I said, "the sickest fucking thing I've ever heard."

"Maybe so, Fin. But that doesn't mean it isn't true."

"When are you going to tell the cops?"

"Today. Now. Emily's going to come with me."

"If I were you," I said, turning away from the ocean and heading back toward my car, "I'd leave that last part out when you talk to the police."

"Wait."

I stopped, whirling around and reaching into my messenger bag, where Owen's knife was safely tucked away with my cigarettes and keys and the last of the blues. I held it out to him, still folded. Beneath the gauze on my hands I could feel the blisters oozing; it was time to change the bandages again.

Every time I looked at my scars, for the rest of my life, I would suffer the shame of knowing I'd earned them protecting the only person who could have saved Betty, but didn't.

"Here," I said. "This is yours. I don't want it anymore."

"Finley, don't." He looked at me pleadingly, finally dropping his mask of indifference, revealing the sorrow and remorse and self-loathing he'd carried all this time, and I realized that when he said he understood the appeal of Betty enlisting someone to end her unhappiness, he had not been speaking theoretically. "I'm sorry. I'm so sorry."

"You were right," I said. "I had no idea how lucky I was, before

I knew any of this. I should have listened to you. I should have left it all alone."

"Don't say that."

"What did it get me?" I screamed. "What good did I do her? And now you think, what, you can just walk into the sheriff's station and tell the truth and suddenly it'll make a difference?" I threw the knife into the sand at his feet, but it might as well have been sticking out of my chest, the way my heart was breaking.

"Don't look at me like that, Finley, please."

I turned my back on him and started walking, wind whipping my hair around my face, struggling to get traction in the sand, and I ignored him as he called after me, shouting my name again and again, until I couldn't hear him anymore, just the steady rhythm of the waves against the shore.

On the way back to Dad's, I stopped on Main Street, still devoid of tourists even though the weather had finally cleared and the temperature had risen. Now that I was leaving, it finally felt like summer, but even in the sunshine Williston looked grim, with the diner shuttered and Charlie's front door propped open, revealing a not-insignificant crowd of day drinkers inside.

I couldn't wait to get back to New York. I didn't care how small my dorm room was, how much I hated my roommate; it would never be as claustrophobic as this place.

I went into the trader to stock up on cheap cigarettes while I was still in Maine. Danny was sitting behind the counter, working on a crossword. He didn't look up when the bell jingled. I wondered if he'd trained himself not to hear it.

"Hey," I said.

"I thought we agreed you wouldn't come in here anymore."

"Cut me some slack," I said, holding up my bandaged hands. "I've had a rough week. Anyway, I'm leaving tomorrow. You won't have to see me again."

"People are saying some crazy shit about whatever happened with Silas that night."

"Oh, yeah? Like what?"

"There's a few different versions going around. Drug-fueled orgy, Native American séance, some kind of satanic ritual."

"Believe me, it wasn't nearly that much fun."

"Some people are pretty pissed about Silas getting arrested. The supply's already drying up."

"I'm sure someone will take his place before too long. In the meantime, everyone can go back to stealing their drugs from their parents' medicine cabinets."

He finally looked up from the crossword. "Is it true you almost killed him?"

"I don't know, maybe. Whatever. He almost killed me first. Can I have three cartons of Marlboros, please?"

"You know the deal. Let me see some ID."

I rolled my eyes and took out my license.

"There's a party tonight," he said. "One last rager before people start leaving for college."

"In the woods?" I asked.

He shook his head. "On the beach, I think. Bonfire and all that."

I slid my money across the counter while he bagged the cig-arettes. "I'll probably skip it. I want to get an early start tomor-row."

"Yeah, makes sense."

"Will you tell Rebecca I said good-bye?"

"Sure."

I stood there awkwardly, wallet tucked back into my bag, holding my cigarettes, no reason to linger but doing it anyway. There was a rack of postcards by the front door, meant to tempt the tourists. I spun it lazily, admiring all the idyllic pictures of my hometown—boats in the marina and sunsets off the water, lush green forests, gulls wheeling overhead in a cloudless sky.

"What is it, Finley? You getting nostalgic? Don't worry, most of us aren't going anywhere. When you come back, we'll be right where you left us."

I ignored the Owen-esque note of martyrdom that had crept into Danny's voice. "Did you ever see her again? Or was it just that one time?"

"You mean Betty's ghost?"

Startled by his matter-of-factness, I nodded.

"Only that once." He glanced over his shoulder and out the window, in the direction of the streetlamp he'd claimed illumi-nated her that night. "I keep an eye out for her, but I don't think she'll come back now."

I looked at him curiously. "Why not?"

"Because she got what she wanted."

"How can you say that? Calder's still free."

"You're the one who needed to see him punished, not Betty.

He did what she asked him to do. I don't think she was ever angry at him. That was you. I think she just wanted the drama her death deserved."

"Well," I said, plucking one of the postcards from the rack, "I did my best."

Dad wanted to go out to dinner that night, do something special, try to shift the focus and celebrate the fact that I was going off to college. I almost said no, and then I thought of my transgressions from the last two months, which were legion, and that the least I could do was sit at a table with him for an hour and eat a bowl of tortellini. He ordered me a glass of wine, and he raised his in a toast.

"To your freshman year of college. The next chapter in your life, kiddo."

I smiled weakly and chimed my glass against his. His subtext was unmistakable. *No more fucking around.*

I woke in the middle of the night, from a nightmare about suffocating that would become deeply familiar. That was the first time I had it, though, right before I left Williston. While everyone else was binge-drinking on the beach and saying their weepy good-byes, I was gasping for air in my sleep. I sat up in bed, clutching my chest and gulping oxygen as fast as I could, and even after the panic subsided and my heartbeat returned to something like normal, I knew I'd never fall back to sleep, so I went downstairs and turned on the classic movie channel, volume on low. I caught the end of *My Darling Clementine*. *High Noon* came on next, and by the time Grace Kelly pulled the trigger at the end, the sky was lightening outside the windows.

I made coffee in the French press and smoked a cigarette on the back porch, eager for Dad to wake up so I could leave. I got dressed and started loading up the Subaru. I had too much to carry on the bus or the train, so Dad had agreed to let me drive back. He would come down to New York in a couple of weeks, see my dorm room, and take the car home to Maine. Knowing I would see him again so soon made our good-bye less difficult than normal. He told me he was proud of me, which I found hard to believe, but I thanked him anyway.

When I pulled out of the driveway, "More Than a Feeling" was playing on the classic rock station. I turned it up and headed home.

A couple of days later, I was hunkered down in my bedroom, air conditioner on high—the tail end of August in New York always came as a shock after a summer in Maine—the overhead lights off, a book in my hand that I wasn't reading. Instead, I was thinking about Owen, and Serena, and even Rebecca, and then berating myself for thinking about them, for not being able to put Williston and its denizens more firmly out of my mind. Mostly I was just staring at the wall and wondering why being back in New York hadn't solved all my problems.

The phone rang in the hallway and my mother answered it; a minute later, she knocked on my door.

"I'm not here," I said, and she came in anyway.

"It's your dad," she said, holding out the cordless in that way that meant I didn't have a choice. Warily, I took it from her.

"Hi," I said.

"Finley," he said, his voice as grave and serious as it had been when he called to tell me about Betty.

The crying kicked in like a reflex. "What happened?" I managed. "Is it Owen?"

"Owen's fine. I need to ask you something, and you need to tell me the truth. Okay?"

"Okay."

Dad cleared his throat. "Your last night in town. Did you go to the party on the beach?" He sounded like he was terrified to hear my answer.

"No. We went out to dinner, remember? And then we went home and I packed."

"You didn't sneak out later? After I went to bed?"

"No, I tried to sleep, but I had a bad dream so I watched movies in the living room until you woke up. Why? Dad, what happened at the party?"

He sighed, relieved that I was genuinely clueless. "Calder's missing."

My gut went cold. "What are you talking about?"

"The last time anyone saw him was that night, on the beach, at the party."

"I wasn't there," I said. "I swear, I wasn't there. It wasn't me."

"Okay, Finley, I believe you. It's going to be okay."

Calder had gone to the beach party. There were dozens of teenagers there, getting drunk in the dark and in the shadows around the bonfire, couples wandering off, kids arriving in one group and leaving with another, depending on who was still sober enough to drive. The police were having a hell of a time putting together a complete list. But several people saw Calder there, and were surprised that he'd shown up at all; this was, of course, the same beach where Betty had died, and suspicion had been growing steadily since his outburst after her funeral. No one at the party knew that Owen had already been down to the sheriff's station and told them everything he'd seen, even Leroy's lending a hand.

I spent the rest of the day on the phone, trying to reach anyone back in Williston who might know what had happened. I tried Owen and Emily and even Serena, but it was Rebecca I finally got on the line. She'd been at the bonfire—but drunk, of course—and Calder had been there, but sort of on the fringes. He didn't talk to many people, just drank a few beers and looked at the water until, she said, it started giving people the creeps. Then she and Danny had slipped away for a while—I asked why, since it had gone so badly the first time, and she said she was leaving for Amherst in a few days, so she thought why not—and when they came back, Calder was gone. He hadn't said good-bye to anyone, and nobody remembered him leaving. He was there, and then he wasn't. It didn't seem like a big deal until the next morning, when his car was still parked by the beach and he was nowhere to be found.

"He just vanished," she said.

I imagined the scene at Charlie's, drunken theories and speculations offered in tones not quite as hushed as intended. Maybe he'd had too much to drink and gotten in the water—Rebecca said there had been a few brave skinny-dippers—or maybe he'd wandered off, from the beach into the woods, gotten hurt and was lying helpless on the forest floor. Maybe one of the other kids at the party knew more than they were telling. The same story the cops had once tried to use to explain Betty's death and the reappearance of her body—that she'd OD'd on drugs and whoever was with her had panicked and buried her—was being told now about Calder.

But then Dad broke the story in the paper—that hours before Calder disappeared, a witness had finally come forward and confessed to seeing him drown Betty. Always a master of subtext, Dad managed to imply, without making any outright accusations, that someone at the sheriff's department had warned Leroy before anyone could pick Calder up for questioning.

The accusations would come later, in the letters to the editor, after the arrest warrant was finally issued, after it finally dawned on everyone that the police were looking for a murder suspect, not a missing person, and that it was their beloved mayor who had, in all likelihood, helped him get away. Eventually, Leroy resigned, citing the need to spend more time with his family and focus on the search for his son.

I told Dad he should run in the special election, but he just laughed.

With Leroy out of office, the Halyard was able to reopen, but through Dad I learned that Emily had taken over running the diner, and that Owen was, at last, applying to colleges, all of them outside the state of Maine. By the time Silas got out of prison, Owen would be long gone.

I never mentioned it to Rebecca, or my father, or anyone else, but I did wonder if Serena had been at the party that night, if she'd finally found the opportunity she'd been waiting for. It would have been so easy—slip a little something into his Solo cup, lead him away from the crowd. If he passed out close enough to the water, the tide would come in and do the rest. I didn't doubt that she could do it, or that she was clever enough to realize how perfect the timing would be, that if Calder disappeared right after Owen went to the police, even the most biased cops in Williston would think Calder was running. What I've never asked anyone, what I've never tried to learn, is whether Serena knew about Owen's revelation. When Betty disappeared, all I wanted were answers, but this time I knew better. I knew I didn't want to know.

That fall I went to class and studied and spent the weekends getting drunk at the obligatory parties. Once in a while I woke up to my roommate, Kate, crouched next to my bed, gently rubbing my shoulder to bring me out of whatever nightmare I was having. She'd ask if I was okay, and I would lie and say yes, and she was gracious enough to leave it at that. I missed Owen, and Serena, even Danny a little, but I held fast to my conviction that I never wanted to speak to any of them again.

One day in November, not long before Thanksgiving, I was lying in bed working on an essay about *Double Indemnity*. Propped up on half a dozen strategically arranged pillows, my kitten mug of coffee within reach, I was approaching, dare I say it, contentment. I was listening to the Sonics on my headphones so I didn't hear the phone when it rang, but Kate answered it and tapped my leg to get my attention.

"It's for you," she said.

I pressed the receiver to my ear without thinking. "Hello?"

"Finley?"

"Yeah?"

"It's Caroline."

As frozen as I felt at the sound of her voice, my expression must have changed dramatically. Kate hastily excused herself, closing the door behind her.

"Caroline?"

"I hope it's okay that I'm calling. Your dad gave me your number."

"It's fine," I said after a moment. "Where are you?"

"Still in Arizona."

"How are the horses?"

"They're okay. I'm doing a lot better, but I'm not really in any rush to go home. How's college?"

"It's good," I said. "I'm trying my best not to fuck it up."

"You know, Cassie finally came home."

"No shit?" I said.

"I couldn't believe it either. Apparently she just came home one day. Right when the weather was starting to turn."

"I guess she's not as stupid as we always thought."

Caroline laughed. "Yeah, I guess not. It's a good thing she turned up when she did. My parents have been talking about moving away from Williston."

"I can't say I'm surprised."

"And I know that Calder's missing, but they won't answer any of my questions about it. So I thought, maybe—"

"I don't know what happened to your brother, Caroline. I'm sorry."

"You've got your theories, right?"

"That's all they are."

"Just tell me, then. What you think happened."

I sighed and put down my laptop. "Fine. You want to know what I think? I think your dad got word that Owen had gone to the police. I think he knew Calder would never hold up if there was a trial, and that this time the charges would stick. So I think he moved fast, and got Calder the fuck out of town before he could even be brought in for questioning. My best guess is that your brother's in Canada somewhere, and that maybe someday, when enough time has passed, he'll come back. But in the meantime, I wouldn't expect any postcards from him."

I left out the last bit of my hypothesis. Calder had only been seventeen when he killed Betty; any lawyer the Millers hired was sure to be formidable and ruthless. Owen's testimony had been the only evidence. It was hard to imagine that Calder would have spent more than a handful of years in jail. I didn't think it was an easy choice—a manslaughter conviction versus permanent exile—but even now, I'm still uncertain that, in the end, the decision was Calder's. After all, Leroy had to protect himself, too.

Caroline was quiet for a minute. "I don't understand," she said finally. "How can somebody just vanish like that?"

"I used to ask myself the same question," I replied, not unsympathetically. "And then I realized it happens all the time."

EPILOGUE.

THE MILLERS DID move away, and Caroline went off to boarding school when she left rehab, instead of joining them wherever they went. Calder never turned up, not that anyone expected him to, and though I was nine out of ten that what I'd told Caroline was true, I did wonder, sometimes, if Serena had gotten to him after all. And once in a great while I thought about Owen, whether he'd slipped onto that beach unnoticed, and killed Calder as some kind of self-assigned penance. Owen was smart, smarter than anyone in Williston probably realized, and I knew him. Stone cold. If he'd wanted to kill Calder, I had no doubt he could have, and gotten away with it, too. Maybe it was the reason he'd decided to go to the sheriff at all—make Calder into a murder suspect again, so everyone would assume he was a fugitive, and no one would look all that hard for a body. For all I knew, Owen had made up the whole story. If I'd seen him again, looked him in the eye and asked him directly, I probably could have learned the truth. But, like I said, I didn't want to know.

I didn't make it back to Williston for a couple of years, and by the time I did, Owen was long gone, off studying literature at Berkeley. Based on our last exchange, I was worried Emily might run me out of town, but she'd taken up with one of the margarita-drinking divorcees who hung around at Charlie's, and her misanthropic facade was wearing thin around the edges. Nonetheless, I kept my visit short. I still do when I go up, staying just long enough to take the Subaru for a drive, visit Danny at the trader, and put flowers on the beach where Betty died. Sometimes I'll go with my dad to a softball game, where I inevitably find myself searching the dugout for Owen and wishing I could watch him go to bat one more time.

I got my own place in the East Village at the end of freshman year, a studio apartment roughly the size of my old bedroom in Williston, on 5th Street between Avenues A and B. I slept on a used futon and all my furniture was made out of particleboard, but I put flowerboxes on the windowsills, burned sage to fight off the smell of cat urine encroaching from the hallway, and hung a framed reproduction of the *Laura* one-sheet above the TV. I used throw rugs to cover the buckling floors and kept a picture of Betty and me on the refrigerator next to the postcard I bought from the trader that final day in Williston. Those two items were the only indication I had ever lived anywhere but New York. These days they're still hanging on my fridge, albeit in a slightly nicer apartment, where I pretend not to notice they've started to fray around the edges.

One afternoon at the beginning of sophomore year, I found a small package from my father stuffed into my mailbox. He still sent every issue of the *Messenger*—the police blotter remained my guilty pleasure—but this envelope had some extra weight to it. I tore it open as I climbed the four flights to my apartment and read the note he'd scribbled on a Post-it.

> *Found this while cleaning out your old bedroom.*
> *Maybe one day you'll tell me about it. Love, Dad.*

It was Betty's college application, still unopened.

I sat at the card table I had set up in my tiny kitchen, armed with a pack of smokes and a bottle of whiskey, and finally pulled the little tab that split open the envelope. Most of the contents were standard—transcripts and teacher recommendations sealed neatly into their own envelopes, forms filled out with Betty's basic information. Her name, her birthdate, her address. Finally, I came to what I thought would be her admissions essay, though it turned out to be something very different altogether.

> *November 15, 1997*

> *It's harder for me to write this than I thought it*
> *would be. Not because I'm having second thoughts,*
> *or because the grim nature of the content has given*
> *me pause, but because words have never been the best*
> *way for me to express myself, and in this particular*
> *situation I have no choice. Let me be more specific—my*
> *own words are not my strong suit. Give me an audience*
> *and a script, and I can reveal myself perfectly. I can*
> *recite a monologue written hundreds of years ago or*
> *reenact a scene from a film you've never heard of, and*

you'll understand me better than if you read this letter
a hundred times. If I'd been allowed to play Ophelia, I
could have shown everyone just how close I am to feeling
my own sanity slipping away. For months now, I've felt
like I'm disappearing. I wish I could have made myself feel
seen one final time. But right now the written word is all I
have to work with, so I'll do my best to make myself clear.

The unlights have been relentless in their efforts.
Every day they cast their long shadow over me, and at
night I hear them scratching at the walls of my bedroom.
I'm exhausted from fighting them, and the prospect of
battling them forever is so daunting. Over and over, I let
them win. Pills wear off. Sex is brief. I just want some
peace. I know I'm weak, and that's okay. Not everybody
can be a fighter.

This letter is meant, more than to illuminate my
motivations, to ensure that no one else is implicated in
what happens to me. No one should be punished, as no
one is to blame—no one but me, of course. The will and
desire were all mine. All I lacked was courage, and so a
friend of mine was kind enough to carry out the details.
I hope that Calder Miller will not have to suffer for the
compassion he has shown me in agreeing to carry out
my wishes. It brings me some measure of relief to know
that once I'm gone there will be a tiny bit less suffering
in the world, and I hope in time others can share that
sentiment.

Betty Flynn

The signature eliminated any hope I had that it was a hoax or elaborate forgery—the romantic, oversized loops in each *y* were enough to convince me. That, and the melodramatic tone she struck with every sentence. *Not everyone can be a fighter.* Perhaps it was sheer ego, but I was convinced she had written that line just for me. As for why she'd allowed the letter to languish with her application, I can only guess. Perhaps she had second thoughts about letting Calder so clearly off the hook; I like to think she knew that I would find it, that she was, in her own way, deferring to my judgment in terms of what to do.

I knew I should send it to Emily or Dad or even Owen. Emily could keep it as insurance, in case Calder ever turned up; Dad could put it in the *Messenger*, prove at last what Calder really was. And Owen would at least have something to corroborate the story he'd told the police.

Betty might have wanted to relieve Calder of the responsibility, but her wishes did not interest me all that much just then. How selfish could she be, to leave me and expect my forgiveness to extend to him, too? I wasn't sure I couldn't muster up enough for even her. And I was sure as hell not going to take the chance that someday a jury might take her at her word. Did the letter have a greater chance of convicting Calder or exonerating him?

Maybe it was just my own selfishness, but I knew I didn't want anyone else to ever read it. I had earned the final glimpse into her troubled heart. All I had to do was picture Shelly reciting portions of the letter to her cunty little friends, and muscle memory took care of the rest. My lighter came out of my pocket, I spun the metal wheel until the flame caught. I held that little orange thumb of fire to the corner of the page until it burned, and I let it burn until there was nothing left but ash.

Nobody talks about the Millers. Nobody speculates about what might have happened to Calder; nobody ever claims to see his ghost. The same collective amnesia, that tacit agreement to pretend it had never happened, was applied to Calder more thoroughly, more permanently, than it had ever been to Betty. Still alive or not, Calder is gone in a way she never will be—like a tumor that's been neatly excised, restoring the body to health. After defending him so staunchly, Williston's only way to cope with the shame is to ignore the whole episode, although I'm sure there have been a few late-night conversations at Charlie's about how they could have all misjudged him so badly. But mostly now it's his name they never speak.

They keep seeing Betty. Even after the theater was rebuilt, there were occasional complaints about lights that flickered without cause, strange noises coming from the catwalk, crucial wardrobe items going missing minutes before the curtain went up on opening night. The students still don't like to be in there alone, and two kids were actually expelled several years after Betty's death for locking one of their classmates in the theater overnight as a prank. I was impressed and heartened when I heard about that; everyone involved was too young to have actually known Betty personally, but apparently her specter looms large over Williston's consciousness, and I'd be lying if I said I didn't take at least some credit for that.

The grave in the woods where Calder and Leroy buried her has been long filled in and reclaimed by the forest, and I doubt anyone could identify the spot exactly, probably not even me. But it's still a place where the kids go at night on a dare, maybe a little drunk or stoned, half hoping they might see her ghost, half terrified they actually will. Sometimes they claim to see her, in one of her old vintage dresses and painstakingly applied red lipstick, but more frequent are the reports of just one of those strange feelings—a sudden gust of frigid air, a hint of movement in the peripheral vision. I always wonder which of the storytellers are the out-and-out liars, and which ones truly believe they've seen her ghost. The liars I can sympathize with; it's the others I find irrationally loathsome, those people with no connection to Betty who manage to convince themselves she would in any way reveal herself to them. Not that it would be so out of character for her. She always did revel in attention and was not particularly choosy about the source. Maybe I'm just jealous because I've still never seen her.

If I wanted people to remember her, then I suppose I got my wish, but it's a cheap sham, cold comfort, whatever. In my occasionally cocky moments, I tell myself I pulled off something of a resurrection, bringing her memory back to life in a place so hell-bent on forgetting her, but it doesn't change the fact that I couldn't save my friend, that in the end the unlights won and took her from me. As a girl, she couldn't hack it, but now, in her own peculiar way, she'll live forever. I don't believe in ghosts, but I'm haunted just the same. Not in the same way I was that summer—grief does fade, and anger, too, much to my surprise.

Loss is a strange alchemy that changes you forever, remakes you into someone, something else, but even that I could have dealt with; sooner or later, everyone does. It's the price of admission for this whole human experience.

If Betty had never asked Calder to kill her, would she still be alive? Would she have found somebody else to do it? How many people need to hear that proposal before you find one who's just curious enough to take you up on it? When I thought Calder was a charming psychopath who had the whole town fooled, I slept better at night. But now I don't think he would have done it if she hadn't begged him to. When I ride the subway, I wonder how many of those strangers are convinced they'd never hurt a soul, unaware they have something sleeping inside them that could be woken up if the perfect circumstances came along, if they were issued a direct invitation in just the right way. I think about what Calder said in the sweat lodge, that this is all made up. It could fall apart at any minute.

I ask myself sometimes, if I could trade the lives of everyone in the sweat lodge that night to have Betty back, would I do it? The truth is, I go back and forth. I like to think that when I reached into that rock pit so we could all get out alive, I evened out some kind of cosmic score that let me off the hook for her death, but I don't know if I believe that, either. Maybe we don't want to know what we're capable of, maybe we're better off not knowing, but on those days when I'm convinced that we all unwittingly have murder in our hearts, I look at the scars on my hands and I remember that it works both ways.

ACKNOWLEDGMENTS.

Thanks to my agent, Brianne Johnson; my editor, Alex Ulyett; and the entire team at Viking, including Ken Wright, Krista Ahlberg, Jennifer Dee, Jim Hoover, and Samira Iravani, who designed the gorgeous and spooky cover of my dreams. Thanks to Sharyn November for giving me the freedom to pursue this project in the first place.

I am deeply grateful to all my friends for their patience, encouragement, and support as I wrote a book that took me to some pretty dark places. Thanks to the fellas of the WSC, the ladies of FMH, and all the misfit toys of Red Hook, Brooklyn, who have made my home so much more than just the place where I live. Special thanks to George Briggs for being my Maine consultant and answering my many questions about growing up there; and to Erica and Craig Berkenpas, in whose Nairobi attic much of this book was written, for giving me a second home halfway around the world.

Thank you to my family: my parents, whose belief in me has never wavered; my brother, who still makes me laugh harder than anybody; and all of my cousins and relatives. They are amazing raconteurs, all of them, and everything I know about storytelling I learned from listening closely at family gatherings.

Finally, thanks to Sarah McCarry for never letting me give up the fight.

ALTHEA CAN'T STOP FALLING IN LOVE.
OLIVER CAN'T STOP FALLING ASLEEP.

ALTHEA & OLIVER

CRISTINA MORACHO

chapter one.

"WOULD YOU RATHER walk barefoot across a mile of Legos or get a tattoo on the inside of your eyelid?"

"That's fucked up." Oliver's words are blurry with fatigue.

"That's sort of the point. Pick one. Don't think about it for too long."

Althea is doing her best to keep Oliver awake until they get back to his house. The windows are rolled down and the car is whipped full of angry March air that beats her blonde hair around her face like a belligerent pair of wings. A screeching punk rock lament is on the radio. She shouts over the music as Oliver struggles to keep his eyes open, his head lolled back against the seat. Her voice and the chill of winter and the metallic thrum of electric guitars grow remote as he drifts off.

He thinks of the delicate skin on the soles of his feet and winces. A mile is too far. "Tattoo. I'd rather get the tattoo."

Althea's race to the house won't change what's about to happen, but she's driving like it means something, mouth cinched into a determined knot, speeding through a yellow light. "We're almost there," she says.

"Let me sleep," he says. "Shush."

"Don't shush me."

"You love it when I shush you."

It doesn't matter. He'll be asleep in minutes, wherever he is. Home in bed is his first choice, but he could do worse than the shotgun seat of his best friend's Camry. An hour ago he passed out in sixth period chem lab, dangerously close to a Bunsen burner.

"I'm so tired," he says.

"I know."

"What about you? Which would you rather?" asks Oliver, enunciating with effort, his tongue thick and uncooperative.

"The tattoo. Obviously." Althea punctuates her point by honking at the driver in front of them, who's creeping along College Road too slowly for her taste.

He unzips his jeans. Lifting his hips off the seat, he shimmies until his pants are around his ankles. He's wearing his favorite cherry-red boxers, and the sight of them is briefly cheering.

"What's wrong with your pants?" Althea asks.

"I'm trying to eliminate obstacles," he says.

"You should have done the shoes first."

"Fuck." Looking down at the hems of his jeans, caught on the heels of his tennis shoes, he finds the task at hand insurmountable. He kicks feebly, and his feet get tangled in denim. He makes a strangled, wordless sound of vexation.

"Just leave it," says Althea. "I'll fix it when we get there."

For her benefit, Oliver sits up straighter, resting an elbow on the open window and propping his head on one hand. "I got one."

"Let's hear it." She turns the volume down so he won't have to shout over Rocket from the Crypt.

"Would you rather . . ." His head slumps forward, but he rights himself quickly. "Would you rather . . ." Althea turns onto their block and his resolve weakens. He'll be upstairs in just a minute, under his down quilt, and he won't have to fight it anymore.

She smacks his arm. "Oliver!"

"Okay, okay." They're pulling into his driveway now. "Would you rather kill a puppy with your hands—"

"Like, strangle it?" says Althea, turning off the engine and unbuckling her seat belt.

"Whatever, or, like, drown it in a bucket." Oliver fumbles for the belt release button.

"I don't like this already."

She comes around to his side and crouches by the open door. Reaching beneath his crumpled jeans, she unlaces his shoes and eases them from his feet. The pants slip off without further opposition. "Okay," she says, patting his ankle.

Oliver emerges from the car in socks and underwear, his backpack still strapped over his black thermal hoodie. He falters, and Althea puts an arm around his waist for support.

"Let's remember this outfit," she says. "I think it's a winner. Maybe more of a spring look, though."

Climbing onto the porch, Oliver gropes for his keys. Across the street, their elderly neighbor Mrs. Parker is sweeping her sidewalk in a quilted navy housecoat and watching the pantsless Oliver with undisguised interest. His hand weaves in front of the lock; as his eyes lose focus, he can hear metal scraping against the door's peeling white paint. "Is she staring at me?"

"Don't you pay that nosy bitch no nevermind." Gently, Althea takes the keys and opens the door herself. "What's my other option? Besides the puppy?"

They ascend the stairs together, him leaning on her heavily now, and she leads him to his room. Pulling back the covers on his bed, Althea ushers him into it. The sheets are soft against his bare legs. When they were kids in flannel pajamas, they used to lie under the blankets in the dark and bicycle their knees against the fabric so they could see the green flash of static electricity. He nuzzles his head into a pillow.

"Or shoot a random person with a sniper rifle from a mile away?" he finishes.

"Those are my choices? Drown a puppy in a bucket or shoot a stranger I can't see?" He feels her weight on the bed next to him, her cool hand against his fevered face while she mulls his hypothetical question, her voice amused but already distant.

"Mmm-hmm. Which one would you . . ." It's impossible even to finish the sentence. When he wakes up, whenever he wakes up, it will feel like a shaky jump from this moment to that one. Then will come that panic of having slept through something important—a final exam, a birthday party, a soccer game in which he was the starting forward. Something is wrong with him, something must be, because it wasn't supposed to happen again and now it has, and he wonders if he should be fighting this harder than he is, but he's so tired and it's completely delicious right now to be in his bed. Sometimes nothing feels as good as giving up, that guilty relief coupled with a healthy dose of I-just-don't-give-a-fuck, and he wants to tell Althea not to worry, everyone needs a vice and this can be his.

"I'll tell you when you wake up. Hold that thought," she whispers, and he's gone.

Althea stays. Lying on her back, she watches the constellation of plastic stars on the ceiling slowly brighten as the remaining daylight drains away and the familiar features of Oliver's bedroom recede into the shadows. The diminutive television perches atop the scratched wooden dresser, its rabbit-ear antenna akimbo, the red standby light of the VCR luminous and eerie. His makeshift desk was her gift on his last birthday—a piece of plywood covered in a collage of his favorite album covers, supported by two sawhorses she'd pilfered from a construction site downtown. A collection of ticket stubs from movies and concerts, pages torn from Althea's sketchbook, and photographs of the two of them are all tacked to his enormous bulletin board. She's memorized the photo lineup: age six, under the Christmas tree at her house, a tiny Oliver wrapped in a string of lights; age nine, Oliver proudly brandishing a cast on his broken wrist while a jealous Althea pouts in a corner of the frame; age twelve, Althea with her hands swaddled in a pair of pink boxing gloves while Oliver cowers, covering his face; age fourteen, standing on Althea's porch the morning they started high school, Althea looking miserable and Oliver strangely enthusiastic; age sixteen, drunk at a Halloween party, dressed as Sid and Nancy, shouting something at the camera.

If he'd stayed awake for five seconds longer, she could have told him the answer to his question, although she suspects he already knows that she would save the puppy. They've been best friends for ten years, and it's not easy for them to surprise each other. The silent digital numbers of the clock radio reconfigure, moving ahead one minute. Althea counts to sixty as evenly as possible—*one banana, two banana*—but still arrives there first, and several more seconds creep by before the clock acknowledges another minute has passed. *How many more of those until he wakes up?* she wonders. Last time it was two weeks. A lot of goddamned bananas.

A day passes, and then another, and another. Every morning when Althea drives by Oliver's house on the way to school, she slows, not expecting to see him waiting for her, but hoping anyway. At night she can't sleep, and at school she can't stay awake, despite her ubiquitous thermos of coffee. A teacher teases her for nodding off in class, suggesting that maybe Althea has caught whatever it is Oliver has. The other students titter and she slouches in her seat, mortified to have called attention to herself. During lunch she eats in her car, stretched across the backseat, propped against the door like she's lying on the sofa in her basement, looking out the window instead of at the television. No one comes to find her. It's not that she doesn't have other friends, but they are more Oliver's than hers. She keeps to herself how unfair she thinks this is, that the one better equipped to go without the other is the one who never has to.

After school she goes home and makes lemon bars; baking

keeps her mind busy, requires the kind of multitasking that finally allows her to relax. At night she makes uninspired attempts at precalculus and chemistry, putting in the minimum amount of effort that will still achieve the desired result, then she shoves her work aside and takes out her sketchbook. Surrounded by music and the smell of freshly sharpened pencils, she turns off the part of her brain that's still picturing Oliver asleep. Eager to prove that she can, in fact, amuse herself, she sketches diligently until she's convinced she's lost track of time, filling pages with the dinosaurs she so often sees in her dreams.

They've been separated before, but this is different. It isn't like when she was periodically shipped off to spend forced time with her mother, in Philadelphia or Chicago or Denver or any of the other places Alice had lived since leaving Wilmington; she was steadily heading westward, like a slow-moving plague spreading across the country. Althea had missed Oliver then, fiercely, childishly, missed their routines and games and easy familiarity, especially in Alice's world of constant upheaval, where there was always a new boyfriend to meet, a new group of friends before whom Althea had to be trotted out, a new hobby or passion of Alice's that Althea was expected to indulge.

Something had changed in October, when her father, Garth, was out of town for a conference and she threw a keg party at Oliver's insistence, his misguided attempt to encourage her to socialize. He had spent the entire day bubble-wrapping Garth's trinkets and hiding them in the attic; they rolled up the Persian rugs and dragged them into the master bedroom. The trick, they decided, would be to devise an activity that would keep every-

one in the backyard rather than roaming around the house looking for things to steal or destroy. Which was how they ended up
filling a cheap vinyl kiddie pool with Jell-O and turning yet another keg party into a wrestling tournament. Plenty of girls were
more than eager to strip down to their underwear and flounder
around in the cherry-flavored mess. Althea was content to swill
her shitty beer on the sidelines and lament that they should have
charged money. No amount of alcohol or urging would get her
into the ring until Oliver asked if she was really so afraid of a
bunch of intoxicated debutantes. That did it. Removing only her
flip-flops, she climbed into the pool, macerated gelatin squish-
ing between her toes, and demanded to be challenged; an hour
later, she remained undefeated. When she was finished, Oliver
jumped in and tackled her, and they splashed around under a
starry southern sky. They tangled with each other, their clothes
soaked and clinging, their bodies dripping and sticky and smell-
ing like too-sweet cough medicine.

The clouds came from nowhere. A flash of lightning; someone said "Oh, shi—" but his voice was cut off by the thunder.
Then it was pouring and everybody ran into the house, including
a dozen girls wearing nothing but bras and panties and Jell-O,
girls who would leave cherry footprints all over the floors, girls
who would sit on the furniture and dry themselves with Garth's
monogrammed towels and eventually leave the Carter residence
looking like the site of a mass homicide. Althea and Oliver stayed
in the pool, getting rained on and trembling with each roll of
thunder. She'd only had a couple of beers but was acting drunker
than she was, for camouflage, because as she watched pink rivu-

lets of rainwater stream down Oliver's temples and wrists, she'd realized something horrifying: She wanted him to kiss her.

He hadn't.

The following day, Oliver was reduced to a quivering mess, terrified of Garth's return; he prayed for a swift execution, while Althea insisted on playing a morbid game of Would You Rather—would you rather watch the other one die, or would you rather be killed first, knowing the other would have to watch you go? They cleaned frantically for hours. Finally, Althea sent him home because he was running a fever. He went to sleep that night and stayed that way for the better part of the next two weeks, and while he was gone she'd noticed there was something different about the way she missed him. It was colored with impatience and expectation, as if they had been in the middle of a conversation, interrupted just as he was about to tell her something important and she was forced to wait for the right moment to ask, "What were you going to say?" She was missing something that hadn't even happened yet and couldn't happen until Oliver was awake and accounted for and finally paying attention.

It had been her mother, of all people, who had intuited the shift, coming right out on the phone one day and asking if she and Oliver were having sex.

"I don't expect your father to talk to you about birth control," she'd begun, and Althea had cut her off at the pass, saying that her health class had covered the subject thoroughly. Nevertheless, Alice had barreled on. "Are you two still having sleepovers all the time? You're too old for that now, you know; you can't be sleeping in the same bed like you did when you were kids."

"Our raging hormones have yet to get the better of us."

"There are places where you can go to get the Pill. You don't even need to involve your father."

"I just told you I'm not having sex. Why would I need to go on the Pill?" Althea responded.

"You know, it can make your breasts bigger, too."

Althea had never told her mother of the shame her flat chest inspired, and she had marveled then at how, in their first conversation in months, Alice could identify the unbearably specific miseries Althea never shared with anyone. Althea had handed the phone to Garth out of sheer embarrassment, and he took the rest of the call in his study with the door closed. He had emerged red-faced and poured himself a scotch, and after that started leaving the basement door open when Oliver was over. Her parents' apparent confidence that she and Oliver either were or would soon be sleeping together only made her more disconsolate as she pitched and turned in her bed at night, wondering why Oliver remained willfully oblivious to what everyone around him appeared to consider a certainty.

"There's nothing happening with me and Oliver," Althea had protested into the phone, and in retrospect it was obvious that her vehemence had given her away.

"Oh, Thea," Alice had said. "Be patient."